CW00552904

By the same author

MALLION'S PRIDE
DARK INHERITANCE
AN AUTUMN IN ARABY
A CERTAIN SPLENDOUR
THE WOMAN IN GREY

CAROLA SALISBURY

Daisy Friday

REISSUED 1987

C

CENTURY
LONDON MELBOURNE AUCKLAND JOHANNESBURG

Copyright © Carola Salisbury 1984

First published in Great Britain in 1984 by
Century Hutchinson Ltd
Brookmount House, 62–65 Chandos Place
London WC2N 4NW

Century Hutchinson South Africa (Pty) Ltd
PO Box 337, Bergvlei, 2012 South Africa

Century Hutchinson Australia Pty Ltd
PO Box 496, 16–22 Church Street, Hawthorn
Victoria 3122, Australia

Century Hutchinson New Zealand Ltd
PO Box 40–086, Glenfield, Auckland 10
New Zealand

Reprinted 1987

ISBN 0 7126 0396 4

Printed in Great Britain by
St Edmundsbury Press Ltd,
Bury St Edmunds, Suffolk
and bound by
Butler & Tanner Ltd,
Frome and London

ONE

I am a creature of impulses. One day when my westbound train
stopped at Westchester, I took up my only luggage – a small
carpet bag – and leapt out on to the platform just as the guard
was blowing his whistle and signalling the driver to move off.
My instant and unheralded departure caused some consternation to the old gentleman who had been sitting opposite me
from London and to whom I had confided that I was travelling
all the way to Falmouth. The poor fellow flew to the window
and regarded me with considerable concern, and he was still
watching me and mouthing some soundless message when the
train steamed out of the station westwards into the dying
sunlight of a summer's day, carrying him out of my life for ever
– much to my private amusement.

It is one thing to abandon the last train of the day upon an
impulse; quite another, when the first wild fancy has fled, to
accept the consequences of one's act. But in addition to my
impulsiveness, I am also a person who can make do and mend.
Accordingly I went straight to the Bull hotel and booked myself
a room for the night, together with a table for supper. Next I
betook myself to my room and washed off the worst of the Great
Western Railway, patted my hair in place, fixed my bonnet
with an extra hatpin – and went out into the warm evening
sunlight.

My road led southwards towards the coast, into that part of
Dorset which looks out upon the world with closed eyes: a place
of secret lanes and half-abandoned villages, of small farmsteads

whose once-thatched roofs are the haunt of bats and owls, and whose gates creak eerily in the evening zephyrs.

It was further than I remembered. My goal lay through three parishes and over two streams. When I was very young and went to Westchester on a single occasion – it was the old Queen's birthday and some kind soul had decided to give every poor child in the county a new sixpence and a stick of barley sugar – it had seemed a very long way to my short and spindly little legs. In after years, I could have done it at a run; yesterday, now some considerable time has fled, it seemed as long and tiring a journey as it had been to the small child of long ago. But presently the final, feckless, winding lane skirted a field that had been laid out before Doomsday, past a sentinel oak that had stood watch on the hillcrest when the fires burned across England to tell of the defeat of the Armada in the Channel, and I was looking down into the Vale of the Blue Boar, so named after the four-legged creature that was carved into the hillside at some immemorial time and which is deep with heather in the summer and crawling alive with adders. Below the Boar, the remains of the village: cottages and barns, the overgrown, green, tumbledown church, rectory – roofless – and the long, gaunt building that had been the abode and the bane of my young life.

No one moved in the village, for all had long since gone. The trade that had made Mordwenn, once departed, had taken the life of the place with it, for there is not enough work on the hill farms to sustain more than a handful of shepherds, and shearers come up from Devon when they are needed.

Nothing ever changes. Nothing remains the same. The old factory, when I came to it, seemed smaller than my memory served me, though in the years since I left it, it had been added to in length. The once-rushing stream that had turned the great water-wheel (itself now gone, and only the eye of faith could discern where it had once been attached to the side of the building) was dried up, silted, and overgrown with reeds. At my passing, a pair of wild ducks took flight from the sedge and flapped, quacking, over a bank of unkempt trees and out of sight.

The door – the great front door that I had so seldom passed through, and only, let it be said, on some Sundays, high days and rare holidays – creaked open to my touch. And I was back with my memories . . .

This was the firing shed, where I had worked for six hours at a stretch without stopping for rest. Then half an hour for a meal, and back again to work for another six.

And at the end of twelve long hours of drudgery – blessed ease . . .

The stairs marked my way. I mounted them, two at a time, for the risers were set close together to accommodate generations of short legs, tired legs. Some of the steps were gone, rotted away by damp and the beetle, and I trod warily, for it would have been an irony, indeed, to have fallen and perished of a broken neck in the very place that should have seen my young life flicker out like an untended flame – as so many others had done.

At the top of the stairs I came to a long, narrow room, the counterpart in shape and size of the firing shed below, save that the roof was low, so low that I was obliged to stoop to make my way – a thing I had never needed to do before.

The beds were still there in two sentinel lines down both sides of the room. Wood-built of solid elm to last and high-sided, so that smaller children should not fall out if they tossed about in bad dreams brought about by sheer weariness and coarse food. Thirty beds each side of the windowless room, and each one numbered at the head with a brass plaque stamped with its numeral.

15 – 16 – 17 – 18 . . .

Heart beating so that I could hear it, I walked slowly down the line, touching each bedhead in passing, striving with one half of my mind to protract the encounter with bed No. 25 so that it might not ever come, though I also ached to see it again – the only thing that had been mine (I lie, only half-mine) in all my childhood.

And then my dragging footsteps brought me to it: the still familiar bed No. 25, where from the age of six onwards I had wearily slept most of twelve hours out of every twenty-four, for an unfailing six days a week, all the year round, winter and summer, red letter days only excepted. A child slave, doomed like my wretched companions, both too young and too old, to labour in the Mordwenn chain-making factory for a pittance that offset some of the parish's expense in feeding, clothing and lodging we outcasts of the greatest nation on earth, with an Empire that knows no bounds.

And this my bed. Did I say it was only half-mine? Indeed it was. For I, who have come far and gained many things, things that are reckoned highly by the world, as well as more valuable and durable riches of the heart and spirit, owned that bed No. 25 only when I lay upon it. For the other twelve weary hours of the day, it belonged to another; another weary head rested upon the coarse, straw-stuffed pillow and huddled beneath the single rough blanket in the eternal darkness that was enlivened only by a single tallow dip whose late presence, all those years later, was revealed by the smudge of blackness on the beam above where it had hung.

There were thirty beds in the dormitory, and sixty labourers – myself included – had once toiled in the factory, sleeping in the great room whose roof was now open to the sky and the high-flying larks that rose in the still summer's air, plain to me then, but all unsuspected in those long-gone days.

For the beds in the Mordwenn chain-making factory were never cold: as soon as one occupant dragged his or her wretched body to labour downstairs, another fell exhausted in the same place.

TWO

I was a foundling, and brought by the well-meaning intervention of some charitable ladies of Westchester parish to the orphanage there. They reckoned me to have been about three weeks of age and gave me the surname of Friday – it being on a Friday that the door of the establishment first closed upon me. I was also given the name of Daisy, and for a similarly practical reason: foundlings at the institution were named in alphabetical order, one per letter. The infant who preceded me (and who had died shortly after admission, so I was later told) was called Clarice. It was Daisy for me, and to the one who came after they gave the name of Emily. I remember Emily, who died of the consumption when she was about seven. We three – Clarice, Daisy and Emily – aptly demonstrated the mathematical chances of a child surviving the then parish system that was called 'indoor relief'.

I seem to remember that I grew up as a normal, rumbustious brat with a healthy – and largely unsatisfied – appetite; tall for my age and possessing a strong constitution which was to stand me in good stead in the hard years that lay in store. Life in the orphanage comprised a regimen of early nights and early morning awakening, with meals of the simplest and cheapest kind largely based on oatmeal, potatoes and other root vegetables, with a few slivers of meat (usually sheeps' lungs, known as lights) once or twice a week, and always on Sunday.

Sunday! An orphanage upbringing would turn anyone into a confirmed and lifelong Sabbatarian. On no other day of the

9

week were we permitted to lie abed for as late as six o'clock instead of the customary 5.30. And Sunday breakfast was always 'sop', which was made of oatmeal and hot water, flavoured with the drippings from the tea-pot, and greatly favoured by the children. On the Sabbath we did no work, but learned the books of the Bible by rote, chanting them through, again and again, till they were firmly fixed in our minds for ever. As long as I live, there will be times – odd, idle moments when the mind wanders at its own will along its own paths – when I shall hear the eternal chant running through my brain, and I shall be back in the big room at Westchester orphanage with the sound of Sunday:

GenesisExodusLeviticusNumbersDeut'ronomyJoshua
Judges'n'Ruth.
(big breath)
SamuelSamuelKingsKingsChroniclesChroniclesEzraNehemiah
EstherJobPsalmsProverbs . . .

At ten we went in crocodile to St Barnabas' church, where, out of regard for the respectable parishioners and their well-scrubbed progeny, we were shut up in a large high-sided stall at the rear end of the nave, into which we were hastily bustled before the main congregation arrived, and from which we were not released till the others were well clear of the churchyard gate, so that their devotions should not be troubled by the sight and the smell of us, ragged, shaven-headed and mostly lousy as we were.

But Sundays were a delight in the main, for in the afternoons we did – nothing. Our guardians left us alone. The weekday chores of cleaning, dusting and polishing the entire establishment till the floors were as slippery as new ice, and every piece of brasswork worn to paper thinness, every step holystoned to virgin whiteness, might never have happened. We simply sat in an orderly, silent circle (for 'idle chatter' was not allowed) and looked at each other till suppertime. In comparison with our common weekday round, the empty, effortless silences of Sunday afternoons were very heaven.

*

To relieve the burden upon the parish, the orphanage children – along with such adult folk from the nearby workhouse as were capable of it – were put out to work in one or other of the small local industries, and the set age for children was six years.

At six, I, Daisy Friday, went to 'residential employment' at the Mordwenn chain-making factory, and there remained till a remarkable turn of the wheel of Fortune (which I will later reveal) lifted me out of drudgery and into a manner of life the like of which, had I been told of it, I would not have believed possible but dismissed as the product of fanciful imaginings.

The craft of chain-making had been introduced into the vales of southern Dorset during the Napoleonic War by a Mr Amyas Arbuthnot, a Devonian, who, reckoning upon the availability of fast-flowing streams to power his machinery and a similar plethora of cheap labour to perform the required tasks, persuaded the government to subsidise his enterprise with the then practically unheard-of sum of a thousand guineas to set up factories in, among other places, the run-down sheep-rearing hamlet of Mordwenn in the Vale of the Blue Boar. Within a very short time, Dorset chain was securing the great battleship buoys of Plymouth, Portsmouth and Chatham – as well as providing food and shelter for the needy of south Dorset and a not inconsiderable fortune for Mr Arbuthnot, even after he had repaid the government loan.

By the time I came to the chain factory, Amyas Arbuthnot had long since been laid to rest in a splendid marble and granite mausoleum in St Barnabas' churchyard, and his grandson had taken over direction of the businesses. Mr Charles Arbuthnot – I knew of him, like all the rest of his workers, as 'Mr Charles' – was no more to us than a far-off figure whom we reckoned to be somewhat on a par with, say, Mr Gladstone or even the late, great Prince Albert himself. In any event, he was the lord of life and death over all of us, the provider, the dispenser of favours, the master at whose whim we either prospered or starved. That much was drilled into us by our foremen and forewomen and accepted as an article of faith by even the youngest.

By the time I came to the factory, also, the range of chain made there had been greatly increased to include such items as rigging-chains for ships, crane-cables, cart and plough cables, halters, curbs, cow-ties, dog-chains and even the links for policemen's handcuffs. Dog-chains were particularly suitable for the less robust of the women and the older children to manufacture, for which they were paid three farthings for each completed article. A good pair of hands, working from ten to twelve hours a day, could produce six chains during that time.

The working of even the lightest chains – heating the iron rods and bending the white-hot pieces, cutting them off and hammering them into shape, link to link – was too much for the youngest of us, as might be imagined. For us there was 'light work', so called.

Light work – merciful heavens! The task I performed for the first three years of my time at the factory rejoiced in the title of 'light work'.

To heat the forges to the intensity needed for making metal white hot calls for a continuous blast of air from a bellows. I worked such a device: a wooden plank pivoted at one end and connected by a chain to an upright, expanding leather trunk at the other. For from ten to twelve hours a day, six days a week, I danced upon such a plank, up and down, up and down, continuously and without pause, till my very bones ached and I sobbed for breath. So much for the 'light work'.

Hardest tried of all were the older women. For them, the task of heating, bending, cutting and hammering the heavy metal was made worse by their lack of dexterity. Unable to handle the intractable material and lacking the agility to avoid trouble, they were constantly being blistered about the hands and body, and burnt by the flying sparks that showered about the firing shed like angry gnats. One such a person as this, she to whom I owe everything I have become in life, whose name I will forever treasure, was Meg Wolfingham, known to her fellow workers as 'Lady Meg' because of her gentle manners, the uncomplaining way in which she performed the tasks that lay just beyond the scope of her strength, the gentle dignity which she brought to a wretched existence – an example that touched us all, young and old, and made us better than we might otherwise have been.

*

'Lady Meg' had been in service at many fine houses, starting as kitchen maid-of-all-work and rising to ladies' maid through her own diligence and application. In the course of her employment, she watched and listened and never asked questions – which, so she forever drummed into me, is the best way to advance oneself in life. 'The unfortunates,' said Meg many times, 'are those who are forever asking questions, for they embarrass others and brand themselves as the ignoramuses that they are.' As a result of watching, listening, keeping her own counsel and learning all the time, she had become able to mix with all classes of people with ease, enjoying the common bond that unites duchesses and kitchen maids, and winning the respect and affection of all.

In addition to her considerable social graces, Meg could also read with fluency, write in a most delightful copperplate hand, and perform small miracles of mental arithmetic. It was a tragedy that ill chance had reduced her to forging dog-chains at the slave rate of three farthings a piece, and the fault was not hers. Ill-health, and the sudden death of a kindly mistress who might well have provided for the old age of her faithful servant, brought Meg to the only recourse of the ageing and infirm of Victorian England: after spending her last pittance on advertising herself 'in any domestic capacity and wages immaterial' (a dreary and familiar formula often seen in the advertising columns of *The Times* and other newspapers, indicating that the supplicant asked only for a roof over her head in return for her labours), she had to fall back on parish relief, indoor relief, that's to say, inmate of the parish workhouse and – in her unfortunate case – transfer to the chain factory.

I have always said that it is really to Meg that I owe everything, and it began this way. By sheer chance, when I was coming up to the age of twelve and about to be apprenticed as a chain-maker, I was shifted down to the end of the long dormitory and away from the small children. It happened that the poor woman sharing Meg's bed had just been taken by the consumption, so I inherited the empty place. From then on, Sunday afternoons were no longer spent in the company of my fellow juveniles; instead the two of us stole away together to a quiet corner of the silent firing shed where, by the daylight seeping in through the grimy window, she taught me the delights of the alphabet, the hazards of addition, multiplication, subtraction and division, and introduced me to the richness of literature from the box of books which she kept beneath the bed – our bed.

There was some bureaucratic oversight and my indenture of apprenticeship was delayed by six months or more. By the time the document arrived, I was not only able to astonish the manager, one Mr Grout, by signing my own name at the foot of it in very tolerable copperplate, but could essay a fair rendition of its contents, a significant part of which I recall to this day:

> ... the aforementioned undertakes during the apprenticeship neither to haunt taverns nor playhouses, nor to squander what remains of her wages after discharging her weekly debt to the Parish in respect of food, clothing and lodging ... nor to play at cards, dice, or any other unlawful games ...

The incongruity of the declaration astonished me then as it amuses me now: how any girl of twelve, after having slaved a full day or night shift at chain-making, should have either the urge or the energy – or, indeed, the opportunity – to spend what remained of about two shillings and sixpence a week on riotous living in taverns and playhouses. It was Meg who taught me to laugh at the irony of it, as she taught me so much else that is not to be found in books – among which is a taste for rightness and order that has bedevilled my life till now, and a sense of outrage when confronted by injustice of the kind that turned my life upside down and brought me to what I am today.

*

The seven years of my apprenticeship had passed. I had become – almost unknowingly, and certainly unwittingly – a woman. And Meg a very tired old lady.

One morning near the Christmas of 1896, news spread round the factory that none other than Mr Charles Arbuthnot was due to visit the establishment and present seasonal gifts to the workers. Mr Charles himself – the spirit of provendor incarnate! Not Mr Gladstone, nor yet Mr Disraeli, but the lord of life and death over us all!

I brought the news to Meg when I woke her at six on a bitingly cold morning and found her awake and in tears.

'Meg, what's the matter, what ails you?' I cried in alarm, while all about us the day-shift workers were rising in the chill gloom to let their bedmates sink into the comparative warmth.

'It's my leg, love,' she whispered. 'I haven't slept the whole night through. I think there's some mischief there.'

I knew that she had suffered a nasty burn from a black-hot chain a couple of days previously, for I had bandaged her leg myself with a strip of cloth torn from the hem of my skirt. 'Let me see it, Meg,' I said.

She raised her skirts and cried out when I gently pulled down a much-darned woollen stocking, drawing it carefully over the bandage that I had wrapped around the right leg just above the ankle. My action attracted some of the women around, who paused in the act of performing their morning's token ablutions and came up to see what was amiss.

'I'm going to take off the bandage, Meg,' I told her. 'I'll be as gentle as I'm able. Tell me if I hurt you.'

She was already weeping and biting her lip in pain almost before I had unknotted the rough dressing, but did not cry out. Slowly, carefully, I unwound the strip of cloth, and saw to my dismay, by the light of the tallow dip, that it was discoloured with blood and pus.

When I lifted it from the wound, Meg gave a sob and fainted clean away. As well she might have, for the burn, which was the size of a five shilling piece (not that I had ever made the acquaintance of a five shilling piece at that time), was red, raw and suppurating.

'Oh, no!' I breathed.

The women pushed closer to look. 'I've seen the like before,' declared one old crone. 'Emmie Stratton, she had such a burn as this, an' they had to take her leg off. Gangrene, it were.'

15

'I remember it well,' said another Cassandra. 'It were done in No. 25 bed, but they was too late. I'll never forget 'er dying screams.'

I bustled the old biddies away with a sharp admonition, but taking a closer look at the wound, decided that there might be something, after all, in their doleful prediction. I, too, remembered the tragic case of Emmie Stratton; though I had been scarcely eight years old at the time, her ending was seared upon my mind in its every last horrible detail. Nor was grave injury leading to amputation and or death by any means a rarity among those working with the hot iron; I could recall at least half a dozen such cases in my time.

Binding up the wound loosely but as adequately as I was able, I bathed Meg's lips and forehead with cold water, and she still lying unconscious. I left her where she was and went down to report her condition to the manager Mr Grout.

I found this worthy in his office, seated at his tall rolltop desk, a quill pen, as ever, between his inky fingers, a worried look upon his parchment-coloured face, and a petulant darting of his eyes behind pebble-lensed spectacles at the sight of me.

'What are you doing away from your work, hey?' he cried. 'I'll dock two pence from your wages unless you can give me the answer straight, unhappy child. Do you not know that you are *stealing* bread from Mr Charles's own lips and the lips of Mr Charles's dependents by neglecting your work and skulking in idleness? Back to your task! And may the Almighty look leniently upon your transgression.' Mr Grout was deeply of the religious persuasion, at the fundamentalist end.

'Sir, it's Meg Wolfingham,' I faltered. 'She's abed with . . .'

'Wolfingham abed, is she?' The eyes behind the pebble glasses blazed with the fire of zealotry. 'Skulking in bed, is she? Lying in somnolent ease at her kindly employer's expense, is she?' He glared at me with distaste. 'And you, unhappy child, have chosen the path of betrayal, have you? "*Which is he that betrayeth thee?*" For he, read she. John, chapter twenty-one, verse twenty.'

The short-sighted eyes softened with an expression that was something like approval. 'Oh, well, it is better to betray than to burn! "*Cast into the middle of a burning, fiery furnace.*" Daniel, chapter three, verse four.'

'Sir!' I interpolated. 'I do not mean what you think I mean. Meg Wolfingham is not skulking, she is sorely sick!'

'Sick, is she?' he cried. 'Sick of what? Not of the excellent and nourishing victuals that Mr Charles's generosity commands me to put before you ingrates, I suppose? Tell me that and I will send a pair of foremen up to the womenfolk's dormitory and Wolfingham shall be brought from her somnolent ease with good birch rods, lying ingrate wretch that she is!'

'Sir, she has taken a terrible burn in the leg,' I said, 'and I'm afeared that it's the gangrene.'

'The gangrene, is it?' he exclaimed, somewhat put about. 'Well, I cannot afford to lose a worker at this time of the year, though it has to be said that Wolfingham scarcely earns her keep even when hale and whole. I will send for Mrs Prosser, the midwife-lady, who has a cunning way with the gangrene. You, child, get you about the task that the Almighty has ordained for you, and leave the matter to Mrs Prosser.'

'Yessir,' I whispered, and backed out of his presence. As I was so doing, he took up a hand-bell and rang it, no doubt to summon one of his minions to fetch Mrs Prosser.

Now I was dubious about the midwife-lady of Mordwenn. She lived in a hovel close by the churchyard wall, which I had passed countless times in crocodile on the way to Sunday mattins, and sometimes the old woman was to be seen sitting on the wall, a black cat by her side, shawled and bonneted, clay pipe in her toothless mouth. We children, convinced that Mrs Prosser was a witch, always quickened our paces when passing her, and our fears were not lessened when she would call out to the forewoman accompanying us comments such as: 'I like the look o' the little one on the end, Missus. Lawks-a-mussy! (Lord have mercy) I'll give you a shillin' for 'er, I will straight!'

It was an anxious morning for me, with my thoughts upon my friend upstairs, so that I was slow and inept about my task of forging handcuff links, a line which, because the weight of chain was ideally suited to my growing strength, I had made particularly mine. I had finished only one chain, and consigned

17

two failures to the melting pot, when the bell rang out for midday dinner, the sound of the bellows ceased, the clash of hammers was at rest, and the workpeople formed in lines for their basin of gruel and hunk of bread.

Not for me. Ducking out of sight of the foremen, I bounded up the stairs three at a time, and was rewarded by the sight of Meg sitting up in bed with the midwife-lady bending over her leg. My friend looked much better, and gave me a heartening smile and a squeeze of hands.

'Mrs Prosser has given me some medicine to drink that has made me quite forget the pain, dear,' she explained. 'And now she is going to apply a poultice.'

The old crone grinned. 'Hoar-bane, that's what I gave you to drink, lovey,' she said. Nor did she pause in her task of mixing up a most unsavoury-looking mess in a chipped earthenware bowl. 'As is called tipsy-flower by the gipsy folk, an' candle-light by foreign folk. Make it like tea, I do. Store it by the gallon jug. Many's the poor soul who's died without pain with the help o' Mrs Prosser's hoar-bane tea. An' now we've the gyssup an' rowanberry poultice with myrtlewort, which is called Much-ease.'

With considerable disquietude, I watched her take a lump of the streaky brown-coloured matter, roll it between her skinny palms till it was soft and malleable, then pat it into the shape of an oatcake and lay it atop the wound. If Meg felt any pain, she gave no sound or sign, but smiled up at me reassuringly.

'You'll be as right as a trivet come Thurday, Missus,' declared the midwife-lady. She glanced sidelong at me. Her eyes, full of ancient sin, washed over me from head to foot, and she winked. 'I seen you around for many a year, lass,' she said. 'You'll go far with them looks, I shouldn't wonder. Give me your hand.' And when I hesitated. 'Go on, do. Ain't many who get the chance of seeing what their fortune holds without crossin' Mrs Prosser's palm with siller.'

Reluctantly, I held out a hand, but the old woman snatched the other, my right hand, and bent over the palm, eyes narrowed.

'You'll wed,' she declared. 'And early. Breed like a doe

rabbit.' She sniggered. 'As to the rest . . .' Here she paused.

'Yes . . .?' I prompted her, and with some anxiety, for a curious change had taken place in the woman. She remained staring at my palm, but her expression, her eyes, were quite different. There was shock, incredulity, something else – disbelief? – written large upon her wrinkled, walnut-skinned countenance.

'What *is* it, Mrs Prosser?' I cried. 'What do you see?'

To my consternation, she made no reply; but gathering up her belongings into a paper sack, she turned and scurried away down the dormitory like a black spider. A pause at the head of the staircase to look back at me, what sounded like a muttered curse – and she was gone, leaving me with a feeling that may well be imagined.

'Pay no attention to her carry-on,' said Meg. 'The poor old thing is full of wild fancies. It comes of loneliness and old age.'

My unease somewhat soothed by her reassurances, I stroked Meg's brow and found it to be heated, still. 'I only hope that her way with burns brings better results than her telling of fortunes,' I said. 'How do you feel now, Meg?'

She closed her eyes. 'Much better,' she said drowsily. 'The tea she gave me drove away the pain. I think I shall sleep now. Mr Grout says I may be excused work for a day or so. A day or so's what he said.'

'And what about your earnings?' I asked. 'Will they be allowed?'

'Oh, no, dear,' she said, surprised. 'I wouldn't expect that. Though he did tell me, out of his charity, that I'd be allowed a bowl of sop in the evenings and it wouldn't be charged against me.'

The bell then having rung for the resumption of work, I left my friend to her slumbers, somewhat relieved at her seeming improvement; but the whole episode, thus far, had kindled in my mind what were as yet only the beginnings of the sense of outrage that was fated, quite soon, to change the course of my whole life.

*

That evening, before the night shift had begun work and we of the day shift were still awake, the announcement was made to the effect that Mr Charles Arbuthnot and his party would be visiting the factory at noon on the following day; all work would finish at a quarter of an hour before noon, all workers were to be up and about, cleaned and alert, with the rooms, staircases and passages swept and dusted by five minutes before the hour. In other words, every effort was to be made to present Mordwenn chain factory as a model place of work, but with as little wasting of working time as possible.

I had made myself a rough bed of old clothing on the floor alongside Meg, who was awake and bright-eyed. The bright eyes I did not much care for, since they suggested a fever. Her brow also was feverish, and her attitude was bemused, her speech rambling, the words almost incoherent. Notwithstanding this, she was able to sip most of the bowl of sop that I fed to her, spoonful by spoonful, after which I bedded her down, kissed her burning brow, and composed myself for sleep on the floor beneath. Worn out, as ever, by my efforts of the long day (I was to change to the night shift after the Sabbath's break, and how I longed for the change), I was soon far away, and not even the booming of the bellows and clash of hammers on steel from the floor below could hold me back for an instant.

*

It was the sudden silence that always awoke one in the chain factory dormitory, as the hammers and the bellows fell silent. Then before the mind had had time to take in the implications of the new day, the body to adjust itself to the aching cold or, depending upon the season of the year, the stifling heat, the night workers came thundering up the stairs and were upon us; demanding their beds and anxious to be in to them before one's own body heat was, like a gift snatched away when almost within the eager hand, denied them.

For once, I was not roughly importuned, but had time to gather my wits and look about me before I sat up and peered over the edge of Meg's bed to see how she had fared in the night. What I saw made me scream aloud.

20

'She – she's *dead*!' I wailed.

This brought no response from the night workers, who were mostly all asleep already; the others, curious, compassionate, or simply glad of the excuse to delay their departure to work, crowded round to see whatever was to be seen.

Meg was lying stark and still upon her back. Eyes closed. Mouth agape. White as any driven snow. And seeming not to breathe.

'Dead!' I repeated. 'Dead . . .'

One of the Cassandras who had made their grim pronouncements on the patient's state the previous dawn leaned over and prised open one of Meg's eyelids.

'Still livin' an' breathin',' she declared. 'Though it'll not be for much longer, I shouldn't wonder.' Whereupon she pulled aside the coarse blanket and bared the injured leg.

'Humph! 'Tis the gangrene if I ever saw it,' she muttered, pointing. 'See how the evil humours is creeping up the leg and down the leg. Watch it, you'll see. When't has reached the groin' – the old woman sketched the conclusion of her declaration by drawing the heel of her palm across her throat – ' 'twill be the end of her.'

I was already halfway down the narrow room before her words were scarcely concluded. I, too, had seen the angry redness that extended, vein by vein, from the centre of the wound upwards and downwards of the leg from the poultice, which, to my touch, had hardened into the semblance of brick, and could not in any way be removed save by inflicting the most exquisite agony upon the sufferer.

I flew into Mr Grout's office, brushing aside a pair of foremen as if they had been nobodies. They stared at me as if I were an avenging angel, which, in a sense, I took myself to be.

'You again, child?' snapped the manager, glaring at me over his glasses. 'Why are you not at your work, hey?'

'Meg Wolfingham is at death's door,' I told him. 'You must summon a doctor – a *real* doctor – or her blood will be upon your hands!'

'What's this?' he cried. 'Did I not have Mrs Prosser fetched, and did she not give the best of her attention to the woman?

What more's to be done, child? Mrs Prosser had to be paid for her attentions, and will need to be paid again, should she be called, which is not my intent. And as for a doctor – what you call a *real* doctor – why, 'tis out of the question. I have no funds to dispense upon such a wild fancy. Wolfingham has had the best of local attention at no expense to herself. More than that I cannot do, for my hands are tied –' So saying, he gestured towards the columns and columns of tightly-drawn figures that lay upon the page of the ledger before him in ink both red and black. 'You do not know, child, cannot begin to imagine, how tightly I am tied about in matters of finance, being obliged to account for every halfpenny and no redress should I be a halfpence out.' He groped for a large bandanna handkerchief that hung like a flag from the tail pocket of his rusty black coat and dabbed his eyes and cheek.

I was greatly touched, discerning a glimpse of humanity beneath the prim exterior of the manager of the Mordwenn chain factory, and my fury faded, though not my resolve.

'All right, Mr Grout,' I said, 'I'll go back to my work, but one thing I ask . . .'

'Ask it, ask it, child,' he said, avoiding my gaze and continuing to dab his cheek.

'That I may be allowed to break off from my work every so often and go up to see how Meg Wolfingham is faring,' I said. 'To see if she is still alive and needing attention, and if dying, at least to die with a friendly hand holding hers.'

Without looking at me, he nodded. 'So be it, child, so be it,' he said.

I left him then, passing the two foremen, who had been listening to our exchange. They made way for me, and their faces, more set to express harsh disapproval than any other human emotion, were regarding me with something approaching awe and respect. Or so it seemed to me in my own highly emotional state.

*

Mr Grout was as good as his word. Every hour of that long morning, I dropped my work and raced upstairs to see Meg;

nor did the foremen make any attempt to stop me, for they had been given their orders.

To my growing despair, it seemed to me that my poor old friend was quietly slipping away from life. Every hour that passed, her breathing (so faint that at first I had not discerned it) faded further, and the pallor of her skin took on the waxen whiteness of death. In the wound itself there was no change: the great brown ugly poultice remained, and the area about it was of a purplish redness and villainously unhealthy-looking.

At eleven o'clock, after seeing her, I descended the stairs quite convinced that I had, with my last squeeze of hands, said goodbye to my friend for ever and that I should find her gone upon my return. With a heavy heart, I applied myself to my work, and was quite taken by surprise when the bells were sounded at a quarter of an hour before noon.

'Lay aside your tools! Stop the bellows! Out brooms and scrubbers!' The foremen moved among us, shouting their orders, with Mr Grout fussing like a frightened hen. 'Get to it, get to it!' he cried. 'Mr Charles and his party will be here in' – he glanced at his big turnip watch – 'in fourteen minutes precisely.'

In the event, it was not fourteen minutes but nearer forty, before a lookout at the main doors reported that carriages were approaching down the village street. By this time, the floors had been swept and the worktables dusted down of iron filings and scrap metal. There had even been time to make some inroads into some of the ancient grime from the windows, thereby providing unexpected views of the Vale, the Blue Boar and all. As to the workpeople, we womenfolk had been provided with the inestimable luxury of a copper full of hot water, together with cakes of carbolic soap, and we fell upon them with delight, pushing and elbowing to have our first hot-water wash since heaven knows when; old women and young girls, the day shift and the night shift (the latter newly-roused for the occasion). And I, Daisy Friday, nursing a grief within my heart – even I could not resist the unexpected treat.

At the order, we lined up in ranks in the firing shed, the females at one end, menfolk at the other (the two genders were rigorously kept apart at all times, waking and sleeping), to await our master and his party.

First came a pair of liveried coachmen, top-hatted and caped-coated, who held open the main double doors to permit the entrance of, firstly, a trio of gentlemen in long, fur-collared greatcoats, who gazed about them in the unaccustomed gloom of the firing shed, then stepped each to one side of the doors to allow the entrance of three ladies, all in furs and heavy tweeds, with most outrageous hats tied down with silk scarves against the winter wind. They also took their places to one side and the other of the open doors.

And then – *they* came . . .

They came with a flurry of wild snow to herald them, like confetti and rice at a wedding. Winter bride and winter groom: she as fair as a Valkyrie; he dark as a pirate. Hatless, he was, with hair drawn back from a high and commanding brow and streaked with a single strand of grey at the right temple, continuing the path of a slight scar just above the eyebrow and into the hairline. Imperious was his high-bridged and very straight nose, masterful the firm mouth and chin. But it was the eyes that demanded attention most of all: set beneath dark brows, they were of the deepest imaginable grey, and incredibly piercing. They swept over us, every one. I shall say till my dying day that I was *physically* aware of the brief instant that Charles Arbuthnot first looked upon me.

So striking was his appearance, so lordly his presence, that one had quickly forgotten the blonde goddess who hung upon his arm. But not for long. Her voice, cool and drawling, with a marked note of contempt, was surely heard from one end of the great firing shed to the other.

'My dear Charles, are all these dreadful scarecrows belonging to you? How too grotesque for words.' And she stared about her with tip-tilted nose wrinkled as if encountering stinking fish. She was in a great cloak of sable, with a sable-trimmed hat, while a whole constellation of diamonds winked at us from her slender throat. I have never in my life, before or since, felt so low, so mean, so downtrodden. And my gorge rose.

If her consort was put out by her outrageous words and

attitude, he did not show it, but gave her a brief bow and handed her to one of his gentleman companions; whereupon he transferred his gaze to the manager, who had stepped forward and was eyeing his lord and master with all the petrified attention of a rabbit regarding an approaching adder.

'Grout, is it not?' Mr Charles's voice was deep, with a rich timbre.

'Yes, Mr Arbuthnot, sir, and it please you, sir.' The manager first surreptitiously wiped his hand on the seat of his pantaloons and then coyly extended it to the inspection of the other's flat stare; when it was not taken, he hastily withdrew the offending member and hid it behind his back.

'Shall you and your party wish to inspect the factory, sir?' he asked, pulling the tattered rags of his dignity about him.

'I think not,' responded Mr Charles, carelessly. 'This is merely a flying visit. We are on our way through Dorset to Lady Moira Fame's' – indicating the blonde goddess in sable – 'where we are spending Christmas. And in any event, chain-making is a subject of which I know nothing.'

'Nor care very much either, my dear,' drawled Lady Moira, troubling not at all to keep down her voice. She smiled archly at him.

'Ah,' breathed Mr Grout, managing to look both disappointed and relieved at the same time.

'However, before we depart,' said Mr Charles, 'my friend and colleague, the managing director Sir Claud Wisher and Lady Wisher are going to present a gift to every member of the work force for the festive season.' He turned to one of the attendant gentlemen. 'My dear Wisher, I turn the proceedings over to you and your lady wife.' Having said which, Mr Charles took a pace back alongside the blonde goddess and engaged her in an intimate conversation. Nor did either of them take the slightest interest in the proceedings till quite a while later.

'A gift! Now we're going to get the gift!' The whisper went round the assembled workpeople, and many were the muttered speculations. It was not to be wondered that, considering our greatest lack, which was for food – any food, particularly food in quantity – most of the conversation in firing shed and dormitory since the news had been announced had been upon the possible nature of the management's Christmas gift, and that victuals of some kind was the most longed-for option. Plum pudding was high on the list of hopefuls, as was blood pudding. Someone had floated the idea of a bit of belly of mutton, or a pig's cheek apiece, but these had been generally dismissed as being fanciful.

We hungry folk waited – even I, with my burden of sorrow, waited – to hear what was to be our gift.

Sir Claud Wisher stepped forward, a rotund gentleman in a fur-collared greatcoat that reached to his stubby ankles, with a red nose and chin that peered out at us from between the high wings of his starched collar, and hugely-knowing eyes.

'The Board of Directors of Messrs Arbuthnot and Son, Limited have great pleasure in wishing you all a Merry Christmas,' he announced, 'and to ask you to accept, on behalf of the Company, a gift apiece for the festive season.'

There followed a concerted intake of breath from the assembled watchers, followed by a sigh of fulfilment. One could be certain that she who had opted for the belly of mutton or pig's cheek was clenching her fists in anticipation.

'To each will be given,' continued Sir Claud, 'an admirable tract written by my friend the Dean of Fenchester, a work of devotion that has proved to be of inestimable consolation to the poor and destitute, and cannot fail to help you people' – and here he pointed round the mass of watching faces, and surely all our mouths were agape with a sudden awakening of cruel disappointment – 'who have the blessed good fortune to be in paid employment, with a roof over your heads, adequate victuals and benevolent care. The volume is entitled *Why We Should Bless our Kind Benefactors.*

'My dear,' he said, turning to the lady who stood at his elbow, clearly his spouse, who wore a cape of white ermine over her tweed suiting, 'will you do the honours and hand to each and every one of these worthy people a copy of the book, please.'

Lady Wisher signified her pleasure in so obliging. Mr Grout and the foremen ushered us into single file; meanwhile the coachmen came upon the scene with two large trays, upon which were piled small mountains of slim volumes which appeared to be bound in mauve-coloured kid leather – as indeed proved to be the case.

I was third in line. First, by chance, was a person named Agnes Dunwich, a widow woman who had lost her whole family in a plague of the fever that had swept mid and south Dorset five years since. Agnes was palsied, deaf and totally illiterate, notwithstanding which she was capable of forging the required six dog-chains a day. She waited, patient and uncomplaining as a stalled milch cow, while the figure in ermine and fine tweeds pressed into her trembling, mittened hands the first of the Christmas gifts, watching Lady Wisher's mouth in the hope that she might glean some enlightenment from the words that were shut out by her deafness.

'Take this, and a very merry Christmas to you, my good woman,' said her ladyship, smiling. 'I bid you pay particular attention to chapters six and seven, which deal in a most moving fashion with the virtues of Obedience and Thankfulness. Next, please.'

Next was a young woman aged beyond her years named Nancy Jeans, whose only child was resident with her at the chain factory. That is to say, the little mite, being below age for work, nevertheless had to remain with her mother during her working hours and be a constant source of anxiety that she might fall into a furnace, pick up a piece of red hot metal in childish curiosity or meet with some such disaster. Nancy, whose constant hope, since the news was known, had been for a gift of food, was in tears when Lady Wisher handed her a kid-bound volume. And I, next in line, had the clear and unmistakable impression that her ladyship believed her to be weeping with speechless gratitude.

'Take the book and read it, my good woman,' said Lady Wisher, handing the volume to Nancy. Adding: 'And read aloud to your little girl' – indicating the rickety mite who clung to Nancy's skirts – 'about the evil consequences of Greed and Ingratitude, both of which vices, regularly found in the young, are touched upon at some length in the closing chapters. Next, please.'

It is a fact that the ingredients comprising one human spirit may not sometimes well accord with those that make up another. No sooner did I meet her ladyship's eye than I knew her spirit had taken against mine. And the feeling was mutual.

'I am of the impression, young woman,' she said, and her eyes (they were of a china blue and limned most expertly with kohl) narrowed slightly. 'I am of the most *distinct* impression that *you* would greatly benefit by diligently learning by heart the chapter devoted to Pride, which often goes with – *Insolence of Manner!*'

She spoke loudly. Her words must have reached the furthest corner of the firing shed. It certainly reached Mr Charles Arbuthnot, for I saw it clear: how he had been listening to something that Lady Moira had been telling him, but upon hearing Lady Wisher's outburst, laid a gently restraining hand upon his fair companion's arm, bidding her to silence. I met his grey-eyed stare for a moment before I replied to the challenge which had just been hurled at me.

And in my reply was all the pent-up bitterness that I had nourished in my heart – till recently all but unnoticed by me – through the years.

'Ma'am, if we are speaking of pride, I think that it is you yourself who might benefit from studying the chapter you mention!' Those were my very words, and I was both shocked and amazed to hear myself utter them.

'Do you hear that, Claud?' wailed her ladyship, much put about. 'Do you hear what that creature is saying to me?'

'Insolence!' cried Sir Claud. 'Downright wicked insolence – the ungrateful young baggage!'

'Should I be grateful to *you*?' I returned with heat. 'Should *any* of us be grateful to you?' And with a sweep of my arm, I embraced the long line of workpeople who stood regarding me as if I had gone out of my mind. 'What use is *that*' – here I pointed to the mauve-bound tract – 'to these people, when not one in ten – nay, twenty – can read a word of the rubbish, just supposing they were of a mind to do so?'

'Eooow!' screeched Lady Wisher in unladylike tones that were more suited to Westchester fish market. 'Hark what the wretch is saying about the dear Dean's wise and splendid thoughts!'

'Silence your mouth, girl!' barked her spouse.

But I was not to be quietened. 'Better than bringing these people high-flown advice about blessing their benefactors, why did you not bring food?' I shouted. 'You and your talk of adequate victuals! How would you fancy going to work on a cold grey dawn with naught but a swallow of sop to hold your breeches up?' He having no reply to that, I then rounded again upon his wife. 'And you, ma'am, you talk of greed as a vice of the young, and I tell you that you speak with more truth than you know. Why, if you were this instant to be struck dead and turned into a side of bacon and a fine pair of cooked hams, a pig's cheek, tripe and chitterlings, the children in this place would fall upon you with greed unashamed and gobble you up, every last morsel!'

Lady Wisher bethought herself to make some reply to that; she opened her mouth to do so indeed, but nothing came out but a strangled gasp.

I warmed to my theme, addressing myself to the arrogant blonde goddess who stood next to Mr Charles Arbuthnot. She was staring at me with an expression of blank contempt; I did not look at him.

'My lady,' I cried. 'Why, instead of taking your guests home for Christmas dinner, do you not all join us here? Is your liking for skilly? We have skilly – not much, but enough to share. Or perhaps you would prefer sop? No? You wrinkle up your nose, my lady. Does your taste run to fine meats then? How would you fancy boiled lights and carrots or potatoes? That's a dish highly esteemed here, my lady. There's folks here who'd fight their best friend for another spoonful of lights and tatties, or snatch it from the lips of their own hungry children.'

Lady Moira's perfect countenance was pale with fury. With regal dignity, she turned to her companion. 'Is this to be endured, Charles?' she demanded.

For answer, he beckoned to one of the footmen, who lowered his burden of slim volumes and hastened to his master's side. 'Escort her ladyship to her carriage,' he ordered. And to the blonde goddess: 'I will join you with the others when I have dealt with this young person, my dear.'

Lady Moira having gone, Mr Charles regarded me. My fellow workmates also regarded me – with the expressions one might turn upon some unfortunate who, having been found guilty and sentenced for a foul and nameless crime, is about to be executed in a particularly atrocious manner.

'Well, miss,' said our master evenly, 'and what have you got to say to *me*, pray? What denunciation do you wish to lay at *my* door?'

'She should be dismissed!' interjected Lady Wisher. 'Thrown out into the street, to starve or find her way to the workhouse, along with all the rest of the idle, trouble-making riff-raff!'

Mr Charles paid no attention to this outburst, but continued to fix me with his gaze.

'I am waiting, miss,' he said evenly.

In for a penny, in for a pound, I told myself; and suiting the action to the precept, I clenched my fists tightly, took a deep breath and delivered myself of the following peroration, which, so far as my memory serves me after all these years, was rendered with scarcely a pause.

'This *gentleman*,' I said in scathing tone, indicating Sir Claud, 'spoke of "benevolent care", care such as we are supposed, by him, to receive in this place. Well, sir, I will tell you of your "benevolent care" and need go no further than the two persons who have just received your Christmas gift.'

I then informed him of the circumstances surrounding Agnes Dunwich and Nancy Jeans, not forgetting the latter's poor child, who was shortly due for the graveyard if ever I saw a sickly mite; and when I had done this, Mr Charles interrupted me for the only time.

'And you hold me, as owner of this factory, responsible for the wretched state of these people you mention – and, by implication, others?' he asked.

'Not directly,' I conceded. 'Truth to tell, they would be worse off in the workhouse, or begging in the streets. Here, at least, they have a roof over their heads. They have food – bad food and not enough of it. But sir, "benevolent care" they do *not* have!

'There is a friend of mine,' I cried, pointing to the stairs that led up to the dormitory. 'A woman of great worth, a woman fit to grace any position of rank in this land (here I threw a withering glance at the wretched Lady Wisher), and a worker in your factory, who took injury in *your* service, Mr Arbuthnot. And what was the "benevolent care" that was offered her? I will tell you: there were no funds available to dispense upon the wild fancy of a doctor's visit. Instead, a few coppers were spent on the village midwife, whose expert attentions are like to cost my friend her life – if she is not dead already!'

More than that I could not say, for my voice was becoming choked with tears, nor with my swimming eyes could I see what effect my words had had upon Mr Charles – not that I cared.

Without another word, I turned on my heels and, pushing my way through the line of patient, frightened people, I rushed up the stairs, two at a time, and into the long dormitory, not pausing till I came to our bed, where lay 'Lady Meg'.

I fell on my knees beside her. In the windowless gloom, by the light of the tallow dip, I saw that she was no better, and if anything worse. Yet she still lived. Her thin bosom rose and fell faintly, and when I called out her name, it seemed to me that her eyelids flickered for an instant and her lips trembled as if on the edge of speech.

Throughout the long afternoon I knelt there, careless of the comings and goings about me. Still on my knees, my hand in Meg's, I must have fallen asleep. When I woke, the day-shift of workers was all abed, and the clash and clamour of the chain-making rose from the floor below.

Presently, there came a tread on the stair, and a gentleman bearing a small black bag came down the aisle towards me, followed by two men whom I knew as chain-forgers, powerful fellows both.

'Where is the patient?' asked the gentleman, pausing by me. 'The woman who has been injured, where does she lie?'

I pointed to Meg.

'Ah!' he exclaimed, and made a move towards her, but I barred his path.

'Who are you?' I hissed, thinking him to be an undertaker's man who, anticipating my friend's death, had untimely come to lay her out.

'I am a doctor,' he said, adding testily: 'Get out of my way, you silly girl!'

A doctor! Was it to be believed that someone out of charity had summoned help – real help – for poor Meg? I watched, spellbound, as the physician examined Meg and her wound, drawing his face close to the latter and sniffing at it suspiciously.

Presently, he stood up and gestured to the two chain-forgers. 'Pick her up,' he said. 'Do it carefully, mind, and carry her down to my carriage.'

'Where are you taking her?' I wailed, distraught to see Meg's slight form being taken up in the hands of the two burly fellows as if she had been a woodentop dolly.

'Why to the County Hospital,' responded the doctor, 'where she can be properly cared for.'

'Is she – is she going to die?' I faltered.

'I do not know,' he replied simply, closing his bag and making to follow the two men and their burden to the stairs.

'But – why? – how?' I whispered after him, fearful, despite my anguish, of waking the sleepers and bringing their fury down upon my head. 'Who *sent* for you to come here, Doctor?'

He raised an eyebrow at the question. 'Why Mr Charles Arbuthnot,' he replied. 'He requested me personally to attend.'

Then he was gone.

*

As might be imagined, I spent a puzzled and uneasy night, tossing and turning in the vacated bed and wondering how it was that Mr Charles had so changed his ways as to extend expensive care to one of his employees. That he must surely have been influenced by my outburst was something I could not ignore, though this solution to the mystery seemed so far-fetched and unlikely that I sought around in my mind for some other. I was still searching in the small hours when weariness supervened and I sank into an uneasy sleep, where I dreamed that I was being chased across the Vale of the Blue Boar by Mr Charles on a horse and took refuge among the adder-infested heather there, letting the horrid creatures crawl all over me and touch my face with their forked tongues rather than stand up and betray my whereabouts to my hunter. I woke up screaming, with the entire dormitory aroused by my cries and cursing me roundly.

Not five minutes later, the night-shift piled upstairs and another day began. However, so far as work was concerned, mine was over almost as soon as it had commenced, for I had scarcely cut the first steel link and bade my attendant child to ply harder on the bellows to raise the heat of the brazier when I was summoned by the foreman to attend upon Mr Grout in the latter's office.

With a dull feeling of an unnamed fear, as when a condemned person mounts the steps of the scaffold in total ignorance of an unimaginable end, my trailing footsteps presently brought me to the dingy cubby-hole where the manager spent his days at his desk.

'You – you sent for me, Mr Grout,' I faltered.

'That I did, that I did,' he responded, peering short-sightedly at me through the pebble glasses. 'Listen to me now, Daisy Friday.'

'I am listening, sir,' I whispered, my heart sinking, finger-nails biting into my moist palms.

'You will immediately gather together all your belongings ready to leave here,' he said.

'Leave?' I stared at him. So this was it, this my punishment for the outburst of the previous day. I was to be dismissed. My indenture of apprenticeship torn up. Indoor relief at the work-house for me. That or begging – and starving by degrees – in the gutters of Westchester. 'Did you say – *leave*, Mr Grout?'

He fixed me with his gaze for a few moments before he replied, and for the life of me I detected no animosity there; rather, his whole demeanour, now that I studied him more

33

closely, was that of grudging respect. It was all very puzzling. Could it be, I asked myself, that my outburst of yesterday had found favour with Mr Grout?

The impression vanished with his next words . . .

'You are finished for ever here!' he responded briskly, lowering his gaze to a sheet of paper that lay before him. 'And you may go where you please, do what you please, for you are freed of your indenture.'

Just as I thought – I was dismissed! And free – as he said. Free to slave for a crust at the workhouse. Or starve outside. There was certainly no paid work for the likes of me, a discharged apprentice, in poverty-stricken mid-Dorset in that year of Grace 1896.

Mr Grout laid aside the paper and cracked his knobbly knucklebones. 'However, if you so choose – and the choice is entirely yours, yours alone – you may present yourself to the local offices of Messrs Arbuthnot and Son, which lie in the High Street, Westchester.'

'For – for what reason, sir?' I asked, astounded.

He spread his hands. 'I do not know for what reason,' he declared. 'I am only a humble wage-slave like everyone else here. Not privy to the secret thoughts of my betters. I merely obey. Obedience is all. As the Good Book truly states: *"To obey is better than sacrifice."* Two Samuel, chapter fifteen, verse twenty-two.'

The wisdom of Samuel enlightening me not at all in my present predicament, and Mr Grout seemingly not disposed to help me out with idle speculation (indeed, he had taken down a cash book and was busily adding up a column of figures, ignoring me completely), I made to leave. One last thought struck me.

'Is there news of Meg Wolfingham, sir?' I asked.

'None whatsoever, none whatsoever,' he replied.

'What's to be done with her belongings – her box of books?'

'I have had no instructions in the matter,' he said. 'When I receive instructions in the matter, I shall obey them without question, as is my wont.'

34

'Oh! Well – goodbye, Mr Grout,' I said, backing away to the door.

He grunted something, but without looking up.

*

Within the hour, I left Mordwenn chain factory with all my slender belongings wrapped in an old petticoat. As I trudged the winding lanes through a thin flurry of snow, under the humped shape of the Blue Boar, my thoughts turned to the strange behaviour of Mrs Prosser the midwife lady when she had gazed into my palm.

What, indeed, had she seen there that had sent her scurrying away in alarm? Was it something related to my present, odd circumstance? What awaited me at the offices of Messrs Arbuthnot & Son in High Street, Westchester? For I was determined to find out, no matter what. After all, there was no further punishment that could be visited upon me for denouncing the management of the chain factory as a pack of grasping scoundrels. I had been dismissed, and that was the end of it.

How was I to know, and how guess, what lay before me? It is certain, reflecting upon the matter with benefit of hindsight, that Mrs Prosser *did* see something in my hand; but she could not have encompassed one half of the glorious splendour and the appalling heartache and perils, the modest beginnings of which awaited me three parishes and two streams ahead along the path to which I had set my footsteps.

THREE

The offices of Arbuthnot & Son in Westchester High Street have long since been pulled down to make way for a Bioscope Picture House, but when I first regarded the establishment in the dying light of that December afternoon, with snow settling on its eaves and being whirled away like spindrift in the westerly wind, it looked as permanent and inviolable as the great pyramid. With considerable trepidation, I mounted the steep front steps and regarded a notice that was painted in neat lettering upon the door: *Knock and Wait.*

I knocked and waited. Presently the door was opened by an elderly male party in a braided tunic and tightly-fitting pantaloons, which note of military persuasion was heightened by a pillbox cap perched on one side of his white thatch and secured by a chin-strap.

'No hawkers and no circulars!' he declared. 'Likewise we has already subscribed to the Parish Poor, Christmas Treat for the 'Omeless, likewise for the Indigent Gentlewomen and et cetera. Good day to you!' Whereupon he made to shut the door in my face, and would have done so had I not smartly interposed my foot in the door.

'I am none of these people,' I declared with some heat. 'I am Daisy Friday – *Miss* Daisy Friday,' I added, to give myself some more weight. 'And I believe I am expected here.'

'*Who's that, who's that?*' The question came from a harassed-looking young man passing by in the passage beyond the door.

He carried a sheaf of papers and gave the impression of being burdened by all the cares of the world.

'Says she's expected 'ere, Mr Walthamstow,' supplied the liveried doorkeeper. 'Name o' Friday, Daisy, Miss.'

'Friday, hah!' A light of recollection burned for an instant in the young man's eye. He scratched his chin (which was of inordinate length), tapped the side of his nose (which was likewise), and said: 'Yes, I recall it now. The message came late yesterday afternoon. Sergeant Walmer . . .'

'*Sah!*' The uniformed doorkeeper snapped to attention and saluted.

'Convey Miss Friday to the counting house and place her in the charge of Mr Nesbitt, who will show her the ropes, her accommodation and et cetera.' His vague eyes lit upon me. 'Welcome among us, Miss Friday. Yes. Ah, now, what was I about to do . . .?' He wandered off down the corridor, vaguely drifting as a leaf before the fickle wind. And in all that exchange, I had neither spoken a word save to identify myself, nor had I been invited to do so.

'Come alonger me, miss,' said Sergeant Walmer.

I came, there being no alternative offered. Furthermore, I was agog with curiosity and a certain excitement to find out what manner of enterprise was being offered to me. So I traipsed along behind the swiftly-marching sergeant as if on drill parade, my bonnet awry with the wind and dusted with fine snow, my worldly goods slung over my shoulder in an old petticoat; looking back on it, I must have cut a most unprepossessing figure.

By way of more corridors, staircases, and an iron bridge that spanned the building with another adjacent, we came at length to a long, silent room down each side of which was set a row of high desks and high stools, where sat fully a score of men and women in the proportion of something like five to one in favour of the former. Upon our entrance, a score of pairs of eyes were raised from their labours, and an exceedingly well set-up young man with sandy hair, bright blue eyes and pink cheeks, lowered himself from his stool and came towards me, extending a hand in welcome.

37

'Miss Friday, is it?' he asked. 'I have been expecting you. The note reached me late yesterday afternoon that you would be coming into the counting house. I'm Mr Harold Nesbitt. How d'you do?' And taking hold of my hand he shook it with vigour.

'How – how do you do, sir,' I faltered, quite bemused.

'Well, since it's approaching dinner-time, we'll leave the business of showing you the ropes till after the recess,' said Mr Nesbitt. 'I 'spect you'd like to see your accommodation, dispose of your baggage, and what not. Miss Amy Pockett will show you there. Miss Pockett: forward! Kindly show Miss Friday to the lodgery. Her room will be No. 7, and the key's on the board.'

'Hello,' said Miss Pockett, who was short, plump and jolly-looking. Like all the rest of the females in the room, she wore an ankle-length grey uniform pinafore over her frock. The first and second fingers of her right hand were marked with red and black ink.

'Hello,' I said.

'Off with you then,' said Mr Nesbitt. He smiled at me. 'I look forward to making your better acquaintance at dinner-time, Miss Friday.'

Miss Pockett led me upon another traipse through the bewildering labyrinth of stairs and corridors, across yet another iron bridge spanning the gap to yet another building.

'This is what we call "the lodgery",' said my guide, and went on to explain. 'Those who don't have homes in the town, like yourself, lodge here for eightpence a week, which is stopped out of your wages. Mind the steps and hold on to the banister, 'tis very steep, this last bit.'

We came at length to the top floor of the building, to a door in a short corridor. Miss Nesbitt unlocked the door and stood aside to allow me to enter first.

'Well, how do you like it?' she asked.

It was a large room – or, at least, it was a large room to my eyes, as wide as the dormitory at Mordwenn, but not to be compared in length, of course. The walls were painted a pleasant shade of pink, and the wooden floor was polished and clean as a new pin. To my sudden surprise and delight, it had *windows*! Two windows, that looked out across the chimneys

38

and rooftops of Westchester to the snow-clad hills in the north. It was some time before I could drag my eyes from the delicious novelty of having a *view* from a room, and when I did, it was to observe that the chamber was sparsely furnished with a cupboard, a chest of drawers, a wash-stand with hand-basin and water jug, and an exceedingly comfortable-looking bed.

'Where,' I asked Miss Nesbitt, 'do all the others sleep?'

'What others?' replied she, clearly puzzled.

'Why all the others who share the room,' I explained, gesturing to the wide space surrounding us, space which, accustomed as I was to living cheek-by-jowl with three score women and girls, my expert eye reckoned to be sufficient for at least six more, ten at a tight pinch.

'No others share the room,' came the astonishing reply. 'They all have rooms of their own.'

'But – you mean . . .?' I began. And then I remembered the lesson that Meg Wolfingham had so often drilled into me: *'Those forever asking questions embarrass others and show themselves as ignoramuses. Watch and listen, Daisy – watch and listen.'* So I held my peace and took a deep breath. When the wonder and magic of it all had arrived at something like its true proportion, I heard myself say, in what I hoped to be a casually approving tone:

'Yes. Very nice. I think I shall be quite comfortable in here.'

Comfortable! Ye gods! Surely the Queen herself could not have been more comfortable in her bedroom at Windsor, or Buckingham Palace!

Looking back on it, I marvel at my coolness, then.

*

Amy (we slipped into first name terms almost immediately after that), by gentle probing on my part, revealed more of the life and conditions to which I had been so unexpectedly translated. For a start, the employment of Daisy Friday had been sanctioned by a note which had arrived in the office of the same Mr Walthamstow whom I had encountered at the door. He, chief clerk of the establishment, had been instructed to expect my arrival – and by none other than Mr Charles himself!

The wage of a female clerk in the counting house, Amy told

me, was five shillings and eightpence a week (eightpence being stopped for a room at the lodgery); Sundays were free, likewise one Saturday afternoon in four was a holiday (though, of course, unpaid). In addition, the employees were given a free midday dinner comprising meat and potatoes and a substantial suet pudding.

To me, who had suffered the orphanage and then the chain factory, where the average wage for a woman was two shillings and threepence for a six-day week from morn till night, and a bed that was never cold in a windowless attic, with lights and tatties for the most favoured meal, the regimen at the offices of Messrs Arbuthnot & Son in Westchester was like being translated to Paradise, and I confess to having been somewhat numbed with the shock of it.

'I expect you'd like to wash and brush up and put your things away,' said my new friend.

'Oh, yes!' I breathed ecstatically. 'Oh, *yes!*' (Would I not, in this my own, my very own, room?)

'I 'spect you'll have a job to find your own way back to the counting house,' she said, 'though you'll soon get used to it. I'll come back and call for you in about a quarter of an hour, in time for dinner. All right?'

I nodded. Watched her leave. When the door had closed upon her – *my* door – I picked up the hem of my skirts and danced around the room, humming a paean of thanksgiving for my new good fortune. A fortune which, contrary to the best precepts that I had heard preached from the pulpit of St Barnabas' church, I had gained by insolence and lack of respect for my betters (or if not, for what other reason? I asked myself). I then hung up my few bits and pieces in the cupboard, washed my hands and face in the basin, straightened my hair in a mirror hanging above the same, and awaited the arrival of Amy to escort me to the midday meal.

*

My first day at Arbuthnot & Son – which terminated with the delicious moment when, newly washed with pure water and cake soap, my teeth scrubbed with salt, and my hair in a pigtail,

I crept between the crisp white sheets of my own, my very own bed – will remain in my memory for as long as I live.

I relived it in the brief, blissful moments before I was snatched away to sleep . . .

The meal was taken in a place called the refectory, which was a long room with two tables set down the sides and a shorter one across the top where sat the principals of the establishment, that's to say Mr Walthamstow, the harassed young man whose acquaintance I had made at the front door, who turned out to be the chief clerk; our own Mr Harold Nesbitt, senior clerk of the counting house; and about six others, none of them female. We others took our places where we wished at the long tables. I sat with Amy, facing two other friendly girls named Harriet and Janet.

Even at this long remove, with memories of a thousand sumptuous and expensive meals between, I still cannot bring myself to think of that meal without making my mouth water.

Such bliss . . .

There was meat, and the meat was boiled beef – the first of my life. I savour, still, the almost sinful ecstasy that came with the pristine touch of its soft and yielding shape upon my palate; the sensuous shock when, my teeth having pierced that first piece, it released its juices and revealed a thousand subtle tastes and sensations, all of them unique in my experience. And the wonder and glory of it: when I had swallowed the first mouthful, there was more, more, more! I truly think that it was almost worth having been half-starved for all of my life till then in order so completely to relish the taste of simple boiled beef and carrots.

After midday dinner, it was back to work. Mr Harold Nesbitt himself performed the feat that he described as 'showing the ropes' to me.

The counting house system at Arbuthnot & Son had the simplicity of method that accorded with the educational standard of the clerks, which was no higher than the rudiments of the three Rs, and in which, to my surprise, I swiftly perceived myself to be as competent as any. Each clerk took charge of a ledger containing the accounts of three or four of the firm's subsidiaries, which might be a grocer's emporium in Poole, a saddler's in Dorchester, a ships' chandlery in Weymouth – or even a chain factory in Mordwenn. I had No. 9 ledger, which comprised the tale of the ingoings and outgoings of two bakeries, an inn, and a chophouse, all in the Westchester area; and it was a tale that was set out in some detail, telling as it did every item of income and expenditure down to the last half-penny and farthing of every day from opening till closing times; credits to the left in black ink, debits to the right in red; every column added up by myself, the totals carried over to the following page, with a running total of profit and loss at the foot of each. The work was hard, exacting and not a little tedious. It engaged us from 8.30 in the morning till six in the evening, with three-quarters of an hour's break for midday meal and a quarter of an hour for a cup of tea and a biscuit at four. Compared with working at the chain factory, it was like reclining on Parnassus and feeding upon milk and honey-dew.

It was not long – no more than about a week – before it became plain to me that Mr Harold Nesbitt regarded me as more than merely a new face in the counting house. To celebrate the Christmas festivities, we adorned the room with bunches of holly and mistletoe culled from hedgerows and oak trees in the vicinity. There was much good-humoured banter concerning the ancient custom of kissing under the mistletoe, in which my friend Amy – a decided flirt – was prominent in her approaches to shy youths and maidens both; urging them to seal their good fortunes for the year beneath the mystic mistle-toe, and snatching kisses for herself into the bargain. It was she who suggested that there should be a long-standing tradition – commencing as from that very day – that the senior clerk of the counting house must set the seal of welcome upon new lady clerks by kissing them under the mistletoe bough at the first Christmas of their employ at Arbuthnot & Son – a suggestion which that worthy gentleman did not appear to take much amiss.

There were two other young women who had joined the firm in that year, and they were the first two in line to receive Mr Harold Nesbitt's benison. When my turn came, Amy directed at me a very decided wink – and I suddenly discerned the true reason behind the 'tradition' that she had instituted.

That, the first kiss I had ever received from a man, differed only in kind from my first bite upon a piece of prime boiled beef: that's to say it was unique in my experience, astonishing as to variety of sensations, and wholly satisfying. Yet, in truth, it was no more than a peck on the cheek.

That same evening when we had closed our ledgers for the day and bundled together the piles of receipts and bills that supported our figures, Harold Nesbitt came up to me.

'Miss Friday,' said he. 'As I understand the roster, you are for a half-day's holiday on Saturday afternoon next. Do I have it right?'

'Why, yes,' I replied, tying the ribbon around a pile of bills with fingers that surely trembled with the onslaught of a sudden premonition.

'Then I wonder, Miss Friday – and my mother also wonders – if you would care to come to tea with us on Saturday afternoon next.' He paused for a moment, and added: 'Mother is musical. Do you like music?'

Aside from hymns and Christmas carols, my knowledge of music inclined only to the occasions when I had heard the song of larks on high and the chatterings of starlings at dawn and dusk; but I had no intention of displaying my ignorance.

'I am enchanted by music,' I replied. 'Particularly' – and I searched my mind for a name from one of the compendiums of general knowledge that Meg Wolfingham had kept in the chest under our bed – 'particularly – um – that of Mr Handel.'

He smiled. And he really did have a most engaging smile that took in the whole of his face, pink cheeks, bright blue eyes and all.

'Well, Mother don't aspire to anything so high-flown as Handel,' he said. 'But she does her best with sundry airs and ballads, accompanying herself on the pianoforte. Will you come?' The blue eyes became very earnest.

'Yes, I will come,' I told him. 'And with pleasure. Thank you, Mr Nesbitt.'

That same night, there was a letter awaiting me in the rack at

43

the entrance to the lodgery, near by where the key board was placed. I did not recognise the sprawling, almost indecipherable handwriting on the outside, and the contents took me some time to interpret, but I managed it – and with a growing delight and relief.

Dear Miss Friday,
A note, and no more, at the bidding of Mr Charles Arbuthnot, who has asked me to apprise you of the condition of my patient Meg Wolfingham.

As you are aware, the woman was in a bad state of collapse when I took her from the factory, and I did not give much for her chances at that time. The wound, so it seemed to me, was in an advanced state of mortification and the ill-humours had reached the upper part of the leg. Furthermore, it was well-nigh impossible to remove the poultice that adhered to the festering parts – it having not only turned to the consistency of stiff leather or wood, but had grown a most noxious-appearing *mould* which could scarcely have improved the state of the wound. You may picture my astonishment (and I freely grant my astonishment) when on Tuesday last, the said poultice fell off of its own accord, revealing the wound to be covered with an area of fine new skin. Furthermore, the surrounding areas were quite free of the discolourations that we associate with the onset of morbidity. In short, the patient was cured of her hurt!

I understand that the poultice was put in place by the old midwife lady of Mordwenn, whose occasional forays into the realms of primitive medicine have not passed unnoticed by me. It is scarcely likely that any other than happy circumstance and benevolent Nature intervened to save my patient. While saying that, one is left with a nagging suspicion that there may be something, after all, in the strange ways of healing handed down by word of mouth from the Dark Ages by such as Mrs Prosser. But it flies in the face of all my learning and experience.
                    Yours faithfully,
                    David Murchison, M.D. (Edin.)

*

'Mother, this is Miss Daisy Friday, who has come for tea with us. Miss Friday, this is Mother.'
    'How do you do, ma'am.'

44

'How do you do, Miss Friday. Harold tells me that you are fond of Handel. No doubt you have heard the *Messiah*?'

'I have not, Mrs Nesbitt,' I replied in truth. 'But I would greatly like to hear that splendid choral work performed. The trouble, as I understand it, however, is to assemble such a large choir, orchestra and pipe organ outside of London, or one of the large cities.'

(Not for nothing had I learned large portions of Meg's compendiums by rote!)

Mrs Nesbitt, small, grey, with twinkling blue eyes the counterfeit of her son's, nodded in approval of my informed summation. 'Do you like scones?' she asked. 'We have warm scones, blackberry jam and clarted cream. And after that I will sing you a few of the old ballads to the pianoforte.' She squeezed my hand, and her touch was dry and delicate. 'I was once on the music halls,' she said. 'Played at the Theatre Royal, Dorchester, likewise the Alhambra, Weymouth. Afterwards, I will show you some of my old posters. *Matilda de Villefort – Chanteuse.* That was not my own name, of course. They gave it to me because it looked rather grand on the posters. Do you take milk with your tea, my dear?'

Sitting in the neat little front room in the tiny terraced house almost within the shadow of the Arbuthnot & Son building, I was warmed and entranced by the, to me, unaccustomed sense of family life, security, permanency. Though even with my limited experience – having only the orphanage and the chain factory for comparison – I could discern signs of near-poverty, it was of the most genteel sort. The furnishings were few and worn, though darned, mended, dusted and polished like museum pieces. The floor was bare of all save one hand-hooked rag rug, but the boards bore the patina of many years loving labour with wax and polisher. And a coal fire burned warmly in the tiny grate.

'Harold began his working life as a draper's assistant,' said my hostess, handing me a dish of tea, 'but, lacking advancement in that trade, he turned to the clerking pursuit. He tells me, Miss Friday, that your coming has made a great improvement in the counting house.'

45

'Oh! Well that's very kind of . . .' I faltered.

'Miss Friday's ledger work is of a very high standard,' interposed Harold Nesbitt, who had turned as red as a turkey cock. 'I entrusted her with some extremely complicated accounts which have given much trouble in the past. But, happily, no longer. Hum!' He re-addressed himself to his tea.

I relaxed in the warmth and the peace, nibbling at the new-baked scones, the home-made jam, the luxury of the unaccustomed thick cream in which a spoon could be stood up. And I eyed the pictures set around the walls: engravings of the theatre and music hall, interspersed with seascapes (on our way to his home, Harold Nesbitt had let drop that his father, a sailor, had drowned at sea); and on the chimneypiece, a whole gallimaufry of knick-knacks: glass paperweights and fairings, ships in bottles, a lustre vase, an American clock that ticked portentously from behind a view of a log cabin that was limned upon its face.

And I felt – for the first time in my life – *at home* . . .

After tea had been cleared away (Harold Nesbitt washed the crockery and I wiped), Mrs Nesbitt sang very tolerably at an upright pianoforte with what I supposed to be a nice touch on the keys. The ballads, all new to me, had titles that I recall to this day: 'Faithfulness', 'Only a Loving Heart', 'The Dying Innocent', and many more.

It was quite dark when the time came for me to leave. Harold insisted on seeing me to the door of the lodgery, though it was only a few steps. While crossing the road, he took my arm to guide me through the dark slush that passing carriage wheels had scored in the newly-fallen snow. Nor did he relinquish it till we parted at my door and bade each other 'good night'.

Reaching my room, I lit a candle and went to draw the curtains of the window that looked down into the empty street which was illuminated only by a lamppost some distance away, at the entrance to a narrow alley. I was about to turn away when it seemed to me that, at the moment before I obscured the view of the snowy night, something – *someone* – moved in the shadowed alley. I looked again. No one there. And then, quite slowly, even cautiously, the head and shoulders of a man

46

emerged into the fitful light of the street lamp, round the corner of the stonework. He wore a wide-brimmed tall hat that entirely masked the features and particularly the eyes; but I knew with the numbing certainty which is the associate of sudden alarm that the stranger was looking directly up at my window.

And it was not Harold Nesbitt, anxious, perhaps, to assure himself that I had safely negotiated the steep staircase to my attic room. Harold wore no such hat.

Even as I stared and wondered, with the hairs at the back of my neck stiffening and my skin prickling, the watcher's head vanished from my sight. Nor did it return.

*

It was scarcely more than a week after that event, in fact it was the Sunday week following, that I took the opportunity, prompted by a note from Dr Murchison, to visit my dear friend Meg in the County Hospital, to which I journeyed by penny conveyance. The hospital, set on the crest of an escarpment, with fine views to the south and the crawling grey sea, was a modern building and equipped by repute with the most up-to-date medical and surgical devices. Having presented myself to a functionary who sat upon a high stool in the entrance hall, and shown him the letter of admission I brought from Dr Murchison, I was directed to the Female Ward: a long dormitory set each side with close-packed beds – yet as much unlike the sleeping quarters at the chain factory as could be. The windows were high and plentiful, the floors swept clean; the patients, each in her snowy-white bed linen, with a white coif upon her head and a night-gown of the same material, looked well cared-for.

Meg saw me early and waved. I went to her bedside and we embraced. To my joy, she looked better than I had ever seen her. There was some colour in her cheeks, which did not seem so lined as I remembered.

'How is your leg?' I asked. 'And how are you in yourself?'

'The leg is quite healed,' she replied. 'As to myself, they tell me that I shall get up tomorrow and be out of the hospital on Tuesday.'

47

I stared at her in alarm. 'And back there to the chain factory!' I breathed. 'Oh, Meg, Meg, how truly awful! And to think that I've escaped all that and am living in luxury. While you . . .' My voice broke.

But she was smiling. And, squeezing my hand, she told me the wonderful news that, like myself, she had won the patronage of Mr Charles Arbuthnot, who, through one of his agents, had informed Meg that a place as housekeeper awaited her at the home of one of his dependent relations, a Mrs Stanhope-Wise, in the village of Penberthy Lee. It was a sinecure, the agent had added, for the house was well staffed with servants, the mistress easy-going, and all Meg would be required to do was run the establishment with a light rein and be companion to Mrs Stanhope-Wise and read to her – for she was blind.

My joy and relief may be imagined, and I was able to tell her the details of my own good fortune: of the clean and orderly work for which I was well paid, fed and housed, of the new friends that I had made. It was when I came to speak of Harold Nesbitt that I stumbled over a phrase or two and realised to my embarrassment that my cheeks were flaming. I was about to gloss over the topic of my friendship with the senior clerk of the counting house when I perceived that Meg was smiling at me in a fond, one could say maternal, manner.

'My dear, I think that either you or Mr Nesbitt must hold the other in very high regard,' she said quietly. 'Or perhaps the feeling is mutual. Don't say any more unless you really wish to, Daisy.'

'I – I have been to tea with Harold and his mother once,' I replied. 'And on the following day, Sunday, we went to church together and afterwards for a walk by the river. Yesterday, being a working Saturday, I also went round to his mother's for supper and he saw me back to the lodgery afterwards. And . . .'

'Go on if you wish, dear. Remain silent if you don't.'

'And he – he asked me to be his wife,' I said.

'You were surprised?'

'In a way – yes. On the other hand – no. I had thought that he – admired me.'

'Did you give him a reply, Daisy?'

I shook my head. 'I didn't say him "yes" or "no", for how could I, having known him for only a few weeks? Oh, Meg, I'm so ignorant in these matters. I hadn't the heart to hurt him, so I begged him to withdraw his offer and to wait till we had known each other for a longer time. Was I wrong to offer him encouragement? Tell me do, for there's none but you I can turn to for advice.'

She took both my hands in hers. Her sweet, ravaged face and gentle eyes melted my heart, yet gave me confidence that I was to receive good counsel – as indeed I was.

'Do you love this man, Daisy? Tell me true,' she said.

'I don't know, Meg,' I replied in truth. 'But I admire him.'

She nodded. 'Then you answered him well, my dear. Admiration is a very fine thing and much may come of it. There are marriages founded on mutual admiration that have greatly prospered to the happiness of all parties, where many entered upon in blind passion scarce outlast the orange blossom that graced the union.

'Continue to admire your Mr Nesbitt, my dear, for he sounds to me an honest, straightforward man who esteems you greatly and is not ashamed to advance his claim. Maybe you will learn to love him, but I tell you this . . .' She paused, and a tear misted her eye.

'Yes, Meg?' I prompted her.

She touched my cheek. 'One day you *will* know love, my dearest child, for you have the heart for it. And when you do, there will be no doubts, no second thoughts for you. You will take your chance in both hands. Though all the fingers in the world point scorn at you. Though all the darkness on earth may hide you from the man you love.'

*

It was dusk when I left Meg. We had talked quietly together, hand in hand, till the ward attendants came round with lighted candles and whispered to the visitors to leave. Kissing her, I stole out into the starry, frosted night and took the conveyance back to Westchester.

I never saw Meg again.

When they came to wake her next morning, they found her dead; passed away in her sleep without any pain; her great heart in that feeble frame having at last succumbed to the years of deprivation and drudgery.

No quiet evening for poor Meg. No dreamy, drowsy afternoons in the sunlit gardens of some lovely country house, to close her days.

It was as if she had lived her life through for only one moment: to lay her hand upon my cheek and pronounce my future; she, more than a friend, better than a mentor and a guide. The nearest to a mother I have ever known, or shall ever know.

FOUR

The week of Meg Wolfingham's death, in the January of that year, what was almost a new Ice Age descended upon the west country and particularly mid-Dorset. Successive blizzards and frosts made the roads impassable, so that folks in outlying hamlets and farmsteads starved to death at their own empty hearths, and old people perished by the score; nor were the dead buried till the thaw set in, for the iron-hard ground defied all the efforts of grave-diggers. Poor Meg herself was not laid to rest till the beginning of the thaw in early February. I attended her funeral, and Harold stood by my side under the bare, black trees, while the rector, his surplice worn over a thick coat, and with a long woolly scarf wound about his neck and chest, wheezed the Service for the Dead over the yawning pit.

Meg's last injunction had set me on a course as regards Harold. Upon his further enquiry as to my feelings regarding him, I answered straight out that I esteemed him highly, but that I was not yet prepared to commit us both to the irretraceable step of Holy matrimony. When he pressed me yet further (but gently, and with great tenderness), I said that I would give him my answer in the spring, and that till then we should walk out together. So began, for us both, a quite serene period in which we were half-affianced. What, in rural Dorset, is called 'Having an understandin', loike'.

I do remember now that I had made some mention to Harold of the mysterious stranger who had spied upon my window on the Saturday eve of my first visit to his home. I made light of it, as one does in the clear daylight when fancies fade. Naturally, he had nothing to contribute to the matter, save to brush away my fears, and there the issue rested and might have been forgotten – had it not raised its head again in a new and terrifying dimension a week or so after Meg's funeral.

*

I am as soft-hearted as the next person when it comes to cuddly little animals. When Josie Edwards, our resident refectory cook, told me that her father's collie dog had been delivered of four puppies and that the 'runt' of the litter, whom nobody wanted, would have to be destroyed, I fell in love with the poor mite without even setting eyes upon it; and when Josie turned up with this little scrap of soft-mouthed, doleful-looking doggy outcast, I was lost to all sterner feelings of logic (for how could I, employed all day, cope with what was eventually going to grow up into a fairly large-sized working dog – and I living in an attic room?). In short, I took on the pup and called him Thursday by the same rule by which I had been named in the orphanage: I first set eyes on him on a Thursday.

The early days were not a great problem, for he was very soon house-trained, and slept most of the day in his basket. I would dash up and see him at midday and give him the scraps off my dinner plate, afterwards taking him for a short romp in the field behind the offices. As the weeks passed and he grew in need of more exercise, we went for walks on the common land outside the town, as far as a dark copse that led down to Mordwenn and beyond. As often as not, Harold came with us.

On the evening in question, I took Thursday alone. He bounded ahead of me, tail lashing vigorously, clumsy legs already outgrown his small body, keen nose scenting the frosty ground ahead. It was already dusk, and I had no intention of going far. Thursday had other ideas.

We came at length to the edge of the copse and I called him to heel, intending to return. Alas for intent. The small figure bounded into the thicket, no doubt in pursuit of a rabbit or a squirrel. I, perforce, had to follow, calling his name.

It was quite a while before I came upon him in a small

clearing. He was looking up at a tree, where, on a high branch, I could just discern against the new moonlight the silhouette of the squirrel which the little demon had no doubt driven up there.

With a fond shake of my head, I took hold of his collar.

'Come, my lad,' I said to him. 'No more hunting for you tonight. It's home for us.'

It was then that there came the quite distinct sound of a dry twig cracking underfoot. Quite close. Out in the darkness beyond the clearing.

'Who's there?' I called. And my voice sounded strangely loud and urgent as it broke the silence.

No response.

Uneasy, but as yet not greatly alarmed, I turned to retrace my steps – away from the direction from which the sound had come – and beckoned Thursday to follow me, which he did. We had scarcely re-entered the thicket before the crack of a trampled twig, and then another, made me look back over my shoulder – to see an angular figure striding swiftly across the clearing in pursuit of me.

And in the moonlight, I saw the outline of the hat he was wearing: a wide-brimmed, tall hat that masked his features in deep shadow!

I ran, shouting to Thursday to follow me closely, and I had the clear impression that he did, for every so often his bounding, parti-coloured form would advance a few paces ahead of me, and then fall back. In this manner we reached the edge of the copse and saw the moonlit common ahead, with the winding path leading up to the town and the beckoning lights of the cottages on the outskirts.

How I won my life that night, I shall never know. The breathless, sobbing progress across the common, with my heart pounding so that it might have burst its way out of me, and my legs growing weaker till, as in a nightmare, it seemed that I was wading through thick treacle and every instant I thought to feel my pursuer's hand close about my shoulder and turn me round to face him – it will all live in my memory, for nothing can erase it. Nor dared I look back, for fear of what I might see, but set my eyes upon the nearest light and steered myself straight for it, disregarding the wayward bends in the path and cutting across gorse, leaping through banks of heather, pell-mell for my very continued existence.

I came at length to the nearest cottage and threw myself at the door, wrenching at the latch with one hand and beating upon the panels with the other.

'Who be there?' came a voice from beyond. A man's voice.

'Open up! Please – *please*!' I pleaded.

'Who be it, husband?' A woman's voice.

' 'Tis a wench. Asking fer to come in.'

(*Please . . . please . . .!*)

I clung there, pounding and pleading, till another voice – that of a young man – joined the duet at the other side of the door, following upon which it was soon opened, and I stumbled over the threshold and almost into the arms of a stalwart labourer in corduroys and a leather jerkin. The man and wife – clearly his parents – stared at me, open-mouthed.

'What ails you, lass?' asked the younger man.

'Looks as if she've stared into the face of Old Nick hisself!' vouchsafed the elder.

'I've been followed,' I panted. 'Someone – a man – came after me in the copse.'

'There's bad folk around,' said the woman. ' 'Tis a folly to go abroad alone o' nights.'

And then, I remembered . . .

'*Thursday!*'

He was not with me!

When I explained to them, the younger man took up a lantern and went out into the night; nor would he let me go with him, but simply asked which way I had come across the common. I remained behind with his parents, and the old woman gave me a glass of raspberry vinegar, which I left untasted, my eye forever straying to the door, a dull ache of fear and remorse in my heart that I had unwittingly abandoned my little friend in my haste to save my own skin.

Presently, the door opened again, and I saw my unspoken question soundlessly answered in his shocked, honest eyes.

54

'Is he – much hurt?' I managed to say.

He shook his head. 'Not any longer,' he replied. 'He be out o' his misery now, poor feller. I saw to that.'

I would have brushed past him to the door, but his brawny arm barred my path.

'Best not,' he said gently. 'In the morrow I'll take a spade and bury him.' He then turned to address his wide-eyed parents. 'What manner of devil have we got roamin' out there?' he asked. 'And if he'd do what he did to a poor dumb animal, what would he not do to a defenceless maid?'

*

The horror of that night did not soon fade, nor the vision of the man in the strange hat, the thought of whose presence haunted my dreams the rest of the time I was in Westchester.

I never again went out by myself after dusk, and seldom alone by day. Harold was a strong shield and weapon against my unwholesome fears; his gentle attentiveness knocked hard upon the door of my conscience, reminding me of my promise. To my alarm, the thought of it weighed heavily; and one day, when I first saw the buds appearing on the branches of the elm tree outside my window at the lodgery, I felt a sense of panic, of being trapped in a circumstance that had slipped beyond my control. Harold did not allude to my promise, but it could not have escaped his notice that the first signs of spring were burgeoning all round us.

And I all unprepared to face up to the decision that I must make very soon.

*

The day that altered my life, so that nothing again was ever the same, dawned as inauspiciously as could possibly have been imagined. It was the time of the quarterly accounting, and we had been working overtime in the office to balance the books of the many and diverse business interests of Arbuthnot & Son. I, particularly, had many problems because No. 9 ledger (traditionally a 'difficult' ledger) simply refused to be balanced. Three successive late nights, with the assistance of the patient

Harold, I laboured upon the problem, and finally discerned that the trouble lay with the faulty returns from the Brewers' Arms Inn at Furstone. Weary but triumphant, I declined the offer of supper at Harold's house and, bidding him goodnight, made to retire to my bed.

I had scarcely lit a candle and drawn the curtains when there came a commotion from the street below: the sound of scuffling and a muffled cry for help. Without any further ado, I ran down the stairs and out into the street to see what was amiss, and espied, on the other side of the roadway, an old gentleman in the grasp of two young ragamuffins, while a third of the like kidney was attempting to rifle the poor man's pockets.

I knew the trio well, for had not they been mere rickety infants at the orphanage at the time that I 'graduated' to the chain factory. Why I even knew one of them by name, and called it swiftly to mind as I waded in to the rescue of the elderly party.

'Take your hands off him, Ned Crocker!' I cried. 'And the rest of you, let the poor man be!'

The lad gaped at me in some dismay, and his companion also. The third ruffian, he who was delving roughly into the gentleman's coat-tail pocket, was made of harder stuff, and greeted my command with a piece of invective that would have brought a blush to the cheek of any female who had not been through the same hard school as he himself. Seeing that soft words would advance my cause not at all, I resorted to action; they were all, after all, only spavined boys, and I a strong young woman. Ned Crocker I boxed in the ear. The pocket-rifler I kicked sharply in the shin. The third member of the gang did not wait to receive his punishment, but turned and fled. After a moment's hesitation, his companions followed after, and I was left alone with the old gentleman.

'Are you all right, sir?' I asked. 'Oh, dear!' To my dismay, upon observing him more closely, I saw that there was an abrasion upon his brow that issued blood, caused no doubt by having his head brought forcibly into contact with the stone wall.

'I – I feel rather faint,' he faltered. He was a man of

considerable age, and frail into the bargain, with a small, delicately-made body like that of a bird. My heart went out to him.

'Come with me, sir,' I said, 'and you can have a sit down and a rest while I bathe your cut.'

The ground floor of the lodgery was the common washplace for the building, and empty at that time of night. Sitting him upon a stool, I drew a basin of water and with a clean handkerchief dabbed his wound free of dust, he all uncomplaining.

'Would you like a nice cup of tea, sir?' I asked him.

'That is kind of you, miss, but I cannot impose any further upon your good nature,' he replied. 'Might I ask the name of my rescuer?'

'Miss Daisy Friday,' I told him.

'Friday – ah, that's a name to remember, an unusual name,' he replied, giving me a very straight, shrewd look. Now that he had somewhat recovered, and a touch of colour had come to his cheeks, I saw that, notwithstanding his years, he was a gentleman possessed of all his mental faculties. Moreover, he was excellently well dressed in a caped coat over a fine broadcloth suit, while his tall hat, which I had rescued from the gutter, was silk and glossy.

'I hope those young wretches didn't get away with any of your belongings,' I ventured.

'I am carrying very little in the way of valuables,' he replied, and patted his lean stomach, across which was swagged a gold watch and chain. 'But I would have been greatly put out if they had taken my dear old timepiece, the rogues.'

'They are almost certainly half-starved,' I supplied, 'and as much to be pitied as blamed. These are hard times in Dorset, Mr – er . . .?'

'Venables,' he responded. 'Call me Mr Venables, Miss Friday.'

'Where are you bound, Mr Venables?' I asked.

'To Dorchester,' he replied. 'Can one obtain a conveyance in these parts?'

'The local carter has a dogcart,' I said, 'but he'll not turn out for as far as Dorchester at this hour for less than five shillings, I shouldn't wonder.'

'That would be most satisfactory,' replied Mr Venables.

So I went across the street to the carter's yard and obtained my new friend's transport to Dorchester. When he was aboard, he took my hand in his and gazed reflectively at me with his steady grey eyes.

'I am greatly obliged to you, Miss Daisy Friday,' he said. 'By your conduct tonight, you displayed a true Samaritan spirit. That is a quality not often to be found, and deserving of the highest commendation.'

With these words, he nodded to the driver and was borne away into the night.

*

There was no escaping it. Spring was upon us. With hesitant, wobbly tread, newborn lambs traipsed after smug ewes; the first early-flowering trees were in full blossom; winter past, the warm benison of the south had fallen upon mid-Dorset; in the shadowed churchyard, new grass was covering the scars of dear Meg Wolfingham's winter grave. And Harold was following me with anxious, questioning eyes.

I was at the crossroads of my life, I knew it. On the one hand, there was the immediate choice of accepting Harold's offer of a marriage based upon respect and esteem, warmed by the certain serenity of an ordered family life together. All too soon, his mother would be gone, and I would take her place dispensing tea and scones, maybe essaying to learn the upright piano and lead my family in hymns and ballads. That was what life offered if I accepted Harold's proposal; and there was naught in it to which I could possibly object.

On the other hand, mindful that I was at a crossroads, I reckoned that there were two other options open to me: I could either do nothing – which is to say that I could refuse Harold's offer and let my life continue its present course along the road that lay ahead – and await whatever else fate might offer me; *or* (and I have to admit that the very thought of it made my blood tingle), I could take the other, remaining path – *and do something different!*

For as long as I can remember, I have known a restless urge to strike out and better myself. With the beginnings I had, and taking into account the independent spirit with which fate has blessed me, it could scarcely be other.

At that juncture, when the necessity for deciding upon one or another of my options (one of which was possibly going to bring great unhappiness upon a fine and gentle-hearted man), I was reminded of a line from Tennyson that I had once come across in Meg Wolfingham's little treasury of learning:

To strive, to seek, to find, and not to yield.

This seemed to express the inner yearning that had always inspired me, and sometimes frightened and puzzled me. On the day that the very last of the trees were in leaf and I could no longer pretend that spring was not with us, I decided to tell Harold on the Sunday following, after mattins, that I could not be his wife. And I was at a loss as to how to explain why this could not be so.

In the event, the necessity for explanations was taken out of my hands by a letter which arrived that same afternoon.

TREACHER MURDOCH & PARTNERS

Solicitors & Commissioners for Oaths

Castle Chambers,
Dorchester, Dorset.
12th April 1897

Dear Miss Friday,

We are instructed to communicate with you regarding a matter which you may consider to be of considerable interest to your goodself.

If you were to call and see the present writer at the above address any time at your early convenience between the hours of 9 a.m. and 6 p.m., you would learn something to your advantage.

We remain, madam,
    your obedient servants,
        Treacher, Murdoch & Partners.
            (sgd.) Giles Treacher

*

59

That arrived on a Thursday. On the Friday morning after, I was on my way to Dorchester in the local dogcart, dressed in my Sunday best, which was a sensible tweed jacket and skirt that I had bought in Westchester market with the proceeds of my first two months' wages. Having shown Harold the letter (which drew from him an amount of head-shaking and doubts as to what some fine town lawyer might regard as being 'to my advantage'), he opted to accompany me, but this I firmly resisted, asking him only to secure for me from the chief clerk, Mr Walthamstow, a day's leave of absence. This he did; and quite a crowd of well-wishers from the counting house, plus Mr Walthamstow and Sergeant Walmer the doorkeeper, gathered to see me off and wish me well – for the details of my strange letter had spread like a straw fire throughout the place, and had been greatly exaggerated in so doing.

As the pony clip-clopped through the winding, leaf-hung lanes, I fell to speculating upon what lay ahead for me in Dorchester. At worst, it might be nothing that would recompense the loss of a day's wages – in which case, I should certainly hang my head in shame upon my return to the counting house; the thought was nearly enough to quench any further speculations. However, my mind presently returned to nibble at the edges of several exciting thoughts that had kept me awake through most of the previous night: all of them centred about the man who, in return for my brash outspokenness (which still had the power to make me gasp at the remembrance of my effrontery), had already shown the mark of his favour and patronage.

What if . . .?

What if (as I had asked myself between ten and midnight) Charles Arbuthnot had some further advancement in mind for me? Something like, say, the post of senior clerk – like Harry – in one or other of his no doubt many enterprises? There was a thought, indeed, to keep a pushy girl awake o' nights!

Or supposing that one of his ageing female relations (someone such as the lady who would have been employing Meg Wolfingham if poor Meg had lived) required a secretary and companion? It was with this notion, between the hours of past midnight and four o'clock, that I had imagined myself making the Grand Tour of France and Italy with my gentle companion, more friend than employer: Paris, Florence, Rome and Venice – the places I had read about, the illustrations I had drooled over; the Champs-Elysées, the Eiffel Tower; the Ponte Vecchio and the Gates of Paradise; the Coliseum and St Peter's Square; the Rialto bridge, nights on the Grand Canal, with our gondolier singing incomprehensibly of love and passion.

I recounted these and many other speculations, till I came to the most unlikely of all, one which I had devised at cockcrow, and which I had carried into the brief hour or so of wearied sleep left to me . . .

Supposing . . . supposing that Mr Charles Arbuthnot, he of the masterful glance and the lordly presence, had looked upon me with such favour that he had there and then determined to bring me forward in life: gradually to wean me away from the influence of the chain factory, to appoint me to positions of ever more worth and responsibility, so that I should learn to acquit myself in all walks of society in order that, at his pleasure, the time being ripe, and he being satisfied with the creature whom he had moulded to his taste, he could make me his wife!

I am to be excused the caprice. After all, I had been awake and wondering all the livelong night. I was, moreover, very young, impressionable and vastly imaginative.

Still, it had been an exciting thought, and it had carried me off to sleep the previous night – as it still had the power so to do. Still turning this fairy tale over in my mind (and I the Cinderella), I fell asleep in the jogging dogcart and had to be woken by the carter when we presently came to the busy streets of Dorchester.

*

'Mr Treacher will see you straightaway, miss. It was Mr Treacher's instructions that you were to be admitted to him no matter what the time of day, what Mr Treacher was doing, nor who was with him at the time. This way, Miss Friday, do.'

The speaker was a dapper little man with a cherubic countenance, a sprightly manner, and a very obvious ginger wig set atop his obviously bald pate. I followed him through cavernous corridors and up narrow creaking staircases to a door at the top of a landing upon which he knocked and was granted admission by a voice from within.

'So *you* are Miss Daisy Friday!'

The speaker, Mr Giles Treacher, upon my being presented to him by his clerk (whose name turned out to be Mr Caldecott), rose and took my hand. He was tall, slender, with butter-coloured hair brushed flat across his brow. His eyes, green, shrewd, twinkling, made a swift appraisal of me; I had the notion that he priced my market stall coat and skirt, noted that my stockings were darned at the heels, and made a good guess that they were likewise cobbled at the toes. I took him to be in his early thirties. He seemed to like me in spite of my poor-looking turn-out.

'Be seated, dear lady,' he said. 'Would you like some refreshment? Tea? Coffee? Chocolate? No? Then let us to business.'

Taking from a drawer in his exceedingly fine and commodious desk a sheaf of papers contained within a cardboard folder, he put on a pair of glasses and perused them swiftly; when he had done, he removed his glasses and beamed across at me.

'You are an extremely fortunate young lady, Miss Friday,' he declared.

'Am I so, sir?' I responded. 'Why so?'

He had a habit, that I swiftly detected, of switching expressions from a comic mask to a serious, not to say tragic, mask at will. Upon my question, the smile disappeared from his lips and eyes and was replaced by a look of the most extreme gravity.

'Miss Friday,' he said, 'I must ask you to prepare yourself for what must prove to be a shock. Do you take spirits? Brandywine, for instance?'

'Spirits have never passed my lips, sir,' I responded. 'Why do you ask?'

'It occurred to me,' he said, 'that a small nip of brandywine – purely for medicinal purposes – might help you to assimilate the news which I have to impart.'

62

'Is it, then – bad news, Mr Treacher?' I faltered, suddenly alarmed.

'Some would not think so, ma'am,' he replied, and switched masks from tragic to comic. 'Some would not think that a legacy amounting to the trifling sum of' – here he consulted the papers before him – 'the trifling sum in the region of one and a half million pounds could be classed as *bad* news!'

*

There is a limit to what the human mind and body can assimilate to any effect. I suppose that the news of being presented out of the blue with an astronomical fortune was no more earth-shaking than the occasion when first I bit upon a piece of prime stewed beef. It was simply a matter of degree. The main effect lay in the uniqueness of both experiences. And, in any event, I simply did not believe Mr Treacher's declaration.

'Sir, did you summon me to come all this way to make mock of me – a poor working woman?' I demanded, rising to my feet.

He was immediately at my side, his restraining hand gently laid upon my arm. 'Be calm, Miss Friday,' he said. 'And be assured that I intend no mockery. It is as I have said. You have succeeded to a legacy of the amount that I have indicated.'

I sank back into the seat, deflated. I suppose that my mouth must have been hanging open.

'Did you say – *one and a half million pounds?*' I whispered.

'That is the sum, ma'am,' he replied. 'And, indeed, through careful investment that I have made on your behalf, the capital must have substantially increased. Er – would you like to see the latest figures?'

I waved aside the notion.

'But who – *who* . . .?' I breathed.

'Ah, I thought you might swiftly pose that question, Miss Friday,' he replied. 'As to your benefactor – I have to tell you that I am not at this time empowered to divulge his name.'

I shook my head, bemused. 'No?'

He shook his head also, firmly. 'No.'

'Oh!'

*

63

At eleven o'clock Mr Caldecott brought tea, both Indian and China, on a silver tray, together with Bath Oliver biscuits, Gentleman's Relish, and paper-thin slivers of bread-and-butter. I watched numbly as Mr Treacher poured for us both, scarcely pausing as he did so in the peroration to which I had been listening for the last half hour or so without so much as a word of interjection. And I am not one who is often found to be short of interjections.

'In addition to the investments I have enumerated, Miss Friday,' he said, 'that's to say, the South African gold shares, the New South Wales Development Trust, the Wyoming Research Cartel, and so forth, I have purchased, in your name, a town house in London and two substantial properties in the West Country. Tea? Indian or China . . .?

'Do you know Bath, Miss Friday? Do try some Gentleman's Relish on your biscuit – but not too much, for it is extremely tasty. Bath is arguably the finest city in Northern Europe, and I do not except Nimes, Avignon or, for that matter, Paris. Furthermore, the real estate market there is extremely buoyant.

'The London house is in Upper Brook Street, Mayfair; a modest, but comfortable establishment, suitable as a *pied-à-terre* if you are up shopping, and managed by a most excellent housekeeper with a small staff of four.

'In your name, I have also purchased a fine terrace mansion in Lansdown Crescent, which, though it does not meet with the same acclaim as the more renowned Royal Crescent, is to the *cognoscente* more refined architecturally, better situated away from the miasmas that arise from the Avon, whilst providing breathtaking views across the river valley. The establishment, which is on three floors, excluding attics and basement, has been fully furnished and staffed under the direction of Lady Wimsey-Fildes, upon my instruction. Her ladyship, who suffered a severe financial embarrassment upon the disgrace and death of her husband, Sir Basil Wimsey-Fildes, Bart., has taken on the commission of acting as your chatelaine and mentor in Bath. Would you like some more tea, Miss Friday?'

I shook my head, and found my voice at the same time.

'Mr Treacher, I insist that you tell me the name of the gentleman who has left me all this money. I *insist!*'

'That is impossible, Miss Friday,' he said. 'Under the terms of the bequest, the donor must remain anonymous for the forseeable future. However' – and here he switched again from tragic to comic mask – 'I am instructed to inform you that, if you are not in agreement with this condition, you are entirely at liberty to decline the bequest.

'Is *that* your wish, Miss Friday?'

What could I say?

*

At twelve o'clock Mr Caldecott brought a decanter of sherry wine and two dock glasses, all upon a silver salver, which he placed on the desk before his employer. Mr Treacher (who had been holding forth for the past hour upon the virtues of Bath as a health spa, a centre of art and culture, the very heart of social life as it has not been lived in this country since the days of Beau Nash, Beau Brummell, not to mention the Prince Regent; with digressions upon Palladian architecture, coupled with odious comparisons with our cousins across the Channel who, as he said, had engaged themselves upon a bloody revolution and regicide at the very same time that Bath had been rebuilt all of a piece in the space of about ten years) beamed at the sight.

'Sherry, Miss Friday?'

'No, thank you, Mr Treacher.'

He helped himself to a bumper measure of the pale wine, sipped, savoured it upon his tongue, swallowed it and sighed contentedly.

'So much, Miss Friday, for your property in Bath,' he said. 'In addition, I have purchased, in your name, a splendid establishment in Cornwall. Do you know Cornwall? What romance is there! What evocations of our mystic past: Tintagel and the Arthurian legend, Avalon and all that.' He took another sip of his sherry, and referred himself to his papers. 'The property is Mortmain Castle, situated on the south coast of the peninsula. Dates back to Norman times and earlier. Passed into the Denvers family, and hugely modernised with up-to-date plumbing in the early seventeenth century.' He smiled at his little joke.

I found my voice again. 'But what shall I do with *three* houses, Mr Treacher?' I asked. 'In all my life, I have never known more than the luxury I presently enjoy – and that's a room of my own under the eaves at Arbuthnot and Sons lodgery.'

At this the lawyer rose, and, still holding his wine glass, proceeded to pace to and fro across the oriental carpet that fronted the fireplace, pausing every so often to mark out a telling point in his address by directing his forefinger towards me.

'I will answer you, Miss Friday,' he said. 'Aside from the prudence of investing a great deal of your liquid capital in stones and mortar – which is the best of all forms of speculation in these times – it is important that you take upon yourself a role that is in keeping with your position. The role of a lady of fortune!'

'Important, Mr Treacher?' I interposed. 'Important to whom, pray?'

'Why to your benefactor, ma'am,' he replied. 'It would be your benefactor's hope that you speedily rise to the highest stratum of West Country society – indeed, of English society generally.'

I could have laughed in his face, but did no such thing; instead, I addressed him seriously.

'Mr Treacher,' said I, 'my benefactor has strange notions about my abilities. Consider: I am a child of the gutter, reared in a parish orphanage and sent to work as a child labourer. The best I ever achieved was to complete my apprenticeship as a chain-maker. Oh, and in that time I also contrived, thanks to the help and inspiration of a woman in a million, to get myself the rudiments of a literary education. And it is this unknown gentleman's wish that *I* should rise to become a flower of high society? Really, he asks too much of me. And you ask too much of me.'

Mr Treacher was silent for a few moments, then he replied.

'Miss Friday,' he said, 'I am privy to most excellent reports of your character and bearing. One witness has it' – and here he referred again to the papers on his desk – ' "That the young woman in question displays an independence of mind, a fearlessness of address, an articulateness of exposition as would not shame a member of the superior sex, and he of the highest education and erudition." '

My gorge rose at the term 'superior sex', which had gained a certain currency in recent years. That aside, I thought I could guess at the source of the 'report' – and stated as much.

'That would no doubt be from Mr Charles Arbuthnot,' I said. 'And he was referring to a recent occasion when I had cause to rebuke him and his like before his assembled workers, despite which he rose to the occasion and marked me for his favours. Correct?'

The lawyer looked affronted. 'I am not permitted to divulge the sources of my reports upon you, ma'am,' he said.

'And is Mr Arbuthnot my – *benefactor*?' I demanded.

He shook his head, and the green eyes flashed defiance.

'I am not permitted to say yea or nay to that question, or any other relating to the identity of your benefactor, ma'am,' he replied. The harshness softened, and he regained his amiable mask again. 'May I, however, add my own brief observation?' he asked.

I shrugged. 'By all means do.'

'I have met this young lady who is the recipient of a fortune which ninety-nine point nine, nine, nine per cent of the population of this planet would embrace with open arms. Nay, would crawl on their hands and knees; crawl through swampland and desert, through Greenland's icy fastness, and swim the widest oceans to obtain; would lie, cheat, deceive, prevaricate, suborn – even kill, to have for themselves. And what have I seen?

'I have seen, and been enchanted by, a young lady whose only consideration is for her worthiness to be the recipient of this legacy, who has doubts about the propriety of accepting it from an unknown source, whose head is not turned by the images of wealth, position and the dubious honours that accrue from the same.

'In short, ma'am, I am become your devoted admirer and servant: willing and happy to serve you far beyond the limits of my brief; to help and advise you in what will surely be a most difficult and trying time in your life. For those who, in the phrase of our national poet, "have greatness thrust upon them", are in as much need of pity as of envy.'

Whereupon, taking my hand, he implanted a kiss upon it. And I would have made some sort of graceful reply, but found to my surprise that I was half-choked with sudden tears.

'Tell me, then, Miss Friday,' he said. 'You will accept the bequest, will you not?'

I nodded.

'Now? Straightaway? You will sign the document which I have here, already engrossed and ready for you but to put your name in the presence of two witnesses?'

I nodded again.

'Splendid!' he cried. And again: 'Splendid!'

*

And so, there and then, I signed the legal-looking parchment which Mr Caldecott brought in upon a summons and stood ready to countersign as witness after his employer had set his own name after mine.

I never read aught of the document save the opening line that began with a great flourish of penmanship with the words: *WHEREAS it is agreed by me, Daisy Friday, a spinster of the Parish of . . .*

The ceremony concluded, Mr Treacher poured sherry for the three of us and both men pledged me with bumper measures and fulsome good wishes, to which I responded with tremulous thanks and a mere taste of the wine, which seemed bitter and unaccommodating to my untried palate. This brought us to past midday, and Mr Treacher proposed that we took luncheon in the grill room of an excellent hostelry in the main street named the 'White Hart'.

The bill of fare (I have it still) included roast saddle of mutton, roast duckling, steak and kidney pudding, stuffed sheeps' hearts, Dover sole with caper sauce, grilled turbot, devilled oysters, smoked salmon, and Dublin Bay prawns in curry sauce. I plumped for the smoked salmon and added yet another gastronomic first experience to accompany the magic of becoming a millionairess in a morning.

Mr Caldecott, who accompanied us to table, wisely reckoning my untutored palate, suggested that I take a glass of Madeira wine with the fish. This I found suave and sweet and very acceptable, so much so that I did not demur when they poured me another.

All through the meal, Mr Treacher held forth about the virtues of Lansdown Crescent, Bath, and Mortmain Castle, Cornwall. If I chose first to stay awhile in Bath, he said, he would communicate with Lady Wimsey-Fildes immediately and apprise her of my coming. Warmed by an ineffable sense of well-being, the like of which I had never in my life experienced before, I readily agreed to his suggestion. Bath it should be. We raised our glasses and pledged Bath.

Most of that meal remains, to me, no more than the sort of transient images which a magic lantern projects upon a screen: a miscellany of faces and colours, smudged impressions, half-conceived realities overladened with fantasy. In short, it was my first – and very nearly last – experience of being rather drunk.

It – the image that jolted me back to almost instant sobriety – occurred while Mr Treacher was rhapsodising upon the architectural excellence of Lansdown Crescent. The curved façade of the terrace, he told me, being unencumbered with the fussiness of columns, elaborate entablature, and so forth, presented to the eye a clean sweep of pure form. I was trying to catch hold of the drift of his argument (no easy feat, for Meg Wolfingham's small treasury had not contained any volumes devoted to architecture), when I had the very clear – and uneasy – impression that I was being *watched*.

Now there were about a dozen others taking luncheon in the grill room, all of them within the compass of my – admittedly unsteady – glance; all were totally engrossed upon either their companions, themselves, or the contents of their plates. Who, then, could be watching me, I asked myself?

I turned to glance behind me, for I was sitting with my back to a window that looked out upon the coach-yard, which was half in sunlight, half in deep shade. And I saw – *him* . . .!

His head and shoulders, the face shadowed by the broad brim of the unusual hat, and the outline silhouetted against the sunlit wall beyond . . .

I may have screamed. In any event, I raised such a cry that all conversation ceased in the room. A waiter dropped a plate in his shock. Mr Treacher reached out and took my hand.

'What is it, Miss Friday?' he asked me. 'What ails you?'

'There's – someone – outside . . .' I faltered.

The lawyer and his clerk gazed towards the window, then exchanged glances. Stung by their manifest unbelief, I nerved myself to take another look.

No one was there.

Mr Treacher cleared his throat. 'Hem. Shall we now address ourselves to the question of a dessert? What do you fancy, Miss Friday? The establishment specialises in a Nesselrode pudding of which they are justly proud.'

I murmured assent to the pudding, and found it to be a rich confection of creamed fruits, mostly chestnuts, all iced. I recollect that it must have been delicious, but I merely pushed it round and round my plate in the pious hope that it would go away; all the time I was thinking of the man in the strange hat – him, and a small scrap of brave, bounding life that had been extinguished out in the darkness of the common that awful night, and might just as well have been me.

My companions, if they were aware of my sudden melancholy, affected not to notice it, but contrived to carry on the burden of a light-hearted conversation that happily called for no contribution from me. I did observe that, though they recharged their own glasses several times, the invitation was not extended in my direction.

Luncheon over, Mr Treacher himself drove me back to Westchester in his own very smart town phaeton, and on the way there proposed the timetable for my translation to Bath. It was agreed that I must give Arbuthnot & Son a week's notice of my intention to leave their employ. After that, I should spend a day or so in Dorchester, residing at the 'White Hart', while I assembled a skeleton wardrobe to take with me for the commencement of my new life.

As Mr Treacher's matched blacks high-stepped through the bewitching countryside, and my head cleared in the bracing air that raced over our soft downland, and all the birds in Dorset seemed to be singing for joy, I was able to forget my fear and attribute the apparition of the man in the strange hat to the second glass of Madeira that I had so unwisely imbibed. And my heart sang with the larks on high and with the meadow pipits in the tall grass.

FIVE

I had been told, when very young, that my arrival at West-chester parish orphanage on that memorable Friday all those years ago was heralded by a thunderstorm of memorable magnitude. The departure of Daisy Friday from the heartland that had fed, clothed and supported her, however exiguously, in the time between, was informed by just another such tempest of thunder, lightning and rain.

I had taken my farewells of all the rest; it was Harold alone who saw me off at Dorchester railway station for the relatively short journey to Bath. We arrived early – too early – and were obliged to sit together in the shelter on the station platform to await the arrival of the train, with the rain streaming down from the eaves and the soaking landscape fading into the misty distance. Thunderclaps were shattering the heavens above and lightning tearing jagged fingers across the dark sky.

Happily, it killed all conversation between us. Not that there was any conversation left. We had said all that needed to be said – and it was not much. Harold, hearing of my astounding fortune, had accepted the news gravely, and wished me well in my new life. He did not take the opportunity of repeating his offer of marriage, nor did I do more than squeeze his hand and kiss his cheek. By mutual accord, we accepted that I had, indeed, taken a new turning at the crossroads and that the kiss, the touch of hands, was my complete answer to the question I had promised to resolve in the spring.

We sat in awkward silence for some time.

'Remember to write to me, Harold,' I said presently. 'You have my Bath address.'

'I wrote it down,' he said, fumbling in his pocket. 'I've got it somewhere.'

'Oh, don't bother to look for it now!' I snapped in an unguarded burst of irritation.

'I'm sorry, Daisy,' he said contritely.

'It doesn't matter,' I said, staring ahead of me towards the distant hills.

It must have been as blessed a relief to him as to me to hear the blast of the engine's steam whistle from afar, and presently to see the train round the bend of a low hill and come puffing grandly into the station.

'Well, here it is,' said Harold, and picking up my two suitcases he raced to the first carriage and essayed to wrench open the door and get me inside out of the rain, baggage and all.

'Don't bother to wait, Harold,' I said. 'You'll only get soaked.'

In truth to tell, he could not have been more wet, having removed his cap so that his sandy hair was plastered to his skull, while his starched collar was wilting round his neck like a sad banana skin and his thick tweed coat was steaming like the hide of a wet spaniel in from the rain. Nevertheless, he contrived to smile bravely.

'Bit o' rain never hurt anyone,' he said.

'That's silly,' I said. 'Who wants to get wet?'

His eyes – those bright blue, adoring eyes – answered me. For my sake, he would have stood in the rain for an eternity. I felt the treacherous tears prickle my own eyes, and was only saved from breaking down by a blast of the engine's whistle and a shudder as the train lumbered slowly into movement. Harold walked with it, keeping pace so as to remain with me, wet and bravely smiling.

I reached out through the window and took both his hands in mine.

'Goodbye, dearest Harold,' I said. 'Don't forget to write, and I'll write to you.'

'Yes, yes!' he cried.

I reached forward upon an impulse and would have kissed him; but the train, suddenly gathering speed, bore me swiftly away. A flurry of smoke from the engine's tall chimney obscured him from my sight till we were clear of the station. The last brief glimpse I had of him as we rounded the first bend was of a tall, tweed-clad figure standing all alone there in the rain. Too far away to be recognisable, he could have been anyone.

*

I have not mentioned that this, my journey to Bath from Dorchester, apart from being the only major expedition of my life, was the first time I had ever travelled by train. The speed of progress was, of course, quite alarming to me. I shared a carriage with two ladies of the farmers' wives sort, and a sergeant of the Mid-Dorset Yeomanry who, having asked and received permission from the three of us, proceeded to light what I vaguely knew to be called a cigareet, and filled the carriage with a pungent smoke which soon became so obnoxious that I was presently constrained to withdraw my permission and civilly ask him to dispose of the offending article, which, it has to be said, he immediately did with like civility; indeed, he asked me where I was bound, and did I know Bath? The sergeant was himself a Bathonian, and when our train emerged from a dark tunnel and out into a broad, green-topped valley up whose slopes ascended, tier upon tier, square upon square, crescent upon crescent, a most noble and spacious city, he was able to point out the twin towers of the Abbey, and name every steeple and spire.

'*Bath – Bath . . .*'

The cry of a gentleman in a cockaded tall hat greeted our arrival. The good sergeant helped down my baggage and opened the door for me.

'Where is Miss Friday? I attend upon Miss Friday. Why ain't she 'ere?' A raucous voice declaiming my name brought my attention to a small, scarlet-faced man in coachman's livery of royal blue and much gold frogging. He was addressing the functionary in the tall hat, who had opened a carriage door and was gazing into it with the air of a dog looking for a lost bone.

'She ain't 'ere,' retorted the latter. 'Ain't nobody a-travellin' first class today.'

'We wuz stric'ly informed that Miss Friday wuz travellin' by this train,' responded his interlocutor. 'And wuz to be picked up.'

'*I* am Miss Friday!' I firmly interposed.

The little man looked at me, looked at my luggage, which was in the hands of the sergeant, looked at the door of the carriage from which I had emerged.

'But, ma'am, you 'as been a-travellin' *third* class!' he breathed, speaking as to a child who had been caught out in the act of stealing apples from an orchard.

I instantly discerned that I had been caught out in a solecism: Mr Treacher had purchased my train ticket, and I had not given a second thought when Harold had bundled me into the first carriage that came to hand out of the rain.

'I *prefer* to travel third class,' I responded with a fine touch of hauteur – or so it seemed to me. 'The company is more amusing.' And to my sergeant: 'Thank you for your help, sir. Pray give my baggage to my coachman. And I bid you a good day.' Whereupon, accepting the sergeant's salute and the doffed hats of the other two men with a gracious inclination of my head, I turned and walked gracefully towards the gate marked 'Exit and Carriages'.

So did Daisy Friday, former chain-worker, pass into history, and Miss Daisy Friday, inheritrix, walk into her future.

*

Waiting in the roadway outside was a row of carriages of various kinds. My coachman, encumbered though he was by my suitcases, darted nimbly on ahead of me and opened the door of a fine landau in which was seated a lady dressed all in black – black toque and veil, black costume with a feather boa of the same sable hue – and holding a black parasol against the bright sunlight which had triumphed over the storm clouds and was causing the rainwater puddles to steam.

'Ah, you are Miss Friday. I had no doubt in my mind on that

score the moment you emerged from *la gare du chemin de fer.*' Her voice was well-modulated, rich, not to say fruity. 'I am Florence, Lady Wimsey-Fildes. In the mature fullness of time, I *may* request you to address me as Florrie.' Her tone was arch, playful. As well as I was able to make out through the heavy veiling that masked her face, the expression was amiable, humorous – and she was of indeterminate years. Late fifties, at a guess.

'I'm pleased to meet you, ma'am,' I said, presenting my hand, which was almost taken by what appeared to be a bundle of black knitting on her lap, but which proved to be a small, woolly dog of attenuated nose and savage mien. I was fortunate in withdrawing my hand in time to escape its snapping jaws.

'Pay no heed to Wink-Wink,' said her ladyship. 'The inclement weather tends to make him *un peu distrait*. Morgan!' she added, addressing the coachman.

'Yes, m'lady?'

'Convey us to Lansdown, Morgan. By the route which encompasses the principal buildings and thoroughfares of interest.'

'Yes, m'lady.'

The dog Wink-Wink, after a last suspicious glance in my direction, relapsed into being a ball of black wool again. Morgan the coachman whipped up his pair, and we swept grandly from the station yard and out down a straight street towards the twin towers of the Abbey that rose above the rooftops. Lady Wimsey-Fildes took from her reticule a violet-sugared almond and popped it behind her veil.

'My late husband, before the disaster, conceived the notion of purchasing a town house in Bath,' said my companion presently. 'Indeed, he was negotiating for a property in the Royal Crescent when the disaster struck. I am, unhappily, now reduced to a modest two-room apartment with no garden. To your right is the house where Lord Nelson lodged whilst recovering from the loss of his arm at the Battle of the Nile. There on the left, of course, is the Abbey. I am not greatly attracted to the Gothic manner, which seems to me to contain a certain perversity of style. Why else should they have stuck

76

bizarre figures of gargoyles about their exteriors? And I do not approve, generally, of the morals of the Plantagenet and early Tudor monarchs who begat them. My late husband, before the disaster, wrote a monograph upon the Gothic cathedrals and abbeys of England, in which he propounded that it would be to the moral benefit of the lower classes for these buildings radically to be refurbished, stripped of their medieval grotesques, and their places taken by uplifting pictures and carvings depicting the family life of our dear Queen. We are now entering Queen Square, named for Queen Caroline. The obelisk in the centre of the green was erected to the memory of Prince Frederick. This brings us to Gay Street, named after John Gay, poet and dramatist, author of *The Beggar's Opera* – in my opinion a most unfortunate work. Noisy! Bedraggled! An incentive to revolution!

'My dear, what is the condition of your heart?' she asked, all out of the blue, laying her hand upon my arm.

'My heart, ma'am?' 'I repeated. 'I'm afraid I don't understand . . .'

'Are you affianced? Is there, perhaps, even in the sheltered purlieu in which you were reared, a gentleman of quality who has kindled a flame within your heart. In short: are you in love?'

My mind took upon itself an image of the 'sheltered purlieu' of chain factory and counting house, dwelt briefly upon dear Harold as 'a gentleman of quality'. And I smiled.

'No, ma'am, I am neither affianced, nor in the state of becoming so,' I told her.

Lady Wimsey-Fildes squeezed my arm. 'Very satisfactory,' she said. 'I am very pleased with you, my dear. A young woman of fortune should not lightly give her hand. That course is for the gel who has nothing but the more ephemeral assets of face, figure and charm to commend her. *She* should seize the first suitable opportunity that offers, for she has nothing to lose but the aforesaid assets, of which *anno domini* and the rigours of matrimony will all too soon deprive her. We now approach the Circus, which is very highly thought of – though I have to confess that a row of terraced houses built in a circle disposes me towards vertigo. Nevertheless, some people quite distinguished for social – and other, less admirable, reasons – have resided here: Clive of India and the painter Gainsborough, to name but two.'

We made a complete ambit of the great circular monolith of warm stone, and I was struck with admiration for its uncompromising elegance, and greatly wished that I had the scholarship to appreciate what I discerned to be an arcane language of architecture that was speaking aloud to the viewer. As to that, I was fascinated by my companion's monologue, and particularly by her references to 'the disaster' that had befallen her late husband. Mr Treacher had spoken of a severe financial embarrassment following upon the disgrace and death of her spouse. What disgrace? I asked myself. What disaster had befallen the titled pair? It seemed to me that I should not have long to wait before her ladyship satisfied my curiosity.

Another thing intrigued me: it was clear that Mr Treacher had not confided in Lady Wimsey-Fildes the facts of my background, and she obviously accepted me as a person who had been brought up in the closeted surroundings of an heiress – a fact which I found astonishing, yet at the same time curiously gratifying. I scarcely had time to dwell upon this before my companion resumed her soliloquy.

'It is important, my dear, that we take early advantage of the Bath Season, when the cream of Society, both of the West Country and London, take up residence in their Bath *pieds-à-terre* and commence a round of dinner-parties, balls, garden parties, *soirées musicales*, and divers routs. To this end, I have issued invitations to a selected list of the *bon ton* to a dinner-party at Lansdown Crescent on Friday of this week. I make no apology for the short notice, my dear. To be in the swim during the Bath Season, one must strike with the speed and unerring accuracy of a stooping hawk. The Duchess of Westford, for instance, has all but monopolised this week by a series of events commencing with a house party at Chillingham Lodge and extending to a *fête champêtre* tomorrow evening. No – I will anticipate your question – we have not received invitations to any of these functions, nor have I sent invitations to those who are enjoying Her Grace's hospitality this week, since we will not wish, my dear, to suffer their over-fed and jaded presence at our table on Friday evening. Enough of that for the moment. We now come to the Royal Crescent, where, as I have told you, my late husband Sir Basil was only prevented from procuring a property by the disaster which fell upon us. As with the Circus, the Royal Crescent has enjoyed the company of the distinguished, and mostly rather boring. One of those who merits interest being the notorious Sir Horace Wynne, who smothered his wife and ran off with her younger sister.'

The Royal Crescent, so it seemed to me, was of a similar and impressive style to that of the Circus, but I had neither the architectural knowledge nor the taste to appreciate it to the full. To me, it seemed rather over-large and bombastic; but my companion's asides about the former tenants of the Crescent served to put the place into perspective and bring it down to earth.

'There once lodged the novelist Katrina Phipps, famous for having had innumerable lovers and a cat that lived for thirty-four years . . .'

A right turn brought us facing a short length of street and, beyond, a steeply-wooded hill topped with yet more sweeps of proud crescents.

'Lansdown,' declared my companion. 'It is a hard pull for the horses. In winter, one is constrained, occasionally, in times of frost and snow, to get out and assist them by pushing. Many's the time when I, as a gel, was obliged to ruin a new pair of satin pumps by trudging after a heavy coach that the poor nags were attempting – and with little success – to haul up the slippery slope of Lansdown Hill.'

She took my hand and gazed at me with what was surely grave intent from behind the thick veiling. And Wink-Wink, apprised of the gravity of the moment, curled his lips in a snarl, displaying a set of very sharp and surprisingly sizable fangs. 'My dear,' she said, 'what are your views on – *necromancy?*'

'Necromancy, ma'am?' I responded. 'I'm afraid I'm not familiar with the term.'

'Ah, you have led a sheltered life, and more power to the elbow of your parents and guardians for the same.' She nodded approval. 'However, as your guide and mentor in matters social, it comes not amiss for me to flesh out your education in some matters which are perhaps best kept obscure from the young. By necromancy, my dear, I refer to the art of predicting events of the future by means of the reading of playing cards, tea leaves, the disposition of one's birth sign, the configuration of one's palm or the protuberances of one's head, but, most specifically' – here she squeezed my hand, leaning sharply towards me as she did so, causing Wink-Wink to emit a loud yap of frenzy – '*by communication with the dead!*'

I gazed at her in some dismay, as well I might, for she continued to grip my hand in a manner that caused me no small hurt.

'Ma'am,' I said, 'I'm afraid I have no views upon such matters.'

'Ah,' she responded, and relaxed her grip. 'Then I must tell you, my dear, that I am the seventh child of a seventh child, by reason of which I am singularly receptive to the emanations from Beyond. Were I to tell you that, ever since I was commissioned by Messrs Treacher, Murdoch and Partners to act as your companion and chatelaine in Bath, I have been in continuous receipt of messages from Beyond, would you not be astonished? Well, it is so, I tell you, my dear. It is so!'

'Oh, dear,' I responded. There seemed not much else I could say in reply to such an astounding declaration.

'There is nothing to cause either of us the slightest alarm, my dear,' she assured me.

'Who – who has been communicating with you, ma'am?' I asked in some trepidation.

'Why – Sir Basil, my late husband. Who else?' was her reply.

'You – you've seen him?' I breathed in awe, despite an inner conviction that her ladyship was gulling me.

'I have not,' she replied. 'But it is by no means unusual for the Departed to communicate with their loved ones through a medium – in this case one's servants, and in particular the housekeeper whom I have appointed to your establishment in Lansdown Crescent, one Mrs O'Grady, a woman of the most impeccable rectitude and a good Catholic. She has seen the apparition of Sir Basil, not once but several times during the past week, as have Nancy the between-maid, Saunders the parlour maid, and Formby the butler. However, I would not take Formby's word, even upon oath, for it is my impression that the fellow is on the bottle, and I must presently address myself to dismissing him.'

'Why, ma'am, do you connect these – appearances – with my coming to Bath?' I asked her. And not without trepidation.

'Why, because the first appearance took place the same day that I received the letter from Mr Treacher apprising me of your imminent arrival,' she said. 'I should tell you, my dear, that I was appointed to the task of furnishing and staffing the establishment in Lansdown Crescent with no knowledge of yourself. One was merely informed that a young lady of fortune was shortly to take up residence there.

'Imagine me – last Monday week it was, and I had just finished reading Mr Treacher's letter – when O'Grady burst into the drawing room without so much as a knock. "My lady, my lady," she cried, "there is a man peering in through the area window into the kitchen. And when I looked at him straight, he was gone – vanished!"

'As you may well imagine, my dear, I received this news with the metaphorical pinch of salt, particularly when I observed the gratified manner in which O'Grady imbibed in one swallow the measure of brandy that I offered her, medicinally, to steady her nerves.'

The thin edge of a nameless dread insinuated itself into my mind. 'What manner of man was this who peered in, ma'am?' I asked.

Her ladyship gave a dismissive gesture. 'I have received no convincing description,' she said. 'Not even when the sightings were reported to me, later, by the servants I have mentioned. However, one thing alone convinces me that it is the departed spirit of my late husband who is attempting to communicate with me through the medium of others.'

'And what is that, ma'am?' I asked.

'The apparition – which has been seen on most evenings of the past week – wears a beard of the naval persuasion,' she replied. 'Sir Basil, as you may or not know, was a prominent yachtsman and a crony of the Prince of Wales. Like his royal intimate, he affected a beard. Need I say more?'

There was a question I had to ask. After a few moments of struggle with my worst fears, I asked it: 'What manner of *hat* does this – person wear, ma'am?'

She looked surprised. 'I really have no idea. The manner of hat was not reported to me. As to that, Sir Basil was extremely catholic in his choice of headgear, and brought back from his journeyings around the world some of the most outlandish hats of the regions he visited. Alive or in the spirit, he could be wearing any of them.

'Ah, and here is elegant Lansdown Crescent.'

*

The Crescent spanned the crest of Lansdown Hill in a noble sweep of golden stone and glinting windows. No. 13, which was just to the left of centre of the terrace, had its front door open immediately upon our drawing to a halt outside. By the time we had alighted, the broad hallway was lined with servants – it struck me, then, and quite forcibly, that they were *my* servants.

Lady Wimsey-Fildes and I passed down the line, while they bowed and curtsied to me as if I had been royalty.

'This is Mrs O'Grady, housekeeper. Formby the butler. Saunders the parlour maid. Nancy the between maid . . .'

'How d'you do, ma'am.' 'Yes, ma'am. Thank you, ma'am.' 'Pleased to meecher, ma'am . . .'

'We will take tea in the drawing room, Formby,' declared Lady Wimsey-Fildes. 'Come, my dear.'

The drawing room, on the first floor front, was about half the size of the entire counting house at Arbuthnot & Son and incomparably better proportioned. The furnishings, which, when my knowledge of styles improved I readily discerned to be in the subtly elegant manufacture of the previous century, were of ebony and gold: ebonised wood embellished with gilded bronze, upholstered wing chairs and sofas in faded gold silks, oriental carpets as thin and subtly-tinted as ancient snake skins. And above all there reigned a massive chandelier hung about with baffling galaxies of crystal lustres that gave forth discreet flurrying tinkles whenever the double doors were opened.

My mentor and I took our places on a wide sofa, and a tea trolly was presently wheeled in by one of the kitchen maids flanked by two others and led by Formby. When Lady Wimsey-Fildes had poured for us both (and a saucerful for Wink-Wink), she raised the black veil which had shielded the most part of her countenance from me. To my great pleasure, she revealed herself to be a lady of most gentle and genial appearance, with a complexion which, though she must have been well advanced into her sixties, was as clear and unwrinkled as that of a well-favoured woman of half her age.

We sipped our tea and nibbled upon cucumber sandwiches of such lacy frailty as to be almost sinful. Presently, she put down her teacup and saucer, rummaged in her reticule and said:

'My dear, I have been remiss in not telling you who I have invited to the dinner-party on Friday on your behalf. Here we are, ah, where is my lorgnette?' She fumbled among the laces at her throat, found the missing article and, putting it to her eyes, read from a sheet of lavender-tinted writing paper.

'The Venerable Archdeacon and Mrs Vallence: now he is a most personable young man and will certainly end up an archbishop – if his admirable wife can be persuaded not to pick her teeth at table. Mr Makepiece Crawley: he is a Master in Lunacy, a curious title attached to some arcane by-way of the Law, who lately married Miss Deborah Wainwright, like yourself an heiress and of suitable age and disposition to be considered for friendship, who will also be present.

'Who else have we now? Ah, there is a gentleman who is much sought after by Bath hostesses, but who, I discover on the grape-vine, did not fall victim to Her Grace's questing tentacles this week. He is Mr Charles Arbuthnot, a Wessex millionaire of most devastating presence and charm.

'Why do you give a start, my dear?'

'Nothing – nothing, ma'am,' I faltered, adding inconsequentially: 'I – I think that someone may have walked over my grave.'

'Well, there is Mr Arbuthnot, whom you must meet and who will be a social acquisition for you in the West Country,' continued my companion, 'and he will be accompanied by a personage from whom he seems, at times, to be quite inseparable.' Here she paused, frowning. 'To be frank, I am not greatly attached to the person in question, whom I consider to possess all the attributes of a well-bred leopardess. Her name: Lady Moira Fame.

'Why, you start again, my dear? And, see, you've spilt tea all over the lap of your charming travelling costume.'

*

I retired early that night. My suite was on the second floor back, with a view down the long garden to the coachhouses and mews. All beyond them lay dark grassland and trees that murmured in the night air; the rumble of wheeled traffic in the cobbled crescent did not carry to the rear of the great curved terrace.

I took a warm bath in the japanned tub that had been filled for me; luxuriating in the rose petal-scented water and regaling myself with an enormous sponge and loofah. Afterwards, in my new peignoir, I extinguished the gaslight in the dressing room and returned to the delights of what was, at that time, the most beautiful bedchamber that I had ever thought to exist in my wildest imagination.

It was all in pale blue and white. The panelled walls were of blue, with the mouldings picked out in white, with discreet touches of silver. An ankle-deep rug which half-covered the white marble floor was – as I later learned – Chinese in origin: a confection of enormous blue cabbage roses on a white ground. The bed was of a delight that almost defies description: a four-poster whose slender uprights were turned like white sugar, enough to make the mouth water at the sight of them, supporting a canopy lined with blue silk, with striped blue and white curtains descending. And to lie upon that bed was to recline in a bower of swansdown.

Before I even attempted to sleep that night, I turned many things over in my mind, most immediate of which was the prospect of encountering Charles Arbuthnot again – not to mention the haughty, patrician Lady Moira. And in my own home!

This man, who had repaid my presumptuous behaviour by interceding for Meg Wolfingham and advancing me from the chain factory to the counting house (especially if, as I sometimes suspected, he was also the author of my present fortune), could scarcely fail to recognise me, even in my new surroundings, by both name and appearance. Oddly, the prospect, though alarming, had nuances and overtones that held a certain dark delight. Lying there in my scented swansdown, I pictured again the first glance of those deep grey eyes upon me, and felt the skin of my whole body, from the roots of my hair to my nether limbs, pucker and tingle at the prospect of a second such encounter. As to another meeting with the blonde goddess whom I had so roundly berated, I found myself not caring one way or another. Let her recognise me, or let her not. In either event, we would see who could most behave like a lady: the 'well-bred leopardess' or Daisy Friday, late of the chain factory!

No fears, then, about Charles Arbuthnot and his Valkryie.

But about *the other matter* . . .?

I am not a superstitious person, for it is truly said that a hard upbringing makes for a hard head; but the very thought of the apparition that had menaced my existence since first I left the chain factory had powers to summon up dark thoughts in my mind. If the sinister stranger – apparition, unworldly visitant or whatever – was pursuing me as far as my new life in Bath and beyond, here was matter to trouble me indeed.

Upon the thought, I swung myself out of my lovely bed and, dousing the lamp, went over and parted the shutters by the merest crack and peered out.

The moon was full and high: a hunter's moon. By its light, every blade of grass and plant in the pleasant garden was etched as clearly as by a graver's hand. The water in the goldfish pond was a sheet of dark glass that reflected the stars and the still clouds. Beyond, the mews was quiet and sleeping, save for a single light burning in the upper floor of the coach-house. Beyond that, behind a stand of still cypresses, was the

85

shadowed graveyard of the church atop Lansdown Hill: the gravestones stood whitely in the moonlight and deep grey in the shadows.

I watched for a while, and with a mounting unease. As my eyes grew more accustomed to the semi-darkness, I seemed to sense *movement* everywhere: in the courtyard of the coach-house, in the lane beyond, in the graveyard – particularly in the graveyard.

Did I not see something flit from the cover of one gravestone to another? I blinked and rubbed my eyes and searched again.

Nothing there. I peered yet again; and then it seemed that yet another movement flitted at the very edge of my vision, only to still itself when I directed my gaze upon it.

I found myself, unexpectedly, trembling. And the palms of my hands were damp with fear. It was then I saw myself for the idiot I was, and how I resembled someone in the lonely darkness of a country lane who looks back over his shoulder, fearful of pursuit by some hobgoblin, while knowing in his heart that he is treading the path where madness lies.

With a curt rejoinder to my own folly, I closed the shutter and went back to bed, where I soon slept soundly till cockcrow.

*

The next few days were taken up in being introduced to the delights of Bath. By luncheon on the second day, Lady Wimsey-Fildes had bidden me address her privately as Florence (as a stepping-stone, I presumed, to the even more intimate 'Florrie'). She introduced me to the Roman Baths, the Pump Room, the Assembly Rooms, and to the very fine emporia that lined Milsom Street, Broad Street and the other principal shopping thoroughfares. Florence had a passion for gloves, and she insisted on buying me several ready-made pairs, as well as ordering more made-to-measure by a Parisian glover who kept a shop opposite the Abbey.

I enjoyed it all (save for the famous waters, a sample of which I tried in the Pump Room and found not to my taste), but was greatly puzzled by the arcane procedure of leaving visiting cards which we followed daily. Though reared in an orphanage and a chain factory, I was not so naïve, even in those early days of my social education, as to imagine that the manners of polite society in elegant Bath followed the same rules as, say, the neighbours of Harold Nesbitt's mother in Westchester, where one might call to ask the loan of a bit of sugar and be invited in for a cup of tea from the pot that forever simmered on the warm hob; I found it difficult, however, to see the reasoning behind the ritual of knocking upon the door of some fine house and presenting one's card to some liveried functionary – and to no apparent purpose. Such baffling details of procedure, as the turning-down of corners, the murmured thanks, and nothing to see for it. Not a cup of tea in sight.

My visiting cards, ordered in advance by Florence and hand-engraved, were of the size and design dictated by protocol and looked – and read – very fine.

They were distributed very liberally throughout the smart parts of the city: bread cast upon the waters. It was not for some days that – to mix my metaphors – the first of our swallows came home to roost. An envelope was delivered by hand to Lady Wimsey-Fildes at 13 Lansdown Crescent. My mentor was instantly beside herself with righteous self-congratulation.

'A most marvellous triumph!' she declared. '*Un veritable grand éclat!*'

'What is it, Florence?' I asked.

'Why we left our cards, as you will remember, at No. 1 Royal Crescent the day before yesterday.'

'Yes. That was the foreign lady, wasn't it?'

'The foreign lady, my dear Daisy, is none other than the ex-Empress of the French, the tragic Eugénie. Her Imperial Majesty is advancing in years and enjoying indifferent health. She has leased No. 1 for the season, but seldom ventures out except to take the waters, nor does she formally entertain, and has declined our invitation to your dinner party and that of the duchess. But – see!'

'What?' I asked.

'She declares herself to be At Home to us tomorrow at 3.30. I tell you, my dear, if Her Imperial Majesty approves of you, you will have *arrived* in Bath, for though a recluse, her every word and action are noted and commented upon. You may be sure that her servants – like all of their kind – will watch your every move, your every word, and Her Imperial Majesty's reaction to the same, reporting it all to their fellow servants in the ale-houses of the city that same night. Over the breakfast tables of polite society throughout the city on the morning after, your social reputation will be made or broken!'

'Oh!' I said in some dismay. And again: 'Oh . . .'

*

Sharp on the stroke of 3.15 on the following afternoon, we descended Lansdown Hill for our tryst with Imperial Royalty. The road being not overcrowded with traffic, we were close to our destination ahead of schedule, so Florence told the coach-man to drive around the block to kill a few minutes. She filled up the available time by reiterating the lesson she had drilled into me the evening before.

'Whatever you do, my dear,' she said, 'make no reference to the Franco-Prussian War, nor to the collapse of their empire and her husband's dethronement and exile. Touch not upon her widowhood. But most of all – *most* of all – do not mention the tragic end of her only issue, the Prince Imperial, who, as you know, was butchered by the spears of the Zulu warriors during the late war in Africa while fighting under the Union Jack for our own dear Queen and Empire. You *will* remember that, won't you?'

'Yes, ma'am,' I responded dutifully.

'Turn into the Royal Crescent, Morgan!' she bade the coachman.

No. 1 was – not surprisingly – situated at one end of the great sweep of honey-coloured stonework that dominated the foot of Lansdown Hill. We had no sooner drawn up outside the steps and had not yet alighted, when liveried flunkeys to the number of six issued from the front door and lined our ascent. We were greeted at the threshold by a vague-looking lady in diaphanous grey, who peered at us short-sightedly, announced herself to be the Marquise de Something or other, and escorted us into a large chamber where sat the striking figure of a woman dressed

88

all in mourning black like Florence. She had a Pekingese dog on her lap, and I had the wayward thought that we were prudent to have left Wink-Wink outside in the care of Morgan the coachman.

The Empress gracefully inclined her head and offered each of us her hand, afterwards gesturing us to the seats that were set before her. The Marquise took her place on an uncommonly uncomfortable-looking stool at her mistress's elbow, where she remained throughout the event, mostly ramrod-backed, hands folded on her lap; seated – but standing in spirit.

'We have never visited Cornwall,' declared the Empress. 'His Imperial Majesty, my late husband, was there during his first exile in England. Tell me of Cornwall, Miss Friday.'

I was struck dumb by the unexpectedness of the question, which was delivered in a clear and pleasant voice only lightly accented – and I looked to Florence for guidance.

'Miss Friday has not yet had the opportunity to visit the estate which she has inherited in Cornwall, ma'am,' said my mentor. 'She is, however, a mine of information about Dorset.'

The Marquise leaned forward and said loudly into the Empress's ear: '*Le comté de Dorset, madame!*' A certain puzzlement left the latter's strikingly blue eyes and she nodded. 'Ah – Dorset.'

There the conversation flagged. Tea was brought in and poured by the Marquise. There were scones, and the inevitable thin cucumber sandwiches. I took the opportunity of covertly eyeing our hostess. Eugénie looked to be in her late sixties, but her hair – clearly once auburn – owed nothing to the artifices of the coiffeur and was only lightly streaked with grey. Her complexion was excellent. Her manner, informed by those steady blue eyes, was queenly and dominant to a degree, and constrained only – or so it seemed to me – by her apparent deafness.

The thin tinkle of stirred teaspoons was interrupted by another declaration from the Empress: 'I am not happy in this house. There is a sad presence here. A note of tragedy to come.'

'Her Imperial Majesty refers to the ghostly presence of the Princesse de Lamballe, who also once stayed here,' supplied the

Marquise. 'The young princess, as you may know, was murdered by the revolutionary mob during the so-called September massacres, and in most appalling circumstances . . .' Whereupon she leaned forward (she was quite near to me) and whispered something so horrible* that I hoped I had misheard it, notwithstanding which, I dropped my cup and saucer, which shattered to pieces on the parquet; one of the line of flunkeys standing in attendance rushed forward and swept up the debris.

If she noticed my confusion, the Empress did not show it. I accepted another cup of tea and a small sliver of cherry cake.

'I have lived with tragedy and sadness,' said Eugénie, and closed her eyes in private agony. A long silence followed. I nibbled a token mouthful of cake, and my teeth came into contact with – horrors! – an exceedingly large cherry stone that had been inadvertently left in the baking. I searched my mind for a means of disposal. To spit it out into my hand was unthinkable, to swallow it absurd. I resolved to keep it where it was till a suitable opportunity arose for getting rid of the wretched thing.

'The loss of the war with Prussia, the loss of our country and empire. My dear husband's sad end –' The Empress seemed to blink away a tear, and took a bite of cherry cake. I was then witness to an incident which immediately called to my mind one of the cardinal precepts that Meg Wolfingham had long ago dinned into me – which was to watch, listen, and learn. In doing so, I mastered in one lesson the difficult art of disposing of unbidden cherry stones and the like – and this from a mistress of the art . . .

I saw the instant that her teeth met upon *her* cherry stone, and felt a pang of sympathy. Her eyebrows rose in astonishment. She then put an elegant hand to her mouth, and with forefinger and thumb took out the offending item, which she then regarded with mild surprise.

'*Mon Dieu!*' she murmured, not one bit put about.

* The Marquise undoubtedly referred to a deposition by one Hervelin. Appearing before a subsequent tribunal, he admitted to having grilled the unfortunate woman's heart and eaten it.

Seizing upon the heaven-sent opportunity, I did likewise: took out my cherry stone and likewise regarded it.

'Well, I'm blessed!' I declared coolly.

Our eyes met. We laughed. A great moment passed between us.

She smiled. Extended her hand. 'Come closer, my dear,' she said. 'You are *très sympathique*. I think that I will tell you of the sadness of an empress who is also a woman.'

I obeyed. Her hand upon my arm, her brilliant blue gaze fixed upon me, she said: 'There comes a time, Miss Friday, when a woman has suffered such loss that she feels that Fate, the world, the malice of her enemies, the punishment of all her transgressions, have combined to destroy her so completely that nothing remains save the very core of her life which – though her balm and consolation – one would not have thought to excite the malice and jealousy of the Fates who had taken so much else.

'Such is not the case. Those from whom everything has been taken, from then shall be taken to the uttermost. It was so with the Empress Eugénie.'

I said: 'You mean the loss of . . .' but was interrupted by the warning pressure of Florence's foot against my instep. I ignored the caution, and repeated:

'The loss of your son, your only child.'

She nodded. 'He was – only twenty-three,' she said. 'Like his father, brave. Perhaps headstrong. Together with a party of comrades, he rode into a Zulu ambush. All might have been well, for the soldiers were well-armed and mounted. But there was no escape. The Prince's horse – its name was Fate, would you believe? *Quelle ironie!* – reared up and threw my son to the ground.'

I pressed her hand that was laid upon my arm. 'Tell me no more, ma'am,' I whispered, and I knew she heard me, if not the very words. 'You are wounding yourself all over again.'

Her fingers tensed, reassuringly, on my arm, and she continued: 'Those who effected their escape from the ambush said afterwards that the Prince managed to regain his feet and, still holding the reins, was about to remount when the Zulus closed in about him, their spears raised. It was soon over, they said.'

I drew breath. 'How terrible,' I murmured. Both Florence and the Marquise were crying unashamedly.

'My son's body was later recovered and brought back to England,' said Eugénie. 'He lies beside his father, where I shall one day join them. I grieved for a year, inconsolable. It seemed to me that I could never come to accept the truth of what had happened till I had seen with my own eyes the spot where my son had both lived and died in one instant. Your dear Queen Victoria, who has known grief also, understood, and gave me permission to journey to Zululand, the war being over.

'I arrived with my escorts somewhere near the scene of the ambush. It was growing dark. There was nothing to see but an open plain that was waist-high in thick vegetation. In the distance, a low hill. They told me that the spot where my son had died was marked by a cairn of stones, but that we would never be able to find it with darkness coming on. Try in the morning, ma'am, they said.

'I would not listen to them, for there was no waiting possible for me. And then . . .'

'And then, ma'am – *what?*' My skin crawled in awful anticipation as I forced myself to frame the question. Florence caught her breath.

'I smelt the scent of violets,' said Eugénie. 'English violets, like those in our garden at Chislehurst – *his favourite flower!*

'There was no doubt in my mind but that my son was guiding me from beyond his far-off grave, and it was so. I ran straight to the cairn of stones hidden among the massed foliage and I fell on my knees beside it – there, in the spot that had been hallowed by the life blood of a Bonaparte who had died for England.'

*

An ormolu clock on the ornate marble chimneypiece tinkled the hour of five at which the Marquise rose without referring to her mistress, indicating with a nod and a smile that the visit was terminated. The former Empress shook us both by the hand and lingered longer with mine, presently turning it over to disclose my palm, which she closely examined. As she did so, I relived the moment in the chain factory dormitory not so very long ago, when the old crone Mrs Prosser had read my fortune in the marks upon my hand. I discerned the same instant amusement – as when both women divined that I should wed and have many children – and then the sudden change of expression from light to darkness, to shocked disbelief, to revulsion.

I snatched my hand away from Eugénie and, thrusting it behind my back, silently challenged her with my eyes to tell me what she had seen there.

Her answer was a sad smile and a shake of her head. 'Better you do not know, my child,' she replied to my soundless question. 'Your strength is great, but could be sapped by doubts and fears. One should not always know what lies beyond the veil.

'All I can say is this, Miss Friday: many forces are ranged against you, but if you remain strong, you will prevail in the end. That is what I believe.'

'Thank you, ma'am,' I whispered.

'You will come and see me again before I depart from Bath? I should greatly like that.'

'Yes, ma'am,' I promised.

She nodded, and we retired from her presence, accompanied by the Marquise. 'Her Imperial Majesty tires very quickly,' said the latter as she walked with us across the hallway. 'And I am afraid that to have spoken of the Prince Imperial has cost her a lot of strength.' The woman – small, grey, birdlike – cast me a shrewd glance. 'I have never known madame to tell the story of the scent of violets to any but her most intimate friends. You must have made a very great impression upon her. But then – you are a very impressive young lady, ma'mselle.'

'*Ma foi*, that she is indeed!' declared Florence.

Wink-Wink, who by this time had overcome his initial revulsion to my presence, deigned to crawl up on to my lap and there accommodate himself during our journey back to Lansdown Crescent. Florence was very cock-a-hoop.

'You have conquered a major citadel of Bath, my dear,' she told me. 'By tonight, the story of your instant friendship with the Empress will be the talk of the servants' taverns. By breakfast time, all polite society will know. We shall be deluged with invitations, mark my words. *Quel frisson!* We must immediately visit Madame Rita, the *couturière* of Milsom Street, and order at least three new dinner gowns apiece. We will do it this afternoon, demanding that Rita's seamstresses work all night for their completion. And at no extra charge – the lower classes are becoming overly pampered nowadays . . .'

She prattled on, interspersing her discourse with her customary French illuminations; and I listened with half an ear, the other ear turned inwards to the recollection of what the Empress had told me:

'*Many forces ranged against you . . . remain strong . . . you will prevail . . .*'

Once, only, did Florence's perorations break in upon my thoughts, when she said: 'You presented yourself most admirably, dear Daisy. If I had any doubts about the success of your first dinner-party (and a young gel's first dinner-party as hostess is always an unknown quantity), those doubts are quite laid to rest.' She leaned over and squeezed my hand, thereby waking Wink-Wink and causing him to bare his teeth at his doting mistress. 'My dear Daisy, you will *triumph* at table next Friday!'

With hope, I endorsed her belief; oddly, it was only the recollection of Lady Moira Fame's flat, contemptuous stare that unsettled my conviction.

*

During our absence, a familiar-looking chest had been delivered to No. 13. Against all likelihood, it proved to be none other than Meg Wolfingham's chest of books that had lately resided beneath our common bed.

There was a note attached. It was from Mr Grout of the chain factory, and addressed to me. In it he stated that, acting upon instructions, he was dispatching the chest to my care, along with its contents. He closed by assuring me of his humble and obedient service at all times – a declaration which, notwithstanding the manifestations of deference to which I was beginning to accustom myself in my new life, had the power to overawe and astonish.

The chest having been carried up to my suite, I excused myself from Florence's company and, locking my door, opened up the chest and took out the lovingly worn volumes that, together with their late owner's deep wisdom, had given me all the education I possessed . . .

The Holy Bible; *The Complete Works of Shakespeare*; *The Voyage of the 'Beagle'* by Charles Darwin; Mrs Beeton's *Book of Household Management*; Plato's *Republic*; the *Iliad* and the *Odyssey*; *A History of the World* in five volumes; *An Outline of Social Etiquette* by Olivia, Lady Tooting; *The Golden Treasury of English Verse* – and many, many more. I knew them all: almost every last word.

Small wonder that I wept to have them with me again – the old and dear friends of my childhood.

SIX

Florence and I together devised the menu; I with close attention to the excellent Mrs Beeton, whose gastronomic extravagances had so enlivened my childhood imagination that I suppose I must have had the best-fed imagination and the worst-nourished stomach of any child in mid-Dorset.

Our kitchen staff – augmented by a Monsieur Jean-Pierre Audubon, who kept a small restaurant for the discerning off Queen Square, and who hired himself out as chef for special dinner-parties – were equal to the large and varied menu, which was to be served *à la Russe*, which is to say that the dishes were cut up on the sideboard and handed round to the guests at their choice; a method which, as Florence pointed out, saves a tremendous amount of confusion at table when as many as three or four dishes and removes are placed there at any one course, imposing a great deal of activity upon the servants, and indeed upon the gentlemen guests, who are frequently constrained to serve the ladies in their vicinity.

The outlines of the dinner settled, and the staff hard at work with the preliminaries, we addressed ourselves to the question of what to wear. Madame Rita and her acolytes had come up trumps with a pair of dinner gowns that were so enchanting as to dismiss all other options – or so we thought on the Wednesday of that week.

Mine was of figured off-white satin, very *décolleté*, and sewn all over with seed pearls. I no longer have the bill for the garment, but I remember calculating that the sum would have well kept the workpeople at the chain factory in food for a year. Florence, putting aside her mourning, had decided upon satin also, but hers was in royal blue and silver, very grand. We both dressed ourselves and held a fashion parade on Wednesday evening. Our minds were made up upon the instant of viewing each other. On Thursday morning, Madame Rita delivered another pair of dinner gowns to order – and we were back with indecision!

It was on Thursday evening that the issue of the dinner-party turned bad on me, and I resolved to have the whole thing out with Florence, and no more subterfuge.

I dropped my predicament into her lap after our supper *à deux*.

'Florence, I have to confess to you that I am an imposter!"

She was sitting opposite me, Wink-Wink on her lap. She had been searching him for fleas, and looked at me with a certain incredulity.

'If you are referring to the fact that your preference is really for my jade green dinner gown instead of the royal blue,' she replied, 'I have to admit that I, too, am guilty of dissembling. My real inclination is for the latter – and, I have to admit, because of its inherent vulgarity.' She laughed.

I shook my head. 'No, it's more serious than that, Florence,' I said. 'When I say I am an imposter, I speak of my – antecedents.'

'Ah!' she said. And returned to rifling for fleas through Wink-Wink's long, curly coat, which was host to many. 'Well, Mr Treacher advised me that there were certain – irregularities – as regards your upbringing, my dear, but I have waited for you to tell me in your own good time, serene in the conviction that there can be nothing in your antecedents (as you choose to call them) that could bring a blush to the most susceptible cheek. Were you or one of your forebears born – in the phrase of the vulgar – "on the wrong side of the blanket"? Is there – to give it the correct heraldic term – a *bend sinister* in your escutcheon? Pay no heed to that, my dear Daisy. A quite surprising number of dukes and duchesses of this realm – the Duchess of Westford included – owe their creations to King

Charles II's penchant for so rewarding his mistresses who provided him with royal bastards.

'Out with it, my dear. Tell Florrie. What is the skeleton in your family closet that so troubles you?'

I took a deep breath. 'Ma'am . . .' I began.

'Florrie,' she interposed with a smile. 'You may now call me Florrie.'

I spread my hands in helplessness. 'Florrie, to begin at the beginning, I – I *have* no family!'

And then I told her all: of the infant in arms who had been brought to the Westchester parish orphanage; of her name, which was no more than an institutional convenience, half a joke, and certainly not her own by family rights; of the wretchedness that followed. I touched upon the chain factory and the conditions under which we had worked. She did not interrupt me. Only when I told her of Meg Wolfingham and the slender limits of my education did she make a move – and that was to shake her head in disbelief.

I closed with the sorry account of my encounter with the man and woman who were to be my dinner guests on the following night, and lightly touched upon the unexpected good fortune which had followed. When I had done, I lowered my eyes, folded my hands on my lap, and waited for her comment.

I had not long to wait . . .

'Undoubtedly,' she said, 'you are of the highest birth. Perhaps even' – here she paused – 'royalty. Though foreign royalty, more like. Yes, there is a certain bone structure to the head, a decidedly Slavonic breadth to the cheekbones. I would suppose that you are a Romanoff. Nothing else would account for your – considering the circumstances – truly astonishing self-possession, your admirable exposition, your air of authority firmly held yet lightly exercised. Yes, you must be of blood royal, or of the highest nobility, equipped by generations of privilege to demand unquestioning obedience.

'So what worries you, my dear?'

'Oh, Florrie,' I replied, 'what you say sounds so very unlikely, though I know you mean it sincerely. I am no more than a bright little dog – like Wink-Wink there – who has been taught a few tricks on how to behave, how to recite Hamlet's soliloquy, the flora and fauna of the Galapagos islands and the books of the Bible by rote. As to the Slavonic breadth to the cheekbones and all that – oh, dear Florrie, I think you are just trying to jolly me along because you have realised that I am scared out of my wits to meet Charles Arbuthnot again, and especially that odious Lady Moira Fame.'

'Lady Moira you will handle like an expert fisherman landing a fighting trout,' declared Florrie. 'Anyone who could charm the poor Empress of the French out of her sadness need have no fears for the likes of Lady Moira.'

'With your help,' I added. 'With your help, I just might.'

'I will do my small best,' she said. 'But I do not have your advantages. Not taken from a royal or noble cradle and deposited in an orphanage, no doubt for political or dynastic reasons.'

'Oh, Florrie, how can you speak of your lack of advantages?' I asked her, amused. 'And you the widow of an English baronet.'

'That I might be,' she replied, 'but my papa was an impoverished curate on a slender living in East Anglia, and I could match you with tales of hardship, line for line. For instance, my siblings and I were only able to attend the parish school on four days out of five during the worst of the winter.'

'Why was that, Florrie?' I asked.

'Because there were only four pairs of boots between the five of us. So we took it in turns to stay at home.'

I trumped her ace: 'I never owned a pair of boots till I was apprenticed.'

She thought for a minute, and then brightened. 'Most days for luncheon we had skilly.'

'I'll wager you never tasted lights.'

'We only had lights once a week,' she replied, adding wistfully: 'Lights were my favourite.'

Upon the impulse, I went over and embraced her, angering Wink-Wink. 'Oh, Florrie, you are such a comfort,' I said. 'How could I possibly have taken on the frightening responsibility of becoming an heiress overnight without you to prop me up?'

99

She patted my cheek. 'You need little or no propping up, my girl,' she said. 'And you'll be able to stand on your own two feet soon enough.'

We relaxed into silence for the rest of the evening; I had my thoughts and she – abandoning the search for Wink-Wink's house-guests – took up her novel, a colourful historical romance of the kind for which she had an enthusiastically declared preference. Small wonder, I speculated, that her head was full of 'cheekbones of Slavonic breadth', 'royal or noble cradles bereft for political or dynastic reasons', and so forth.

Dear Florrie.

Happy to have confided in her, I half-wished that I could have brought myself to touch upon my nagging fear of the creature in the strange hat, but I could scarcely bring myself willingly even to think of him. As for the 'apparition' who had haunted the precincts of No. 13, *he* had not been reported again since my arrival there.

And that struck me as being rather odd . . .

*

At seven o'clock on Friday evening, bathed, dressed, and my rather intractable tresses brought into some kind of order in a chignon with side curls before and behind the ears by a Miss Veronica, *coiffeuse* of Walcot Street, who also attended upon Florrie, I sat in the drawing room with Florrie opposite to await our guests. My mentor, who had in the event plumped for the royal blue gown, looked like a veritable queen with her white hair plaited on high beneath a shimmering tiara.

I watched my fingernails for a while. And then there came the distant tinkle of a bell from the panel in the basement, followed by a clatter of hurrying feet on the stair.

'Our first guest,' said Florrie, consulting her fob watch. 'One minute only after the set hour. Must be hungry. Or thirsty.'

Presently: '*Archdeacon and Mrs Vallence,*' intoned Formby the butler. And an astonishingly young, blond and pink-faced cleric entered the drawing room with a pretty redhead upon his arm.

Introductions and light conversation followed. 'Gervase is

delivering the sermon in the Abbey at Sunday evensong, Miss Friday,' vouchsafed Mrs Vallence breathlessly. 'You really must come. He's taking as his text that awf'ly amusing joke in *Punch* – the one about the curate's egg, when the bishop says at breakfast: "I'm afraid you've got a bad egg, Mr Jones," and the meek little curate replies: "Parts of it are excellent, my lord." And Gervase, the clever pet, is going to relate Mr Jones's response to the good that's in even the worst of us.'

'*Mr Makepiece and Mrs Crawley, ma'am.*' From the doorway.

The Master in Lunacy looked to have been made out of dusty parchment deeds. His youngish countenance was grey and severe, his stiff manner likewise. The high points of his formal collar reached almost to his ears, and he smelt most markedly of mothballs. His fiancée, the heiress, in total contrast, was a pippin-cheeked, rather hoydenish girl who looked as if she might have left her horse (and a pretty lively one at that) tied up to the railings outside. She shook my hand with vigour and opined that it was going to be a marvellous year for trout-fishing, didn't I think?

'*Mr Tristan Melmoth, ma'am.*'

Tristan Melmoth's entry – indeed, everything about Tristan Melmoth – was unforgettable: massively built like an operatic tenor, with a shock of sleek grey hair swept back from a fine brow that was set off by a prominent widow's peak; impeccably tailored, and walking with a marked limp and the aid of a stick.

'Miss Friday. Such a pleasure. So kind of you to have asked me.' He bent over my hand and implanted a kiss in the air an inch above my knuckles. His eyes, swept by unbelievably long lashes, were widely-spaced, luminous, and of a tawny, tiger-like hue. I felt instantly attracted by the man, as one might be drawn towards a beautiful and dangerous animal – for instance, a tiger.

'I understand you've been abroad, Mr Melmoth,' I ventured, by way of polite conversation, but feeling like one who has ventured a hand inside the bars of a cage to make a tentative attempt to stroke a sleek, scented coat.

'India, ma'am,' he supplied. 'I have been staying awhile with my friend the Maharajah of Ammapur, whom I advised on various improvements to his summer palace in the hills.'

'You are an architect, sir?' I asked.

He smiled. 'An artist, ma'am,' he replied. 'And a dilettante at that, but my small works have been admired the world over. I take what has already been made – be it a palace, a land-scaped parkland, a finely-cut diamond, a beautiful woman – and re-create it in a fantasy setting of my own devising, what the French would call a *mise en scène*.'

'How so, sir?' I asked, intrigued.

He gestured with an elegant, slender hand that was neverthe-less well-muscled, bronzed, and pelted with fine dark hair. 'The palace – as with the one at Ammapur – I surround with mystery. I dam a river to produce a lake. In the lake are islands set with temples and pleasure domes, miniature Trianons, from which the music of sitar and drums steals languorously over the dark waters.

'To a landscaped parkland of the English shires, I introduce a note of romance, of danger. Ancient copses are torn down and replanted with the lush trees and undergrowth of the tropical rain forests, the whole enclosed within a glass conservatory that dwarfs the contemptible little Crystal Palace of Mr Paxton. Its interior is alive with the calls of the tropics: the scream of macaw, parakeet and blue-crowned motmot, the shriek of baboon and capuchin. High in the treetops, the dark eyes of a captive ape glower across a yawning gulf where a royal python is richly coiled in the upper branches of a banyan. A thousand varieties of coloured fish illuminate the depths of heated pools. And all this within half a mile of a sleepy Cotswold village.

'I take the sixteenth largest diamond in the world and incomparably the most beautiful, and set it within the gold jaws of a Gabon viper, whose fangs are of ivory and eyes of emerald surrounding a pair of matched rubies.

'As to my setting for a beautiful woman . . .'

'*Lady Moira Fame and Mr Arbuthnot, ma'am.*'

I tensed myself, and felt my scalp tingle, my breath quicken. Meeting Florrie's eye, I saw her nod and smile with encouragement. My head went up. I stepped forward to greet the couple from whom in all Society I had the most to fear.

'How do you do, Lady Moira – Mr Arbuthnot. I am Daisy Friday.'

'How do you do.' Cold her voice, frigid her hand inside the silk glove. And her chilly eyes swept over me, taking in my coiffure, my complexion, pricing my frock, my jewellery – and dismissing them all. With a wild surge of relief, I perceived that not only did she reject me as insignificant – *but she did not recognise me!*

'Miss Friday – your servant, ma'am.' His hand enveloped mine with a gentle firmness and I met the gaze of the deep-set, piercing grey eyes that I had never forgotten.

Nor had he forgotten me – I knew it on the instant!

'Are we all assembled my dear?' asked Florrie, peering about the company through her lorgnette.

'Only Miss Powker is missing,' I supplied.

'Ah, dear Amelia will be late at the Last Trump. We will wait ten minutes more and then go into dinner without her.'

From the corner of my eye I saw Lady Moira being button-holed by the fascinating Mr Melmoth, and her Valkyrian frigidity visibly thawed upon the encounter. I was also disturbingly aware that Charles Arbuthnot was gazing at me intently, and I would have moved away in sheer fright had we not been reunited again by a passing footman who offered a tray of champagne between us both.

I took a glass. So did he. Our eyes met. He smiled: it was a curiously disarming smile that took years from his age without in any way detracting from the disturbing awesomeness of his commanding presence. I felt like a child before a momentarily kindly master.

'How are you enjoying your sudden rise in fortune, Miss Friday?' He murmured the question so that only I should hear.

'Well enough, Mr Arbuthnot,' I replied. And had the thought to add: 'The rise would have been more sudden and alarming, but for the intervention of the kind person who first set my feet a considerable way up the ladder of fortune.'

He shrugged. 'It was little enough, and you amply graced the counting house, so my reports have it.' He smiled again. 'As, from a brief acquaintance, one might have foreseen.'

I may have blushed. 'My belated thanks,' I said. 'And also for the kindness that you extended to my poor friend Meg Wolfingham.'

'I was sorry to hear that she had passed away.'

I nodded. A silence fell between us. Behind me, I heard Lady Moira's loud, aggressive laugh.

'Does – *she* know about me?' I asked him.

'No.'

'I thought not.'

'She never saw you clearly. Moira's eyesight's very bad. She's only prevented from wearing spectacles through sheer vanity.'

I took a sip of champagne – the first of my life – and was enchanted by the way the bubbles tickled the back of my throat.

'*The Honourable Mrs Powker.*'

'Darling Amelia's here at last,' declared Florrie. 'Now we can go into dinner.' Taking me by the arm, she effected a swift introduction. ' 'Melia, dear, this is darling Daisy, whom you will grow to love. Daisy, this is my old chum Amelia.'

The Hon. Mrs Powker was of Florrie's age, with frizzed white hair and an engaging smile. 'How d'you do?' she said gruffly. And to Florrie: 'Brought you some roses, dear. Left 'em in the damn' hansom. You're lookin' a bit peaky. Been overdoin' it?'

'Mr Melmoth, you will escort Mrs Powker,' said Florrie, taking charge in her inimitable manner. 'Daisy dear, you will go in with the Archdeacon, you'll be on your left. Mr Arbuthnot, will you escort Miss Wainwright? Lady Moira . . .'

Presently, two by two, we filed in through the double doors to the dining room, where candlelight shone warmly on sheer white napery and old silver.

I led the way to the head of the table, my arm resting upon that of the handsome young archdeacon. My first dinner-party.

If I had known what faced me, I think I would have turned and run!

*

Through the soup and fish, conversation was general across and along the table.

'Where d'you hail from, Miss Friday?' This from the pippin-cheeked Miss Deborah Wainwright, seated on my right. There was a quite discernible pausing of spoons and forks to mouths, an abatement of mastication, as most people waited to hear something about their hostess who had appeared in Bath Society right out of the blue, without antecedents, reputation good or ill, or anything to commend her at all save a supposedly considerable fortune.

'From mid-Dorset,' I replied. 'Near – um – Westchester.'

'Ah, then you must have hunted with the Westchester and Colne,' declared Miss Wainwright with a glance of approval. 'In which case you know m'cousin "Boopers" Benedict, who was master there till he broke his neck and had to follow the hounds in a donkey-drawn Bath chair.'

'I have never hunted,' I admitted.

Upon my declaration, some spoons and forks paused again in their passage.

'Never *hunted*?' repeated Miss Wainwright. 'How *very* odd.'

From the other end of the table, the odious Lady Moira framed the question that must have been teetering on one or two pairs of lips. 'Dear me,' she said. 'And if you didn't hunt in mid-Dorset, what did you do with your time in the winter, pray?'

'I addressed myself to keeping warm,' was my response.

There was a little polite laughter at my sally, and a faint flush of annoyance briefly chased across Lady Moira's porcelain cheek; it came as no surprise to me that her ladyship did not take lightly to idle banter; she quickly returned to the probing attack.

'If you hail from mid-Dorset, but nevertheless never hunted with the Westchester and Colne,' said she, 'you must, notwith-standing, have met Sir Claud and Lady Wisher of Marnsfield Hall. Sir Claud is managing director of one of Mr Arbuthnot's companies – as you might recall.'

Did I not well remember meeting Sir Claud and his lady? The memory of that encounter in the firing shed was still a fresh canker in my mind – and I had no doubt the feeling was shared by that unlikeable couple. Before composing an answer to the Valkyrie's question, I flashed a glance down the table to Charles Arbuthnot, who was seated between Miss Wainwright and the archdeacon's wife. With what looked like quite unnecessary concentration, he was slicing his mackerel into neat squares: no help or guidance from *that* quarter.

'I – I met Sir Claud and Lady Wisher on one occasion,' I replied.

'That would have been at Marnsfield?' persisted my interlocutor. 'I ask, because if so, it is possible that I was also present.'

'It was not at Marnsfield,' I replied. And to cover my rising apprehension about the direction of her questioning, took a deep sip of my champagne.

'The reason I ask,' said Lady Moira, 'is because I have a very clear impression of having met you before. Something about you – your voice . . .' She tapped her cheek thoughtfully and fell silent.

'When shall you be taking up residence at Mortmain Castle, Miss Friday?' asked Charles Arbuthnot, blessedly filling the nerve-searing silence in which – as I was convinced – my blonde tormentor was going to remember where we had previously met.

It was Florrie, seated at the opposite end of the table from me, who took up the answer; dear Florrie, who clearly saw as well as I – and, indeed, Charles Arbuthnot – that Lady Moira's line of questioning was leading me towards social disaster at this, my first dinner-party. 'My friend will probably go down to Cornwall at the end of the season and winter there,' she supplied. 'We have ascertained that, despite general belief to the contrary, the coast of south Cornwall, due presumably to its prevailing maritime winds, does not suffer in winter from the extremes of temperature that one experiences in, say, London or the eastern counties. I recall when I was a gel in Lincoln, at the time my papa was a canon at the cathedral (I believe you were once clerk to the chapter there, Archdeacon), we had the most appalling arctic winter in the year of '45 – or was it '46 . . .?'

Florrie prattled on, snatching inspiration out of the air and embroidering her theme in a most amusing and diverting manner; all the time commanding the willing attention of her listeners, whom she presently had in tucks of laughter when she recalled the tale of how the dean and chapter of one of England's most ancient and prestigious of religious foundations, while travelling in a body to the consecration of a new parish church in the diocese, were caught in a blizzard and obliged to spend the night in a wayside inn, where the local ale so inspired these ten upright gentlemen of the cloth that they were constrained to entertain the no doubt wide-eyed and open-mouthed peasantry with their renditions of popular music hall ballads.

But two of Florrie's listeners, at least, gave her less than their full attention. There was I, whose hand strayed frequently and unwisely towards my wineglass; and there was Lady Moira, who continued to gaze at me with what I knew to be short-sighted concentration as she puzzled her brain for the answer that must surely, sooner or later that evening, occur to her.

*

During the entrées, the conversation around the table remained particular, that is to say, one or other of the more articulate guests carried the burden of a monologue to which the others attended. I would have wished for the talk to have become general, so as to have hidden my anonymity amongst the common chatter, but it was not to be. Accordingly, I unenthusiastically pushed lamb cutlets around my plate, drank too much of the unaccustomed champagne, and hoped for the best.

The talk returned to my castle in Cornwall, about which most of the guests expressed a curiosity which was satisfied by the fascinating Mr Tristan Melmoth.

'I know Mortmain well,' said he. 'Not, I hasten to add, from personal acquaintance, though I shall hope to rectify that omission at an early date –' He treated me to a long-lashed, sidelong glance when he said this. 'No, my knowledge of that superb building is gleaned solely from my architectural studies and my insatiable fascination for the Arthurian legends of

Cornwall. Oh, yes, my friends, there is no doubt that Mortmain Castle enjoys as good, if not better, claim to a connection with the shadowy image of King Arthur and his Camelot than the more widely-famous site of Tintagel on the northern coast of the peninsula. If my information is correct, Mortmain is also profoundly and widely – *haunted!*'

'Haunted?' exclaimed Florrie.

'Dear me! Not that I believe such things. But there is more in heaven and earth, as they say.' This from Mrs Archdeacon Vallence. 'Do tell more, Mr Melmoth.'

Melmoth glanced towards me again and smiled. 'I have no wish to disturb our hostess and owner of Mortmain with what may well prove to be mere myth and fable,' he said. 'But if Miss Friday is willing that I should proceed . . .'

Bemused, I nodded my assent. A footman refilled my empty glass, and I saw that Lady Moira was still narrowly regarding me.

'As to the fabric of the present building,' continued Mr Melmoth, 'the present structure stands upon a crag to the north-west of Lizard Point, and the oldest parts date to a Norman keep erected by one Gilles, Count of St Lo – a soldier of fortune who had fought under the banner of William the Conqueror at the Battle of Hastings, for which service the lands surrounding Mortmain Crag were his reward. The letters patent from the King contained a riddle which specified that Gilles could have as much land as could be enclosed by a single ox-hide. The astute soldier of fortune solved the riddle: he slaughtered the largest ox obtainable in all England and Normandy and had its hide cured to the fineness and softness of velvet. He then ordered his wife and her seamstresses to cut the hide into the finest and thinnest single strip with the sharpest and most delicate of scissors. The resulting strip – it was more like a silk yarn – was laid in a vast circle about Mortmain Crag and encompassed an area so great that legend tells us it took a good man on a powerful horse over five hours hard riding to get round it.

'Having obtained his land, Count Gilles built his castle upon the footings of a citadel that had been totally destroyed by assault in pre-history. Evidence of that savage assault was discovered by the Count's workmen in the shape of a mass grave within the confines of the old walls, where the skeletons of up to a thousand warriors bore mute testimony to the scale of the siege. And when the new master of Mortmain caused a chapel to be built and consecrated within the newly-raised walls, there was no means by which the roof beam could be persuaded to remain in place. Day after day, the beam was put up and secured; night after night, some unknown agency rejected it and it was found in the dawn light to have fallen into the roofless nave. Count Gilles's chapel at Mortmain remains a stark, roofless and unconsecrated shell to this very day.'

'Ah, I have heard of this,' interjected the archdeacon. 'Some attempt was made, during the last century, to roof and conse-crate the shell of which you speak. Indeed, a roof of sorts was erected and stayed there till the ceremony of consecration, which was to be performed by the archdeacon of Exeter cathedral, in which see the parish of Mortmain then was. I have read an account of the ceremony – or, as I have implied, the *attempted* ceremony. No sooner had the archdeacon and his acolytes entered the building than darkness fell outside, the candles guttered and died, and a dreadful chillness took hold of the place. When the officiating priest attempted to recite the Collect, his voice was drowned by a vast chorus of disembodied voices screeching in some alien tongue, and while he persisted, they persisted. In no time the congregation had fled, and most of the acolytes also. The archdeacon followed soon after. And then the roof fell in. That is the bald account, as I remember it.'

A murmur of unease passed round the table like the breath of panic, and despite my present predicament, I joined in it.

'So much for the chapel,' said Mr Melmoth hastily (one had the clear impression that he much preferred to hold the stage without the assistance of Archdeacon Vallence). 'No one goes near it now, nor has any further attempt been made to complete or consecrate the place. It is said that on certain nights of the year, at the time of the summer and winter solstices, a chorus of chanting is to be heard in the vicinity. "Pagan chanting" is how it has been described.'

'The manifestations undoubtedly relate to the pre-Christian era,' supplied the archdeacon, earning himself a resentful side-glance from Mr Melmoth. 'The whole Arthurian legend is bound up with the struggle between the Forces of Light and the Powers of Darkness. I would say that vestiges of the latter persuasion still exist in remote corners of Cornwall and elsewhere.'

'Quite so, quite so, sir,' responded Mr Melmoth, giving one the very clear impression that the archdeacon's generality would have been better supplied by him.

And then – another voice . . .

'If I may interject,' said Charles Arbuthnot, and every eye around the table – my own in particular, I'm sure – was immediately upon him, 'there is a tale of another manifestation relating to Mortmain which came my way some few years ago. If I have my hostess's blessing' – he smiled sidelong at me – 'I should like to recount it, for, in my opinion, it admits of a refreshingly simple explanation, uncluttered by speculation concerning Arthurian legendry, the myths associated with the Dark Ages, and so forth.'

'Oh, do tell, Mr Arbuthnot!' breathed pretty young Mrs Vallence, and she spoke for us all around that table – the women in particular. Nothing could have been more marked than the contrast between his delivery and that of Mr Melmoth: the latter's presented with a studied theatricality and affectation, his with a firmness and simplicity of address which had the power to spellbind.

'Very well,' he said, glancing again at me. 'I address you all to the latter half of the seventeenth century, when the West Country was torn by the struggle between King and Parliament that we know as the English Civil War. Broadly, Cornwall was for the King, and Cornish cavaliers drove a swath of victory from Stratton in the north of the peninsula to Lansdown Field, which is only half an hour's walk from where we sit tonight.

'At this time, at the commencement of the war, Mortmain had passed by inheritance to the Denvers family, and the then incumbent, Lord Denvers, while too infirm by reason of a hunting accident to take up arms for his king, was a staunch supporter of the cause, sending monies to the loyal forces in Bodmin and Launceston and evicting those of his tenants and their families who were pledged to Parliament.

'One of these, the Penburys, who farmed to the north, had a son named Richard, who was secretly in love with Denvers' daughter Felicity, and she with him. When his family were thrown out, Richard went to his lord and pleaded for reinstatement. Felicity added her pleas to those of her lover. Suspicious of her passionate entreaties, Lord Denvers challenged the girl, who then admitted her connection with Richard and begged her father's permission to marry the young yeoman, since – as she had the courage to declare – she was carrying his child.'

The silence that followed was broken only by something very near to a sob of anguish from Florrie. 'And what happened then, sir?' she asked. 'Did Lord Denvers give his blessing upon the match?'

'That he did not,' responded Charles Arbuthnot. 'He had Richard whipped from his door. His daughter he had locked in the upper chamber of one of the towers, where she remained till the end of her days, which were numbered. Richard, though at heart a man of peace, was so embittered by the treatment that he had received at Denvers' hands that he joined the pikemen of the Parliamentary forces who were invested at Stratton, and was gravely wounded in the defeat that was inflicted upon them there. It was during the retreat from Stratton – and Richard was dragging himself along with the aid of two sticks – that news was brought to him of his lover's fate: she was near to her time, and her merciless father was denying her any attention, but keeping her locked in the tower, half-starved, alone, despairing.'

'Did he go to her – did Richard go to the lass?' cried Deborah Wainwright, who had been listening to the account with visible concern upon her honest, homely features.

'He did,' replied Charles Arbuthnot. 'He dragged himself – and he a dying man – the width of the peninsula and half its length, begging such help as he could along the way and arriving at the gates of Mortmain Castle in the dark hours of a May night. Servants found him in the dawn light, fingers still in the act of scrabbling at the studded oak. By the marks in the sandy earth leading to the castle, they reckoned that Richard must have crawled on all fours for the last mile.

'He was, of course, stone dead.'

Despite my private concern, Charles Arbuthnot's spellbinding account had drawn me towards those two ill-starred lovers of long ago.

'What of the girl – what of Felicity?' I asked him. 'And her child?'

'They perished both,' he replied. 'Nor did Lord Denvers raise a finger to help them. His own daughter and her love-child he caused to be buried outside the hallowed confines of the parish church. The last resting place of Richard Penbury is not recorded.

'*But their spirits live on!*'

'You mean – they haunt Mortmain Castle?' breathed Mrs Vallence.

Charles Arbuthnot nodded. 'All of them, Lord Denvers' restless ghost included,' he said. 'Denvers, so the story goes, makes his presence known by a dark shadow that stalks the castle courtyard, pacing up and down as if in agony of conscience. Felicity and her stillborn child are no more than an uneasy presence – a whispering sigh, a quiet weeping, a passing unease – in the staircase leading up to the tower where she was incarcerated. As for poor Richard Penbury . . .

'In the month of May, they say, the figure of a crawling man may be seen o' nights both around – *and inside* – the castle!

'That is all I know. Perhaps it is enough for Miss Friday's peace of mind – in which case I may already have said too much.'

I met his grey-eyed gaze and hastily looked away, suddenly and unaccountably frightened by what I might see there – or, perhaps, what I might not have seen there.

*

'From whom did you receive your inheritance, Miss Friday? This place – the castle in Cornwall?'

Lady Moira threw her bombshell at me just as the table was

applying itself to the second course. I, caught in the act of gazing down in bewilderment and some compassion upon the pair of tiny trussed and roast pigeons that had been set before me, and caught entirely unawares, took some time to frame an answer to her searching question. And while I ferreted around in my mind, I swear that every knife and fork around the table was stilled again, and every eye was upon me.

'I – I don't know,' came my answer at length. A poor reply, it had at least the virtues of brevity and truth.

'Don't know?' The Valkryie's wide, baby-blue eyes fixed upon me short-sightedly. She frowned in utter disbelief. 'Don't *know*? How very odd.'

The awkward silence that followed my declaration and her reaction to it was broken by an interjection from Mr Makepiece Crawley. The Master in Lunacy, who had scarcely contributed a word so far, seemed eager to draw a veil over my embarrassment. 'When the Tsar of Russia visited London last year,' he said, 'my lady wife and I had the inestimable honour to be presented to His Imperial Majesty, did we not, my dear?'

'That is so,' responded his lady. 'His discourse was most diverting. He told me that there was nothing he liked better than a toasted English muffin.'

No response; no one was remotely interested in the vagaries of Tsar Nicholas II – only in the source of my inheritance.

'Miss Friday and I took tea with the poor Empress Eugénie the other afternoon,' said Florrie, moving smartly into the breach. 'Most affecting. Her Imperial Majesty, who, as you must all be aware, can seldom be constrained to speak of her misfortunes, and most particularly about the death of her beloved only child the Prince Imperial, was completely forthcoming in the presence of our present hostess, whose charm and unaffected sympathy brought a simple and frank reposing of confidence from that star-crossed lady. For the first time, as I was given to understand from her companion the Marquise de Sevray, the Empress told a story relating to her son's death that she had never before recounted to any other than her most intimate friends. Now – what do you think of that?'

A murmur of vague appreciation greeted Florrie's declaration, but the general response was half-hearted; the pack was in full cry after more toothsome game. I took another deep swallow from my champagne glass. Even Florrie looked defeated.

'I have a very great regard for the ex-Empress,' said the archdeacon. 'Though not a co-religionist, the lady is, nevertheless, a by-word for the virtues which I myself personally hold in the very highest regard.'

His observation was greeted by a wall of silence.

It was then that the Hon. Amelia Powker, who had contributed nothing to the conversation throughout the three preceding courses, but had munched her way doggedly through at least two of each and their removes, mopped her mouth and brow with her napkin, took a deep swallow of claret, motioned to a footman to replenish her glass, and gave forth the interjection that was to be my social downfall that fateful evening. It was directed to the saturnine and bewildering man who, despite my present alarms, had not for one moment been far from my thoughts, seated as he was only two places distant on my right.

'Mr Arbuthnot, sir,' she announced.

'Ma'am,' he responded.

'I have in mind that I'm greatly indebted to you, sir.'

'Indeed, ma'am?' replied Charles Arbuthnot, obviously amused. Sensing a protracted diversion, I took another profound swallow of my champagne out of sheer relief.

'Why yes. I was advised by m'cousin Winstanley to purchase shares in one of your companies. And greatly to me advantage.'

'That would be the Earl Winstanley, ma'am?'

'Yes, m'cousin Roland, the admiral. Bless me, I made a very tidy sum on that transaction, and I'm greatly indebted to you, bless me if I ain't.'

Everyone had returned to their mutton, their pigeons, their fowl. The Hon. Amelia, who had a manner of address that put one in mind of one of her cousin the admiral's battleships ploughing the seas for England – stolid, immovable and implacable – was not one to be interrupted, not even by the odious Lady Moira.

'I'm extremely glad to hear it, ma'am,' said Charles Arbuthnot. 'Which company of mine is this, pray?'

'Why the Westchester Chain-Making Company,' replied the other. 'Situated, as I understand it, in the village of Mordwenn. I know little or naught about the making of chain, but if my receipts are anythin' to go by, you must make uncommonly good chain, sir.'

I reached for my champagne glass, and found to my surprise that it was empty. Quenching an impulse to look towards Lady Moira, I resolved to hang on by my fingertips and wait.

There was not long to wait . . .

'I remember now! That chain factory! Last Christmas! *She*!'

Her finger was pointed accusingly at me, but her remark – accusation – was thrown at Charles Arbuthnot.

'What are you trying to say, Moira?' he responded evenly. 'And that being determined, do you think that this is the time, or the place, to say it?'

As when a hawk, circling a field of crows scavenging among the cut stubble, will silence the cawing, so did this exchange still even the slightest sound – the clink of silver upon china, the tinkle of glassware, the movement of the soft-footed servants, even breathing itself – in the dining room.

Her face was a picture of impotent rage seeking to express itself. Oddly, she had (as yet) no eyes for me.

'You *know*, Charles!' she breathed. 'You knew – you have known all along – who this creature is. Deny it – deny it, if you dare!'

'Yes, I have always known,' he replied. And he flashed me a straight glance that told me nothing of his thoughts.

'And yet you brought me here, knowing what you know?' she cried. 'Brought me to this – *creature's* table, to be humiliated. To be reminded of the ill-bred insults she heaped upon me, upon the Wishers, even upon yourself that day.' Her eyes blazed in my direction. 'I saw you only imperfectly that day,' she cried. 'It's scarce to be surprised at that I did not instantly recognise the unwashed scarecrow with the loud, illiterate mouth – now that she is got up in poor imitation of a person of quality.' She rose, white and unstoppable as boiling milk. 'Take me home,

Charles,' she ordered. 'Now. At once. It is the least you can do, to wipe out the gross indelicacy of bringing me to this ignorant upstart's table!'

A cold fury had been kindled in my mind during her peroration. I neither knew, nor cared, nor did I look to see if Charles Arbuthnot was moving to obey her command; my sole intent was to answer that woman's insult in kind. I rose to my feet, and was instantly aware that my legs, as far as the knees downwards, seemed to have taken on an independent life that was subject neither to my wishes nor to my control. In short, as I realised later, I was experiencing for the first time the general effect of drinking (as I afterwards elicited from the butler) the larger part of a bottle of champagne in a little over an hour and a half.

As a follower of my life story will appreciate, I have a better than average recollection of events, particularly of conversations. At this stage, I should hasten to add, I am indebted to my dear friend Florrie Wimsey-Fildes for the nice details, the turns of phrase, the nuances of expression contained within my reply to Lady Moira Fame.

It went, so I am led to believe, something like this:

'Madam, I am sorry that you have to go, but before you do, there are a few points touching upon our late encounter that I must set to rights. First, the remarks I addressed to you that day in no way repaid the open and hurtful contempt you displayed to us, the poor, half-starved wretches who stood before you. I was more rude, by far, to Mr Arbuthnot here, and yet he turned the other cheek and rewarded my insolence with his charity – charity of the finest and most acceptable sort, being anonymous and calling for neither thanks nor recognition. In all, it was poor, pompous Sir Claud Wisher and his lady who received the worst of my tongue – and maybe they deserved it most of all, since their callousness was compounded by mealy-mouthed cant and hypocrisy.

'But you, Lady Moira, I think you had from me what you deserved, maybe a little less. Well, you have had your revenge before these people, my guests. And I wish you well of your vengeance.'

(By then, I was standing with difficulty, and only doing so by holding on to the table with both hands.)

'One thing, however, I must put to rights before you leave. You have described me as being ill-bred, loud-mouthed and illiterate, an ignorant upstart, a creature.

'I will tell you, ma'am, that I may well be ill-bred, but I have no proof of my breeding. An upstart I certainly am, and perhaps loud-mouthed, perhaps even a sort of creature.

'*But illiterate I am not!*'

(Here, I am told, I pointed at her accusingly, and she stared at me, wide-eyed, like a rabbit at a stoat.)

'Why I can out-literate you any day of the week, ma'am. Are *you* familiar with the fauna of the Galapagos Islands, the arguments of Plato, the glories of the *Iliad* and the *Odyssey*? *I* am! And also, in great part, with the history of the world, and have had Lady Tooting's outline of social etiquette instilled in me since an early age.

'Why, from early childhood I have been able to recite the books of the Bible from memory.

'Can *you* recite the books of the Bible from memory, Lady Moira?

'Genesis Exodus Leviticus Numbers Deut'ronomy Joshua Judges 'n' Ruth (*Big breath*) Samuel Samuel Kings Kings Chronicles Chronicles Ezra Nehemiah Esther Job Psalms Proverbs (*Another breath*) Ecclesiastes Solomon Isaiah Jer'miah Lam'ntations 'Zekiel Daniel Hosea Jo'l Amos Obadiah Jonah Micah Nahum Habakkuk Zephaniah Haggai (*Bigger breath*) Zechariah Malachi Matthew Mark Luke 'n' John Acts Romans Corinthians Corinthians Galatians 'Phesians Philippians Colossians Thessalonians Thessalonians Timothy Timothy Titus Philomen Hebrews James Peter Peter (*Loud inhalation*) John John John Jude Revelation . . .'

Which having been completed, so I am informed, I slid gracefully to the floor for the first – and last – time in my life.

*

I awoke, and I was in my blue and white bed. The surely midday sun shone obliquely through the part-drawn window curtains and upon Florrie, who sat by the window in a button-back sofa, Wink-Wink asleep on her lap, and addressed herself to a piece of petit-point needlework with which she – in her own phrase – 'wasted the odd hour or so between living and being'.

She looked up to hear me stir, and twinkled.

'How is your head?' she asked.

'It – hurts!' I replied ruefully, after having tried to raise it.

'You took too much champagne,' she said. 'I would have warned you, but you were too far away and it wasn't opportune to send you a *billet doux* down the table via a footman.'

'I wish you had, Florrie,' I replied with fervour. 'And I tell you here and now that neither champagne nor any other intoxicating drink will ever pass my lips again so long as I live.'

Her eyes opened very wide to hear my declaration. 'In any other person, Daisy,' she said, 'I would regard that solemn avowal as a mere caprice, brought on by the conjunction of a soured liver and an intractable head. In your case, my dear, I am persuaded that it is a vow you will keep.'

'You can be sure of that,' I said, sitting up. 'Oh, the pain! Did I make a great fool of myself at table last night, Florrie?'

'You were greatly provoked,' she replied. 'When that's been said, you acquitted yourself with a certain dignity that didn't pass unremarked among your guests. But, nevertheless . . .'

'Nevertheless, it would have been better if I had kept my mouth shut and left Lady Moira to make a fool of herself on her own,' I supplied.

She nodded. 'Next time, in similar circumstances, you will do just that, my dear,' she said. 'For I have never met a young person less likely to make the same mistake twice.'

I thought glumly of my future as a hostess, as a lady of smart society. 'Do you think that I have failed in Bath, then?' I asked her.

'A certain check upon your social progress,' she replied. 'I would put it no higher than that. To counterbalance it, of course, there was your remarkable éclat with the Empress Eugénie, which is the talk of the town.'

'But notwithstanding, you perhaps think that I should ab-

118

sent myself from Bath society for a while?' I suggested, sensing the drift of her thoughts.

She spread her hands and shrugged. 'As always, my dear, you contrive the most elegant solution to a problem. Yes, indeed, it would be a highly suitable move. You have not yet visited your romantic castle in Cornwall, and your departure there will cause scarcely any comment. One month, two months, is a long time in Bath society. By the end of the season, a dozen other minor scandals will have filled their minds to the exclusion of last night's little scene. And Lady Moira is not popular in Bath, if only for the reason that the Fames are *arrivistes*, the family's advancement having been obtained by providing uniforms and equipment at cut prices – though at outrageous profit to themselves – during the Napoleonic War.'

I nodded. 'Cornwall it is, Florrie. But shall you accompany me, dear?'

She shook her head. 'Not yet,' she said. 'The anniversary of Sir Basil's demise falls the week after next, and I always go into retreat in the weeks preceding and following, when I deeply meditate upon the imperfectibility of the human state and its transient nature – to my spiritual advantage.' She brightened considerably and added: 'But I will join you there later on, and will greatly look forward to it. So will Wink-Wink, who simply adores the seaside.'

I thought for a moment, and then posed a question to which I had no great wish to know the answer. 'What happened last night, Florrie – in the end?'

Immediately, she seemed to become interested in searching Wink-Wink's coat for passengers. 'Why, you were carried upstairs to bed,' she said with an air of elaborate casualness.

'Not by you, surely?'

'No. By a gentleman. But it was all perfectly proper, my dear. I accompanied you.'

'Which gentleman?'

'Mr Arbuthnot.'

'Oh.'

Silence. Florrie encountered a quarry and instantly gave

chase. The capture and kill having been accomplished, she gave me a sidelong glance. Finding that she met my gaze, she looked away again.

Presently, she said (again with studied offhandedness): 'Bath gossip has it that Mr Arbuthnot is pursuing Lady M. for all he's worth, and that if he's not careful she'll catch up with him and drag him to the altar. But that's just what they say. Myself, I would suppose that the gentleman in question would make a more sensible choice for a life partner. What do you think, dear?'

'Mmmm,' I commented.

*

By the afternoon post that day, I received a letter from Harold Nesbitt. More a Round Robin than a letter proper, it had been countersigned by all my friends and former colleagues at Messrs Arbuthnot & Son: that's to say, from Mr Walthamstow the chief clerk down to Sergeant Walmer the doorkeeper and including Amy, Harriet, Janet and the rest of the girls.

> Dear Daisy,
> We often wonder how you must be getting along in your new life in Bath, and talk about the old days in the counting house when you would have us all in tucks with your cheery ways. It doesn't seem the same without you. Sgt W. was saying only the other day that your smile was the best thing for starting his day.
> If you have time do please drop us a line or two and let's be knowing how you're getting along. Whatever happens nobody in A. & Son has any doubt that you'll be as successful and popular in Bath as you were in Westchester.
> Cheerio, then. And hoping this finds you as it leaves us in the pink.
> Your friends . . .

Then came Harold's signature in his neat, clerkish hand, with the others' names following after. There was a postscript from Harold alone, and its tone was quite different from that which had gone before:

P.S. This is just from me, Daisy, the others won't be seeing it. Just to say that I quite understand how it is that you'll not be able to give me the answer I wanted so much. And I know it's not just because your good fortune makes you think you're too good for a poor clerk like me. I'm just not the fellow for you and never have been. No complaints, we've had some good times together and I'll never forget you. Trouble is that every other woman I meet will have to stand comparison to Daisy Friday with her eager eyes and the smile that you could warm your hands against. Knowing you has changed my whole life for the better and I'll treasure the memory always.

Mother sends her love. You will know my feelings in the matter.

Yours aye,

Harold

I shed more tears than I would have believed possible over both messages of affection, my gratitude exceeded only by the puzzlement of having inspired such a wealth of emotion in such nice people. About Harold, I pondered long and hard, thinking of ways to ease the burden of his existence, now that I had the means to do so. Even a few guineas – the amount I had expended upon that fateful first dinner-party – would have provided undreamed-of luxuries for his mother's little house in Westchester. Not very much more, and Mrs Nesbitt could pay a daily woman to come in and do the household chores for a twelvemonth – and that would be a blessing for a woman of her age and increasing infirmities.

I pondered on all this, but in the end good sense prevailed: there was no means by which I could send financial assistance to Harold without offering affront; no contrivance by which I could do such a thing anonymously, for he would immediately divine the source of his blessing and return the money with injured pride.

I settled for writing a short, very sincere letter, setting out my reasons for declining his offer of marriage and providing him with the consolation – if consolation it might be – of my continued friendship. Six drafts I made of this proposed missive, and six drafts I screwed up and threw into the fireplace. In the end, I shelved the project till I had had time to compose it more felicitously in my mind.

Next day, I departed for Cornwall. The letter to Harold busied me at odd moments in the weeks that followed. The weeks lengthened into months.

The letter, in the event, was never written – an omission that I shall continue to regret bitterly for the rest of my life.

SEVEN

On a balmy evening in early summer, I journeyed out of the steep valley of the Avon and pursued the setting sun towards the wild western land that juts out into the wastes of the Atlantic, and whose rock-girt coast is the bane of seamen the world over and the graves of innumerable of their forebears.

I travelled alone in a handsome sleeping suite that had been requisitioned upon the advice of the coachman Morgan, whose many accomplishments included an intimate acquaintance with the ins and outs of the Great Western Railway system. The suite comprised a day parlour that could be translated to a sleeping compartment by the letting down of a bunk, and a small bathroom with the usual offices. There was another such suite adjoining in the same coach, but all I saw of my neighbour was a shadow upon the drawn blinds when the train drew in at Bath Spa station and I boarded it at ten o'clock at night. The train was due to arrive at Falmouth in the early hours, but one was at liberty to remain abed there for as long as one chose.

I waved till the small group who had seen me off – Florrie, Morgan, the tweenie who had acted as my lady's maid – faded behind in the smoke-shrouded gloom of the station yard, and then addressed myself to bed; but not before I had admired the last view of Bath that is afforded the traveller at night: the sight of that wonderful old city rising from the river, tier upon tier, crescent upon crescent, and square after square; all lit up in diamond necklaces of winking lights.

The bunk was astonishingly comfortable, and I was greatly

wearied after a trying day of deciding upon what must be packed for my stay in Cornwall, doing some last-minute shopping in the town, scribbling a short note to my solicitor Mr Treacher, informing him of my change of abode (for so he had asked me to do when the time came). You might think that these activities were no great burden for one who had slaved twelve hours a day in a chain factory, but you would be wrong; if there is anything I have learned in my translation from poverty to riches, it is this: the trials of the rich, which are equalled by the trials of the very rich, are different only in kind from those of the poor, the cold and the half-starved; the human mind and frame is of such imperfection that it is seldom entirely satisfied with its lot (and is, indeed, often grossly dissatisfied). How else to account for miserably unhappy millionaires and suicidal monarchs? And yet there are, paradoxically, exceptions to the rule: the odd souls (I have known many such) who are deemed poor and wretched by the world's standards, but who romp barefoot through life as through fields of clover, and throw their caps over the moon for joy.

I digress . . .

No sooner were my eyes closed than I slept, and woke from a pleasant dream of warmth and comfort to the high whistle of the locomotive, a squeal of brakes, and a change of motion which suggested that the train was slowing to a halt. I had scarcely registered this fact when, from the corner of my eye, *I perceived that I was no longer alone in the compartment!*

Instantly, I sat bolt upright. The newcomer – no more than a dark shape set against a drawn window-blind through which shone the faint loom of a light from outside – was standing by the open door which clearly led to the adjacent suite and which I had previously tried and found to be locked.

As the first scream rose to my lips, the intruder advanced upon me with hands outstretched, and I saw to my alarm that he – undoubtedly a man, for he had the height and shoulders width of a male – was wearing a broad-brimmed tall hat by which I had come to know and fear him.

He was my tormentor, the killer of my dog and my own would-be murderer!

My fingers grappled for the let-down table at the side of my bunk, where lay – as I remembered – a candlestick, a carafe of water and a glass, and sundry small items of personal adornment. My grasp closed around something which, in the dark, I instantly perceived to be the neck of the carafe.

Then he was upon me, and the reek of a heavy, sickly aroma assailed my nostrils. One hand was at my shoulder (and I felt and heard my nightgown rip under his fingers); he thrust the other towards my face, to my mouth. A cloth enveloped my mouth and nose. Its aromatic stench filled my whole world. I felt my senses slipping away from me as I descended into a whirlpool of spinning lights. As I sank into an oblivion which I knew instinctively would be the end of my life, my whole will was directed to my right hand, which still clutched the slender neck of the carafe. As I wielded it, I felt the water pour down my bare arm, and the entire contents cascaded upon me as, striking blindly at my assailant, the vessel shattered to pieces against him.

He cried out in agony. The aromatic pad fell away from my face, and I saw him in the increasing light from outside as he staggered back, holding his hands over his eyes.

The train slowed to a halt with another tortured squeal of brakes.

'*Exeter – this is Exeter! Change here for Exmouth and Moretonhampstead!*' The announcement was delivered from outside the carriage in stentorian tones.

I shrank back against the wall of the compartment as the mystery figure, still in a state of considerable distress, brushed past the bunk with no further regard for my presence, wrenched open the carriage door and flung himself out into the night and the lamplight of a station. A staccato clatter of footfalls, and he was gone.

When I dared to wrap a shawl about my shoulders and peer outside, I met the gaze of two men in the livery of the Great Western Railway Company. One of them, obviously the senior, wore much gold braid upon his cap; his companion carried a lantern, which he presently held up to illumine my face. What both men must have seen written on my countenance certainly gave them cause for alarm.

'Good heavens, ma'am – what ails you?' exclaimed the senior of the two.

'I – I have been attacked in my compartment,' I replied.

'Was it by the fellow who leapt out just as the train drew in? Ran like a hare, he did. As if the devil was behind him. Ran straight out of sight.'

'Just like a hare, as you say, sir,' echoed his assistant. 'Straight out of sight.'

The Station-Master (I now identified him upon closer acquaintance, for he had his rank emblazoned upon his cap badge) peered inside my compartment and observed my very considerable luggage disposed upon the floor and the racks. 'Would this gentleman 'ave been travelling with you, ma'am?' he asked. 'Your 'usband, perhaps?'

'Oh, no!' I cried. 'I'm travelling alone to Falmouth. This – person – forced his way into here from the compartment next door. I think, I think . . .'

'Yes, ma'am?' Both pairs of eyes were upon me, very watchfully.

'I – I think he was attempting to kill me,' I said. And despite my conviction, the assertion, to my own ears, sounded silly and hysterical. I think they thought so, too.

'Ah, be that so, ma'am?' breathed the Station-Master. 'Be that so indeed? Us will take a look in that next compartment. By your leave, please, ma'am.'

They brushed past me and went through the door by which my midnight visitor had entered. They soon returned. Their attitude towards me had undergone a change in the brief time between.

'No luggage in there, ma'am. Nothing,' said the Station-Master. 'Your attacker travelled light. Nor 'ad the bunk been slept in. I'd say he sat up – and waited his opportunity.'

'Just as you say, sir,' vouchsafed his assistant. 'Sat up and waited his opportunity.'

'There was only – this,' said the Station-Master. In his hand he held a small green bottle, uncorked. I caught the sweet, sickly stench that had filled my whole world minutes before.

'Chloroform, ma'am. I reckon as 'ow you might be right. The scoundrel meant business sure enough!'

*

Time, tide and the regulations of the Great Western Railway Company being attendant upon the vagaries of no man, the train was obliged to resume its journey on schedule. We steamed out of Exeter Station with the Station-Master and his assistant running along abreast of my window, the former assuring me that he would telegraph on ahead to the police in Falmouth and apprise them of the dastardly attempt upon me. I nodded my fearful thanks and closed the window. As I did so, my glance fell upon a notice attached there:

It is dangerous to put your head out of the window when the train is in motion. G.W.R.

Unaccountably, the warning had the power to make me shudder as if someone had walked over my grave.

To say that I slept for the remainder of my journey would be like asserting that one had enjoyed tranquillity in a gale while voyaging in a rowing boat. Wearied, I drifted off right enough; but every change of motion of the train, every time the wheels clattered over a rough part of the track, each time the loco-motive's whistle sounded, I was awake and near to screaming; and such sleep as I had was haunted by the vision of the creature in the weird hat.

It was a positive relief, in the grey dawn light, to see the sweep of a wide harbour, a forest of ships' masts and the hint of the grey sea beyond; and to feel the train slowing down and sliding to a halt under an ornate engine shed.

'*Falmouth – this is Falmouth.*'

I was washed and dressed when there came a discreet tap upon the compartment door. Opening it, I met the gaze of a thick-set young man of medium height in a Derby hat and Norfolk jacket. He was fair-haired, with a bronzed complexion, mutton-chop whiskers and a disconcerting, green-eyed gaze. At his elbow stood a uniformed policeman.

'Good morning, ma'am,' he said, doffing his hat. 'Do I address Miss Friday, whose carriage is waiting outside to convey her to Mortmain Castle?'

'Yes, sir,' I replied. 'I'm Daisy Friday.'

'Sergeant Penbury, ma'am. May I come in and hear what you have to say about the occurrence at Exeter?'

The uniformed man remained outside, as Sergeant Penbury (Penbury? Penbury – where had I heard that name before, and recently? I asked myself) took the seat opposite me and produced a notebook. His green eyes narrowed as I handed him the chloroform bottle which the Exeter station-master had given to my charge. In a few brief words I was able to tell him all I knew of the attack upon me.

'Do you have any idea who the assailant might have been, Miss Friday?' he asked, when I had done.

'No,' I replied. And added: 'But I have seen him before – several times.'

He looked up from the page of his notebook. 'Tell me,' he said.

I told him – everything; as I had not found the courage, resource, detachment, effrontery – call it what you will – to tell even dear Florrie. He listened without saying a word; but made notes from time to time. I sensed that his attention quickened when I told of how the stranger had pursued me over the common at Westchester and how poor little Thursday had met a violent end.

'And he was seen in the vicinity of your house in Bath?' he asked, when I had finished. 'By whom, Miss Friday?'

'By various of the servants,' I replied. 'Oddly, after I arrived at Lansdown Crescent, the visitations ceased – save that I thought I saw something in the graveyard late one night. But I could easily have imagined it.'

'That might be significant,' said the sergeant, making a note.

'What might?' I asked.

'The fact that he watched the house before you arrived and ceased to do so after you came. It suggests that he knew of your future movements, but not the actual timing of the same. In other words, he is someone fairly close to you – but not *too* close to you. And that would eliminate several would-be suspects, perhaps. Tell me, Miss Friday, who knew of the actual day on which you planned to take up residence at your house in Bath?'

I named them all, commencing with lawyer Giles Treacher and Mr Caldecott his clerk, the employees at Arbuthnot & Son, Florrie Wimsey-Fildes and the rest. Sergeant Penbury noted them all.

'We may discount all those people,' he observed. 'Together with their intimates, I fancy. But with whom does that leave us, I wonder? Who would wish you harm, Miss Friday?' He mused, chin in hand, regarding me with the green-eyed gaze that gave away nothing. 'And why chloroform?' he added.

'What are the effects of chloroform?' I asked. 'I know nothing of it, save that it is used as an anaesthetic. Can it – *kill*?'

He nodded. 'Its safety margin is relatively narrow,' he said, 'which accounts for the many fatalities resulting from its use in inexperienced hands.' He stroked his whiskers thoughtfully. 'The significance of your assailant's use of chloroform, however, might lie not in its fatal properties, but in its ability to render the victim unconscious and helpless.'

'For what purpose, sir?' I demanded, alarmed anew.

He pulled a long lip. Clearly, he was not to be drawn upon this point.

*

The road from Falmouth harbour to Mortmain Castle lay, in the first place, along the coastal road, providing wide and uninterrupted views of the English Channel to the east. My coachman, a Cornishman and taciturn to boot, nevertheless was constrained upon enquiry to point out to me Rosemullion Head, the Helford River estuary, and later, as the road bore us southward, the distant roofs and towers of Helford town. The sun had barely risen a handsbreadth before the well-marked road became a dirt-track and we were lurching through wild and seemingly abandoned countryside of derelict farms, sodden meadows, roofless byres and what, even to my untutored eye, was clear evidence of many years of neglect.

The coachman had a phrase for it. One-eyed he was and, as I

have said, taciturn. He turned in his seat and, pointing with his whip, encompassed the passing scene of desolation.

'Mortmain land!' he growled. 'Accursed land!' And he spat. I made no reply.

Presently, through the gap between two low hills ahead, I saw the brassy glint of sea and a distant sail on the heat-haze of the horizon. Did I but know it then, the twin hills formed the northernmost boundary of the Mortmain home park, as distinct from the land which William the Conqueror had granted to Count Gilles, that soldier-of-fortune who had encompassed it within the span of an ox-hide.

The home park announced itself by a high wall of drystone that shut out all else save the upper battlements and turreted towers of the fortress that was my other home. Seeing it thus, imperfectly, from afar, with the seabirds winging round its high finials, I was struck with a sense of awe and wonder at my new estate. It was a feeling that was greatly enhanced when soon after the carriage passed between twin gatehouses and through high, open gates of gilded ironwork – and I saw Mortmain Castle plain.

Where to find the tongue to describe it? Though not vast, its shape and proportions bedazzled the eye into imagining it was both wider and taller than it really was. Firstly, it was set upon a dark crag of rock that rose, at its seaward end, almost vertically from the shore, and it being high tide at the time, the sullen waves were throwing themselves upon its foot. A high curtain wall surrounded the whole complex of buildings which comprised a central keep in the Norman manner (as I later learned, this was a copy of the Norman White Tower of London), surrounded by a coronet of smaller towers all connected, and surmounted by pinnacles. At one end of the complex, near the sea and built to the edge of the outer wall, was a slender, roofless building massively buttressed. I knew without being told that this was the haunted chapel that by no will of man would allow itself to be roofed or consecrated.

'Mortmain!' spat my coachman, and made it sound like a curse.

*

The way into the castle led up a steep incline, under an archway, across a drawbridge that spanned a deep abyss where the high tide scoured the footings at its base, through another arch built into the screen wall and out into a pleasant courtyard set with trees and unexpected lawns. There was even an ornamental pool with a plunging fountain: as the coach passed close by on our way to the great doorway of the central keep, I saw golden carp meandering lazily in its pellucid depths.

There was no one there to greet me. I paid off the coachman when he had set down my baggage; he drove off back across the drawbridge with not so much as a thanks and a backward glance. Storm clouds were massing to the west as I picked up my small valise and ventured to strike upon the massive, iron-studded double doors with a heavy knocker fashioned in the shape of a satyr's head. The sound echoed and re-echoed in the far fastnesses of the void beyond.

Presently, one of the halves of the door creaked open to an unseen touch, and a sweep of worn stone floorway lay open to my gaze. Beyond that, a row of stained-glass windows illuminated the dim interior with a mysterious blue gloom. There was no sign of anyone within.

'Hello!' I called, tentatively. And, again: 'Hello in there!'

No response.

Easing the door further open, I took a couple of steps into a vast hallway and looked about me. High in the raftered ceiling, rows of ancient banners hung like tattered grey ghosts in the stillness. A shaft of coloured light from a stained-glass window illuminated one of these talismans of a long-gone military glory: it depicted a red dragon, greatly faded, upon a white ground.

I walked further into the hall; as I did so, the sound of the door creaking shut behind me made me turn with a start.

There was a small child – a girl of about seven or eight – who had been hidden from my sight behind the open door. Her small hand reached and closed the latch.

'Well, thank you for letting me in,' I said, amused. 'And what's your name, little girl?'

No reply.

I tried again. 'My name's Miss Daisy Friday,' I said. 'I am the owner of Mortmain Castle, as you may know, and I've come to live here for a while. It's very big, isn't it? Do you live here, too – with your mother and father, perhaps?'

The child made no reply, but continued to gaze at me with curiously lack-lustre eyes, and her lips were forever seeking her thumb, which stole from time to time into her mouth. A pretty little thing, with golden curls like a cherub and dressed in a simple, clean pinafore frock, she offered promise of a charming nature, but gave none of it away.

'Well, I expect we'll get to know each other better when I've been here for a while,' I said, defeated.

Still no reply; but she was no longer looking at me, but at someone – something – behind me . . .

'Phoebe doesn't talk, ma'am. You'll have to forgive her for that.'

I turned to look at the speaker, who turned out to be a woman in her sixties, with bone-white hair drawn back into a bun, taut features, and prominent eyes that forever sought out a spot to one side or other of my shoulders, never directly meeting my gaze. She wore the attire of a senior servant: black bombasine, a stark white apron and coif, and a chatelaine of keys suspended from a thick black leather belt at her waist.

'I'm Mrs Steeple, ma'am,' said she. 'Phoebe is our grand-daughter and lives with us, by your leave. Will you be wishing to see your rooms? I'll send Steeple to fetch up your baggage. Your pardon for not greeting you, but I didn't hear Ben Flack's carriage coming up the drive. Phoebe, she sees and hears everything.' This speech was delivered in a flat monotone, utterly devoid of expression or sentiment. She struck me as a woman whose heart and soul had been pared away as a knife takes the stone from a ripened plum.

'Thank you, Mrs Steeple,' I replied, determined to be bright before the unassailable front of her chill presence. 'And thank you, too, Phoebe, for letting me in,' I added, turning.

But the child had gone.

Mrs Steeple took my small valise from me and, motioning me to follow, advanced through the hall to a wide, richly balustraded stone staircase that led up into a bright loom of light which revealed itself as a long corridor set with tall windows. Rows of painted portraits lined the walls, each in an ornate gilded frame; I passed beneath the frowning glances of fine ladies and gentlemen of past times, some in court wigs of the last century, others in costumes of even greater antiquity – a few of the men wore armour.

My guide presently came to a halt before a panelled wall hung with resplendent tapestries depicting scenes of the chase. She touched a panel and the whole section swung open to reveal a spiral staircase leading up.

'This is the private entrance to the east tower, ma'am,' she informed me. 'The whole tower is given over to the mistress's quarters, and the last Lady Denvers, who had it converted for her use, had this staircase built so that she could receive her lovers without the knowledge of the servants.' As she made this observation, the woman's pinched mouth pursed with prim distaste.

The way up to the tower was no more than three sweeps of the spiral, which was well lit by glazed arrow slits in the stout, deeply-recessed walls. We emerged into a semi-circular chamber with the usual stone flagging – but now it was scattered with oriental rugs of unbelievable softness to the tread and patterned in a myriad of subtle colours faded to the mute tones of dried flowers.

'Your sitting room.' She opened double doors leading to another semi-circular chamber furnished in the most delectable taste: a sort of oriental fancy, with painted woods and carvings in porcelain and jade: a style I later came to know as *chinoiserie*, that had been widely popularised by the then Prince Regent, our great Queen's uncle. A most elegant and comfortable-looking day-bed was set before a wide window that commanded a view of the coast as far as the point of the Lizard to the east. Away across the mist of early morning, innumerable vessels of all sizes, under both sail and steam, were ploughing their mackerel furrows up and down the grey waters of the English Channel.

'This is lovely,' I said. 'Most charming.'

133

'You'd like to see your bedchamber and dressing room, I shouldn't wonder,' said Mrs Steeple, and abruptly turned to lead me away.

The bedroom, dressing room and usual offices were on the floor above, and done out in the same excellent taste as the sitting room, with a variation of styles, insofar as *chinoiserie* was replaced by the more formal manner of the eighteenth century. My bed rivalled that in Lansdown Crescent and was hung with dove grey curtains to tone with the panelled walls in grey and white enlivened by silver. In the dressing room there was – the first of its kind I had ever encountered in my life, nor have I seen many since – a sunken bath of Turkish tiles with gold-plated taps that issued forth both hot and cold water *to the touch!* (I later learned that this de luxe plumbing had been imported from the eastern seaboard of America, where they are so much further advanced in these niceties of civilisation than we of the old world.)

'Thank you, Mrs Steeple,' I said when the tour of inspection was over. 'If you can arrange for my baggage to be brought up, I should like to bath and change and relax for a while after a most trying journey here.' (Ye gods! If the wretched woman had but known that I had narrowly escaped murder or the like during the previous night, she might have spared me the look of half-concealed contempt that greeted my remark.)

'Yes, ma'am. I'll have Steeple bring your things up directly,' she said. And with the merest sketch or caricature of a curtsy, she turned on her heels and was gone.

Alone, I took off my hat, gloves and shawl, and reclined on a chaise-longue that occupied in the bedroom a similar position to that of the day-bed in the sitting room immediately below, but with a more extensive view over the sea and coastline. And there – safe at last in what was unexpectedly and astoundingly my own home – I thought back again to the events of the previous night.

The uncommunicative but undeniably impressive Sergeant Penbury (and where had I heard that name before? – not for the first time did I curse my inability to recall names), had made it plain that my unknown assailant followed close behind every

134

move I made – yet not too close. But he must have been aware of my impending departure for Cornwall, and had improved upon his performance at Bath, by arranging to travel with me on the same train and in the same carriage, adjacent to my own suite. His attempt upon me had only been foiled, surely, by the sheer chance that he had miscalculated his timing and made his attempt just as the train was about to slow down and stop at Exeter. There was also the detail of the water carafe which I had had the great good fortune to break over his head.

I lived again the terror of those moments; but such is the merciful blessing that the mind offers one in even the most wayward of circumstance that I slipped easily from fears to ease and from there to a light slumber, from which I was aroused by the sound of a tap-tap on the door, followed by a querulous, croaking voice: a male voice.

'Be this where you'll be wanting the baggage, ma'am?'

He was a man of declined years: grey-haired and stooped, a defeated look about his eyes. He was dressed in decent corduroys. I took him to be Mr Steeple, and, presumably, the spouse of the severe woman whom I had already met.

'I'm Steeple,' he added, confirming his station. 'Mrs S– be my lady wife and housekeeper. I do be odd-job man, being fit for naught else since I were taken of a bullet at the assault upon Delhi in t'Indian mutiny, me being then in the Royal Devon & Cornwall Light Infantry, commander Colonel Amos ffolkes-Walmer – wi' two small ffs i' the ffolkes. Where would you like it put, ma'am?'

'Over there, by the cabinet,' I instructed him, being immediately aware from his manner that the poor man was not entirely right in his wits; and, indeed, this impression hardened when I saw a cruel scar that ran obliquely across the side of his head, above his left ear: a mark that could have been left by a passing bullet.

'Ain't been no one living in the castle since the last Lady Denvers was took,' said Steeple. 'Or so we was told. The wife and me, we was in service with the Bravingdon family. You'll have heard o' them, ma'am. Major Bravingdon, he who was killed climbing in the Alps, and I were his officer's servant in the old R.D.C.L.I. A finer gennleman never drew breath nor died so tragic. Will there be aught else, ma'am?'

'No, that will be all, Steeple,' I replied. 'Thank you.'

'Thank you, ma'am,' he said, touching his forelock.

Upon an impulse, I halted him at the door.

'Steeple . . .'

'Yes, ma'am?'

'The pretty little girl – your grand-child . . .'

'Phoebe, ma'am?'

'Yes. Your wife tells me that Phoebe doesn't speak. Why is that? Is she a deaf-mute perhaps, the poor mite?'

He shook his head. 'Phoebe were born as right as a trivet, ma'am, but were robbed of her speech and much else, and all of a night. It happened this way, ma'am . . .

'Her father were skipper of a coaster plying betwixt Bristol and Plymouth, round Land's End. Our only child, who were Phoebe's mother, God rest her soul, travelled always aboard the barque *Philomel*, and indeed knew no other married home. And Phoebe went with them.

'One night, late i' the year, when the gales fill the church-yards with such sailors and their folks as the sea renders up in its own good time' – here Mr Steeple's voice broke and a tear coursed down his worn cheek – 'the *Philomel* foundered off Gwennap Head, which is sou'east o' Land's End. The crew panicked and lowered the only lifeboat, leaving the skipper and his small family to fare as they might. There was one other boat remaining, a tiny dinghy as my son-in-law used for his fishing when in harbour, and not safe to carry a cat in deep waters, let alone two grown persons and a child.

'The rest we can only guess at, ma'am. Not that night, nor the day after when the storm still raged, but on the eve following, the dinghy were washed ashore on the tide in Helford River and the child Phoebe lyin' in it, all a-swooned with cold and terror.

'Our girl and her husband we never did find. And Phoebe, she's never uttered a word again since that time, nor likely ever will. 'Tis a hard trick for fate to play upon an innocent child, ma'am, don't you think?

'I'll be goin' now.'

At the door he paused again of his own accord. A look of sudden puzzlement overcome by recollection passed across his countenance.

'There were something else as the missus charged me to do,' he said. 'Ah, I remember – a letter did arrive for you soon after you came, ma'am.' And he produced the same from his coat pocket and handed it to me.

The postmark was Dorchester and the superscription from Messrs Treacher, Murdoch & Partners. It was from Giles Treacher in reply to mine:

> . . . that you have shifted to Mortmain Castle, where I trust that you will find everything in order [he said]. The housekeeper, Mrs Steeple, though a somewhat forbidding character, is a tower of strength to whom you may look without hesitation for any support. Her husband, who is a wounded veteran of the Mutiny, does the best he can and that's all as can be said for him. The rest of the castle's staff, all local folk, are hard-working and trustworthy.
>
> However, my reason for writing to you, ma'am, is that I feel at this juncture that I must apprise you of certain facts concerning the source of your inheritance. I should like to call upon you on Monday or Tuesday of next week, and will not impose upon your hospitality for more than the day in question.
>
> I remain, madam,
> Your obedient servant,
> (Sgd.) Giles Treacher

I thrilled at the thought of it! Within days, I was to learn something of the personage – or personages – who had raised me from a less than a nobody into somewhat more than a somebody.

But – taking into account the cautious note of Giles Treacher's letter – *how much* was I to be told?

*

Bathed, rested, changed and refreshed, I betook myself to explore my new home. Using the secret staircase (there was another, visible flight of steps, I learned, that descended quite openly into the main hallway), I went out of the great double doors and into the castle courtyard, where I enjoyed watching the golden carp and the feathery diamond droplets of the fountain as they splashed into the ornamental pool; and delighted in the faerie whisper of the silver birch trees taking the light winds from over the castle walls. I afterwards sat upon a stone seat fronting the central keep, which had an arched stone doorway out of which from time to time emerged serving wenches and kitchen maids of various sorts and ages, who, clearly aware of my presence in advance (having, presumably, espied me through the windows), curtsied low and giggled in my direction. In this manner, I suppose, every lass in the castle kitchen took a closer look at her new mistress on the pretext of going about her mistress's business. I found the experience quite diverting, and counted no less than six separate faces.

From my vantage point, I saw much of the comings-and-goings in Mortmain: a little higher from where I sat, on a low rampart set with two cypress trees between which was stretched a clothes-line, there appeared two fresh-faced girls carrying a wicker basket between them, from which they took sheer white washing that they proceeded to hang, giggling and gossiping all the time, till, espying me, they clasped their hands across their mouths and ran in confusion, carrying their empty basket; at ten o'clock by the brass-faced clock over the gatehouse, there was delivered – after much whirring and clacking of machinery – ten silvery strokes upon well-tuned bells; soon after, from that part of the central keep which I divined contained the kitchen quarters, there issued that most subtle and beguiling aroma of frying onions which – *pace* Mrs Beeton – is the essential beginning of a good sauce. I wondered what treat lay in store for me at luncheon . . .

Then my gaze was directed towards the coronet of four towers – my own, the east tower included – which acted as satellites to the central keep. At first glance, I took their appearance to be identical in all respects, till I became aware that the one diametrically opposite mine (and, by its position, the west tower) was different from its companions by reason of the fact that its windows were all closely shuttered. Scarcely had I registered this than the doorway at the foot of this tower opened and Mrs Steeple emerged and locked it behind her. She saw me almost at once, but gave no sign of acknowledgement and walked swiftly towards the kitchen entrance of the keep.

Having exhausted all the possibilities of my present vantage point, I got to my feet and strolled across the courtyard, in and out of the shade of the trees, till I came upon the roofless hulk of the unconsecrated chapel. Almost immediately, I was overcome by a curious heaviness of spirit: it was as if a cloud had suddenly obscured the warmth of the sun – yet the sun still shone brightly. I shuddered and drew my shawl more closely about my shoulders.

The chapel door opened to my touch. It was bare inside: four walls and a stone floor, lancet windows and a double arcade of stout columns supporting nothing but the sky. And empty. Yet in my imagination, it became suddenly peopled with the colour and panoply of a great religious occasion: I seemed to see priests and their acolytes in bright vestments, heard their chanting and savoured the sweet incense. All at once, the vision crazed, cracked, and fell apart. I seemed to hear cries of panic, the great crashing of stonework and timbers, the rushing of many feet, the groans of the injured.

'At what time shall you require luncheon, ma'am?'

Mrs Steeple stood behind me, framed in the open doorway, her hands folded before her, her fugitive eyes seeking something over my shoulder. I sensed that she took some delight in having surprised and alarmed me.

'Whenever suits your arrangements, Mrs Steeple,' I replied coolly. 'At what hour will you be ready to serve?'

She shrugged. 'It's cold cuts and stew mostly,' she replied. 'Both will keep.'

'Shall we say one o'clock?' I suggested.

'As you wish, ma'am,' she replied, and turned to go.

'Mrs Steeple,' I began.

'Ma'am?' She paused.

'I should like to explore the entire castle, part by part, room by room. Alone – without a guide. I delight in seeking things out for myself. Presumably some of the apartments are locked –

the west tower, for instance. Do you have a spare set of keys?'

'No, I do not.'

'Then will you see to it that a spare set is obtained, please?'

She nodded. 'Steeple will have them cut in the village.'

'Thank you,' I said. 'One thing more, Mrs Steeple. Why are the windows in the west tower all shuttered?'

I detected a slight pause before she replied. 'There – there's nothing in there but spare furniture and pictures. Mr Treacher, when he was here first, he said that some of the pictures were very valuable and best kept out of the sunlight. So the windows have been shuttered ever since.'

'I see,' I replied. 'Well, that's most interesting. I should much like to view this spare furniture and these valuable pictures, Mrs Steeple. Can this be arranged? After luncheon, for instance?'

'Well . . .' She paused.

'Surely there's no impediment to my seeing the inside of the west tower,' I persisted.

'No, ma'am. Only that – that it's all very dusty,' she said.

'You went in there this morning,' I retorted, 'and don't look any the worse for wear.'

Her slight hesitations, the evasion about the dusty state of the tower's interior, the shifty manner which she now wore very clearly, all added up to my growing conviction that the house-keeper of Mortmain Castle was hiding something – something connected with the west tower.

'After luncheon it is, then,' I said firmly. 'You will attend me with the keys.'

'Very well, ma'am,' she replied.

*

Drink . . .

That was it. Searching out all the options, I came upon the most likely of all: Mrs Steeple was a secret drinker and kept her supply of alcohol locked away in some cabinet within the west tower. That morning, without a doubt, I had been witness to her slipping in there for a surreptitious tipple. Having decided that, I felt mean to have so brutally searched her out. The poor woman (for whom, it has to be said, I had taken an instant aversion that seemed to be mutual) had known the dreadful experience of losing her daughter, a tragedy that was compounded, furthermore, in the small person of the stricken Phoebe, by a constant and piteous reminder of that sad loss. Small wonder, lacking a strong man to sustain her, but only poor wounded Steeple, that she had turned like so many others to the consolation of the bottle. Having of late become an avid reader of the newspapers and the weekly and monthly journals, I was well aware that the demon drink was one of the blights of our society, particularly among the labouring classes.

At luncheon, to which I was summoned from my sitting room by a pretty housemaid who introduced herself as Nellie Throstle, and which I took alone in a pleasant apartment off the great hall of the central keep with no less than four servants in attendance upon me, including Mrs Steeple, I could not but notice that the housekeeper was much put down in spirits and looked as if she had been crying.

I was served an excellent ragout of mutton followed by cold ham and West Country cheeses. Declining wine (which I had steadfastly done since my disastrous behaviour at my first dinner-party), I took a small cup of coffee to close and felt sufficiently mellowed to repent of distressing Mrs Steeple.

'Mrs Steeple,' I said, 'that was a most excellent luncheon.'

'Thank you, ma'am,' she responded flatly.

'You are probably very busy this afternoon. I shall be quite happy to view the west tower, along with the rest of the castle, at some other time. When the new set of keys have been cut, for instance.'

'This afternoon will suit as well as any, ma'am,' she said with a shrug. 'If you have the time.'

'Very well then,' I responded. 'Let us go now.'

*

The west tower, as I have already intimated, was of identical structure to its companions, that's to say, four storeys high and circular in shape. Upon our entering the ground floor, Mrs Steeple threw wide the shutters to disclose a semi-circular chamber stacked high with crates and chests which, she explained, contained a library of books that Mr Treacher had purchased along with the estate of the late and last owner Lady Denvers (she of the secret staircase to her private quarters). The adjoining room on the lower floor, also semi-circular of course, was similarly furnished; the floor above, literally packed to the ceiling in both rooms, was overflowing with cupboards, sideboards, dressers, commodes, chairs, tables and wooden pieces of that ilk. The floor above contained pictures, and such an army of pictures: mostly stacked face-to-face in serried ranks like ill-assorted soldiers on parade. A few – a very few – were properly hung on the walls. One of these, a portrait of a young woman, caught my eye immediately the shutters were open, on account of the striking beauty of the model and the excellence of the artist's execution.

It showed a lady in the glory of her early-ripened womanhood, and she could have been scarcely more than eighteen or nineteen. She was dressed in the costume of a bygone age, though I was hard put to know the period. Her gown was of pale blue silk, cut low in the neck and with puffed-out sleeves that were slashed to reveal an undergarment of gold tissue. Her light brown hair, the colour of ripened wheat, was gathered in a chignon and allowed to fall in corkscrew curls across the forehead and before the ears. But it was the steady gaze of her lustrous green eyes that most commanded my attention: they seemed to speak out to me across what had surely to be centuries, and their message was quite clear, the artist had caught it perfectly: those eyes declared her calm fortitude and her endurance against all odds. She was all woman – and a fighter.

'What a marvellous portrait!' I declared aloud. 'Mrs Steeple, I must have it hung in my sitting room. Will you please have it carried there this very day?'

'I would not advise it, ma'am,' she replied.

'Why so?' I demanded, surprised.

'Well, ma'am,' she said, 'Steeple and me, we're not from these parts, not south Cornish folk, but we've heard enough of local talk to know that there's ill-luck concerned in anything regarding the lass in yonder picture. Why – didn't she starve to death in the upper chamber of this very tower we're standing in, all those years ago?'

I remembered then – and the name came straight to me as if inspired by the painted lips in the portrait.

'She's Felicity Denvers!' I breathed. 'And she died for the love of a lad named – named – what was it? – Richard something. I have it – Richard Penbury!'

And then I knew why the name of the young police sergeant of Falmouth had struck a chord of memory in my mind. And, gazing up at the portrait, another resemblance came to me very forcibly: the eyes in the picture – those steady, cool eyes, green-shaded – were identical to those of Sergeant Penbury!

*

I had my way with Felicity Denvers' portrait: two footmen carried it over to my sitting room at once. What was more, I took a fancy to a couple of pieces of furniture: a pretty little cabinet and a handy gate-legged table that I rescued from the jumble in the west tower and translated to my own quarters. Mrs Steeple scowled and grumbled, but it cut no ice with me.

I did not find the secret hoard of strong drink that I had suspected her of keeping in the locked tower – though in truth one would have been hard put to discover such a cache in all that jumble. Her hesitancy, her obstructiveness, I now put down to the mutual animosity that lay between us. Clearly, she resented my coming to Mortmain in the first place, though why this should be so was a mystery I had no means to fathom.

To close the exploration of the west tower, she had taken me to the top floor, where a two-roomed apartment lay bare of all furnishings save a plain iron bedstead with no mattress, and a roughly made table and chair of some antiquity. It was with something of a shock that I considered the possibility that these might indeed be the furnishings which had served poor Felicity Denvers and her unborn child during those last days of her hideous confinement. On the way back down the spiral stairs, I seemed to sense a presence of sadness that was quite tangible, and I thought of the supposed ghosts that haunted the scene of that ancient tragedy, and whispered a prayer for the shades of the doomed lovers.

Perhaps the experience leaned heavily on my spirits, for I felt constrained to remain within my own quarters for the remainder of that day, busying myself in writing to Florrie, giving her an account of my journey and arrival (though carefully omitting any hint of the appalling experience on the train, for her comfort's sake), and a note to Giles Treacher inviting him to stay over in Mortmain for as long as he needed. I then filled up the rest of my day by reading a few chapters of Mr George du Maurier's novel *Trilby*, which I had borrowed from the Bath lending library along with several other volumes to occupy my idle hours in Cornwall.

By seven o'clock, I was restless, and paced my sitting room, back and forth, in a turmoil of mind that I found difficult to justify, though upon reflection the reason was not all that difficult to fathom: an heiress I might be, translated from drudgery to affluence, but my life had been threatened, and for all I knew might still continue to be threatened.

To pacify my mind and quench my fears, I essayed an exercise that dear Meg Wolfingham had taught me in the past, which was to sort out all the good things in my life and lay them out for my own inspection and delectation.

Well, firstly, there were my friends, whom I greatly treasured: there was Florrie; Giles Treacher, also, I could count as a friend; at some remove, and unhappily so, there was Harold Nesbitt, who would walk through fire to my aid if I so much as raised a finger to summon him.

There was – Charles Arbuthnot . . .

I came to Charles, to the thought of Charles, by devious means, as a cat will approach a saucer of cream: well aware of the certain delight that resides there, but oddly dubious of the whole enterprise, perhaps in the fear that the image is – just an image. And may be snatched away from one's importuning grasp.

The exercise proved successful, however, for I was in much improved spirits when the maid Nellie came to ask what I would like for my evening meal. She explained that, upon instructions from Mr Treacher, the rule at the castle was that full menus for luncheon and dinner were daily to be prepared no matter who was in residence. I could have what had been prepared for that evening; on the other hand, cook would produce anything to my fancy.

With a rueful thought of how such an option would commend itself to the workers of the Mordwenn chain factory, not to speak of the orphanage, I asked for a small portion of raised pie, which was on the menu of the day. This I partook of in my own sitting room, with *Trilby* propped up on the sauce boat before me.

At ten o'clock, I prepared myself for bed, my first night in Mortmain Castle, my very own castle. Outside, the moon was high and bright: it picked out in finest detail the shimmering leaves of the trees in the courtyard below my bedchamber window. By its light, also, I could see the dark shapes of the carp in the still water under the now sleeping fountain. Opening the window to allow the night air to freshen my repose, I eased myself into the languid comfort of my four-poster bed and composed myself for slumber.

The moon was still framed in the window when I woke some time later, summoned from sleep by a sound which had struck me as that of a heavy door being slammed. I sat up in bed, ears strained to catch a possible repetition of the sound. Nothing came. I was half-inclined to fall back again and close my eyes when some imp of curiosity impelled me – much against my better inclination – to get out of bed and tiptoe over to the window.

I looked down. Nothing appeared to have changed: the leaves still shimmered, the carp seemed not to have shifted since I saw them last, the moon had moved only the breadth of a hand.

But everything was – quite different . . .

A hellish change had taken place in the courtyard of Mortmain Castle. A great evil was crowding in upon that tight enclosure, casting its spell before.

I saw it come. It came from out of the shadows that masked the locked and barred doorway over the drawbridge: a thing that crawled on its hands and knees, swaying from side to side with every painful movement. He – it was a man, or had the semblance of a man – was clad in garments that were ghostly grey and ephemeral-looking. The head was bowed, and I could see nothing of the averted face, nor did I wish it; my only desire was to tear my gaze away from the horror below me, to bury my face in the pillows, shut out the sight and hope to extinguish the memory of what I was fated against my will to watch to the bitter end.

I watched as he – it – slowly circled the ornamental pool, pausing only to raise its head as a wild animal will sniff the scent of water, and then resumed its crawl: across the grassy patch and into the shadows that lay below the roofless hulk of the unconsecrated chapel.

I closed my staring eyes only once – and when I opened them again, the apparition had vanished.

EIGHT

Charles Arbuthnot's words came back to me:

'. . . He dragged himself, dying, across the peninsula . . . begging help along the way . . . arrived at the gates of Mortmain . . . they found him in the dawn light, fingers still in the act of scrabbling at the studded oak.'

And again:

'In the month of May, they say, the figure of a crawling man may be seen . . . *both in and around the castle!*'

In the clear light of a May morning, even after a night of alarm, the message had a false ring, for nothing in the view from my window now touched in any regard upon the horror of the night before. A gardener's lad was sweeping the pathway along which the apparition had crawled, and he was whistling at his work. The two young laundry maids whom I had seen the previous day ran across the green with a clothes basket held between them, and laughingly exchanged a joke with the gardener's lad. Little Phoebe walked slowly across the green, carrying something, absorbed.

Yet – it had happened. I *had* seen the ghost of the tragic Richard Penbury.

Why then, since it was poor Richard who had been gravely wronged, had his appearance been heralded by that tangible manifestation of evil? There had been no evil in him – only a devotion that transcended the act of his dying.

Did the key lie with the man who had set in train the events that led to Richard's death and that of his lover and her child?

I put it to myself: had the spirit of the evil Lord Denvers also been there in the castle courtyard last night – unseen by me, yet manifesting the vile pall of his presence?

*

I spoke of my experience to no one, since there was no one I felt inclined to trust, least of all Mrs Steeple, most certainly the last person in Mortmain in whom I would have confided. Little Nellie Throstle commended herself to me as a possible future confidante even though she was very young, and I touched lightly upon the supposed hauntings when she served me breakfast, but received nothing but the dismissive smile of a simple, uncomplicated young girl whose life was too full of delight in earthly pleasures to be concerned with ghosts and suchlike.

It was through Nellie's influence that I was guided towards an enterprise that was to become a very great part of my life. It happened this way: I commented on the excellent breakfast, and while clearing away my tray, she suggested that I might like to accompany her in a tour of the castle kitchen and meet cook and her staff. To this I readily agreed; accordingly I was introduced to the vast, stone vaults where the whole effort of a cook and no less than five assistants – pastrycook, vegetable cook, sauce cook, dessert cook and general dogsbody – plus innumerable kitchen maids, scullions and apprentices, worked to the principal end of – at that present time – feeding one solitary person. And that person was me! The thought stayed with me for the remainder of the morning and set in train a process that inspired me to action. I reasoned this way: it took a staff of around a dozen, plus an outlay of, say, £10, to prepare meals for one person every day. Might not a similar sum of money, and considerably less staff, prepare a simple and nourishing meal for a hundred needy persons? And by needy persons, I was thinking of the children of Westchester parish orphanage – or even the workers in the Mordwenn chain factory.

As to the practicalities of the matter, I looked to my mentor in matters gastronomic, the indefatigable Mrs Isabella Beeton, whose master work *Beeton's Book of Household Management*, published in 1861, has remained the definitive authority on matters domestic to this day and will likely remain so as long as there is an oyster to be opened, a recalcitrant servant to be scolded, or a cooking stove to be black-leaded. To my delight, I discovered that the great woman had already provided me with an answer to my question; in the chapter upon soups, Mrs Beeton tells how, in the winter of 1858, she made, each week, in her copper, 8 or 9 gallons of a nourishing, cheap soup for distribution amongst about a dozen poor families of the village where she lived; a soup, moreover, that was greatly liked, and gave to those poor wretches a warm, comforting repast, in place of the broken cold meats and bread which was their staple diet – for the tragedy of the very poor and needy is that they have no concept of the culinary art as a means to cheap and nourishing meals.

The 'Useful Soup for Benevolent Purposes', so entitled by its author, comprised ox-cheek, any pieces of beef trimmings, a few bones, liquid from the larder stock-pot, ¼ peck of onions, 6 leeks, a large bunch of herbs, ½ lb of celery (the outside pieces and green tops suffice very well), ½ lb of carrots and the same of turnips and coarse brown sugar. And ½ pint of beer; 4 lbs of rice or pearl barley, ½ lb of salt, 1 ounce of black pepper, a few raspings and 10 gallons of water. Cooking time (the meat and bones first, the vegetables after half an hour, along with the sugar and beer, and the rice and raspings two hours before serving) was 6½ hours in all. The total cost being around one penny ha'penny per quart, which was enough for four persons. So much for the culinary arrangements of Mortmain Castle!

Fired by my inspiration, I straightway penned a letter to the governors and managers of the Westchester parish orphanage, the establishment which I had selected as what one might term the 'guinea pig' for my great experiment in benevolent charity; in it I set forth my plan to donate a monthly sum sufficient to provide one half pint of Mrs Beeton's Useful Soup for Benevolent Purposes daily to every child in the orphanage, making only one stipulation: that the Beeton recipe (which I enclosed a copy of) should be faithfully adhered to, contingent upon the seasonal availability of the ingredients.

I then sealed up the letter and put it out for posting, mindful of that famous saying: 'Tall oaks from little acorns grow'.

*

'A Commander Todd is here, ma'am. He presents his card and asks to be received.'

I took the visiting card from the footman and scanned it.

'Ask the Commander to come in, please.'

'Yes, ma'am.'

And what kindly wind, I asked myself, brought this gallant American naval gentleman to Mortmain? Todd – Todd? Did I know of, had I ever heard of, a Commander Jack B. Todd, United States Navy?

'Commander Todd, ma'am.' From the door of the main drawing room of the castle, where I had been taking tea.

'Miss Friday, ma'am, it's very kind of you to receive me at no notice whatsoever, but my motive for calling occurred to me only this morning.' My visitor advanced to take my extended hand. He was tall – as tall as Charles Arbuthnot – and strongly built; dressed in a Norfolk jacket and knickerbockers, with thick stockings and immensely stout boots of the kind one associates with the sporting gentry. His face was clean-shaven, wide, bronzed, and sparkling with health and good humour. I took to him at once.

'How do you do, Commander,' I said. 'Take a seat. Would you like some tea? Bring some fresh, Davidson, will you, please.'

Jack B. Todd disposed himself in an armchair opposite mine and filled it to overflowing, looking about him appreciatively as he did so.

'Great place you have here, ma'am,' he said. 'This room, for instance, the decorations, the ceiling paintings, the panelling and so forth, they're eighteenth century at a guess, but the structure itself is older, much older, surely.'

'The central keep, where we are, dates from the eleventh century,' I replied. 'Or so I'm told.'

'The *eleventh* century,' he repeated, with the air of a man who has just heard an utterance of the Delphic Oracle. 'Well, I must say that's really something. Nearly half as old as the Christian message. It certainly makes one feel that one's standing in the presence of history – or, in our case, sitting.'

We both laughed. He looked curiously boyish when he laughed; much younger than his years, which I put at around the mid-thirties.

'And why have you come to see me, Commander?' I asked, pouring tea. 'With milk? Sugar or lemon?'

'Without sugar and with lemon, please. Now that's a question and a half, ma'am, and needs to be provided with a little background. Firstly, I'm assistant naval attaché to the United States Embassy, and here down in the West Country on furlough. What I'm after is cliffs.' He grinned.

'Cliffs?' I echoed.

'Steep, rugged, soaring granite cliffs – the like of which you enjoy in Cornwall in great amounts. You see, ma'am, in addition to being a sailor – at this present time, a *political* sailor' – he accented the word and pulled a scornful lip – 'I'm also a climbing man.'

'You mean you climb rocks – mountains and things?'

'Exactly, ma'am.'

'Well, that sounds very exciting. Have you ever heard of a climber named – what was it? – Major Bravingdon? The reason I mention him is because my housekeeper and her husband used to be in service with the Major's family.'

At this, the Commander's eyes lit up, and he laid his teacup and saucer upon the side table before he cried reverently: 'Have I heard of Major Tom Bravingdon? Ma'am, you are speaking of arguably the greatest rock climber of his generation – and his generation of Englishmen produced some unforgettable climbers. Why, Bravingdon's virgin routes up the Jügspitz, the lesser Pläatz, the Matterhorn and the Eiger are enshrined in the hallowed annals of the international climbing fraternity. Bravingdon was a prince among climbers. Climbing was his whole life.'

'And also his death,' I added wryly. 'Or so I'm told.'

The Commander shrugged and looked down sadly at his big, clasped hands. 'True, true,' he said. 'The Jügspitz claimed him in the end, that killer mountain, insignificant as to height compared with the great peaks of the Alps, but deemed unclimbable to this day.'

'Did Bravingdon never conquer it?' I asked, intrigued.

'His party of four were last seen alive five hundred feet below the summit,' he said, 'with the worst of the climb – the great overhang – still ahead of them. Minutes later, the mist came down and shut them from the view of the watchers with telescopes in the valley below. Their bodies were found next morning below the scree, and all five were buried together in the village.'

'Did they not reach the top?' I asked.

'We shall never know,' he said. 'But if Bravingdon didn't make it, then that mountain *is* unclimbable – and has remained so to this day.' He stared down into his teacup and we were silent for a while.

'However,' I said at length, 'you say that you are after cliffs. Is there any way in which I can assist you, Commander?'

'There most certainly is, ma'am, if you'd be so kind,' he replied. 'The cliff below your castle, on the seaward side, struck me very forcibly when I was walking along the beach this morning. Now there is a classic coastal cliff, the likes of which, for interesting variations of climb, I have scarcely ever seen in Europe, Asia or the Americas. It's only a little bit of a cliff, sure, but a veritable microcosm of everything that rock climbing is all about. I should greatly esteem your permission to scale it.'

'But of course, Commander,' I replied. 'Any time you like. When? I should like to watch you.'

He grinned (really a most heartening grin). 'Well, if you're doing nothing in the next twenty minutes or so, ma'am – call it a half-hour – I'll be willing to oblige.'

'You mean – *now*?' I asked. 'But – don't you have to provide yourself with equipment? Ropes? Special clothing? That kind of thing? And shouldn't your next of kin be informed, in case – well, you must know what I mean, Commander. I should feel *responsible* if you came to any harm!'

As regards my fears, he was all solicitude; not a hint of mockery or amusement at my ignorance of his chosen sport. 'Miss Friday,' he said earnestly, 'be assured that I have all the equipment I need for the climb: that's to say, a good stout pair of nailed boots, a light heart and a certain expertise. Your cliff is not a difficult nor a particularly wearisome climb. It has merely the virtues of uniqueness. I shall walk it at a stroll in something under half an hour, and you may set your watch by me.'

'Very well, sir,' I responded, greatly heartened. 'Why are we waiting?'

*

That part of the cliff upon whose crest the ancient fortress was built rose almost vertically from the sandy beach below. At that hour, the tide was on the flood, but there was still ample walking space down there. By dusk, the waves would be breaking impotently upon the granite footings of Mortmain as they had done from time immemorial.

I stook my stand upon the walkway alongside the roofless chapel, by the machicolated battlements that overlooked the beach and the sea beyond. Peering down, I saw the tiny figure that was Commander Todd. He had descended by a staircase hewn out of the granite wall and was staring up at the problem that he had posed for himself. Presently, jamming his tweed cap more firmly upon his head and spitting upon his palms, he set both hands and a boot toe against the edge of an almost vertical slab of rock about the size of a three-storey house, and immediately commenced to scale it; fingers and toes insinuating themselves into the barely perceptible crack at the edge of the slab. He gained the top of his first hurdle and paused for a brief moment to size up his next move. And I glanced at my fob watch: it had taken him exactly five minutes.

The Commander's problem was clearly now a matter of circumventing an overhanging portion of rock that afforded no holds whatsoever, so that only a fly could have stayed alive upon it (as regards the issue of immediate peril, there was already a thirty-foot drop below him – or more). I had the notion that he would skirt the overhang; no such evasion occurred to him! To my intense alarm, he commenced a crab-like passage diagonally across the face of the overhang, clinging with toe ends and fingertips to declivities and faults in the granite face that were certainly not visible from where I was standing. I lost sight of him when he was obscured from my view by the upper part of the outward-leaning rock; and expected at every breathless moment that I should see him cartwheeling down to his doom. After much longer than I liked, however, I saw a hand reach up and grasp the lip of the overhang; next moment his smiling countenance sprang into view, and then the rest of him.

Twelve minutes had gone by. He was considerably less than halfway up.

I was deeply puzzled by the American's next move: instead of continuing directly upwards along a course which, from my vantage point, appeared to offer ample hand and footholds, he again traversed diagonally across the cliff face (achieving no height at all to speak of as he did so) towards a deep cleft in the granite that rose, almost like an open chimney, to within fifty feet from where I was.

His manner of ascending the 'chimney' was ingenuity itself: wedging his whole body within the cleft (where he fitted with inches only to spare all round), he then literally *walked* vertically upwards, bearing his whole weight alternately upon his feet, his hands, and his back, which was pressed against the wall of the chimney behind him – a most striking manner of ascent which looked intolerably difficult and tiring; dangerous, also, for one slip and he must inevitably fall straight down the cleft with no hope of recovery, and be torn to pieces on the jagged sides.

Heart in my mouth, I leaned as far out into the abyss as I was able, to follow his progress. He moved quite slowly (too slowly for my taste; the suspense was unbearable), and when, to my intense relief, he swung himself out of the head of the chimney, my watch said that he had been twenty-two minutes on the cliff face.

'Well done!' I called down to him. 'But be careful of the last bit.'

'I shall be so careful, ma'am, that it will hurt!' he called back. And then – it happened . . .!

He had leaned forward to take two hand-holds when his single toe-hold appeared to desert him. Next instant, the American was suspended upon a near-vertical slab by his fingertips, with feet scrabbling to find extra purchase.

I bit my lip to choke back a cry, fearful that to do so might alarm him. I watched the expression on his face, for his face was clearly in view and it seemed that I had only to reach down and I could touch him. Not by a contortion of the eyes or mouth did he betray any sign of strain or alarm; all I saw there was the face of a man who was concentrating upon a quite commonplace problem to which he would speedily find the solution. And find it he did: within seconds, both feet were firmly established again. He swung himself up, moving quickly, scurrying – as it seemed to me – in the manner of a spider.

He was soon clambering over the balustrade and at my side.

The ascent had taken him – as he had predicted – under half an hour.

*

I saw him off the premises. He had come on a bicycle, borrowed, so he told me, from the Blue Boar inn down at the village, where he was lodging.

We shook hands at the gatehouse, by the drawbridge.

'I hope I didn't alarm you, ma'am,' he said. 'The folly of climbing without a rope isn't so much of a folly when one is tackling quite simple problems that one's overcome many times before. It's the new, unknown problems that lead to the downfall of unroped climbers. That old cliff of yours is a textbook of all the classic puzzles that have been satisfactorily solved since the sport began to be taken seriously around the beginning of this century.'

'I was alarmed for you,' I admitted. 'But, at the same time, the experience was tremendously exhilarating. In a curious way, it made me want to be there instead of you. I think I should like . . .'

155

I paused. The thought had come to me quite unbidden: it seemed absurd, yet at the same time very typical of me.

'Yes, ma'am?' he prompted.

'I think I should like to learn to climb,' I said. 'Here – on my own cliff. Do you think you could teach me, Commander Todd?'

He grinned. 'I would deem it a pleasure, ma'am.'

*

It had been a day of many new developments: my first essay into the field of benevolent charity, the meeting with my new American friend and the prospect of learning a new and exhilarating sport, and my first whole day as resident owner of Mortmain Castle. I went to bed that night with the shutters and curtains firmly closed, fearful of further ghostly manifestations in the courtyard below. I need have had no fears, nothing disturbed my untroubled sleep and I awoke with a feeling of curious well-being.

It was Sunday, so I ordered a carriage and went to mattins at the parish church of Mortmain village (which lies within the bounds of Count Gilles' oxhide strip and was part of my inheritance, lock, stock and barrel). As I passed over the castle drawbridge, I discerned a movement out of the corner of my eye, and looked back to see little Phoebe's pale face peering out at me from one of the arrow-slits in the high stone wall of the gatehouse; thumb in mouth, she watched me go and made no sign of greeting or recognition.

The rector of St Matthew's, who had been apprised ahead of my coming, himself greeted me at the church door and escorted me to the private pew of the Denvers family (which was mine by right of succession); in some considerable state, it was set back at the rear of the congregation and well above their heads so that, if the notion took me (as it must have taken so many noble Denvers in the past), I could have nodded off to sleep, unseen, beside the pot-bellied iron stove placed there to warm the Denvers against the biting cold of winter, and under the great carved oak escutcheon of that now defunct noble breed.

The rector, who was clearly of the fundamentalist persuasion, sermonised at some considerable length upon the promised hell-fire, about which he appeared singularly well-informed. The choir sang well, and so did the congregation. At the close, I was introduced to the rector's wife and their four strapping sons – and was pleased to see Commander Todd amongst the emerging congregation.

'Are you still of a mind to take lessons in climbing, ma'am?' he asked me with a note of challenge.

'That I am, sir,' I replied. 'If you are still of a mind to instruct me.'

His eyes twinkled. 'Shall we say tomorrow morning?' he said.

'I have my lawyer coming to see me tomorrow and Tuesday,' I replied. 'If nothing else intervenes, I shall be free from Wednesday.'

'I'll call upon you Wednesday morning at ten.'

'Stay for luncheon, do.'

'Thank you, ma'am.'

He saw me to my carriage and handed me in, raised his hat as we drove off and then, turning, went on his way into the village. As I glanced back, his tallness and straightness put me greatly in mind of Charles Arbuthnot; his manner of striding with head erect and hands loosely clasped behind his back was very similar. I found the resemblance somehow disturbing, though I was at a loss to know why.

The rest of the congregation – villagers and local farmpeople all – remained clustered by the lych-gate of the church, to gawp I suppose, and take the measure of the new owner of Mortmain land.

I did not see a smiling, friendly face amongst them. And that, I fancied, was the legacy of the noble Denvers.

Before I was summoned to Sunday luncheon – while I was throwing scraps of bread to the carp – the rattle of carriage wheels and the clatter of hooves on the wooden drawbridge signalled an arrival. A solitary figure in a tall hat sat behind the coachman. He alighted to see me and, enquiring of Miss Friday and learning I was she, announced himself as Hawn, Mr Tristan Melmoth's valet, and gave me a letter from his master.

The message was brief, and simply informed me that Mr Tristan Melmoth had taken up residence for the summer at Penford Lodge, near Mortmain village, and greatly wished to renew our most interesting acquaintance.

Not unpleased at the prospect of meeting again the stimulating Mr Melmoth, I bade Hawn convey my best wishes to his master.

*

The rest of Sunday passed uneventfully, the night also. Giles Treacher arrived by the station carriage at around midday. What's more, he brought his clerk Mr Caldecott with him, and the latter was carrying a briefcase. I received them in the main drawing room.

'Miss Friday. How nice to see you looking so spiffing. The role of chatelaine greatly becomes you.' Twinkle-eyed as ever, his flatly-brushed, butter-coloured hair giving him an endearingly boyish look, Giles was just as I remembered him from the first time we met; nor had Mr Caldecott, he of the sprightly manner and ginger wig, changed by so much as a false hair. I greeted them both with pleasure and offered them a glass of sherry wine.

'Well, what is new in Dorset?' I asked.

'In Dorset, not much,' replied Giles. 'But we have murmurings of things afoot as far as Bath.' He glanced towards his clerk.

'That we have, that we have,' confirmed Mr Caldecott.

'For instance?' I prompted, sipping at my coffee.

'One hears,' said Giles, with a touch of archness, 'that a certain gentleman has taken a house in Cornwall for the rest of the summer.'

'Not unadjacent to Mortmain, ma'am,' added the clerk.

I smiled, happy to trump what they clearly thought to have been an excellent lead. 'Mr Melmoth,' I said. 'I know. He sent a message round to me yesterday afternoon.' And I had the pleasure of seeing them look one to the other in puzzlement.

'Mr Melmoth?' exclaimed my lawyer. 'But who is Mr Melmoth, pray?'

I perceived that my trump had somehow gone amiss, and enlightened him as to Tristan Melmoth's identity; both men exchanged glances again and shrugged their shoulders indifferently.

'I was referring, ma'am, to a gentleman of mutual acquaintance,' said my lawyer.

'Who, then?' I demanded.

'Mr Charles Arbuthnot,' he said, and smiled. 'It is odd, is it not, that of all the places to spend the summer, Arbuthnot has chosen this particular corner of west Cornwall, and not a stone's throw from Mortmain. And now you have this other gentleman, this Mr Melmoth.' He gazed at me archly over his wine glass. 'Quite a gathering of bees around the honeypot, isn't it, Miss Friday?' he chuckled.

*

After luncheon (during which Giles made a great play of his clerk being an ardent coarse fisherman and did I think that he might try his hand with rod and line in the castle's stewpond in the home park? – to which I made the response that Mr Caldecott might indeed, and was welcome to select for himself what rods and lines he chose from the gunroom), we touched in the main only upon trivialities.

Save in one respect . . .

The name of dear Florrie came up, and Giles was so warm in his obvious admiration and sympathy for my friend and mentor that I felt constrained to put the straight question to him about Florrie's deceased spouse.

'What exactly *did* happen to Sir Basil Wimsey-Fildes?' I asked. 'You spoke once of his disgrace and death, and poor Florence refers to what she calls "the disaster". What disaster was this – if I may be so bold as to ask?'

Giles cracked a walnut between his palms with devastating expertise, and cocked an eye towards his clerk, who became suddenly interested in chopping his Gruyère cheese.

Getting no assistance from that quarter, my lawyer began: 'It's an odd tale. Sir Basil was a career diplomat. Worked in the Colonial administration ever since he left 'varsity. They say he was the mainstay and inspiration of Britain's rule over our territories and islands in the Pacific. Leastways, he made a considerable name for himself in the Windway Isles, where he was revered as a god by the natives and won for himself some extraordinary title. What was it, Caldecott?'

'*Sua che mani hissar hohocho*, sir,' supplied the other. 'Which being translated means, so I understand: "Incorruptible chief man of Great White Queen". The lady in question being our present most gracious sovereign, ma'am.'

'Quite so,' continued Giles. 'However, Sir Basil's career was terminated by Lady Wimsey-Fildes' tendency to seasickness in her declining years, which rendered her incapable of accompanying her husband on the long sea hauls between the outlying islands under his administration. He resigned his appointment, returned to England with his lady and took on several city directorships.'

'Of which one was Messrs Fox-Fothergill, merchant bankers, sir, on which you also had a seat,' added his clerk.

'Quite so,' replied the other. 'And this rendered me particularly close to the denouément, which was preceded by Sir Basil's death by drowning in a sailing accident off Cowes in – in . . .'

' 'Ninety-three, sir,' supplied Caldecott.

' 'Ninety-three it was,' confirmed Giles. 'I remember it well, because it was in September of that year, after Cowes Week, that we unearthed this most appalling scandal at Fox-Fothergill. By a process of manipulation which, Miss Friday, I won't burden you with the trying details of, half a million pounds had found its way out of the firm's coffers and into the distant horizon.'

'Not a trace was ever found,' said Caldecott.

'That is so,' said Giles. 'The fraud was most skilfully contrived: a matter of transfer of funds from one source to another, from London to Paris, Paris to Marseilles, Marseilles to Cairo, Cairo to some unbelievable place with some unpronounceable name in East Africa – and there the trail ended. The funds just disappeared, as I have said, into the distant horizon. Pfue!' He snapped finger and thumb.

'And Sir Basil was held responsible?' I ventured.

Giles looked at Caldecott, Caldecott looked at Giles. Both shrugged. 'Naturally, the recently dead man's dealings were among the first to be probed,' said Giles. 'And some pretty fishy things emerged. Nothing, I hasten to add, that one could put a finger on. And, anyhow, the poor fellow was no longer with us and he had left a charming lady widow. No, the whole affair was tidily hushed up to some degree. That's to say, the directors dipped their hands into their pockets and made good the losses to the shareholders. An attempt was made to gloss over the whole affair, but people will talk, and I'm afraid that most of it was talked in the sort of places that matter most. I believe I'm right in saying that Her Majesty never acknowledged Lady W–F– again till last year at Royal Ascot, and the poor dear's had an unbelievably hard time re-establishing herself in Society.

'So much for the Wimsey-Fildes scandal.' He smiled at me. 'I hope I've answered your question. But they never did recover Sir Basil's body, you see. He was sailing single-handed in a day-boat when he was obviously caught in a squall off the Needles. The boat was dashed to pieces on the rocks. It could have been accidental death, or . . .'

'Suicide?' I suggested.

'The way the cards were falling,' he said, 'the fraud couldn't possibly have remained hidden for more than another few weeks. Yes – that's more or less what we thought: Sir Basil took the coward's way out, and the rest of us rallied round to save dear Florence.'

*

The great play about Caldecott being an ardent coarse fisherman was quite obviously just a polite contrivance got up between the two men: Giles Treacher wanted me on his own when he spelled out the true facts of my inheritance.

Luncheon over, we retired again to the drawing room. The clerk departed with rod and line for the stewpond, I poured post-prandial coffee for us both and invited Giles to help himself at the tray of liqueurs.

'Well?' I opened challengingly. 'What have you to tell me, Giles?' It was the first time that I had addressed him to his face by his Christian name.

He was clearly put about by my directness, and took refuge in what I was to recognise as his familiar lawyer's conceits: which is to say he took from his briefcase a sheaf of papers, put on his spectacles, and gazing at me over the top of the lenses assumed what I recalled as his 'tragic mask'.

'Miss Friday, dear lady . . .' he began.

'Call me Daisy,' I prompted him. 'A gentleman who has led me towards one and a half million pounds would – even if I did not esteem him personally, as I esteem you – deserve as much.'

He switched expressions from tragic to comic, hunched his shoulders and chuckled.

'Well, then, Daisy,' he said, 'let us, as the French put it in their witty, Gallic way, return to our muttons. You will recall that, at our first meeting, you posed certain questions to me regarding the identity of your benefactor or benefactors. I told you then that I was unable to supply that information, and that the anonymity of your benefactor was a condition of the bequest.

'I have to tell you now that circumstances have radically changed, and that I am able to give you some information about the identity of the gentleman in question. Some – guarded information – I may add.'

One question immediately sprang to my mind. 'Is he Charles Arbuthnot?' I demanded.

'No, he is not.'

'Aaaah!'

(Why did this reply give me such a heartfelt sense of relief and release? I asked myself. It was very odd. Did I so dislike certain aspects of Charles Arbuthnot that the very thought of being beholden to him for so very much was distasteful?)

'You have, however, met the gentleman in question – though briefly,' said Giles.

'Is he – here today? In the vicinity? Shall we meet again?'

Giles's comfortable countenance was genuinely creased in

the tragic mould when he replied. 'No, Daisy,' he said. 'For he passed away last week. Which is why I am now permitted to disclose his name – though little more.

'He has gone. But you will remember him, as I have said. You met each other once only. I think this likeness may refresh your memory.' And he took from a small envelope in his briefcase a photograph which he handed to me.

The photograph represented two men standing side by side in a sunlit landscape that had a distinctly foreign look about it. Both were in casual clothing of tweed jackets, knickerbockers and soft caps. The man on the left of the pair I instantly recognised as my present companion; he and the other were gazing at the camera with expressions of extreme gravity – or so it seemed to me.

My attention was directed to the second man. It was some moments before recognition took place in my mind.

'I know him!' I exclaimed. 'Yes! Westchester – outside my windows that night! Those three ragamuffins setting about the old gentleman. I rushed downstairs and made some shift to rescue him. It was nothing really. The lads were a trio of starvelings. Orphanage brats. I did more harm to them with the toe of my boot than they ever did to him.

'But he seemed uncommonly grateful for the help I was able to give . . .'

I stared hard at Giles Treacher; who gazed back at me with complete impassivity.

'Giles,' I said, 'you are not trying to tell me in all seriousness that this old gentleman – his name, as I remember, was Ven – Ven . . .'

'Venables. His name was James Venables, Daisy.'

'You are not telling me that Mr Venables bequeathed one and a half million pounds to me – *while he was still living* – simply because I saved him from being robbed and manhandled slightly by three back street urchins? Giles, I simply do not believe that. It is absurd!'

'Absurd or not, you *must* believe it, Daisy,' he replied. 'For I have the documents here in my briefcase, duly signed, witnessed and sealed, to which, also, you yourself added your signature of acceptance in my office, again duly witnessed by Caldecott and myself.

'The matter is legally signed, sealed and delivered, Daisy. The unlikelihood of the transaction is immaterial in law. Comment is superfluous. Disbelief is irrelevant. Established legality is all.'

Rising to my feet, I walked the length of the drawing room and back again, my mind racing in a turmoil of puzzlement and indecision.

'But don't you see, Giles,' I protested, 'what you now tell me puts an entirely different complexion on the matter. You secured from me an acceptance without any explanations whatsoever, save that I must either accept or reject – just like that.'

'Then what has changed, Daisy?' he asked.

'What has changed!' I cried. 'Ye gods, Giles! Am I now to accept a fortune from a complete stranger for extending to him the kind of assistance that anyone in their right mind would extend to a weak old man . . .'

'Anyone?' he interposed. 'Are there so many good Samaritans with us? How many young girls would risk themselves by . . .?'

I brushed that argument aside. 'That isn't the point, Giles. Now I know the truth of the matter, I shall withdraw. An old man's whim – maybe he was in his dotage, this James Venables, I don't know – isn't sufficient to translate me to all – *this*!' I gestured about me. 'Not for *nothing*! Why, what of his relations? Wife? Children, maybe? What are they going to say in the very near future now that Mr Venables has passed away and they await in expectation for their rightful inheritance?'

'There are no relations,' replied Giles flatly. 'No wife. No children. No one who could by any stretch of the imagination be said to have any claim whatsoever upon the estate in question.

'No one but yourself, Daisy.'

*

In the end, by the sheer persistence of his lawyers' logic, he talked me round, and the logic he cemented in place with sentiments that I could not resist.

'James Venables was my friend and the friend of my family all my life,' he said. 'To me, he was always "Uncle Jamie". After what looked like becoming a lifelong bachelorhood – though not, as he put it, "*crusty* old bachelorhood" – he met and married a lady twenty years his junior. They were ecstatically happy, and it was the second greatest day of Jamie's life when Maude presented him with the daughter for whom he had always longed.

'Jamie was rich, and not only in the love and affection of his new little family and his friends. He had succeeded to a fortune, but till he met Maude his wealth scarcely had any meaning for him, since his needs were few and simple. Mindful, now, of the age difference between Maude and himself, and with tremendous plans for the baby Naomi's future, it was a source of great comfort to him that, if he went first, as seemed certain, they would never want in all their days and Naomi – whom he idolised – would have within her grasp every prize that our society could offer. As she grew older and more precocious, Jamie would often say to me: "Giles, that lass of mine – I wouldn't be surprised if she doesn't become the first woman Member of Parliament. Or even Britain's first woman Prime Minister!"

'Alas for Jamie's hopes . . .'

I reached out and touched Giles's hand. 'My dear, I have a notion that the rest of this story is going to be very hard for you to tell,' I said. 'If it's too hurtful, I'd much prefer to spare your feelings and hear no more.'

'You have to hear it, Daisy,' he said, 'for every word is true, and for the sake of my friend's wishes, you must continue to accept the legacy. Listen, please. The rest of the story is as short as it's sad.

'Yes. They died. Both. Maude in childbirth, and the new baby with her. Naomi lived to be almost your age, and fulfilled in her short life many of the hopes that her doting father had dreamed for her.

'Her death was stupid. Wasteful. A cruel jest on the part of the Fates. Adventurous to a reckless degree, she took to the sport of ballooning, and to Uncle Jamie's alarm, was flying every evening she could spare.

'I was with Jamie when the news came through on the wire to his club. Her balloon took off from the heights of the Avon south of Bath. She and her companion were last seen heading southwest towards the Bristol Channel and South Wales. They had not been located before darkness fell. Neither they nor any trace of their balloon were ever found. It is believed that the sea took them for ever.

'And there you have it, Daisy Friday. The rest is straightforward. I told you that some of my information would have to be guarded, and it must be so. Suffice to say that, by a certain means, Jamie Venables and I came to hear of this young woman – this Daisy Friday – who had risen from orphanage and slave-factory to a respectable occupation, and whose character commended itself to all who met her . . .'

'Charles Arbuthnot included,' I interposed wryly.

He nodded. 'I will now concede that it was Arbuthnot, whom I know well in business, who gave us the glowing report upon your character,' he said. 'Following upon which, Jamie went down to Westchester to see this paragon, this Daisy Friday, for himself.

'The rest you know.'

I sat down. Poured myself another cup of coffee. Found it to be cold.

'And what did he say about me, then?' I asked. 'Your Uncle Jamie, as you called him, when he got back, how did he report on this Daisy Friday? Please – I should like to know.'

'He said that Daisy Friday was everything he could have wished for in a second daughter,' replied Giles. 'He said that she was brave, forthright, modest, without "side", intelligent, pleasing to be with. You know – for I have told you already, Daisy, that those sentiments echo mine exactly.

'Jamie said: "Giles, Daisy Friday must have that legacy. I wouldn't be true to Naomi's memory if I stood by and allowed that lass, who has done so much to raise herself up, to be like a rocket that soars to its early zenith, only to fall, spent, in a drab backwater like Westchester. Given the means, the push, Giles,'' he said, ''our Daisy Friday could go anywhere. Do anything.'' That was what he said, believe me, Daisy.'

I nodded. 'But I think there's much you still haven't told me.'

'Yes,' he conceded. 'And there are some matters upon which I may never be able to enlighten you. For these, you will have to take me on trust. But, believe me, Daisy, when I say again that what I have told you today is the truth.

'Now, my dear' – and at this he reached out and touched my hands, and there was no lawyers' guile, no lawyers' chop-logic in his manner of address, but only simplicity and affection – 'You will keep the legacy, won't you? For his sake.'

I nodded, too near to tears to trust myself to speak.

*

Mr Caldecott returned from the stewpond in time for tea, but without any catch. Giles, who had accepted my invitation to stay overnight, said that they had business with the Duchy Records Office in Truro regarding the transfer of the Mortmain land from the executors of the Denvers' estate to myself, a matter of some complexity which would take the greater part of a day, and that they must depart early in the morning. I had unearthed a very pretty inlaid ivory backgammon set, and with it a set of rules which I had taken some trouble to master after a fashion. Giles declared himself to be something of a back-gammon devotee and we played together till dinnertime, while Mr Caldecott, no doubt wrung out by his efforts at not catching fish, dozed in an armchair before the fireplace. We essayed six games before the dinner gong was sounded, and I am ashamed to say that I won them all – not possessing the expertise diplomatically to allow my opponent to beat me now and then.

Over dinner (which, for my guests' diversion, I asked to be served right at one end of a massive refectory table in the glory of the great hall of Mortmain, with the flickering light of innumerable candles picking diamond pinpoints from the polished silverware and napery), Giles was most diverting with his stories of the legal and business worlds of London and the West Country, ably assisted by his clerk's timely interpolations.

We all retired early. I said goodbye to them, for a carriage had been ordered at six in the morning, to enable them to catch the milk train for the Cornish capital. In the event, after a refreshing night's sleep, I woke at the sound of the carriage and watched from my window as the two men mounted with their briefcase and overnight bags and were carried away across the castle drawbridge and into the morning mist rising from the water meadows of the home park.

I little knew that there was one of them whom I was fated never to see again.

*

That morning the clouds rolled in from the west, threatening a rainstorm. Restless, I threw my old purple shawl over my shoulders, put on a bonnet, and left the castle by the kitchen gate, taking the winding path that led over the moor to the village. I had not gone far before I had the curious feeling in my bones, my fingertips, in the small hairs at the back of my neck, that I was being watched. I paused and looked about me. Nothing in sight but the barren moorland dotted with the few mean fields that were farmed by the small-holding tenants of the estate. To my left, the jagged outcrop of the 'Devil's Fingers' darkly pierced the skyline.

Was it my heated imagination, or did I see a changing shape among those tumbled granite cairns?

I looked again, this time to my front, along the winding path that led over the hill to the village in the hollow beyond.

A figure stood watching me from the path on the hillcrest, part-silhouetted against the stormy sky. I knew him at once. He was not my secret enemy, nor was he Jack Todd, though he bore a great resemblance to the latter, as to shape and size and in the way he carried himself.

I knew in the instant that it was Charles Arbuthnot, and that he had been watching me ever since I had emerged from the kitchen gate of the castle.

He saw that I had seen him. His hand came up and he doffed his cap. I essayed a tentative wave. He walked down the hill towards me, down the winding path.

I remained where I was, for some compulsion bereft me of all movement. Putting it in another way, I suppose that I did not want to appear too over-eager to be near him. As he drew closer, I saw that he was subtly changed. The articulate, fascinating, darkly saturnine man who had so entranced my dinner table on that otherwise disastrous occasion, was transformed from the formally-dressed man-about-town to a tweed-clad country gentleman.

'Dear Miss Friday,' he said, when he drew close. 'How very nice to see you. I had heard from a mutual friend that you were still in residence at the castle and I was on my way to leave my card. Are you well? You are looking remarkably well.'

I gave him my hand. 'I'm very well, sir,' I said. 'And Mortmain is very fine. You will be amused to hear that the castle is undoubtedly haunted – as you took pains to warn me.'

He gave a look of gently-mocking concern. 'Oh dear me,' he said. 'I trust that the ghost – whichever it was – did not frighten you too much. The requisite of ghosts, particularly those who presume to inhabit splendid establishments such as yours, is that they must be stylish in their habits. Yes, I would say that style is tremendously important in a ghost.'

I looked him straight in the eye – and I have to admit that I was immediately discomforted and looked away. 'Sir, I think you are gulling me,' I said. 'You don't believe that I saw a ghost.'

'Oh, Miss Friday, I do, I do,' he said, with what must have been sincerity.

Oddly, there was a lightness between us such as I had not known on the previous occasions of our meeting. Perhaps it was his relaxed, gentle manner, the well-cut but well-worn tweeds that he sported. I felt greatly at my ease with him. By unspoken, mutual consent, we went neither back to the castle nor towards the village, but took a sheep track that led along the shallow valley and remained in sight of my home.

'And what else has happened since you have been in Cornwall?' he asked.

'I've taken up rock climbing,' I replied.

'Rock climbing?' He looked surprised. 'Whatever persuaded
you to go in for that extremely hazardous pastime?'

I told him – all about Jack Todd and my climbing lessons –
and he listened with apparent interest, but – or so it seemed to
me – with a most flattering concern for my safety, and he
continued to reiterate that I was taking considerable risks in my
new sport, to all of which I found myself listening with pleasure
of a unique and elusive sort. The very notion that the great Mr
Charles Arbuthnot was concerned for Daisy Friday's safety I
found curiously – how to put it? – intriguing . . .

'Shall you be staying in Cornwall for long, Mr Arbuthnot?' I
asked.

'It depends upon events,' he replied. 'I have some business
interests in the Duchy which, mostly due to my own neglect,
have fallen into a state of confusion. I must say, I wish that I
had the services of your lawyer Mr Treacher to help me through
the tangled thickets of legal confusion. By the way, how is
Treacher?'

I was about to reply to his question, and to add that the
person in question was still in Cornwall, and might well be
easily reached, when – *it happened* . . .

It must have been a mole hole, or perhaps the entrance to an
adder's nest. In any event, the hole was of a size exactly to fit my
shoe when I trod into it, stumbled, and would have fallen
heavily on to the rock-studded ground and done myself quite an
injury, had not Charles Arbuthnot seized hold of me round the
waist, and, supporting me, borne me up.

'Are you all right?' he asked.

'My – ankle – I think I've twisted it,' I said. 'Nothing much,
but – it's rather painful.'

He instantly shrugged off his tweed coat, and laying it on a
tussock of grass, helped me to sit down upon it. He then took my
foot – it was my right foot – and gently removing the shoe,
probed my ankle.

'Does it hurt when I do that?' he murmured.

'No – not very much,' I replied.

'And there?'

'No – not at all.'

'I don't think you've broken a bone,' he said, 'but you should keep off it for a day or two. No – rock-climbing.' He smiled.

'I will take your advice,' I said.

He put my shoe back on again, and paused while he was doing so. 'Quite remarkable,' he said.

'What?' I asked.

'Your foot,' he said. 'I've never seen such a small foot, but then – I don't often have the opportunity to examine ladies' feet at close quarters.' He straightened up, and his tone of voice became suddenly very matter-of-fact. 'Can you walk with a little help,' he asked, 'or shall I carry you back to the castle in my arms?'

'I – I'm sure I can walk,' I whispered.

That was it: the beginning, the middle and the end of our encounter. But – so far as I was concerned, at least – nothing was ever the same between Charles Arbuthnot and me again.

I walked back to the castle leaning on his arm. He saw me in, delivered me into care, and took his leave, promising that we should meet again while he was in the Duchy.

*

The dreadful news, when it came, broke upon me in two parts, and the early stirrings came at noon. The village constable, one P.C. Mortimer, rode into the castle on his bicycle and, asking to see the 'mistress', gave me the garbled first version which had come to him by way of the telegraph line from Truro to Falmouth and thence by messenger to his police post in Mortmain village.

The message said simply that there had been a daylight robbery in Truro and that the thief had got away with a package of important legal documents in the possession of a Mr Treacher, a lawyer of Dorchester. During the course of the robbery, Mr Treacher had been injured while going to the aid of his clerk, Mr Caldecott.

As may be imagined, I was horrified at the news and pressed P.C. Mortimer to seek for further details. All that long day, I fretted round the castle, climbing from time to time to the highest point of my east tower to peer out across the home park in the hope of seeing a conveyance emerge from the gap between the two low hills that marked the boundary of the home park.

I was actually standing there – and peering – when the dogcart came into view. As it drew closer, I perceived that the small vehicle contained one man and he was driving. I could clearly see his Derby hat and the thin cigar that was stuck jauntily in the corner of his lips. Before he reached the drawbridge, I had identified him as Sergeant Penbury of Truro, and went down to greet him.

He alighted and took my proffered hand.

'A bad business, ma'am,' he said.

'Is – is Mr Treacher all right, Sergeant?' I asked fearfully.

He looked puzzled. 'Oh, that gentleman took no more than a blow on the head when he tried to prevent the thief from leaving,' he said. 'But the poor Caldecott fellow, he never recovered consciousness and died on the way to the hospital.

'And the thief – whoever he was – got away scot free with the briefcase stuffed with documents.

'Are you all right, ma'am? You look faint. Here – take my arm and I'll help you inside.'

*

Later, Penbury gave me the full story in detail. The crime had taken place in the Black Dog hotel in Truro, where the two men had booked two rooms in the anticipation that their business at the Duchy Records Office might be protracted. They had scarcely gone to their separate rooms to deposit their overnight luggage when Giles Treacher, whose room was at the far end of the corridor from that of his clerk, heard a shout for assistance, followed by the sounds of a violent struggle coming from that direction. He reached Caldecott's door in time to see his assistant being beaten to his knees by an assailant, who, having just contrived to drag the briefcase from his victim's nerveless

172

fingers, was belabouring his unprotected head with a 'life-preserver' – a leather cudgel topped with a bolt of lead.

'Treacher never saw the villain's face,' said Penbury, 'for his features were overshadowed by a broad-brimmed hat. As he tried to protect his clerk, the assailant aimed a heavy blow to his shoulder that incapacitated him completely. As he sank in agony to his knees, the other made good his escape with what he had obviously come for – the documents in the briefcase.'

'Poor, poor Mr Caldecott,' I whispered. 'How could anyone have harmed such a kind, meek man who didn't have it in him to hurt a fly – or even catch a fish.'

'Meek he may have been, ma'am,' said the sergeant dryly, 'but he didn't part with that briefcase without giving his life!'

We sat in silence for a while – we were in the drawing room, and Penbury had declined the offer of tea, but sat on the edge of his chair, notebook on his knee, pencil in hand, watching me with his inscrutable green eyes.

'Where is Mr Treacher now?' I asked.

'In the hospital at Truro,' replied the policeman, 'resting after the treatment he received for the damage to his shoulder. He'll stay there overnight and be off back to Dorchester in the morning, where he has important business to attend.' He was silent for a moment, and then added: 'Mr Caldecott's remains will accompany him back to be laid to rest in Dorchester.'

I nodded. There seemed nothing else to say.

'And now,' said Sergeant Penbury in a completely different tone of voice from that which he had so far used, a brisk, no-nonsense, let's-get-to-it kind of voice that immediately aroused me from my despondency, 'let us seek to find who this scoundrel is who killed and wounded to get those documents – which, as I have been informed – relate to your recent inheritance, ma'am.

'And I may add that there is little doubt but that the man who burst into Caldecott's room in the "Black Dog" and the man who assaulted you on the train are one and the same.'

I stared at him. 'The – *the hat?*' I faltered.

'The hat!' he responded. 'So now, since we now know that it's your inheritance that concerns this fellow, may we assume that he has ambitions to get his own hands on that inheritance – and proceed from there?

'To begin, ma'am, is there anyone in your life – an enemy, a presumed friend, a relation – most particularly a relation – who might suppose himself (or *herself*, for we cannot at this stage entirely dismiss the possibility that the person in the strange hat is a woman; a hat is a fine disguise) to be entitled to that inheritance?'

I shook my head. 'I don't have a relation in the world, sir,' I told him. 'You see, I have no one, for I am a foundling. Nobody's child.'

'Nobody's child?' He looked at me searchingly, and I was reminded where I had seen the counterpart of that watchful, green-eyed glance. 'There is no such thing as "nobody's child", ma'am. Everyone who is born on this earth alive is *somebody's* child.'

'That's as may be, Sergeant,' I responded, somewhat nettled. 'But, unlike your own fortunate case, I am unable to point to my parentage. Relations I undoubtedly may have – but they are as unknown to me as I presumably am to them.'

'However,' he said, 'you will concede, ma'am, that any relations you may have are more likely to know of your existence than you of theirs.'

I thought that remark through, and finally conceded that he must be right.

'So,' he said, 'we must try to find if you have any relations. Your lawyer Mr Treacher has never alluded to any? Or the possibility of any?'

I shook my head.

He was silent for a moment, and then asked: 'From whom, since you are, as you put it yourself, nobody's child, did you receive your inheritance?'

'I don't think I can tell you that,' I replied. 'Upon that point, you must speak with Mr Treacher.'

He nodded. 'I will do that ma'am,' he said. 'It seems to me that Mr Treacher holds the key to much of your life.'

'That he does indeed,' I replied. (And knows more than he's

willing to speak of, even to me, I reminded myself.) 'But his whole intent is for my welfare, you can be sure.'

'I wouldn't doubt it for one moment, Miss Friday,' replied the other. He got to his feet to go, putting his notebook in the capacious side pocket of his tweed coat and his pencil in his breast pocket along with an array of others. 'I'll take my leave, ma'am. Thanks for your help.'

'I'm bitterly sorry this has happened,' I replied, 'all the more so if, as seems likely, I'm indirectly responsible. Poor Mr Caldecott. Was he – married?'

'A widower, as I understand. And no children.'

'That's a blessing.'

He nodded.

I escorted him to the courtyard where one of the grooms was tending to the cob in the traces of his little dogcart. And a wayward thought came to me, which I decided to express.

'Sergeant Penbury . . .'

'Ma'am?'

'Are you in some way related to the Penbury family who farmed some of the Mortmain land around the time of the Civil War?'

'I am, ma'am,' he replied. 'And my brother still does so.' His gaze was firm, direct.

'Then you must also be descended from Felicity Denvers,' I declared. 'I say this because you have her eyes. You see – I've a portrait of her, and the resemblance struck me immediately.'

He smiled: it was a taut, humourless smile. 'Why, that couldn't 'ardly be so, loike, could it, ma'am?' he said, reverting to the warm, West Countryman's burr that was certainly not his habitual manner of speaking.

'Why not?' I asked.

'Why, 'twould make me one o' the gentry, and that wouldn't do at all, would it, ma'am?' he said, and there was a note of mocking bitterness in his voice. 'What's more, everyone knows as how the Honourable Felicity Denvers's babby died when she did, so 'twouldn't be possible that any of her looks descended to me, would it now?

'Good day to you, Miss Friday.'

175

He climbed up into the driving seat, shook out the reins, clicked his tongue, and was gone.

I watched the dogcart out of sight beyond the gatehouse arch, then turned to go back into the keep; as I did so, I saw Phoebe's small, pale face regarding me from one of the second-floor windows – but she immediately moved away.

NINE

'I'm to appear at the Diamond Jubilee, at St Paul's Cathedral on June 22nd next. Would you believe it? I shall probably be presented to the Queen. My mother, who is a stern republican and anti-monarchist of the old order in the United States, will nevertheless be thrilled to her very bones to hear that her blue-eyed boy has shaken the hand of Britain's longest-reigning monarch.'

The speaker was Commander Jack Todd. It was Wednesday, and he had called to give me my first climbing lesson, as arranged.

'Mmmm,' was my comment on that.

He was more sensitive and observant than I would have given him credit for. We were sitting on the edge of the ornamental fountain in the courtyard when he reached out and touched my hand.

'You aren't yourself today,' he said. 'I heard about the murder in Truro and gathered that the two men involved as victims of the attack had been your guests. Do you want to forget about the climbing lesson today, mmm?'

I shook my head. 'I'm sorry I'm out of kilter,' I admitted. 'You're quite right, that awful business *has* upset me, but I'll be the better for shaking myself out of it, with your help, Jack.'

We were Jack and Daisy already. By some curious alchemy on his part, we had been so during the brief period that we had sat by the ornamental pool, drunk a cup of coffee and thrown biscuit crumbs to the carp.

'O.K.,' he said. 'Let's go, Daisy. Lesson one starts right here.'

I gazed at him blankly.

'Did you say – *here*?' I stared about me. Did he require that I should, for my first lesson, climb the face of the gatehouse, or the central keep, perhaps?

'That's right,' he said. 'Stand up and face me. Feet slightly apart, hands down by your sides.'

I shrugged and obeyed, eyeing him warily. For the enterprise, I was wearing a pair of cycling bloomers that dear Florrie, in a moment of wild abandon, had bought for me at an emporium in Bath (*'Pour le sport, ma chèrie'*), and I felt about as much at home in them as an admiral on a donkey.

Jack did not get up, but sat there and watched me quizzically.

'Right!' he said. 'At the order "Go", bend the knees and, keeping the torso upright, sink towards the ground till your fingertips touch the ground.

'GO!'

I went – slowly and with as much grace as I was able, and hugely grateful that I was not wearing a skirt, let alone a bustle. I could not have been the first woman in the civilised world who quietly blessed the excellent sensible dress devised by the late Mrs Bloomer.

'Remain where you are,' said Jack. 'And on the order "Rise", return slowly to the upright posture as before.

'RISE!'

I obeyed. And achieved the upright posture that, according to Mr Charles Darwin, had taken Man countless millenia.

'What next, teacher?' I asked.

'Repeat the exercise,' he ordered. 'GO! – BEND! – RISE! – BEND! – RISE . . .!'

Following his orders, I complied with the terms of the exercise and continued till he called upon me to stop. I did so, and stood watching him, rather out of breath but otherwise unscathed. To my surprise, he was regarding me with some admiration – not unmixed with a certain cynicism.

'I might have expected it,' he said.

'I beg your pardon?' I asked.

'The exercise – it would have flattened most women unused to that kind of physical activity. But I'd overlooked that you, as a member of the British upper classes, have been riding to hounds and jumping hunters over five-barred gates since you were knee-high to a foxhound. You were great – great! And I declare you to be in a fit physical state to start climbing.'

'Thank you, sir,' I responded, amused. I made no effort, at that juncture, to disabuse him about my 'British upper-class' origin being the explanation for the unusually good state of my leg muscles; an early childhood devoted to a twelve-hour-a-day stint of jumping up and down on a bellows-plank will do as much – and more – for the leg muscles as all your fox-hunting!

*

'Take it easy. Rest. If you do nothing, you can't come to any harm. Relax. Think of how well you've managed so far, and how the rest of it's going to be just the same. Think positively. And whatever you do, *don't* look down again!'

This was several days later (Friday or Saturday, as I recall), and the fourth or fifth intensive lesson. Jack was supervising my first complete ascent of the cliff; he was ahead, and staking out our progress with a rope attached to pins hammered into cracks in the granite wall of the 'open chimney'; the idea being that, if I fell – as seemed likely to me on several occasions – the rope that joined us would bring me up short.

I had just had a very bad moment. Halfway up the chimney, when I seemed to be going well, I looked down to gloat over what progress I had made – and saw to my horror that I was jammed by no more than the pressure of my fingertips, toes, and the small of my back in a sheer-sided funnel down which, if I relaxed a muscle for so much as an instant, I should instantly fall to a very painful death (I never gave a thought to the rope).

Fortunately, Jack saw it all. He must have seen the terror in my eyes and certainly could not have missed the uncontrollable tremor of my limbs. He spoke to me. Told me what to do. And I obeyed him.

Moments later, the terror faded, and I resumed my climb. With ever bounding confidence, I swarmed up after my guide and reached the top of the chimney in triumph. The last section of the ascent, by comparison, was like walking upstairs.

When we reached the battlements – which were lined with wide-eyed castle servants who had been neglecting their duties in the no-doubt anxious anticipation of losing their mistress and being thrown out of employment – Jack shook my hand, kissed me on both cheeks, and told me I was a born climber.

I believed him without question, for this was also my opinion. I may say that, after my first conquest of irrational fear in that open chimney, I never again – save on one very bizarre occasion, of which more later – knew fear whilst climbing.

Before we parted that day, Jack said to me, quite casually: 'Are you going to the Diamond Jubilee celebrations in London, Daisy?'

'I hadn't given a thought to it,' I replied. 'Why do you ask, Jack?'

'Well, because if you were going, I could arrange for you to have a pass to St Paul's Cathedral, and you'd maybe see your old Queen as close as you see me now. And maybe she'd say "hello".'

'How very kind of you,' I said. 'I'll think about it and give you my answer in a day or so.'

'No hurry,' he said. 'Tell me at Mr Melmoth's garden-party. I take it that you've been invited, of course, since I'm given to understand that Melmoth's a friend of yours.' When he made this last observation, I was aware that his eyes were very watchful.

'Tristan isn't a great friend of mine,' I replied carelessly. 'Indeed, we met only on one occasion, and that was at a slightly disastrous dinner-party at my house in Bath. I found him – very amusing.'

He huffed and puffed for a while, the way some men will when they have something on their mind and cannot bring themselves to unburden it. However, he managed to overcome his compunctions, and came out with the following:

'Ah – Daisy, I know you'll take what I have to say in the spirit in which it's offered, that's to say, I offer it as your very sincere friend and, I may add, a great admirer of your goodself.'

'Of course, Jack,' I responded, greatly amused at the delightful – if stuffy – turn of phrase that my American admirer employed.

'Ah – in short, Daisy, I have to tell you that Melmoth is pretty well known in certain sections of male London society, in which as a representative of the United States, I'm obliged to mingle.'

'And much to the credit of the United States, Jack, I'm sure,' I interposed in all sincerity.

'Ah – thank you, Daisy,' he replied, with a look that may have been informed by the suspicion that I was gently pulling his leg. 'What I want to say is this – that Melmoth guy – now, he's got a pretty bad reputation with women! *There*!' Having delivered this pronouncement, he folded his arms and looked down at me with the air of a man who, for the love of a good woman, has betrayed the masculine code of mutual support and patronage. I could have hugged him.

'Thank you for the tip, Jack,' I said. 'I'll keep it in mind in all my dealings with Tristan Melmoth, you can be sure of that.'

He nodded, clearly relieved at having discharged his duty as a friend and admirer. We parted company on that agreeable note.

My invitation to the Melmoth party had, in fact, arrived a couple of days before by the hand of his valet. It announced that the affair was to be held in the gardens of Penford Lodge, a matter of only ten minutes drive from the castle.

What intrigued me most, and continued to do so, was a postscript on the printed card in what I took to be Tristan Melmoth's own flamboyant hand:

You will be amused to learn that I have secured the acceptance of our mutual friend C— A—, who has also taken up summer residence in the vicinity of the Siren of Mortmain. *Tant mieux.* *A bientôt. Votre* T— M—

Though I did not greatly like the allusion to 'the Siren of Mortmain', reminding me, as it did, of Giles Treacher's reference to 'the gathering of bees around the honeypot', I could not escape the fact that the thought of seeing Charles Arbuthnot again filled me with a curious mixture of worried anticipation and pleasurable unease.

But at least, I told myself, this time I should meet him without the presence of the appalling Lady Moira.

Alas for ill-supported hopes!

*

Penford Lodge – as I gleaned from a copy of *The Landed Gentry of Devon & Cornwall and their Principal Seats of Residence*, a dusty volume which I managed to unearth in Mortmain's rather frugal library – was situated one mile north-east of Mortmain village in the parish of St Mary, Walmespole; a former hunting-lodge of the Tremellion family; eighteenth-century with modern additions.

To Penford Lodge, the following Wednesday, I was conveyed in an open landau, very conscious that I cut a not unimpressive figure in an afternoon frock of white organdie sprinkled with tiny blue roses that had been made for me by Madame Rita of Bath, and a cartwheel hat adorned with enough Bird-of-Paradise feathers to have decimated that species. The sun shone, and I kept up my parasol in the pious hope of reducing my naturally bucolic complexion to the fashionable pallor. As the horses clip-clopped through the dusty lanes and past eyeless cottages of strangely silent villages (I had been told that Cornish folk hide behind their net curtains at the sight and sound of alien passers-by), I read and re-read two letters that had come on the morning's post. One was from dear Florrie: a six-page effusion including the latest gossip from Bath, to wit: the Dean of Wells had died, and young Archdeacon Vallence was tipped as his successor; the Empress Eugénie, tiring of Royal Crescent, had returned to her home in Chislehurst; the annual summer Fair had passed almost unregarded, save that a lion-tamer in Bravestock & Wimewold's International Circus had been assaulted and partly devoured before the horrified eyes of the Bath bourgeoisie. And she greatly missed me, and would join me in Cornwall just as soon as she was able.

My other letter was from the governors and managers of the Westchester parish orphanage; in reply to mine, their Chairman, a Mr Brindley, put his signature to a most effusive epistle of thanks for my most kind offer of financial assistance in the support of feeding the deprived children of the parish, and would Miss Friday honour the same institution by accepting the title of Patroness? And would Miss Friday one day honour us with a Visit of Inspection? Yours most sincerely, etc. I folded up the letter and marvelled how a few paltry guineas a year could raise one's standing from that of ex-inmate to honoured Patroness. I further resolved to extend my activities in the field of simple benevolent charity, in which, so it seemed to me, I was uniquely qualified as an expert; because I knew what all the governors and managers, the do-gooders and the religious cranks, the placemen and the would-be wielders of power could and would never know: that the one over-riding obsession of the very poor and wretched is the vision of a decent, satisfying meal – and to hell with the pious tracts about blessing the benefactors, being obedient and thankful, eschewing greed and ingratitude, and all that.

So resolved was I upon extending my first essay into filling the bellies of the disadvantaged that I there and then set to and composed a possible list of other so-called charitable institutions that might well succumb to the offer of my few guineas for the immediate benefit of their wretched inmates. I did this on the back of Mr Brindley's letter, and was still working on it when we came through the handsome wrought-iron gates of Penford Lodge, and I was handed down and most rhapsodically greeted by my fascinating host.

'My dear Miss Friday! You will never know with what desolation of spirit I awaited your note of acceptance. If you had chucked, I should have cancelled the entire fanfaronade. But you accepted! You are here – and the gaiety of nations has not been eclipsed!' With which extravagance of expression, he implanted his airy kiss an inch above my hand. 'To the garden,' he said. 'Come and meet some new friends – and some old ones.' He winked saucily, and I had a sudden premonition of mischief on his part.

The garden of the house (itself a sizeable but unimposing square box with pillars and a sort of dome in the middle) was laid out in terraced lawns lined with long yew hedges and interspersed with fountains and gesticulating statuary of the undressed sort. There must have been all of a hundred people present, amongst whom a veritable battalion of liveried footmen passed with trays of champagne that were being gratefully received – which may have accounted for the high note of frenzied chatter that rose in the still summer air like the cry of parakeets.

'My dear Miss Friday, may I present Sir Wilfred Tollemache, Lord Lieutenant of Devon. And this is Colonel Avery of the Cornish Light Infantry. Mr Robert Partridge, Mr John Bulgin, Mr Kimble Thomas – all West Country gentlemen of tremendous distinction. Commander Todd I think you already know.' He winked.

'Hello, hello. How do you do – how do you do?'

'I'm glad you came,' said Jack Todd. 'This party is already halfway to a bear-garden. This is what comes of serving champagne ad lib through the whole afternoon. By nightfall, it'll be Sodom and Gomorrah all over again.'

I saw his point. Already, the younger members of the gathering were playing hide-and-seek and blind-man's buff in and out of the yew hedges and round and about the statuary; while a couple of youths in hunting scarlet had taken off their boots and were wading in a fountain bowl, splashing each other and giving wild whoops; one of their companions was urging them on with shrill notes from a hunting horn.

'I'll give you time to circulate the guests and then I thought maybe we could slip away and have tea somewhere,' said Jack.

'Oh, that wouldn't be very civil of us,' I said, and my eyes were searching the chattering throng for a certain face.

'Are you coming to the Diamond Jubilee in London?' he asked.

I answered absently: 'Yes, I think I should like that, Jack.'

'I'll fix you that pass,' he said. 'We'll meet up at St Paul's.'

'Thank you, Jack. You're very kind.'

Tristan Melmoth insinuated himself between us and gently

took my elbow. 'I mustn't let our transatlantic friend impose upon too much of your attentions, my dear,' he purred, and his tigerish eyes swept the both of us. 'Come and meet an old friend.'

His hand at my elbow, still, and limping heavily with the aid of his cane, our host led me through ranks of chattering people to a small group adjacent to a complicated statuary work comprising a jumble of struggling men and women. Twenty paces from them, and I saw the back view of a man: very straight and upstanding, broad shoulders, hands loosely clasped behind him – and in an instant the small world about me opened up into glorious sunlight.

'Yes, *he's* here,' murmured Tristan Melmoth in my ear. 'And have I not watched you searching for him with your eyes, even when the fascinating Commander was trying so hard to com-mandeer your entire attention? Regrettably, however,' he added, 'I have been obliged to countenance – a gate-crasher! Where *he* goes, *she* – alas – will also insist upon going! *Tant pis!*'

Lady Moira was in scarlet silk with a dramatic white hat composed almost entirely of huge ostrich plumes. Her eyes met mine unwaveringly and I detected a gloating triumph there; but I had neither eyes nor ears for her or any part of her. When she gave me her gloved hand, when she even went so far as to implant a Judas kiss upon my cheek, it was as if she had never happened; my whole being, my total attention, was wrapped up in the glory that had suddenly surrounded me and illuminated my life in the short walk that had brought me from the everyday world of this and that to an unimaginable wonder that was, even now, opening up – like an eternal succession of mystical doors in some galactic puzzle-box – revealing fresh sights and sounds and feelings which left me in breathless hope that it would go on for ever and ever . . .

'How are you liking Cornwall, Miss Friday?'

'Very well, Mr Arbuthnot. And you?'

(Surely he must see the reflected glory in my eyes. And why had I never before noticed, I asked my bemused heart, that apart from the slight scar above his right eyebrow which reached into the hairline, there was also a corresponding echo of that same scar lightly touching the clean-cut angle of his firm jaw.)

'Nobody, but simply nobody has stopped talking about your dinner-party,' vouchsafed Lady Moira. But I had no ears for her, and he and his eyes were blessedly only for me.

'Did you have any refreshments?' he asked me. 'The *pâté de foi gras* has been specially imported from Strasbourg. Melmoth spares neither effort nor expense. One's reminded of the Roman emperors, who used to have snow brought by relays of fast runners from the slopes of the Alps to chill their guests' Valerian wine.'

'I've never tasted *pâté de foi gras* to my knowledge,' I replied.

'Till today, neither had I,' he said. 'Let's go and find the fellow who's giving it out.' And with those words, taking my arm, he led me away from the group, from Lady Moira, from everyone, and out through the anonymous, jabbering throng, to a quiet glade that lay between two long lines of clipped yew hedges. There there was only one small statue on its plinth – of an old man quizzically regarding a skull – and a live small boy and girl playing touch-and-run in and out of the arcaded yews.

'I was sorry to hear about Treacher and his man,' said Charles. 'It must have been a very great shock to you. I heard the details from Treacher himself when I was obliged to make a lightning visit to Dorchester t'other day. I gather (though he told me nothing, he's a lawyer all through) that the matter concerned your inheritance in some way. I trust that you are in no way threatened?'

(He was worried for me!)

'I – I don't think so,' I replied, thrusting into a dark corner of my mind all thoughts of the man in the strange hat and concentrating upon Charles's concern for my safety.

He nodded gravely. 'And what are you doing with yourself at Mortmain? Knowing you as I do – which is slightly – but guessing more about you than you would suppose, I do not imagine that you spend your time in sewing a fine seam, or watching your wide acres grow.'

'I've taken up benevolent charity,' I said.

'And what is that?' he asked. 'And how does *benevolent* charity

186

differ from charity in general, which one had always supposed to be by definition benevolent?'

His tone, all at once slightly – how to put it? – hectoring, and with just a suspicion of male patronage, raised my hackles. I replied with a touch of tartness that I made no attempt to hide: 'The difference, Mr Arbuthnot, between charity and what I call *benevolent* charity, lies in the object of the transaction. The former – from my slight personal experience of organised charity – is a means to keeping the poor and hopeless half-starved and acquiescent, well-stuffed with the pious tags so beloved of your friends Sir and Lady Wisher – such as being grateful to your benefactors and don't for heaven's sake make any trouble or cause a rumpus just because your belly's rumbling and empty.

'Benevolent charity, on the other hand, Mr Arbuthnot, in my humble submission, goes to the root of the problem of poverty, which is how to feed the inner man. A full belly, say I, means a contented man, woman or child.'

He nodded – but doubtfully. 'There is something in what you say,' he conceded. 'But, you know, it was the concession of limited benefits to the masses by King Louis XVI of France that brought about the French Revolution. Desire feeds upon itself and begets even more unacceptable demands.'

'Fiddlesticks!' I declared. '*I* have studied the French Revolution as closely as you, sir. *I* have read Mr Carlyle's definitive work in two volumes. The Bourbons' concessions were too little and too late. If king, nobles and church had attended to the people's wants early enough and vigorously enough, the French Revolution would never have happened.

'Show me a man, woman or child with a full belly – and I will show you someone who will not answer the call to man the barricades!'

With which declaration, and finding that I was near to tears of deep emotion, and that my hair was falling down from under my hat, and that my nose had probably turned a silly red, I backed away from him.

'Please excuse me,' I said.

And fled.

*

When I look back on the dreadful close of that fateful afternoon, I wonder if there was something I might have done to prevent it.

I suppose that having made the shattering discovery (and I reckon I must have suspected it long before) that I was hopelessly in love with Charles Arbuthnot, and having expressed the boiling-over of my emotions by the classic means of deliberately provoking a lover's quarrel, I might be excused for not having paid closer attention to the comings and goings of the people about me.

Emerging from the house, where I had fixed my hair and dabbed some rice powder on my nose, I sought about for Jack Todd, but not finding him, was an instant prey to Lady Moira.

She descended upon me like a swooping hawk, and had clearly seen me enter the house and been lying in wait for me to come out. She seized me on the terrace, waved to a passing flunkey to bring us both champagne, guided me by the elbow to a stone bench that overlooked the receding vista of the landscaped garden as far as an artificial lake adorned with preening swans that acted as a full stop to the whole boisterous statement, and addressed me severely in these terms:

'What are your intentions towards Charles Arbuthnot?' she demanded to know.

'What do you mean – intentions?' I countered feebly enough.

'Don't bandy words with me, woman!' she snapped. 'It's as plain as a pikestaff that Charles has set his cap at you after a fashion – and why shouldn't he, a man of the world? So! He was – titillated – by the wide-eyed waif who spoke out against him in his own factory. He advanced her in some degree by having her grubby face cleaned and putting her into an office. And then what? I suppose in the fullness of time, he'll have his way with you like he has with all the rest.

'But what are your intentions towards *him*, pray?'

I was so staggered, so affronted by her brutal assault that words failed me for as long as it took for a shadow to fall across us and a gloved hand to place two brimming glasses of champagne on the low table set by the bench.

'Yes, yes, put them there,' said Lady Moira fussily. 'And

bring something to eat, will you? Some of that *pâté*. Oh, and some smoked salmon.

'Where was I?'

'You were asking about my – intentions,' I prompted her. 'And, by the way, Lady Moira, what are *your* intentions towards *him*?'

She dismissed that with an imperious flourish of her hand; as if such a question had no right to have issued from my mouth, and with a sneering smile upon her exquisitely-moulded lips, she picked up a wineglass and treated me to a glance of superior pity.

'It is already arranged,' she purred. 'Charles and I are to marry immediately after the Diamond Jubilee celebrations are over. The Prince of Wales, unfortunately, is unable to stand as Charles's best man, but the Duke of Westchester is deputising for His Highness.

'Would you like me to send you an invitation?'

She raised her glass in gloating mockery.

'To you. Your very good health. Remember, my dear, in love – as with so much else in life – *second* prizes don't really count!'

She drank deeply.

I still wake at night with the memory of what followed, and sleep always evades me after that. For so long as I live, I think that I shall never shut out the vision of Lady Moira Fame's hideous end.

There was the choking; the suffusion of blueness to her face as, rising stiffly, she clasped a hand to her throat and, staring-eyed, tried to cry out. All that came was the strangled squeal of a slaughtered animal.

Two paces separated us from the balustrade of the terrace: she took half of the rest of her life to cover it; was poised there for a moment – before she folded up like a wooden-top dolly and toppled headlong on to the grass below, right at the feet of a horrified group of guests who had been laughing there.

She was dead, and still staring-eyed when I went down there.

Jack Todd, it was, who firmly led me away despite my entreaties.

*

I lay for a long while on the sofa in a shuttered room and could not stop crying for the world. Presently, they brought a doctor to me, who gave me a soothing draught that helped. After him came – of all people at such a time and feeling as I did! – Charles Arbuthnot.

'I would not have had this happen for the world,' he said. 'I've simply come to say that I'm dreadfully sorry that you were witness to Moira's shocking end. The only consolation is that it must have been instantaneous, and without pain.'

Without pain! Merciful heavens, could he but have seen the look on that poor creature's face when she took that final plunge!

I turned my face to the wall, and said nothing.

'I have to go now,' he said. 'It's necessary for me to send a telegraph informing Moira's mother of the tragedy. You do understand.'

'Yes – I understand,' I replied.

'Well, goodbye for now, Miss Friday,' he said. 'I will call upon you soon.'

I did not reply. He went out. When I heard his footsteps receding down the corridor outside, I had another paroxysm of weeping from which I had scarce recovered when there came a discreet tap on the door.

It was Sergeant Penbury. 'Sorry to trouble you, Miss Friday,' he said, 'but there are certain things that I have to know right away, and only you can give me the answers direct.'

'Of course,' I said. 'Do sit down.'

He pulled up a straight-backed chair and sat down near me. From out of his pocket he produced the tattered notebook that had come to resemble his badge of office.

'Miss Friday,' he said, 'I don't want to intrude upon your grief. Lady Moira was a friend of yours, I take it?'

I shook my head. 'No. In all honesty, I couldn't describe her as a friend. To be frank, she detested me. And I have to admit that the feeling was more or less mutual.'

'I see. And yet, at the time she died, you were sitting together on the terrace, having drinks.'

'Yes.'

190

'Chatting in a – well, if not in a friendly, in a – shall we say? – civilised manner?'

'No. Not civilised at all.'

'Oh.' He was silent for a few moments, and then: 'Did you take your drinks, your champagne glasses, to that seat on the terrace, or were they brought to you? This is quite important.'

I thought for a moment; after what had happened, it seemed so frivolous for him to be dealing with such a triviality.

'Um – they were brought to us. Lady Moira gave the order to one of the footmen before we sat down.'

'This footman – would you know him again?'

'Why, no. I had my back to him.'

'And you didn't see him when he brought the drinks – is that what you're going to tell me now, Miss Friday?'

'Yes. That's quite right. He brought the drinks and laid them on the table near to us. I was listening to what Lady Moira was telling me. Why should I be looking at the footman? Sergeant, I really don't understand . . .'

He raised a mildly admonishing hand. In the shuttered gloom, I could scarcely see the expression in his green eyes, but I thought that it might not be unlike that of the girl in the picture . . .

'Please, Miss Friday. Bear with me. You didn't see the footman who brought your champagne – you didn't see him from first to last?'

'No.'

'But Lady Moira saw him? Addressed him? If she were alive, she'd be able to point to this fellow and say "this is the footman who brought our champagne"?'

'Yes. Undoubtedly,' I replied, still puzzled as to why he should be persisting in this – as it seemed to me – irrelevant questioning.

Sergeant Penbury closed his notebook, secured it with an india-rubber band, and placed it in his side pocket. His pencil went to join the others. 'Thank you, Miss Friday,' he said. 'There'll be an inquest, of course, and you'll be summoned to repeat this evidence before the coroner.'

'Really?' I replied, astounded. 'But . . .'

'Eventually, there may, and it's to be hoped, *will* be a criminal prosecution,' he said. 'Your evidence will be called for then, also. You do understand that, do you, Miss Friday?'

I shook my head, by now totally bemused. 'No, Sergeant, I *don't* understand!' I retorted. 'Lady Moira – for whom, for heaven's sake, I had no reason, no earthly reason, to have any very great regard – died before my very eyes just now. Of a heart attack, or something of that kind, I suppose . . .'

'She was murdered,' he interposed. 'Poisoned.'

I gaped at him. 'Murdered – you said *murdered?*'

He nodded. 'By prussic acid,' he said. 'There was enough prussic acid in the champagne glass she drank from to – in the words of our police surgeon – "to kill an elephant". And that isn't all . . .'

'*Poisoned!*' I stared at him, still unable to come to terms with what he was telling me.

'What's more, your own glass was similarly treated,' he said. 'If you had joined Lady Moira in drinking that champagne, you also would be on your way to Truro public mortuary like she is, poor woman.

'Why didn't you join her in a drink, Miss Friday?' he asked.

Someone replied: 'I don't drink – not any more.' And I suppose it must have been me.

*

The draught that the doctor had given me presently brought me easeful sleep; when I woke, the sun had gone down and the room was in deep shadow. Rising up and opening a window shutter, I looked out into the garden. Immediately before me was the terrace where the last, grotesque Dance of Death had marked the end of Lady Moira Fame's life; beyond that, the long stretches of yew-bordered, grassy walks swept down to the ornamental lake and the swans. Nothing there, now, but silent desolation; no guests, nothing – save for a napkin that balled and rolled like a piece of tumbleweed in the fitful evening air.

I examined myself in a pier glass and found myself not looking as bad as I had imagined. A dab of rice powder and a flick of the hairbrush made me more or less presentable, and the

192

Bird-of-Paradise hat covered a lot of sins. I went out to see what was happening in Tristan Melmoth's summer retreat.

I heard his voice as I opened the door, and saw him at the far end of the passageway, silhouetted against an archway leading out to the garden. His back was towards me and he was addressing a companion: a shortish man in black, whom I took to be his valet. Some fragments of his discourse came to me.

'One must leave here. One couldn't stand the appalling shame of being gawped and pointed at by the dreadful yokels whenever one rode out. I shall go to Scotland. See to it that the house is . . .'

And then he saw me, and limped down the passage to greet me: a big man, a slow walker, sailing like a full-rigged ship, with his smaller companion trailing far behind in his wake.

'My dear Miss Friday! How are you? I have been *desolate* for you. Oh, and you are looking so well after your dreadful ordeal. Would you like some tea?'

'Thank you no, Mr Melmoth,' I replied. 'I really must go.'

He spread his hands in a gesture of dismay. 'But you must rest, my dear,' he declared. 'Let me ask them to prepare a suite of rooms for you for the night.'

'No – please.'

'Very well, my dear. Hawn – have them bring Miss Friday's carriage round to the front.' Taking me by the arm, Mr Melmoth walked me slowly down the passage, talking all the time. 'It has been a social disaster for me,' he said in confiding tones. 'The police treated my guests with scant courtesy, so you may well imagine how the servants fared at their hands. Happily, most of them have been in my employ for many years and their bona fides are impeccable, for all possess testimonials dating back from the beginnings of their lives in service. Not so, however, some of the footmen whom we secured from a domestic agency in Falmouth. Some very louche characters there, I fancy. However, *they* were bundled with scant ceremony into a police Black Maria and driven off in most unaccommodating haste to headquarters. It's to be hoped that the perpetrator of this dastardly crime is among them and will speedily be winkled out.'

I broke in on his monologue: 'Has everyone else left?'

He smiled. 'If you refer to dear Arbuthnot, as I fancy you do, he departed almost immediately after the tragedy, when it was quite apparent that nothing could be done for the unfortunate woman, and was driven to Truro to telegraph the news to Lady M's aged mama who apparently lives in San Remo. Miss Friday, my dear, at second glance, you do look rather peaky. Are you *sure* you won't rest overnight?'

'You're very kind, but no,' I said.

'Well, I shall be leaving tomorrow,' he said. 'I can't possibly stand the pointing fingers and the muttering that's sure to follow. I have the police people's assurance that my testimony will not be required at the coming inquest (I suppose you'll be called, my dear, since you were actually on the scene of the crime). I shall spend the rest of the summer in Scotland, in Monteith, where Lord Mountstrachan has been pestering me for ages to liven up the rear elevation of his dreadful barrack of a castle. I have in mind a gazebo after the Italianate manner, and perhaps a water garden leading down to the loch. It will be very amusing.'

We came to the front door and emerged out on to the curved drive. My carriage, waiting near, was brought forward.

'Goodbye, my dear,' said Tristan Melmoth, taking my proffered hand. 'I hope we meet again soon, and in more pleasant circumstances.'

'Goodbye,' I said. It was on the tip of my tongue to thank him for his hospitality, but I restrained myself.

He leaned towards me, large handsome face a mask of concern.

'But who would *wish* to murder Lady Moira?' he asked. 'She had certain social – disadvantages – as we both know well, who have seen her in full spate. But what servant would take umbrage over her irritating little ways – to the extent of wanting to kill her?'

'And me also, for that matter,' I added.

Mr Melmoth affected a monocle, which he sometimes wore in his right eye, sometimes dangling across the front of his impeccably starched shirtfront. On this occasion he was wearing it. At my words, he stared at me, wide-eyed, and the monocle fell and swung on the end of its black moiré ribbon like a pendulum.

The police, it seemed, had not told him about the prussic acid in the other glass of champagne.

*

The sky was overcast and threatening rain by the time the carriage passed through the tall stone gateposts that marked the beginning of the long, curved drive up to the castle; each gatepost was topped with the snarling leopard crest of the Denvers, their granite features crumbling with age and weather.

It was quite obvious, from the moment when we swept under the gatehouse arch and into the courtyard, that news of the tragedy at Penford Lodge had already reached the castle. All the servants were there to watch my return: they clustered at the windows and doorways, paused at their work in the yard and on the lawns; the laundresses in the raised garden stopped taking in their sheets and turned to search their mistress's face, to read what was written there.

The Steeples were standing at the foot of the steps leading up to the main door of the keep. I thought I saw Phoebe standing like a small wraith in the gloom beyond the doorway, but the image flitted out of my sight.

Mrs Steeple's eyes held an unframed question, which I ignored.

'Have them bring a pot of tea up to my sitting room, will you, please,' I said to the housekeeper as I alighted from the landau. 'I'm going to have a rest, and won't require dinner. Will you see that I'm not disturbed.'

She sketched a curtsy. 'Yes, ma'am.' And lowered her eyes.

I walked past them into the hall and down along the corridor, through the secret entrance behind the panel, and up to my sitting room, where I threw off my Bird-of-Paradise hat and laid myself on the chaise-longue. The lustrous green eyes of Felicity Denvers gazed down at me from the wall opposite. She must know – who better? – how I felt.

Besides all else on that dreadful day had come the revelation that I was in love. And that it was a hopeless love. I closed my eyes and heard Moira Fame's high-pitched, mocking voice again:

'*I suppose in the fullness of time, he'll have his way with you . . . like all the rest . . .*'

I put my hands over my ears, but there was no shutting out that voice:

'*Charles and I are to marry . . . would you like me to send you an invitation? . . . Second prizes don't count . . . Have his way with you like all the rest . . . all the rest . . .!*'

'NO-O-O-O!' The cry burst from me. I sat bolt upright and opened my eyes – to see little Nellie Throstle standing in the doorway and gazing at me in awe and alarm. She was carrying a tray of tea.

'I – I did knock, ma'am,' she faltered. 'But seeing as how you didn't reply . . .'

'It's all right, Nellie,' I assured her, straightening my hair in confusion. 'Come on in.'

She obeyed, and put the tray on the side-table by the chaise-longue. 'Are you all right, ma'am?' she asked with concern written all over her pretty, friendly face. 'Is there anything else I can get you, like?'

'No, I'm all right, thank you, Nellie,' I told her. 'I – I must have dozed off and had a bad dream. Nothing to worry about.'

'Very good, ma'am.' She curtsied and left me.

The tea tasted like nectar and cosseted the edges of my bruised mind. I sat cross-legged on the chaise-longue, held the cup in both hands and sipped it like a child, savouring every mouthful.

I must never see Charles again if it could be avoided, that much was certain. To be with him, to be near him, would be to open the wound again (not that the wound was healed, nor likely to be for a very long time).

And yet – and yet . . .

His plan of marriage dashed so brutally, might he not soon be seeking consolation elsewhere? Of the marriage sort – or of the *other* sort?

Did I – Daisy Friday – want to take my place in line, along with (the phrase made me wince, but it had to be thought) 'all the rest'?

'No,' I said aloud, quite suddenly calm now that it had been said. Daisy Friday might offer her heart only once; but the man who took it must love her as completely as she loved him. So it's goodbye Charles Arbuthnot, and goodbye to a love that blossomed, flowered and fell in the space of time it takes to have a silly lovers' quarrel and for a vindictive, jealous woman to spread her venom – and then die.

I lay back against the pillow and thought of Moira Fame's dreadful end, as if by the intensity of the image I might burn it from out of my mind; it was no use – over and over again, I could see her standing and staring at Death, hear the unearthly cry that rose to her ghastly blue lips, watch her fall like a discarded doll. The next image that had to follow was one *where I, too, had drunk the poisoned wine . . .*

And then there were two of us in a hideous *pas de deux* of Death: staring-eyed, screeching our last, circling each other, stiff arms outstretched.

The last image of all: the two of us joined in dissolution, lying side by side on a marble slab in a mortuary.

Restless, I tossed from side to side, fighting to shut out the memories and the speculations of what might have been. It was no use: too much had happened that day to be thrust on one side. Furthermore, there was the ever-recurring thought of the continuing danger in which I stood. My enemy – my secret, faceless enemy, who had pursued me relentlessly from the desolation of rural Dorset to bustling, busy Bath, and now to the wild West Country – would surely continue to do so till he had fulfilled his intent – as he had so nearly done today.

What should I do? Flee from him for ever? Fly to the ends of the earth, leaving no trace of my passing? I had the means. No one to say me nay. No family, no friends with bonds to keep me tied. I could creep away at any time. Now. Tomorrow. No need to pack, or to make a fuss of parting – that would only alert my faceless enemy, who was everywhere.

I warmed to my theme, which provided a blessed release

from my terrors: saw myself taking what I had declared to be a casual stroll down to the village – this for the benefit of the servants. Once there, a hired dogcart to Truro. From thence by train to, say, Penzance. In Penzance, I would pay the skipper of a fishing boat to convey me by night to a port on the French coast opposite – in Brittany, somewhere like – and I strove to remember the details from the dog-eared school atlas that I had pored over with Meg Wolfingham all those years ago – Brest, that was it. From Brest, I could take ship anywhere in the world: the South Seas, Tahiti, Christmas Island, Tonga, Madagascar – the names flew from the treasure house of memory. Somewhere beyond the setting sun there was a place where I could be safe: a paradise island beyond a coral reef where no one ever came; a place inhabited by warm-hearted and gentle people who would accept me unquestioningly.

Secure from harm at last . . .

I must have slipped, all unknowing, from thoughts to dreams. When I stirred and woke up, it was dark and rather cold. I heard the rain outside, slicing thinly against the thick glazing of the window above my head. But it was neither the darkness nor the rain which had roused me: a recess of my mind quite clearly echoed to a sound that I had heard.

An alien sound – in the room!

'Who's there?' I breathed; lest I should call some evil down upon me, I kept my voice low.

And then, by the thin moonlight that pierced the rainclouds and my window, I saw – IT.

It came from the direction of the open door, and it moved slowly on hands and knees, crawling sideways, like a crab. There was not enough light to pick out more than its silhouette as it advanced with slow and deliberate motions. Towards me!

I drew myself back against the wall, fearful to move, fearful to cry out in case I incited it to leap upon me. There was no escape: it barred my way to the door and I would as lief tried to pass it as thrust my hand into a nest of adders. All I could do was wait in petrified agony to see what it would do.

And then, I had left it too late to do anything but scream.

Still only a dark shape, but now more clearly recognisable as a man – or the semblance of a man – it was almost within reach of the couch on which I was huddled. Breathless with horror, I saw it seem to gather itself up painfully and, resting upon one arm, reach out the other, fingers extended, to seize the edge of the chaise-longue.

And then I began to scream.

I was still screaming when there came a commotion from outside the door, on the main staircase up to my suite; shouts of alarm and the clatter of running footfalls. Someone was carrying a lantern: by its loom, I could pick out what looked like a couple of burly gardeners and a fellow in footman's livery. There were at least two women.

The effect of the light, on the other hand, threw the thing at my side into even deeper shadow, so that mercifully I could not see its face, though I could feel its breath upon me, and could hear the curious snuffling sound – like that of a questing dog, or a pig – that it was making. I covered my face with my hands and willed it to go away.

'Are you all right, ma'am?' Mrs Steeple's voice. She sounded greatly concerned.

I lowered my hands. Over by the door, two of the men were half-carrying, half-dragging the thing back the way it had come. It appeared to offer no resistance. I shuddered.

'I'm sorry that happened, ma'am,' said Mrs Steeple. 'I wouldn't have had it happen for all the world, I swear it. But – well, he got loose, see? But I swear he wouldn't do any harm to a soul.'

I drew a deep and shuddering breath, and felt much calmer.

'Mrs Steeple,' I said, with a composure that quite surprised me. 'Would you be so good as to tell me who – or what – that creature is, and from where did he – or it – escape, as you put it.'

A look of evasion crept in at the edge of her expression which had formerly been all concern, and she did not reply.

'You will tell me, Mrs Steeple,' I persisted, 'for you are not leaving this room, save to pack your bag and baggage and begone, unless I know the identity of that creature who invaded my privacy.'

'Well – I'll tell you, ma'am,' she said at length. 'But I beg you to repeat it to no one outside these walls, for 'twould bring shame on me and my family, and I could not live with it.'

'I will be the judge of whether I tell or keep silent,' I replied implacably. 'But you will answer my questions, or leave here tonight.'

In the end, I heard her tale.

*

The creature was her brother, she told me: born a monster after her mother had been chased, brought down and gored by a bull while carrying him. The primitive code of the countryside in deepest Cornwall – which was of a muchness with the code of medieval times, when the hideously deformed were regarded as offspring of the devil, and dating even further into antiquity when the weak, ailing and imperfect infants of the ancient Spartans were put out on bare hillsides to perish – put great pressures upon the parents of such unfortunate infants; many such were permitted quietly to die of benevolent neglect during illness. As the verse goes:

> Thou shalt not kill; but need'st not strive
> Officiously to keep alive.

Almost certainly, a considerable number of these afflicted were dispatched by more direct means, as often as not with the connivance of some such midwife as old Mrs Prosser of Mordwenn. Such a fate had escaped Mrs Steeple's brother; whether by reason of a strong constitution or by the reluctance of the family to bend to local tradition, the monster lived and throve after his fashion, and was now – if such a term could be applied to such a tragic creature – a mature man.

I now saw it all very clearly.

'And he abides in the west tower!' I accused her. 'Which you always keep locked!'

She had the grace to avoid my glance. 'Yes, ma'am,' she whispered.

'On the top floor,' I continued remorselessly. 'And when I

demanded to be shown the tower, you had your brother shifted to some other hiding place for the occasion. Correct?'

She nodded. 'There – there's an underground passage from the west tower to the gatehouse,' she said. 'We took him there. But – but he's a creature of habit, and doesn't like the gatehouse. That night, he broke loose and tried to find his way back to the west tower . . .'

'I first saw him then,' I said, and shuddered at the recollection.

'And he did the same tonight,' she said. 'He's very determined, you see, ma'am, for all that he's as gentle as any kitten. Only he must have lost his way . . .'

I thought of the horror that had crawled, crab-wise, across the floor towards me, its hand reaching out to probe – and I shuddered.

It was then that the woman reached out and laid a hand on my arm. 'Don't send him away, ma'am,' she pleaded. 'How could such a creature live amongst others? You should see him plain. In the daylight. And then you'd realise that the world outside these walls would never accept him as a human being with a soul, with feelings like the rest of us, that can be hurt, that can laugh and cry. Out there, ma'am, they would stone him and revile him. Without me to look after him, he'd die in some hedge bottom and be thrown into an unmarked hole as if he were the carcass of some sheep that had perished on the moor.' The tears were running, unchecked, down her deeply-lined cheeks.

'You love him, Mrs Steeple,' I said, and it was not a question.

She nodded. 'Inside, he is the dearest, kindest, most generous creature who ever lived,' she said. 'If you send him away, ma'am, I shall go with him, and if I can find no place that will take the two of us, we'll starve together.'

I thought for a minute. 'How many others in the castle know your secret, Mrs Steeple?' I asked.

'The old hands,' she said. 'James the footman and Harris the head gardener. Mrs Treviss of the still room, one of the gardener's men, Meg Wainwright the dairymaid. Steeple and me. That's all.'

'And Phoebe?'

'Phoebe knows. But she – she's too young to understand right proper, you see, ma'am.'

I paced to the far end of the room and lit a candelabrum. The dancing flames illuminated the portrait of Felicity Denvers that looked down at me from above. The green eyes seemed to carry a message. I turned back to the tragic figure of the housekeeper.

'Your brother can stay here, Mrs Steeple,' I told her. 'Keep him well and keep him safe.'

I cut short her tearful thanks, her pledges of eternal devotion to my service. It has to be said that, though I greatly pitied the woman for the tragedies that had been heaped upon her in the persons of both her brother and her poor grandchild, my first impression of her, which had been unfavourable, had not greatly changed despite all. So does fate deal unfairly with those most in need: Mrs Steeple, who deserved all the compassion that could possibly come her way, remained essentially unlike-able; and unlikely to receive compassion in consequence.

When she had gone, I turned and looked up at the portrait again.

'Well, Felicity,' I said, 'do you approve of what I did? You should, for the impulse came from you. I had the clear impression of you asking me to extend to that poor woman the charity that never came your way.' I turned to go and get ready for bed, but at the door, I paused and looked back.

'What *did* become of your baby, Felicity? If the baby died, as legend has it, why does Sergeant Penbury have your eyes?'

Answer came there none.

TEN

The dark events of the previous day were quite put to shame by the brightness of the following morning, when the swallows were out early and diving across the surface of the ornamental pool, scooping up tiny mouthfuls without pausing; there was a diamond droplet of dew on every clipped blade of grass of the smooth lawns, and the sky met the sea in an horizon of haze that promised a heat wave.

The morning so warmed me in spirit that I took my mug of coffee direct from the kitchen, together with a thick slice of freshly baked bread generously spread with farm butter as yellow as saffron, and went up on the ramparts.

On one side, there was nothing but cliff, a strip of beach being gradually encroached by the incoming tide, and then the waste of ocean that reached to France directly ahead and to America on the right. On the other side was the desolation of moorland that flanked the home park, its horizon bounded by craggy outcrops of rock like devil's fingers (so-called by the local folk) rising out of the earth. Supping my coffee, munching on my bread-and-butter, I was able to distance myself from the world of people and abandon my thoughts to the scenes around me, and to the wine-like air, the warm sun, the utter silence broken only by the murmur of the waves on the shore below, the bird songs on high.

Alas for my brief interval of tranquillity . . .

A head appeared at the top of the staircase and, looking

round, found me. It was the footman James, one of those who were in the secret of the creature in the west tower.

'Ma'am,' he said, 'there is a Mr Arbuthnot just ridden in, who asks to see Miss Friday.'

'Is there, now?' I replied, nettled, for I had by then quite made up my mind how I was going to respond to any advances from that quarter. 'Then please convey Miss Friday's compliments to Mr Arbuthnot and tell him that she is not available.'

'Yes, ma'am.'

Peering cautiously over the edge of the battlement above the courtyard, I saw Charles standing by the pool, his horse tethered to the mounting block nearby. He was wearing a grey riding coat, and I also saw that there was a mourning band of black material around his left upper arm. Hatless, he was gazing down into the pool where the carp lazed, and tapping the side of his boot with his whip. He looked round when James emerged from the door of the keep with my answer to his request.

I was too high up to hear the exchange, nor was I well positioned to see the face of the man in the riding coat, though I clearly discerned the footman's expression as he carried out my instructions. A few moments' pause, while James listened to the other's comment, and then, bowing obsequiously, the servant turned and walked swiftly back into the keep. Charles Arbuthnot turned and resumed his contemplation of the carp.

I waited on tenterhooks for James's return. He was soon back.

'Well?' I demanded of him.

'Ma'am, Mr Arbuthnot says that he is in no hurry this morning and will happily await Miss Friday's pleasure.'

'Damn the man!' I muttered.

'Ma'am?'

'Nothing. You may go, James.'

Again, I looked over the edge. Charles Arbuthnot had seated himself on the balustrade of the pool and was calmly lighting a cigar with the air of a man who had settled himself in for the day. Fully five minutes passed as I stood in contemplation of the man who had stolen my heart and whom I now wished to be far away and out of my sight so that I could resume the business of living without thoughts of him.

But he would not go. Nor did he have the appearance of a man who had the slightest intention of leaving. It was barely nine o'clock: if he was – as he said – in no hurry that morning, he might well wait around till luncheon.

There was nothing else for it: I must confront him. Now and for ever.

I straightened my hair, wiped the crumbs of bread from the front of my dress, and on the way down glanced in all the mirrors as I passed them, remarking to myself with satisfaction that I looked not too bad and that the rigours of the previous day – and night – lay lightly upon my features.

Charles rose to his feet as I came out into the sunlight again and approached him.

'Good morning,' he said, smiling.

'Good morning, sir,' I responded.

He looked at me a trifle askance. 'Miss Friday,' he said, 'I hope I do not discern from your manner that you are still at odds with me.'

'At odds with you, sir,' I replied. 'On what score?'

'On the matter we were discussing at the garden-party,' he said. 'When I implied that the great social upheavals of this world are not to be placated simply by the widespread dispensation of a little free soup and bread.'

'I will agree to differ from you on that issue,' I responded coldly. 'It is of no importance.'

'Then there is no quarrel between us?' he asked.

I shrugged. 'Why should there be, sir?' I replied, 'since I have known nothing from you but generosity.'

He nodded, seeming to accept my word, though still casting me a doubtful glance, as well he might, for my attitude was stern and unbending.

'It was a bad business yesterday,' he said. 'And I am told that it could have been worse, since your life also was threatened. Who could have perpetrated such a dastardly crime?'

Ignoring the question, the answer to which had puzzled my

mind in vain through many dark hours, I said: 'Lady Moira's death must have come as a great shock – a tremendous blow – to those who held her dear.'

'Yes, indeed,' he replied. 'I dispatched a telegram to her mother, who lives in Italy. The poor woman doted on Moira, her only daughter, and will be distraught.'

(And are you also distraught? I wondered. And if so, why have you come to pay court to Daisy Friday? Your fiancée is not yet cold in her grave, and you are already pursuing one of 'the others'!)

'Well, I won't keep you, Mr Arbuthnot,' I said. 'No doubt you are busy arranging for your – for Lady Moira's funeral and the settling of her affairs.'

'That task has naturally fallen to me,' he said. 'And it is a burden I bear with a heavy but willing heart. I had thought, however, that when the sad obsequies are over, I might call upon you more frequently, Miss Friday.'

('More frequently' – I almost gasped aloud at his shameless effrontery. Did he really think that I was a piece of ripe fruit so ready as all that to yield to the picking? If so, he was gravely mistaken.)

'I'm afraid that will not be possible, Mr Arbuthnot,' I said. 'I have taken up charitable work of the kind you so despise, and it will occupy so much of my time in future that I shall have little opportunity for social life. It's a pity – but there it is.'

He looked at me long and hard with those deep grey eyes that had had the power to awe me right from the first, and I felt my resolve weakening and my determination trickling away like water in the palm of one's hand.

'Miss Friday,' he said evenly, 'no matter what you have said to the contrary, I am still of the opinion that you are at odds with me for some reason.'

I shrugged. 'If that is what you choose to think, there is nothing I can say to dispel the impression,' was my less than frank retort.

He unfastened his horse's rein from the ring bolt on the mounting block and gathered the leather in his hand ready to mount.

'You have learned much since you left the chain factory,' he said, 'but one thing in particular.'

'And what is that?' I asked.

'You have learned to dissemble,' he replied. 'You are no longer the young virago who spoke straight from the heart and spoke with truth no matter how much it hurt. You have learned to keep your own counsel. You have become – civilised. And in many ways, it's a pity.

'Good day to you, Miss Friday.'

With that, he sprang into the saddle, saluted me gravely with his whip, and clattered off down the path and across the drawbridge.

I watched him go with mixed feelings: with some relief, some misgivings, and much regret.

*

The inquest on the dead woman was carried out by an *ad hoc* coroner's court on the Friday following in the tiny schoolhouse in Mortmain village, the children being given the unexpected bonus of a day's holiday from lessons for the occasion; they remained throughout the proceedings with their little wide-eyed faces pressed to the windows, staring in awed puzzlement at the grown-ups playing out their elaborate and incomprehensible game of charades.

I was the first to be summoned to give my evidence and delivered it in just about as much time as my last, fateful encounter with Lady Moira Fame had taken. The coroner – that same local physician who had given me the soothing draught after the murder – quizzed me closely about the footman who had served us the champagne, but, as before, I was only able to declare that I had seen a shadow and a gloved hand. No more.

Nor did anyone else add a scruple to the weight of testimony concerning the tragedy. Sergeant Penbury read aloud from his notebook about the events I have set out. Questioned, he said yes, he had interrogated everyone present at the scene of the crime, including the agency waiters, who might be described as the only strangers at the garden-party – but to no avail. One of these men, only, had been found to have a criminal record of theft; but since he had been working in the kitchen throughout the afternoon under the close supervision of Mr Melmoth's chef, he was exonerated from all suspicion. As to the rest of the temporary servants, all declared unequivocally that they had not served champagne on the terrace to the two ladies in question – as, indeed, did Mr Melmoth's regular staff – and no witnesses could be produced to denounce any one of them as a liar.

Not much was made of the fact that my glass, also, had been poisoned, since it was apparently not within the court's brief to consider anything other than the cause of Lady Moira's death; the coroner did, however, congratulate me upon a narrow escape.

The verdict was never in any doubt, and was arrived at without any delay: 'Murder by person or persons unknown' was the formula.

They could have added: '. . . and attempted murder by the same.'

*

I had spotted Charles Arbuthnot seated among the public at the back of the court, and Jack Todd also. They were not sitting together, and as we filed out of the room, both made a move to approach me. In the slight milling of people in the playground outside the door, I deliberately allowed myself to be button-holed by the American, forestalling any possible approach by Charles Arbuthnot.

'Jack, will you escort me home, please?' I asked.

'Why, I'd be delighted,' was his reply. 'Don't you have a carriage?'

'Yes, but I feel rather upset by this morning's business,' I explained, noting from the corner of my eye that Charles Arbuthnot was watching us from the edge of the throng, but making no move to approach. 'Keep me company, do, and stay for luncheon at the castle.'

He took my arm. As we walked to my waiting carriage, we had to pass quite close by the man who had never been far from my thoughts, day and night, since I had rejected him at Mortmain. He raised his hat and wished us a grave 'good day'. Nothing more.

On the road out of the village, Jack said: 'Still interested in climbing, Daisy?'

'Of course,' I replied. 'Why do you ask, Jack?'

'I have in mind a rather spectacular, but not too difficult project,' he said, 'and wondered if you'd care to join me.'

'Tell me about it,' I said, eager for distraction, grateful for anything – anything – to drive away the image of those dark grey eyes that had been fixed upon me back at the schoolhouse.

'Well, a piece down the coast,' said Jack, 'there's a rather spectacular pillar of rock close inshore and surrounded by the sea at high tide. Folks call it "Old Jacob". It's around two hundred feet high and really no great climb – just enough to frighten off the kids and the tyros, but well within your capabilities as I've observed you, Daisy. Like to join me?'

'I'd love to, Jack,' I said, and I meant it. My need, after what had happened, was to *do* something, to get away, to throw myself into some kind of activity. Already I had extended my charitable enterprise by writing to six more orphanages and workhouses and presenting them with my proposition for donating 'Useful Soup'; but this was rather like sitting in the dress circle and watching other people perform; what I needed was to become personally involved in something – and climbing presented itself as a challenge: myself against nature.

'Well, that's bully,' said Jack enthusiastically. 'The point is that "Old Jacob" is a miniature version of a much more forbidding pillar up in the Orkneys called "The Old Man of Hoy", which really is a challenge to an experienced climber. The "Old Man" 's all of four hundred and fifty feet high and I intend to lick him before I finish my stint at the embassy and go back to the Fleet.' He grinned. 'Maybe you'd like to come up to the Orkneys and see me make the attempt, Daisy.'

'I don't know about that,' I replied. 'But, tell me, Jack, how far away from here is "Old Jacob"?'

'Oh, three – four miles. Why, Daisy?'

'Jack, take me to see him!' I cried. 'Now!'

'Why, sure,' he replied, and suited the word to the action. 'Driver, take the next turning right and follow the cliff road westwards. Do you know "Old Jacob"? Right – that's who we're off to see. Stop on the cliff-top right above him, will you?'

He sat back in his seat, grinned at me like a little boy off on a treat, and squeezed my hand companionably.

This is better, I thought. No need to run to the far ends of the earth to escape from my faceless enemy; this is good enough: to be with someone whom one can trust, who makes no demands, who is the perfect antidote to that pair of searching grey eyes and a hopeless love for a man who regards me as just one of 'the others'. Who will protect me.

Three miles or so along the barren cliffs, with the grey sea crawling below, the narrow road turned sharply towards the cliff edge and the coachman drew rein and pointed. Jack helped me to alight and we walked to the very lip of the abyss and looked down.

Far below us, the Atlantic breakers lashed the foot of the high point upon which we stood, for though the day was calm, there is never stillness in the seas around that coast: the great waves crashed against the granite base, clawed with long white fingers to ascend, retreated in frustration and were engulfed by those that followed.

' "Old Jacob"!' said Jack, pointing.

A short distance from the base of the point, and entirely surrounded by foaming water that beat and lashed upon it from all sides, was a tall pinnacle of rock which, though scarcely half the height of our own promontory, had, by reason of its awesome isolation, a forbidding majesty all its own. The very notion of going down there and setting foot upon its flattened summit seemed an effrontery that flew in the very face of Nature and could only court certain disaster.

'We'll start just before the high tide,' said Jack laconically. 'While the sea's coming in over the sand and we can walk out there. By the time we reach the top, "Old Jacob" will be isolated like he is now, and we can sit up there and eat our sandwiches with the whole big Atlantic going crazy all round us. Then, when the tide goes out, we climb down and walk away dryshod. How does that strike you, Miss Friday, ma'am?'

The delightful simplicity and practicality of his plan drove away all my fears. Suddenly, 'Old Jacob' was placed in his proper dimension, and I could not wait to conquer him.

'When, Jack?' I asked. '*When?*'

'Would tomorrow suit?' he asked. 'To hit the tides right, we'd have to start around about a quarter of an hour before high water, which will mean beginning the climb at half past nine in the morning. That too early for you?'

Too early for pampered Daisy Friday? I thought of the freezing cold dawns back in the chain factory at Mordwenn and could have laughed in his dear, earnest face. Instead, I said: 'No, that will be splendid, Jack. Let's go!'

*

It was too late to go all the way back to the castle for luncheon and we were both hungry from the bracing fresh air, so we had an al fresco meal at a public house called the 'Goat and Compasses' in a nearby hamlet: bread-and-cheese washed down with strong dry cider out of a barrel; and Jack told me about his forebears and his upbringing. His father was a major in the Federal army who had been killed in front of Chattanooga, and his widowed mother had had to go out as a scrub woman to rear her infant son; and there they both might have stayed – as Jack himself put it: 'At the bottom of the heap' – but for the advent of an old admirer of Mrs Todd, who courted and married the widow and took the son as his own. Though raised in the mid-West and never setting eyes on the sea till he was sixteen, the first glimpse of the wild ocean lapping the shores of the eastern seaboard inspired the young Jack Todd to follow a naval career.

'I went to sea in a training ship,' he said, as we sat beneath a tree in the pub garden and sipped soda water. 'You wouldn't believe the spiritual experience of first clinging to the top-trees of a full-rigged ship in an Atlantic gale. I was scared to hell and wished myself anywhere but where I was. Yet all the time, I knew I was in the right job. And so it was.'

He's a nice man, I told myself, and it isn't only the strong cider that's making me maudlin. He'll look after me and keep me safe while ever he's here in Cornwall.

And I said: 'I think I'd better be getting back to the castle. They'll wonder where I've got to. I'll drop you off at the "Blue Boar" on the way back, Jack.'

'Sure,' he said. 'And we'd better get an early night. We've a hard day ahead of us tomorrow, Daisy.'

*

I had written to Giles Treacher extending my deep sympathy over poor Mr Caldecott's cruel end and wishing Giles a speedy recovery from his own injury. There was a letter from him waiting for me on my arrival back at the castle later that afternoon:

Dear Daisy [it read],
Thank you for your kind thoughts. Caldecott's funeral was on Tuesday. A quiet ceremony, with only a few friends and the people from the chambers who have worked with the old fellow all these years. A good man who made a fine, brave end. I pray that the blackguard who did for him will speedily be brought to justice.

The theft of the papers from the briefcase means that I shall have to prepare another set for your signature and it is imperative that you do this at an early occasion. Accordingly, I am proposing to travel down to Cornwall on Monday next and will be at the castle around midday. If you are going to be away on that day, or if it will be inconvenient for any other reason, would you please send me a telegram to that effect?

Trusting that you are well.
Your sincere friend,
Giles T—

P.S. I read in the press about the curious murder of Lady Moira Fame. Most mysterious and the newspapers are not saying much about it. Perhaps you will be able to enlighten me when we meet.

*

I had arranged to be woken the following morning at six o'clock. Shades of Mordwenn chain factory! The day was blustery and threatening rain, though the sun broke through the clouds while I was breakfasting in my sitting room, and I saw the far headland bathed in a shaft of heavenly light, and a million diamonds sparkling in the boisterous sea as the sun touched each separate wavelet.

I wore my knickerbockers, a thick jersey and a short tweed jacket, a pair of boots like Jack's, which my friend had purchased for me in Truro, and a Tam o' Shanter bonnet. My hair I screwed into a plait at the back, and I put cold cream on my face to protect the skin from sun and salt water. Thus attired and girt-about with a haversack containing my luncheon of ham sandwiches, Cornish pasty, a rather sleepy last year's apple, and a flask of soda water, I set off on my adventure.

As the carriage took me out of the courtyard, I could not drag my gaze away from the west tower, from the shuttered windows on the top floor, behind which the poor creature who dared not show his hideous countenance was doomed, through my charity, to eke out his days in solitary darkness . . .

Jack was waiting for me, as arranged, at the junction with the cliff road. He was in Norfolk jacket, breeches, climbing boots and cap, and carried a coil of stout rope like a bandolier over one shoulder.

'Looking forward to it?' He grinned as he got into the carriage.

I nodded eagerly.

'I had a word with the coastguard in the pub last night,' he said. 'He's an old salt. Knows this coast like his own front parlour. He says that the rain will hold off, but it'll be windy on top of "Old Jacob". Good thing you're well wrapped up, Daisy.'

We came presently to the point that looked down upon our quarry. 'Old Jacob' was quite different standing in his plot of smooth white sand, with the encroaching sea a good fifty yards away, but coming on in slowly advancing lines, every new surge bringing the edge of the great ocean implacably nearer.

I dismissed the coachman, telling him to pick us up at the 'Goat and Compasses' at six o'clock that evening. There were rough-cut steps in the face of the cliff, down which we descended to the beach. Once on the level with 'Old Jacob' 's base, the full import of our enterprise struck me most forceably: it was an awesomely towering and difficult-looking climb, and – at least from where I was standing – not a hand and foothold in sight.

'Are we really going to go up there?' I asked.

Jack laughed. 'We'll walk it,' he said. 'Taking it easy all the way, using the rope and with plenty of rests, we shall be at the top well before noon. After that, it's a lazy lunch, and all downhill after. Come on, Daisy, or the sea will beat us to it.'

Indeed, the first wavelets were lapping the seaward base of the great pillar as Jack – acting as leader – set first foot on the towering shaft of granite and hauled himself up to his initial handhold. Two more lifts and he was six feet up. I, roped behind him, waited till he signalled me, and then followed his course precisely. Ten minutes later, when he called the first halt for a brief rest on a narrow ledge upon which you could scarcely have set a window box, we looked down upon our labours to see that the hungry waters had now entirely surrounded our abode and were continuing their inexorable progress up the sand to the cliff base – a process I watched with mixed feelings: on the one hand, we were now committed to the climb, and on the other, we had become the prisoners of the sea, condemned to cling to our inhospitable pillar of rock till the conjunction of time and tide set us free.

'On we go,' said Jack, and, echoing my own thoughts: 'The exit door has just slammed in our faces!'

The first fifty feet or so of the great pillar afforded more hand and footholds than struck one at first sight. This was caused by the action of the sea in scouring away the weaker parts of the granite face to leave crevices and indentations. Nevertheless Jack, who dictated the pace, moved slowly and cautiously – for my sake, of course – picking his upward route with tremendous care and not hesitating to change direction sideways if he saw a better option; carefully securing the rope through the pins that he hammered into fissures in the rock, he paused to watch and assist me every time I followed his last move. In this manner, we came to yet another miniscule ledge and took another rest.

'How are you doing?' he asked.

'Better than I had hoped,' I answered. 'Oh, Jack – just look down there. The sea's coming after us!'

Sure enough, the boisterous waves, now entirely the masters of the space separating the pillar from the mainland, were surging in a boiling maelstrom immediately below us, and reaching upwards with every new assault, so that the foaming spindrift splattered the rock face not ten feet below where we clung.

It was at that moment I knew the compulsive fascination of climbing: the deliberate courting of danger in the most bizarre circumstances, so that the mind is cleansed of all lesser fears and idle imaginings, and there is only the harsh reality of living or dying – with the choice in one's own hands, and in the exercise of one's own skills. And with that revelation, I was cleansed of all my other fears.

'The next part will be more difficult,' said Jack. 'From here on, the sea never reaches, even in the high spring tides. Watch your step, and remember, Daisy – you can't come to a lot of harm if you simply do nothing.'

He was right. No longer had the questing fingers of the sea scored nooks and crannies out of the granite; the rock was smooth and sun-baked from time immemorial. Nevertheless, Jack's expert eye discerned every small indentation, each miniscule fault, which he put to good use. The going was slow, but we made gradual progress. At one stage, we entirely circled the pillar without advancing upwards, till my leader found the path he sought. After about an hour's climbing, we had come through the worst of a nearly vertical section that had been almost totally devoid of hand and footholds. Jack was kneeling on the edge of a slight inward slope which would afford us another rest. I was climbing up to meet him. He was holding the rope that joined us, gathering it in as I came closer.

One more step to go. I was reaching up for the last handhold. And then – *it happened . . .!*

CRA-A-A-KK!

Something struck the rock close by my head: I was immediately showered by splinters.

I screamed. My foot slipped.

Next instant, I was dangling on the end of the rope with the boiling sea a hundred feet beneath me.

'Be still!' cried Jack. 'Don't struggle!'

He was holding the rope, which was stretched taut between my armpits and the pin hammered into the rock above his head.

'Now,' he said, in a very calm voice, 'reach up your hands, Daisy, and just as soon as you can get a hold, grab it. Take it easy now.'

Slowly, inch by inch, he lifted me, bracing himself against one foot only, which he jammed against the rock, the hobnailed heel biting against the unyielding granite. Inch by inch, I rose, till it seemed to me that I might be able to reach a handhold. I stretched further. My fingertips touched. Then my palms. Then I was part-supporting myself.

'Easy, Daisy,' muttered Jack. 'We've nearly got you.'

The blessed moment came when my feet scrabbled, slipped, scrabbled again – and found holds. Jack let go of the rope and, putting his hands under my armpits, dragged me to safety.

Panting, I took my place beside him.

'What – what happened?' I breathed.

'It's my opinion that . . .' he began.

CRA-A-A-KK!

Another sharp report – it came from the cliff. Instants later, there was a slamming impact nearby, and a flying chip of granite tore a scarlet furrow across Jack's hand.

'Duck your head down, Daisy!' he cried. '*We're being shot at!*'

*

A whole minute passed by, and me with my face pressed closely to the rock, so closely that I could see every particle of the hard-textured granite and the subtle discolourations limned there by the passing millennia. Neither of us spoke during that time, but waited for another report that might herald the end of one or both of us.

Presently, Jack raised his head and looked round towards the towering clifftop. I followed his gaze. There was no sign of anyone up there, but there was plenty of tumbled rock and dark gullies – enough cover for a company of soldiers.

'Maybe he's shot his bolt,' said my companion. 'Maybe he's just waiting till we make better targets. In any event, I reckon the sooner we put "Old Jacob" betwixt us and him, the better. Come on, Daisy. Let's move.'

So saying, he edged his way along the slight slope towards the seaward end, and I followed after, consciously shrinking inside myself, hideously aware that my unprotected back was turned towards the hidden marksman.

CRA-A-A-AKK!

'*Down!*' shouted Jack. And we both flattened ourselves against the granite. Something slashed close overhead with the sound of an angry hornet. Another shot followed. The bullet struck rock and screamed away into the high blue sky.

'That feller means business!' said Jack. 'Take my hand, Daisy.'

I obeyed him, and he bundled me ahead of him, paying out the rope between us. As I edged forward, it suddenly came to me that his intent had been my preservation: the gallant American was now shielding me with his own body.

Only one more shot was fired – and missed – before we swung round a craggy edge and had placed 'Old Jacob' between ourselves and our would-be assassin. We were safe – provided we stayed where we were.

It was a quarter to eleven in the morning.

Low tide – low enough for us to get off the pinnacle and retrace our steps to the cliff – was due in about four hours' time.

*

I bound his wounded hand with my handkerchief. We settled down to make the best of our enforced halt. Jack rigged up a cat's cradle of rope suspended from four pins hammered into the rock above our heads, from which he hung two loops of rope upon which we were able to sit in a fair degree of comfort and complete safety.

From time to time, he took a cautious peep round the angle of the rock to scan the shore. On two occasions, his appearance was greeted by a shot from our enemy.

'He's still there,' was Jack's grim comment. 'It remains to be seen if he'll stay till low tide.'

'If he comes down on to the beach when the sea's gone out, he'll be able to pick us off like flies on a wall,' I ventured.

'That had also occurred to me,' replied my companion. 'We shall have to make dispositions to meet the occasion, Daisy.'

Jack was not to be drawn any further upon what 'dispositions' he had in mind, but suggested that it might be a suitable hour for refreshment; accordingly, we opened up our haversacks and offered each other a taste of the comestibles therein. I accepted a very thick slice of polony sausage from Jack's hoard, he took a Cornish pasty from me, and we both drank from my soda water. In this manner, slung on a piece of rope halfway up a 200-foot granite pillar in south Cornwall, with the Atlantic surf raging below me and an implacable enemy waiting not far distant to put a bullet through my head, did I partake of what has surely been so far – and I devoutly hope will for ever be – the most bizarre meal of my life.

'Who is he, do you think?' asked Jack, when we had had our fill.

'The man with the gun – if man it is?'

'Who else?'

'The same who poisoned Lady Moira. The same whose real intent, I'm convinced, was really to poison me,' I replied. 'The fact that he – or it still might be a she – thought to ensure success by putting prussic acid in *both* glasses is proof of the killer's utter ruthlessness.'

'Why is he trying to kill you, Daisy?'

'Because of my inheritance. I've thought about it long and hard, but there is nothing else in my life – nothing – that could possibly warrant the attention this man has given me. That's what I think, and that's what Sergeant Penbury thinks. And this will be the fourth attempt he's made to kill me, Jack.'

'Very neatly contrived, too,' said my companion wryly. 'One clean shot at each of us and we'd have fallen down there and never have been seen again. The Atlantic doesn't yield up the dead – not along this coast.'

I shuddered at the thought.

'Cold?' he asked.

'That, also,' I admitted. 'Your coastguard was right – it *is* windy on "Old Jacob" today.'

'Come closer to me,' said Jack. And when I did so, he put an arm around my shoulder and drew me to him. 'That better – warmer?'

I nodded.

'Put your head on my shoulder and try to rest,' he said. 'We've got quite a while to wait yet and there's no point in getting all het up. So long as it's flood tide, we're as safe as if we were back home by the fireside.'

I obeyed him, grateful for his strength and comfort. It is possible, even, that I may have dozed off; in any event, it seemed that scarcely any time passed before he roused me and said: 'The tide's going out now, Daisy. Here's where we start making our special dispositions.'

*

Jack re-rigged us both to a single rope, with which we made a descent to sea level. By this time, the tide was running out fast; my companion dipped the toe of his boot in the water and I marvelled to see the great swirl of wake as the torrent surged past it. Next, to my surprise, he stooped and took off his boots, tied the laces together and hung them round his neck.

'You – you're not going to try to swim?' I cried. 'Not in – *this*!'

He nodded. 'Just as soon as the tide-race slackens,' he said. 'Which it will in the latter part of the ebb. By then, the water will be under six feet deep between here and the shoreline – I'll practically be able to wade all the way.'

'But – what are you going to *do*, Jack?' I demanded.

'Like we said, if our friend comes down on to the beach when the tide's out, we don't have a chance. So I'm going to carry the attack into his camp and surprise him. On the other hand, I may find him gone.'

And, despite my entreaties, he was not to be dissuaded, nor would he discuss the matter further.

Another ten minutes or so passed. Without a word, Jack

unhitched himself from the rope and lowered himself into the water. It reached to his shoulders, and, despite the slackening of the flow, he appeared to have some difficulty in remaining upright.

He looked up at me and grinned. 'Wish me luck,' he said. 'Come to think of it, wish us both luck.'

And then, ducking head and shoulders under water, he was gone. One stockinged foot broke surface briefly as he kicked out in the direction of the shore, round the bulk of 'Old Jacob' 's craggy base; there was a flash of tweed suiting as he showed once more – and then he was gone from my sight, leaving me sick at heart with anxiety for his safety.

Minutes slipped by, and not an instant when I did not expect the air to be split by the crack of gunfire – but none came. The level of the water was receding fast, and I could see small fish nosing about the sandy bottom. Finally, I could bear it no longer and, freeing myself of the rope, let myself go and landed knee-deep in the Atlantic. It was as cold as any ice.

'DAI-SY!' The call came from the shore, and it was Jack's voice. I waded clear of 'Old Jacob', and saw his tall figure standing on the clifftop, waving wildly to me.

'It's all right – he's gone!' he shouted.

Then I was wading, running through the swirling waters with joy, relief and release. Jack came down the steps to greet me as I stumbled on to the sand; wrapped his arms about me and held me tight.

'Oh, Jack – I was so worried for you.'

'There was no call for it,' he said. 'I swam and crawled under water almost to the shoreline. If he'd been here, I might have got him, but he was gone. And only these to mark his passing . . .'

In the palm of his hand he held what I took to be a pile of empty cartridge cases. 'Rifle cartridges,' said Jack. 'A military rifle at a guess. This fellow means business.'

'What now, Jack?' I asked him.

'Your carriage will be here at six,' he said. 'I propose that we repair to the "Goat and Compasses" and there avail ourselves of a little of Scotland's famous specific for driving away colds, chills, and the doubts, fears and regrets that trouble the heart and mind of Man.'

Later, in the bar parlour of the pub, seated before a blazing log fire that the landlord, seeing our condition, had insisted on lighting in the huge open grate, and sipping a hot toddy, a thought occurred to me.

'Jack,' I said, 'how could that man have possibly known that we were going to attempt "Old Jacob" today? Really, I sometimes think that he has super-human powers of perception. He seems to know everything I'm going to do in advance!'

My companion pulled a long lip and looked shamefaced. 'I have to confess to you, Daisy,' said he, 'that the fault lies with me.'

'How so?'

'Well, I was in the bar at the "Blue Boar" last night,' he said, 'and talking to the coastguard, as I told you. But I made no attempt to keep my voice down, and the bar was crowded. It was market day in Mortmain village, you see, and there were a lot of men from out of the district, as well as the locals. In other words . . .'

'In other words,' I supplied, 'my secret enemy could quite likely have been standing at your very elbow last night.'

'That's about the size of it,' said Jack ruefully.

*

We scarcely spoke to each other in the carriage on the way back. I delivered Jack to the front door of the 'Blue Boar' and went on my way to the castle. Driving somewhere between the village and the home park, with the towers of Mortmain coming in sight above the trees, a light broke in upon my dark thoughts, the scales fell from my eyes, and I saw quite clearly where the solution to my dilemma lay.

One man, and one man only, held the key. And I, Daisy Friday, would wrench that key from him. At once.

Immediately upon my arrival, I went straight to my sitting room and penned a curt telegram, which I then gave to a footman with instructions to drive to Truro and have it dispatched right away. The message was to Giles Treacher in Dorchester. It read:

I HAVE DISCOVERED ALL. TO BLAZES WITH MONDAY. YOU WILL COME
IMMEDIATELY, AND THAT IS AN ORDER = DAISY FRIDAY

The telegraph service in the West Country proved to be of
such a high order that a reply came only shortly after dinner
while I was preparing for an early bed after my gruelling day. I
read it with some wry amusement:

CATCHING FIRST TRAIN AVAILABLE TOMORROW. I BEG YOU DO NO-
THING, CONFIDE IN NO ONE, TILL I HAVE EXPLAINED EVERYTHING =
DEVOTEDLY GILES

In spite of all, I slept well that night, better than I had for
nights, safe in the knowledge that, by a subterfuge on my part,
the cat was already halfway out of the bag, and poor Giles
Treacher was falling over himself in his anxiety to reveal
everything to me. But why, I asked, composing myself for
slumber, was he so adamant that I must not reveal my supposed 'discovery' to anyone? Well, I should have the answer to
that also, soon enough; by reference to the railway time-table, I
estimated that Giles would be at the castle by noon.

As it turned out, he was preceded by another visitor – a
visitor both unexpected and dearly welcome.

*

'Florrie! Florrie, dearest – how are you?'

'My sweet Daisy. Let me look at you. (Shame on you,
Wink-Wink! How could you snap at dear Daisy, who has
always been so kind to you and given you titbits and taken you
walkies etcetera?)

'Ah, my dear, the Cornish air suits you very well. There is
quite a bloom in your cheeks.'

'Oh, but it's so nice to see you, Florrie,' I said, hugging her
but keeping well clear of Wink-Wink this time. 'Why didn't you
write me you were coming? I would have driven to Truro to
meet you.'

'It happened upon the spur of the moment, my dear,' she
replied. 'Yesterday afternoon, I was still happily ensconced at

my favourite retreat of St Brigid's, near Sidmouth. Just before compline, I had an altercation with Reverend Mother. In no time at all, I had packed my bags and was on my way back to Bath post-haste. This morning, I woke up with the compulsion to come and see you – particularly after what Mrs O'Grady told me over my breakfast tray about the dreadful end of Lady Moira Fame. I hasten to add that I knew nothing of the tragedy till then. The nuns of St Brigid's live by a very strict rule, and newspapers are not permitted within the convent's confines. I much doubt if they will be apprised of the Second Coming till it has both come and gone, but what can you expect of a Reverend Mother who becomes quite hysterical on discovering that one of her paying guests keeps a little bottle of whisky in her cell for medicinal purposes?

'I digress . . .

'Daisy, tell me – is it true that you, yourself, came within an ace of sharing Lady Moira's terrible fate – or is that just newspaper hysteria aided by idle gossip?'

'It's quite true, Florrie,' I told her.

My friend drew a deep breath and closed her eyes in anguish. 'Oh, merciful heavens!' she breathed. 'What is happening to the modern world when a young gel of means and property cannot rise from her bed in the morning with the certain knowledge that she will retire whole and hearty to the same at night, and not be assassinated by nihilists and revolutionaries?' She laid a hand on my arm and gazed at me in considerable anxiety. 'I take it that the cowardly murder was the work of nihilists and revolutionaries?' she quizzed me. 'Put my mind at ease on that score, for I declare that I could not rest easy in my mind if I thought that *ordinary* folk, as opposed to nihilists and revolutionaries, went around poisoning young gels of means and property for no discernable reason.'

Amused despite myself, I said: 'There *is* a reason behind it all, Florrie, and it has nothing to do with nihilism and revolution.'

She clutched my arm more tightly, and Wink-Wink growled in his throat. 'Then who – *who*?' she demanded.

'As to who, we may not soon discover, Florrie,' I replied. 'As to *why*, I have every hope of learning the answer to that question' – and I looked across at the pretty French ormolu clock that discreetly ticked upon the chimneypiece of my sitting room – 'some time after midday. And I promise you, Florrie, that you, my very dear friend, will be present as a witness when the tale is unfolded.'

'Aaaah!' she breathed, awed.

'And now,' I said brightly. 'Let us have some coffee and you can tell me how you fared during your retreat – discounting your contretemps with the Reverend Mother concerning the medicinal whisky. Was the experience valuable, Florrie? Did you come to any conclusions, during your meditations, about the imperfectability of the human state?'

'I came to certain very definite conclusions about the Reverend Mother,' she retorted tartly, and Wink-Wink barked his approbation.

*

I had sent a carriage to pick up Giles Treacher from Truro station. At seven minutes past twelve by my fob watch (which I had been consulting every five minutes for the last hour), there came the crunch of wheels and hooves on the gravel outside. Looking down, I saw the lawyer alight, carrying a briefcase under his arm. I had instructed them to usher him straight up to my sitting room. He was not long in coming. My first impression was of a frightened man – and I thought I saw in this an advantage to me in the game of bluff which I was about to enter into with him.

'Good day to you, Giles,' I said, offering my hand.

'Hu-hello, Daisy,' he faltered. 'How are you?' He looked anxiously towards Florrie, who sat looking very regal on the sofa with Wink-Wink quietly snarling at the newcomer. 'How do you do, Lady Wimsey-Fildes,' he said doubtfully.

'Mr Treacher,' she responded, graciously inclining her head.

'Her ladyship will remain with us during our conversation,' I informed him.

'But – but . . .' he began in protest.

'That is my wish!' I declared.

224

He gestured towards Florrie. 'But – um – have you – have you . . .?'

'I have told her ladyship nothing,' I retorted. And sat down, leaving him standing with his briefcase still under his arm. 'Now, Giles, where to begin? Shall be begin by determining *your* part in the mystery surrounding my inheritance? For instance, concerning the account of how your late friend Mr Venables, bereaved of beloved wife and daughter, sought around for a suitable young woman upon whom to bequeath his fortune of one and a half million pounds, and whose eyes just happened to light upon Daisy Friday. That account is not entirely true, is it?

'*Is* it, Mr Treacher?'

'Parts – parts of it are true,' he faltered weakly.

'*Parts* of it,' I repeated. 'Like the curate's egg! Tell me, has Sergeant Penbury of the Devon and Cornwall Constabulary approached you concerning the source of my inheritance – as he informed me he so intended?'

'Yes, he has.'

'And you gave him the same account as the one you gave me – Mr Venables and all that?'

'Substantially – yes. That was the account I gave the sergeant.'

'Substantially. I see.' I looked at him searchingly for a few moments, and added: 'Am I correct in assuming that your part in this affair – in telling me a part-truth concerning my inheritance – might well land you in trouble with the Law on a charge of misrepresentation?' (I was skating on very thin ice here, since my slender knowledge of law was derived solely from a volume in Meg Wolfingham's precious book box entitled *A Layman's Primer of Contract & Tort*.)

Poor Giles flinched at that; but the direct challenge seemed to sharpen his resolve – which was not at all what I aimed for; rather, I wished to add to his discomforture. In the event, he straightened himself up, took a deep breath and answered firmly and frankly:

'I think not, Daisy. Not at this stage and after the passing of so much time. However, if this affair ever became public property, it is not beyond the bounds of possibility that I might be struck off the rolls as a solicitor for unprofessional conduct.'

'Oh, dear!' I exclaimed, and meant it. 'I think you'd better sit down, Giles, and tell me all about it.'

So he did.

*

'In the first place, Daisy, Jamie Venables was not your benefactor, though all the other details I confided in you were accurate and truthful in every particular, to wit: Jamie's late marriage to a younger woman, the daughter of his old age whom he idolised, the tragic deaths of his loved ones, his wish to settle his quite considerable fortune upon a worthy person or persons. To coin a metaphor, Daisy, these matters were the bricks and mortar with which I fabricated an edifice that was part-substance, part-illusion.'

'But why did you *need* to deceive me?' I asked. 'And why, before he died, did Mr Venables need to come to Westchester to look me over and take my measure as a person?'

He said: 'To confirm that you were indeed the worthy person that had been represented to us; worthy enough to justify the quite considerable risk of public disgrace and obloquy that would descend upon we two conspirators – and others – if our conspiracy failed.'

'And what conspiracy was this, Giles?' I asked.

'You don't know a thing, do you, Daisy?' he asked quietly. 'The telegram was a trap, was it not?'

'A trap – yes, Giles,' I admitted. 'But you will tell me all, nevertheless. What was – is – this conspiracy?'

He rose and, walking over to one of the windows, looked out across the castle courtyard. Hands loosely clasped behind his back, he replied to my question without looking round.

'It concerns your parentage, Daisy,' he said. 'Your father, the only son of a proud and arrogant couple, both of impeccable lineage and tremendous fortune, had the temerity to – in the phrase of the snobbish – "marry beneath him", for which reason, his parents swore that he would never touch another penny of the family fortune while they lived – and they kept their word.'

'Who was my father?' I asked tremulously.

He ignored the question, and continued his tale: 'To be brief, the news of your father's untimely death almost exactly co-incided with that of your birth, Daisy. Your young mother, distraught, brought her baby to the grandparents in the hope of softening their hearts – in vain. They drove mother and infant from their door and told the wretched widow to go back to the gutter where she was reared and take her brat with her (I quote their very words, which they quite unashamedly recounted to their friends in polite society).'

'Monsters!' ejaculated Florrie Wimsey-Fildes. 'Insensate brutes! That such people should be alive and hold such views in the nineteenth century!'

'Go on, Giles,' I urged him. 'What then?'

'The young mother, weighed down with grief and never very strong, took the consumption,' said Giles. 'It was of the chronic or galloping variety and she lingered only a few weeks. At her death, the parish authorities approached the grandparents with a view to them taking in the child. I – I am reluctant to continue, Daisy . . .'

'Tell me all, Giles,' I said.

'Surprisingly, the grandparents received the child into their home, and seemingly with a good grace. But that was merely a subterfuge to cover a vile intent. In due course, they cast the infant out; but they did worse than that: with the influence that their wealth and position enabled them to exercise, they caused the baby to disappear from the county of Somerset, and to re-appear as a nameless foundling in mid-Dorset.'

'At the parish orphanage,' I said slowly. 'And after that the chain factory.'

'That is so, Daisy.'

'Who was my father, Giles?'

Disregarding my question, he turned and walked the length of the room to the fireplace, turned, and went back down again; he seemed to be assembling his thoughts, for his mouth formed silent words, his brow was furrowed in concentration, and his hands, still clasped behind his back, tapped nervously one against the other.

227

Presently, he resumed his tale: 'Your father was abroad when news came that he had had a dreadful accident and was dying. Your mother, who was near her time – indeed, the baby was already overdue – was totally unable to make the journey, so she pleaded with Jamie Venables and me to hasten to his bedside to comfort his last hours and bear the promise of her undying love. We, your father's friends, who esteemed him above all others, departed without hesitation.'

'And were you – in time?' I asked.

He nodded gravely. 'We were in time,' he said, and treated me to a long and searching glance, following upon which he again set about pacing the room; while I watched, every nerve in my body screaming out for him to resume his story – which in time he did.

'There then came the matter of making financial provision for his wife and child. The family estate and fortune being entailed, it would normally have passed from his parents to him on their deaths, and there was nothing they could do to prevent it. They, however, still lived – and for a considerable while longer. Till, in fact, Daisy, you had been missing for – I think I am right in saying – around seventeen years.

'However, with the death of the old people, and the entailed estate passing to the heir – which was you, Daisy – Venables and I redoubled our efforts to locate this child who, due to the vile machinations of the grandparents, had been deprived of her true identity and bundled out of the way so deviously that it was as if she had disappeared from the face of the earth.

'It took years – years – to find you, Daisy. And then, having done so, Jamie Venables and I brought you, by devious means, to your rightful inheritance.'

For the third time, I framed the question that was uppermost in my mind: 'Giles, on my knees, I beg you to tell me and keep me in suspense no longer – *who was my father?*'

'Yes, Mr Treacher,' interposed Florrie. 'Who – *who*? For pity's sake do not torture the poor gel any further.'

For answer, Giles laid a hand on my shoulder and gazed into my eyes. 'Your father, Daisy,' he said, 'was one of the finest, bravest, truest men I have ever known. Older than I, he was both father and brother to me. My guide and my mentor. For him – or for any of his loved ones – I would give my all, fly to the uttermost ends of the earth. Furthermore, I would lie, cheat, deceive, dissemble, perjure myself – and with a clear conscience. Such was the quality of your father, and such the loyalty that he inspired in his friends.

'His name – Bravingdon. Major Tom Bravingdon.'

'The mountaineer!' I cried.

I stood aghast. Stupefied with shock. Somewhere from afar, Florrie was saying: 'What a revelation! I knew the Major well by sight, though we were not acquainted. Oh, the tragedy of his death. The whole country mourned him, you know. The very embodiment of the parfit gentil knight, *sans peur et sans reproche*. Oh, I had always thought that dear Daisy was descended from the very highest and most noble – but I could not have imagined – this!'

I found myself saying: 'Giles, you may imagine how proud and happy this news has made me. That I am no longer a parish foundling with a made-up name, but the daughter of a national hero. To me, it is all the difference between being alive and half-alive, acceptable and an outcast, myself and an enigma.

'But Giles – Giles – for mercy's sake, for the sake of the esteem in which you claim to hold me, for the friendship that has grown up between us, a friendship that led to poor Mr Caldecott's death and so nearly to yours – why did you not tell me that my dead father was Tom Bravingdon?'

He did not reply for a long time, and when he did, his voice was hoarse with emotion and so near to tears that I would as lief have interrupted him as silence a penitent on his death bed.

'Tom and his party of four disappeared into the mists of the upper Jügspitz with ample time to reach the summit – if that proved to be possible – and make the descent before nightfall. Next morning, the villagers found the bodies of Tom's four companions at the foot of the mountain. Tom they found some time after, on the glacier above. Dreadfully injured and dying. The following day, in response to Annie Bravingdon's plea, Jamie Venables and I were on our way to Munich by express train in the hope of being with him at the end.

'We found him – alive. But in such a state that one would have wished him dead a thousand times over. The headlong tumble down the cruel slope of the glacier – a thousand feet of ice studded with frozen knives – had not mercifully been terminated, as it had in the case of his companions, by a sheer, killing drop over the precipice at the end. No, he had lain all that night with his wounds, the bleeding staunched because the wounds had frozen. And, added to that, came the long night of frostbite, delirium – and madness.

'Such was the state in which we found him when we came to that hospice in the Bavarian Alps. Alive – where a lesser man would have perished up there on that glacier. His very strength of will, the courage that triumphed even over the madness, had reserved him for a torture more fiendish than the mind of perverted man could ever have devised.'

He was silent. I shuddered. Away in the corner of my vision, I heard Florrie quietly sobbing.

'It's to be hoped that he – my father – didn't suffer for very much longer after you came to him,' I said, 'and that your presence was a comfort to him at the end.'

Giles shook his head. 'I have to tell you, Daisy,' he said sadly, 'that he never, by look or by word, gave the slightest sign of recognising me.

'Nor ever will.'

The import of his last declaration took some moments to assemble itself, and when it did, I still could not believe what I thought I had heard. I stared at Giles, who was looking at me in a most odd manner: head on one side, eyes guarded, watchful, defensive.

'*What* did you say?' I breathed.

'I said in effect that your father, Major Tom Bravingdon, will never recognise me,' he replied.

'*Will* never . . .?'

There was utter silence. Florrie had ceased to weep.

'Your father still lives,' said Giles. 'But it is a burden of life I would not have wished upon any creature of this earth.'

Alive!

Still alive!

And then, like a great drum-roll from out of a dark forest, the knowledge burst in upon me, and I was running from that room and out into the winding stairs and the twisting corridors; out into the sunlight and across the green grass, with passing servants staring after me in wild speculation of my state.

The door of the west tower was unlocked and ajar. I raced up the steps, two at a time, to the top floor. Mrs Steeple was coming out of the door with a tray of broken food scraps and an empty bowl. Her eyes widened with alarm to see me and read the truth and resolve in my expression. She put out a hand to check my progress, but I thrust it aside.

'No, ma'am – no!' she entreated. 'Leave it to us. There's nothing you can do – nothing!'

The room beyond was in deep shadow from the shuttered window. Nothing had changed since I was last there, save that little Phoebe was sitting on the single chair by the table, and there was a humped form in the shadows of the iron bedstead, lying there.

Upon my entrance, the child looked up, and, seeing me, leapt to her feet and ran towards me, eyes wild.

'Hello, Phoebe,' I said placatingly, assuming that I had alarmed her in some way. 'Don't worry. There's nothing to worry about.'

And then, she spoke – or, more precisely, she screamed:
'*Go away! You shan't hurt him! He's my friend!*'

'Oh merciful heaven!' came Mrs Steeple's voice at my elbow. 'That I should ever hear words pass her dear lips again!' And she was on her knees beside the child, pressing that small head to her wasted bosom, keening and crying to her, rocking back and forth.

I left them; took a few more paces forward and stood beside the bed, screwing up my resolve, framing the first words in my mind.

The form in the bed gave no sign of awareness of my approach. One hunched shoulder was presented to me, that and the matted hair at the back of the head.

I advanced a hand, tentatively, and laid it upon his shoulder.

'Sir, I think that you are my father,' I whispered.

231

And then he turned his head, and I saw him in a shaft of sunlight through a crack in the shutters; and I knew the truth of what Giles Treacher had meant when he said that he would not have wished such a burden of life upon any creature of this earth.

ELEVEN

It was late when I was prevailed upon by Florrie to have something to eat. The routine of Mortmain Castle not having been diverted one iota by the alarms and excursions that had taken place, there was a full three-course menu with entrées and removes readily available at any hour of the evening upon demand for myself and as many guests as I had chosen to invite. Florrie pleaded tiredness and went to bed. Giles and I sat down to a late supper in the small hall, and were served cold meats by Mrs Steeple. My companion was provided with a bottle of claret.

Mrs Steeple's demeanour was that of a woman torn between a heart-rending sadness and a new, iridescent joy that coloured her whole being. Giles was later to explain the former; she, herself, was unable to contain herself about the latter.

'To think that my darling child can speak again!' she cried, needlessly busying herself by dusting the serving table with the hem of her apron, and weeping the while. 'And still talking ten to the dozen. I left her with Steeple just now, and she was prattling on how they mustn't do any harm to "my friend" – as she calls the Major. She says they talk to each other when they're alone. Of course, that's just child's make-believe, but it goes to show how close she feels to him, no matter what his looks and the way he behaves.'

'I should like to speak with Phoebe tomorrow, when she's rested, Mrs Steeple,' I said.

'Of course, ma'am,' she replied. 'I'll bring her to you when you're ready to see her. Would there be anything else tonight, ma'am?'

'No, thank you, Mrs Steeple,' I said. 'You may go to bed. Oh, how is my – how is the Major? Is he comfortable?'

Her sad eyes were turned upon me, and her sadness won ascendancy over the joy of her grandchild. 'He won't be moved, ma'am, no matter what. We prepared a nice ground floor suite in the south tower, along with a bathroom and sitting room, like you ordered, but he wasn't for being taken out of his own room, no matter how Steeple and me tried to urge him. He fought us, ma'am, and there's strength left in him yet, as well I know.'

'The prisoner, in defiance of the popularly held belief,' said Giles, 'does not always readily leap to lose his chains. At the fall of the Bastille and the freeing of the derisory few prisoners held there, one old fellow had to be carried out of his cell in tears of entreaty to be allowed to remain.'

Mrs Steeple curtsied and withdrew. I regarded Giles thoughtfully.

'She was well schooled, and presumably by you, Giles. You all had your stories off pat. With her, the unfortunate creature in the west tower was a brother who had been injured before birth.'

He had the grace to look embarrassed, though not, it has to be said, ashamed. 'The Steeples are devoted to your father,' he said. 'She was his nursemaid, of course, and the pair of them worked for him right up to the day that he departed on the fateful expedition to the Jügspitz. They would have done – and will still do – anything, said anything, sworn anything, for his sake. As I would. As Jamie Venables would have.'

I pushed the untasted food around my plate. Suddenly blinded by tears of pride and gratitude – pride that I should have been sired by a man who could inspire such devotion, gratitude that that devotion had been expressed so completely and unreservedly – I felt too humble, too beholden, to complain that the deception had been practised upon me also.

'What are the extent of his injuries and disabilities, Giles?' I asked, pushing aside the plate and taking a sip of water. 'Please don't prevaricate with me. Is there ever to be any hope?'

234

'You saw him, Daisy,' he replied simply.

I closed my eyes. 'Yes,' I breathed. 'I would not have believed that a human face could remain so disfigured in life. Only one undamaged eye to show that he is a living creature – let alone a man. And as to the rest of him, Giles? He doesn't speak, of course – that much I discovered. What else is lacking?'

'He is also deaf,' said Giles. 'Nor does he appear to have any sensibility concerning the things and people surrounding him. Mrs Steeple swears that he knows her, but I am afraid it is a pious belief that comes from great love. It is not only his terrible injuries, which have turned him into a chronic cripple, but that night of horror on the frozen mountain has destroyed his brain. Perhaps it is a mercy. Perhaps it would have been beyond his mind's compass to recall that night without reliving it all over again in all its agony.

'Can you not now begin to appreciate why Jamie and I entered into this conspiracy, Daisy? Picture the two of us when we first saw him in that hospice in the shadow of the mountain that had destroyed him and his companions. He was dying – the good brothers assured us of that. It was only a matter of hours – minutes, perhaps. The miracle was that he had lived so long. Nevertheless, we resolved to delay telegraphing the news to his wife till he had gone, despite her many and repeated communications begging to know of his state.

'The hours lengthened into days. Inconceivably, his condition grew even worse. And then came the news that Annie Bravingdon had been safely brought to bed of a girl child, so we took the fateful decision of anticipating the seemingly inevitable by telegraphing that Tom Bravingdon had died and was to be buried along with his four companions in their common grave.

'The headstone in the churchyard below the Jügspitz bears those five names, though one still lives – if it can be called life.'

'Oh merciful heaven!' I breathed. 'How terrible – terrible!'

'Heaven showed little mercy in preserving him,' said my companion. 'At least, that is my opinion, though who am I to judge? When it became clear, after another week, that the patient was rallying slightly (and the good brothers attributed it to their prayers and the intercession of the saintly founder of their Order), we returned to England, leaving the shattered remains of our friend in the care of the hospice. During the journey, we searched our consciences, and both arrived at the same conclusion independently: it was out of the question for that young mother ever to be permitted to set eyes upon the horror that her splendid husband had become.

'And we stayed with that resolve – Annie Bravingdon went to her grave believing that she was a hero's widow.'

One question still burned in my mind, and I expressed it – not for the first time:

'All this I can understand and appreciate – but why did you lie to me about the source of my inheritance? Why didn't you simply tell me that my father was Tom Bravingdon who was killed while climbing in the Bavarian Alps in the very same week that I was born?'

'The solution you pose would have suited the case very well, Daisy,' replied Giles, 'but there was an overriding consideration that rendered such a simple explanation quite impossible.

'I will explain . . .

'With the death of your grandparents, Daisy, my old friend and I were in a cleft stick. By falsely announcing Tom Bravingdon's end, we had deprived him in one stroke of his birthright. A dead man cannot inherit.

'By this time, we had brought him from Bavaria and placed him, at our expense, in the Steeples' loving care in a small house outside Salisbury. The issue of the inheritance so troubled my conscience that I determined to make a clean breast of the affair to my godfather, a gentleman high up in the judiciary with a special weight in the part of the establishment that deals with probate – which is the official proving of wills and successions. I should add that this gentleman, who will remain nameless, had once been my mother's suitor, but she had chosen to marry his best friend, notwithstanding which he remained my mother's devoted servant, never married, and regarded me more as a son than a godson. I tell you this, Daisy, so that you will understand the motives behind his subsequent conduct in this matter.'

He paused to take a sip of his claret; I waited in breathless anticipation for him to resume his tale.

236

'I went to the judge and told him all,' said Giles at length. 'Confessed to our conspiracy and threw us both on his mercy. He railed at me for being a young fool, at Jamie for being an old fool who should have known better. Next, without giving any indication of his intent, he insisted upon journeying to Salisbury and seeing for himself the creature who had once been Major Tom Bravingdon.

'I shall not soon forget his reaction to the sight of that piteous wreck of a fine man. He who had seen many terrible things and heard many terrible tales of life and people, who had innumerable times donned the dread black cap and condemned murderers to be hanged, wept to see what had become of England's hero. And when he had satisfied himself with our evidence that the man before him was indeed the pathetic remains of the great mountaineer, the judge agreed to be a party to the conspiracy.

'With his connivance and that of certain of his trusted colleagues, the records of probate were amended to state that Major Tom Bravingdon's death *followed* that of his parents – in other words, that he had been the surviving heir to the family fortune.

' "But," said my godfather, "there the matter must end. The records tell that Bravingdon inherited, but is now dead, and those records will remain in the vaults of Whitehall, where they will gather dust for centuries. However, he still lives – but the records say he is dead. So, as far as the world is concerned, dead he must remain."

'I then asked the judge what must be the course to take in the unlikely event of our locating Tom Bravingdon's missing daughter. (I should tell you, Daisy, that you scarcely came into our calculations at this stage: we were convinced that you had died, like so many, in your infancy.) Could she inherit from her father?

'He gave his judgement and it was this: "If you discover the daughter, she must be told nothing of her parentage. No one else can be permitted to share this secret and enter into this conspiracy. I will arrange for you, Giles, to have complete power of attorney over the Bravingdon inheritance. You will administer it for Tom Bravingdon and, should his daughter be found, for her in her turn. *But the daughter must not be told of its source.* Our falsified record of Bravingdon's death lies in the vaults beneath Whitehall, and there it will remain for posterity to read. Only one option is open to you: if the daughter reappears, you can exercise your power of attorney and make over all, or part, of the fortune to her – but you will have to concoct a false source, a supposed benefactor."

'And that, Daisy, is why Jamie Venables, on his death-bed, urged me to provide you with an imaginary benefactor – himself.'

We were silent together for a long time, and then I said: 'Why, then, after all, have you told me all this in defiance of your godfather the judge's command?'

'For two reasons, Daisy,' he replied. 'Firstly, the judge is now dead. Secondly, none of us had taken into account the possibility that someone might seek to kill you to gain the inheritance. This was something that we could not have foreseen, and entirely changes the situation. To protect you, to bring this killer to justice, it will perhaps be necessary to make a clean breast of the conspiracy to the authorities, so that the police can track down whoever it is has a claim – or thinks he has a claim – to your inheritance. And would murder you to get it.'

'But – who could that be, Giles?' I asked – and it seemed as if I was asking it for the hundredth time.

'I don't know, Daisy,' he replied. 'I just don't know and have no means of guessing.'

*

Next morning, Sergeant Penbury came.

I was with Florrie in my sitting room when a footman brought me news of his arrival, and I went down to the great hall where he was waiting. His thick-set figure in the inevitable Norfolk jacket strangely dominated the great chamber as he stood there, his back to me, gazing up with what appeared to be considerable intent at a tattered battle flag that hung from near the rafters. He turned upon my approach and those searching green eyes swept me from head to foot.

'Good morning, Sergeant. You wish to see me.'

'Good morning, ma'am.' He took my proffered hand. 'You – and Mr Treacher, if that is possible. I understand that he is staying here.'

'I will send for him,' I said.

'Is there somewhere where we can be assured of being alone?' he asked. 'Alone and with no chance of being disturbed? What I have to tell you is – highly confidential.'

'We can go into the solar,' I said, greatly intrigued by his air of mystery. 'And I will send for Mr Treacher. Come this way, Sergeant.'

The solar was a light and airy chamber on the third floor of the keep, overlooking the sea and with the southern aspect that gave the chamber its name: the sun shone into it for most of the day; even in winter, so I was told, it was unnecessary to provide any other form of light and heating. The police officer and I settled ourselves in easy chairs and were engaged in what was, for my part at least, extremely strained and nervous small-talk when Giles joined us.

A polite exchange between the two men was followed by an awkward silence, as the sergeant produced from his pocket a sheaf of papers which, having perused briefly, he then replaced, gazed first at one of us, then the other, and delivered his surprising opening:

'I have to congratulate you both, sir and madame. You must have powerful friends in high places. I'm most impressed.'

Giles and I exchanged uneasy glances.

'Please particularise, Sergeant,' said my fellow conspirator, with more assurance, surely, than he felt.

'Sir, I had occasion to question you recently regarding the source of Miss Friday's inheritance (it was after the incident at the "Black Dog" in Truro, when you were injured and Mr Caldecott lost his life), and you told me that a certain Mr Venables was the lady's benefactor, following upon which the Devon and Cornwall Constabulary communicated with Probate at Whitehall, enquiring further of this inheritance. Back came the reply – I have it here – that our information was incorrect, that Miss Friday had inherited the estate of the late

239

Major Bravingdon, and that this information was to be treated in the strictest confidence and not to be divulged to anyone but the officer directly working upon the case – that's to say me. Furthermore, every attempt to obtain further and better particulars from Probate has met with a blank wall of silence – a circumstance that is unique in our experience. So I repeat, sir and madame, you must have friends in high places.'

I made no reply to that. Giles shifted uncomfortably in his seat and said: 'That apart, Sergeant, what use have you made of this information so far, pray?'

The shrewd green eyes narrowed with amusement, and crinkles of good humour appeared at their outer corners. 'Very well, sir, we'll speak no more of the unusual circumstances surrounding Miss Friday's inheritance. I know my place and do not wish to fall foul of faceless bureaucracy. As to what use I have made of the information, my answer is – plenty.

'I know the name of the man – yes, it is a man – who has been plaguing Miss Friday, who killed your Mr Caldecott to obtain the documents in your briefcase. And, by the way, what *were* those documents, Mr Treacher?'

'Deeds,' said Giles. 'Engrossed, signed and witnessed, which transferred the Bravingdon estate to Miss Friday. Anyone who read them would know the story of the inheritance from beginning to end.'

'Our man went to desperate lengths to peruse those deeds,' said Penbury. 'And they will have undoubtedly strengthened his resolve to rid himself of Miss Friday – unless we catch him first.'

'Who – who is this man, Sergeant?' I breathed.

'I will begin at the beginning, ma'am,' replied Penbury. 'The information that your fortune was derived from the Bravingdons and not from Mr Venables' – he cast a stern look at Giles – 'was my starting point. I had already wasted much time and effort in making Mr Venables my starting point' – another glance towards Giles – 'but I began again.

'My enquiries about Major Bravingdon revealed nothing that was not already common knowledge: he married a Miss Annie Beasley and had issue of one daughter' – he glanced towards me, but made no comment – 'and was killed in a climbing accident in Bavaria. As far as I was able to ascertain, he formed no other attachments and had no other issue. His life, quite clearly, was entirely blameless and he lived as he died, in the highest esteem.'

' "A parfit gentil knight," ' I quoted. ' "*Sans peur et sans reproche.*" '

'Quite so,' said the sergeant. 'However, when I traced back further, to the Major's parents, I discovered a very different kettle of fish. The wife drank and the husband, a former Guards officer and man-about-town, had had mistresses galore, both in London and in Somerset. One of the latter, a Mrs Caroline Studeley, a widow of the parish of St Edmund, Taunton, gave birth to an illegitimate boy child thirty-two years ago. Furthermore, upon examining the parish records, I found that Mrs Studeley had quite brazenly entered the name of the child's father as – Captain Hubert Arthur Bravingdon. The child's name is given as Paul Hubert Alexander.'

'And he is the killer, you think?' asked Giles.

'Undoubtedly,' replied the other. 'The accounts of his life and career, his relationship with his mother – all of which I have gleaned in considerable wealth of detail from friends, neighbours, acquaintances and business associates – leave not the slightest doubt but that he's my man.'

'For example?' interposed Giles.

'For example,' responded Penbury, 'what would you think of a lad aged nine who was brought before the magistrates for gross cruelty to a litter of kittens?'

'That's him!' I exclaimed, and they both stared at me in amazement. 'He – he also killed my dog,' I added lamely. 'And most cruelly. It must be – it *has* to be him!'

'Continuing Master Paul Hubert Alexander's career,' resumed the sergeant, 'we find him, at the age of eighteen, entering the employ of Messrs Standish and Wilding, auctioneers, of Tiverton, Devon. Three months later, he was dismissed for fraudulently converting the proceeds of a sale in which he had acted as cashier. He also narrowly escaped a serious charge on this occasion for assaulting Mr Charles Standish, senior partner of the firm, with a hatchet.

'I will continue with the catalogue of his crimes, which is extensive, in rather less detail. Assault and battery – six months prison sentence; armed robbery – two years; grievous bodily harm – five years; innumerable minor felonies all involving violence. And then – murder!'

'Murder!' Giles and I echoed the word in unison.

'He was arraigned before the High Court on a charge of murdering a Miss Gladys Henshaw, to whom he claimed to have been affianced,' said Penbury, 'though the engagement was denied by the dead girl's parents. It was the prosecution's case that Paul Studeley (he assumed his mother's married surname), in his insane pursuit of the girl's hand in marriage – or perhaps merely of her favours – subjected her to months of heartless persecution, and then, when she still resisted him, lured her to a quiet place and savagely killed her. The jury, however, completely taken in by his pleasing and forthright delivery when giving evidence on his own behalf, and being convinced that such a fine young fellow was incapable of so horrible a crime, acquitted him. And the last we hear of Paul Studeley is that he has emigrated to Australia. From whence, if my surmise is correct, he has since returned and is pursuing Miss Friday – and her fortune.'

'On what grounds?' demanded Giles, echoing my own objection. 'Having disposed of this lady, how could he possibly hope to succeed to the fortune – an illegitimate?'

'Ah, that question brings us to the character of the mother,' said Penbury, 'and she is as important to my case as the would-be inheritor himself.

'Mrs Studeley (though she described herself as a widow, I have been unable to trace any record of her marriage) was a failed actress and ballet dancer – presumably of the lowest sort. In later years, she made something of a living as a fortune-teller, reader of tarot cards, tea-leaves, palmiste – that kind of thing. Neighbours described her as a woman with the wreckage of a considerable beauty that she sought to rekindle with the aid of paint and powder, kohl and henna. As a consolation for her lost beauty and a substitute for her success as an artiste, say those who knew her, Mrs Studeley lavished all her hopes, all her frustrated ambitions, upon her son Paul. The boy, from infancy to manhood, they say, was grotesquely spoilt and pampered. "One day," she told the neighbours and anyone who cared to listen, "my Paul will be a millionaire. When he is twenty-one, I will tell him the secret of his birth, and he will go to claim his rightful inheritance." To one woman – now deceased: I had it second-hand from her daughter – she said that she had gone through a form of marriage with a very rich gentleman and that, no matter what the neighbours whispered, her Paul was legitimate. I need not add, Miss Friday, that there was not the slightest truth in that assertion. Captain Bravingdon married his wife ten years before he ever set eyes on the Studeley woman, and they both lived unhappily ever after till their deaths.'

'And so,' said Giles, 'your case is that, believing his mother, Paul Studeley is now relentlessly pursuing what he believes, quite wrongly, to be his rightful fortune?'

'Yes,' said the other. 'It is my case that Studeley, discovering that Miss Friday was about to inherit . . .'

'He knew that early enough!' I interposed. 'Why he was following me around and menacing me before even *I* was told!'

The police officer frowned. 'Yes, that is something I can't explain: how he came to discover your secret. However, by some means, he did – and from that day, Miss Friday, your life was in danger. You took your place, in his mind, beside poor little Gladys Henshaw – the victim-elect of a man with a fire burning in his disordered brain, the fire of wanting: "I want, therefore I must have!" And I'm afraid that, somewhere along the way, he quite lost touch with reality – and because of that, I'm worried for you, Miss Friday, I really am.'

'Why do you say that, Sergeant?' demanded Giles, while I sat and stared in horror. ' "Lost touch with reality." '

'He started off rationally enough – if you can call murder a rational activity,' said Penbury. 'The attempt in the train to Truro, though badly mistimed, would, if it had come off, have been put down to accidental death.'

'How so?'

Penbury cast a doubtful glance at me and seemed reluctant

to answer at first. 'There are three tunnels after Exeter,' he said at length. 'Having rendered the lady unconscious with chloroform, he would then have hung her head out of the window . . .' There was no need for him to say more; I shuddered at the image he had presented with such economy of expression.

'But the killing of Lady Moira – that could never have been dismissed as accidental,' said Giles.

'Exactly,' replied Penbury. 'That marks the beginning of his irrationality. It is almost as if he had abandoned all hope of gaining the inheritance by stealth and was now hell-bent on destroying the person who, to his disordered mind, has usurped it. I may add that, to my way of thinking, his attempt to shoot Miss Friday on "Old Jacob" comes into the same category. Yes, ma'am, I had a full report on the occurrence from Commander Todd.'

'And so this monster, this murderous fiend, is still at large and still among us,' said Giles. 'Do you not have a description of his appearance, Sergeant?'

'Only that he is of pleasing looks and forthright manner,' replied the other. 'Furthermore, it is likely that he has inherited from his mother a talent for acting, however slight.' He then added a definition that I was to remember, with alarm, in the dark hours of the nights that followed: 'He could be the down-at-heel fellow who brushed past you in the street last week – or he could be the cultured gentleman who sat opposite you at a dinner-party the day after.

'He has no face, no definite appearance, and almost certainly is no longer using his given name.

'We only know that he exists.'

*

'Shall you be needing *this* again, ma'am?'

Nellie Throstle, acting as my lady's maid, had been sorting through my wardrobe and my very considerable baggage, some of which had still not been unpacked. I was seated before my vanity mirror, brushing my hair and thinking how to mend the ravages of my sleepless night, when she came into the dressing room bearing over her arm a garment which, when she held it up, proved to be a plain, roughly-made dress of grey calico which, after a brief moment of blank puzzlement, suddenly burst upon my consciousness and unlocked a whole houseful of doors to memory.

It was the dress – my only other dress – that I had worn for more years than I cared to remember at the Mordwenn chain factory. To be precise, it had been my Sunday dress; the one I had worn to work on weekdays was so patched, torn and deeply grimed with iron dust and swarf, and singed with proximity to hot metal, that I had consigned it to the dustbin. My Sunday dress, the grey calico, I had myself washed and ironed and placed at the bottom of a trunk as a reminder of drear days thankfully behind me.

'No, I won't be needing it, Nellie,' I replied, 'but I'll keep it. That dress brings back very odd memories of a time gone past. Leave it with me for now.'

'As you wish, ma'am.' The girl wrinkled her pert little nose, enough to demonstrate her disapproval, but not enough to be offensive; matter-of-fact Nellie had no time for sentiment. She handed me the dress. 'Will there be anything else, ma'am?'

'Yes, ask Mrs Steeple to bring Phoebe to see me when the child has had her breakfast. If it's convenient.'

'Yes, ma'am.' She curtsied and left me.

My Sunday dress . . .

I turned it over and over in my hands, feeling the tired fabric beneath my fingertips. I stood up, then held it up against me and examined the result in the cheval-glass. It was ridiculously short, for it had been supplied to me by a parish charity when I was yet not fully grown either upwards or outwards.

And to think that, in this dress, I had braved the concerted fury of Charles Arbuthnot and his companions that memorable day near to Christmas. Wearing this dress, I had tongue-lashed the insufferable Lady Wisher and her equally appalling consort; clad in this frowzy confection of cheap calico, I had challenged Lady Moira Fame with her silks and furs, her aristocratic birth and her implacable sense of superiority, her overwhelming contempt. Well, she now rested in her untimely grave, and all because I had spoken up that day.

And Charles . . .

How must I have looked to him, in this dress, when I had spoken out against him, his caste, his exploitation of the half-starved wretches who gaped in awe to hear my denunciation? Surely not for my appearance had he chosen to lift me up to the eminence of his counting house and commend me to Giles Treacher.

Charles . . .

The dress fell from my fingers. I closed my eyes and allowed my thoughts to drift towards the forbidden subject of the love that had sprung alive in my heart on that never-to-be-forgotten tragic day when we had stood in a crowded garden-party and it had been to me as if we were alone together in Arcadia.

Best not to think of it! I dragged myself back to the there and then, for had I not sworn to myself innumerable times – times when I was lonely and despairing, the moments before sleep when the mind is at the mercy of its whims and weaknesses – that I must rid myself of all thoughts of Charles Arbuthnot? And I repeated to myself, over and over, the dreadful formula that was calculated to stifle my love, my warmth, my longing:

'He'll have his way with you . . . like all the rest . . . all the rest . . .'

It was no use. I had to see him again, even if only to quarrel with him. But how was it to be contrived? At our last meeting, I had as good as sent him packing from my door. Perhaps I could persuade Jack Todd to hold a small dinner-party at his quarters in the 'Blue Boar'. Yes, that was it. And the trick would be to engage Charles in conversation about the attacks upon my life. Might not sympathy and compassion soften his acquisitive heart: Nimrod the hunter of womenfolk disarmed by concern for his intended victim?

I was meditating upon this for heaven knows how long, when there came a knock at the door and Mrs Steeple entered upon my summons. With her, shy and pale in a crisp pinafore dress and button boots, was her granddaughter.

'Phoebe to see you, ma'am,' said the woman, and to the child: 'Say "good morning, ma'am" to Miss Friday, like a good girl.' But Phoebe only hid her face in her grandmother's skirts. 'She's shy with you, ma'am,' said Mrs Steeple, 'and you'd scarce believe, would you, that she's been chattering sixteen to the dozen ever since she woke up this morning? It's a miracle, that it is. Oh, ma'am, you'll never know the debt of gratitude we owe you for being the cause of giving back our child the blessing of speech.'

'I did little enough, Mrs Steeple,' was my reply. 'I was simply there.'

'Ah, but you see, ma'am, Phoebe thought that you'd come to take away her "friend", as she calls the Major. And 'tis my belief that the shock of it made her cry out in protest, if you follow my meaning.'

'Then I'm very gratified,' I said. 'And how is – how is the Major this morning?'

Her face fell, the joy faded from her eyes. 'The same as ever, ma'am,' she replied. 'Nor will ever be any different, I shouldn't wonder. He just sits and stares with that one eye of his into nothingness. Not a sound, nor a sign. Just – nothing. But Phoebe, she still goes on about the talking they do together. Silly girl.' She stroked the child's hair affectionately. 'Who's a silly little girl, Phoebe?'

The child remained with her face pressed against the woman's skirts and made no response.

'I'm going to leave you now with madam, Phoebe,' said her grandmother. 'She wants to talk to you. Mind you watch your manners and answer up brightly like you did to me and grandpa this morning.' She smiled at me. 'You'll find she'll unburden herself when the shyness is worn off, ma'am.'

'I'm sure she will,' I said. 'Phoebe is a very nice little girl and we'll get along splendidly.'

With some reluctance, the child allowed herself to be dis-entangled from her grandmother and ensconced in one of my easy chairs. Mrs Steeple curtsied and made as if to leave. At the doorway, she paused and turned.

'Ma'am – I . . .' she began.

'Yes, Mrs Steeple?'

'I want to say that I'm sorry for the deceit I practised on you, ma'am. I mean as regards saying that he – that's the Major – was someone other than he is. I did it because . . .'

'I know why you did it, Mrs Steeple,' I interposed. 'And it doesn't matter. You did your duty by my father, as you had been instructed, and I have nothing but gratitude for your devotion.'

'Thank you, ma'am,' she whispered, near to tears. And was gone.

'Well, Phoebe,' I said brightly, turning to attend to my small guest. 'What shall we do first? Would you like to tell me all about your friend?'

No reply; she became absorbed in tracing her finger along the smocking that decorated the front of her pinafore dress; lips pouting in concentration upon the small activity, and no attention paid to me.

'You talk with your friend, you say,' I persisted. 'What do you say to each other when you're alone together?'

Her only response was to address herself even more diligently to probing at her smocking.

'Oh, come, Phoebe,' I said, brightly encouraging. 'Surely you can tell me. Do you' – I searched for likely topics – 'do you tell your friend what you've been doing during the day? What you've been playing at, what you've had for your meals and so forth?'

Her head bowed even lower. The finger that probed at the tucking of the pinafore halted in its movement and froze there. She had entirely shut me out. I had the wayward impulse to snatch that hand away and shake some sense into her – an impulse immediately quenched.

'I don't think you really do talk to your friend,' I said banteringly. 'And I'm quite sure he doesn't talk to you.'

This direct challenge went the same way as the rest of my approaches: it drew forth no response whatsoever, not even a further withdrawal.

'I think you're telling fibs about you and your friend,' I declared. 'He can't speak. Everyone knows he can't speak.'

At that, she bowed her head so that her small face was entirely hidden from me, and I could no longer tell, by her expression, if my barbed comment had drawn out any emotion. It was then I decided that I had gone about the interview badly,

248

and I put it down to my inexperience with children. I should have been more oblique in my approach, I told myself, taken more time, perhaps done quite a lot of talking myself, told her about my stay in Bath, my visit to the ex-Empress of the French – things to intrigue and interest her, to set her mind at ease and break down the barrier of her shyness. Instead, I had closed the door to a tactful approach, and it might take days – weeks – for me to win her confidence.

And I could not wait that long: there was something I had to know, something I had to put to the test. Now. Immediately.

The door having been shut in my face, I had no recourse but to attempt shock tactics to open it again. My sudden, blundering appearance in the west tower the previous day had so alarmed her that her speech had returned in order that she might express the alarm and dismay which had totally overwhelmed her.

I would attempt the same tactic again – this time deliberately.

'Well, Phoebe,' I said, 'I think you had better leave me now. When next you see your friend, I should like you to tell him that I am taking him away with me quite soon. We shall go together to my house in Bath, or perhaps . . .'

'NO!'

She screamed the word at me. Her small face turned to look up into my face, and I saw, with a sudden lurch of remorse in my heart, that her cheeks were streaked with tears.

'Don't take him – please, ma'am,' she said brokenly.

'Oh, Phoebe, Phoebe – as if I would!'

She ran to me then, and I gathered her to me, my own tears prickling my eyes.

'He doesn't have anyone but me,' she said. 'And he's so hurt, ma'am. There's never been anyone as hurt as what my friend is. If you take him away, he'll have nobody. There won't be anyone who he can talk to that'll understand him. He'll be alone inside himself for ever!'

'I won't take him away,' I promised her. 'And even if I do, you shall come with us, Phoebe.'

A brilliant smile began to be born behind the tears as she

249

looked up at me and held me more tightly. 'He doesn't like leaving his room in the tower,' she said. 'But he might, if you and me both went with him.'

'Do you think so, Phoebe?'

'Oh, yes, ma'am.'

'How do you know?'

'Well, he said to me this morning, he said: "That young lady who came yesterday is my daughter and I should like to see her again." So you see, ma'am – he likes you. He *really* likes you.'

It was madness to search for a forlorn hope in the fantasy-weaving of a small and discernibly imaginative child – but hope will search for truth in whatever unlikely place it might be found.

I seized her hand. 'Then I shall go and see him now, Phoebe,' I cried. 'And you shall come with me!'

*

The upper room in the west tower was in deep shadow, as ever. The figure hunched on the bed did not stir when we entered, and a pang of hopelessness soured my anticipation. I determined to waste no time in bringing the issue to the test, and in as businesslike a manner as possible. Accordingly, I crossed over to the window and, throwing wide the shutters, I let the morning sun stream into that bare room, flooding the figure on the bed in its pitiless light, revealing to me for the first time the full horror of what the man who was my father had become, so that I blenched at the sight. He, in his turn, flinched away from the sudden sunlight and made to cover his single eye with one grotesquely malformed arm – so, supposing that he was capable of discerning my revulsion, he might have missed my change of expression.

Steeling my nerve, I approached the bed. Deliberately allowing my eyes to slip out of focus (a habit of mine when I am unavoidably brought in contact with an unpleasant sight), so that he was no more than a dark blur of indeterminate shape and colour, I said brightly: 'Good morning, Father. Phoebe brought me to see you. I hope you slept well.'

(Why, oh why did you come here? I asked myself. Fool, fool,

250

what good can come of it? Why don't you leave him to his misery? Why do you torment yourself with hope – and all because a hysterical child plays a game of make-believe?)

And then, I heard the beginnings of the same curious snuffling, pig-like sound that had so revolted me when I first encountered it in the darkness of my sitting room. And it persisted.

'He's talking to me!' cried Phoebe. 'My friend's trying to say something!'

I closed my eyes in agony. There then followed the travesty of a dialogue between the child and the man-turned-monster, and Phoebe's part was largely composed of 'Yes', 'No', and 'Please say that again'. Soon my revulsion turned to embarrassment at the bathetic charade to which I had wittingly made myself a party, and I wished myself far away from that place and that time; it was no use, I had to remain and suffer it to the end, for Phoebe's sake.

Presently, the animal sounds ceased, and the child nodded and said yes, she would.

She came to me and took my hand.

'My friend says to tell you that you're very pretty,' she said.

'Oh, how kind,' I said in a voice that sounded very unlike my own.

'He says that you're very like your mother.'

'Well, that's nice.'

'He says – um . . .'

'Yes – what else does he say?' I asked indulgently.

She frowned, puzzling her mind to recollect. 'I – I can't say it very well,' she muttered, and clicked her tongue in annoyance. 'It's a bit difficult to remember.'

'Well, never mind, Phoebe,' I said. 'Perhaps it will come to you later. I think we may be tiring your friend. Perhaps we'd better go.'

'No, no!' she cried urgently. 'He most particularly wanted me to tell you this bit. I'll ask him again. And I'll remember it this time.'

So she went back to her 'friend', and there followed a

251

repetition of the mumbling mumbo-jumbo, another span of hideous embarrassment to see the poor creature being made the butt of a child's fantasy.

Presently, she turned back to me again, her face alight with a confident smile. 'I've got it right now,' she said. 'This is what I'm to tell you – hem!' And she cleared her throat, frowned very hard, screwed up her small face into an expression of deep concentration, and said: 'Um – but at my, er, back I always hear time – time's something chariot hurrying near and yonder – yonder all before – before . . .'

I found myself saying it with her, as if in a dream, or, more nearly, in the half-waking state between sleep and sleep, when the mind is attuned to music that is never heard by the woken ear:

> . . . *Time's wingèd chariot hurrying near,*
> *And yonder all before us lie*
> *Deserts of vast eternity.*

'That's it, ma'am!' cried Phoebe. 'That's what he said. Fancy you knowing.'

Through my new tears, I fought, still, against the likelihood of what I had just seen and heard. The child had committed the poem to memory, of course. But – she could not read, had never been schooled. Then she had overheard it – yes, that must be it. No other explanation offered itself. Against all probability, that was the way it had to be; to consider any other explanation was to accept the unacceptable: that by some means Tom Bravingdon had actually communicated the verse to his friend the child. And a most unlikely vehicle for communication: Andrew Marvell's 'To His Coy Mistress' – hardly a suitable poem for a father to quote to his daughter. And yet – my father had been a man of action, doubtless not given much to quoting poetry; was it not possible that the Marvell was simply an unconsidered fragment, a memory of his schooldays?

Had it been – was it – his method of trying to communicate with me?

I looked directly at him. The featureless countenance told me

252

nothing, but the eye, his single, blue eye (coloured exactly as my own) was fixed upon me, and surely I discerned there, red-rimmed and without an eyelid as it was, the pure light of reason.

'Phoebe!' I said, not shifting my gaze from him.

'Yes, ma'am?' she whispered.

'Turn your back on me, Phoebe,' I said. 'Face your friend, and don't look round, no matter what.'

She obeyed me without question.

I took from the pocket of my skirt a handkerchief: a silly, flimsy thing of pale blue silk edged with white lace, and held it up.

'Phoebe, ask your friend to tell you what I'm holding in my hand,' I said.

'Yes, ma'am,' she replied, and I put the handkerchief back in my pocket.

There then followed the by now familiar procedure, which was terminated by the child looking round – rather too quickly, I thought.

'Well, Phoebe?' I asked.

'He says, can you come a bit closer, ma'am, 'cos he can't see so far.'

'Very well,' I said resignedly, my brief-lived hope fading fast. 'Turn your back and I'll do it once more.'

Again I held up the handkerchief, this time at only a couple of paces from the bed. The single, red-rimmed eye seemed to search it out. I replaced the handkerchief again while the pantomime was repeated. Phoebe turned round to face me. She was smiling.

'Ma'am, he says it's a hanky.'

I exhaled a long-held breath. 'What sort of hanky, Phoebe?' I found myself asking.

'He says blue – with a white edging.'

And then I fell on my knees beside the bed and, blinded by tears, I stretched out my hands to him.

'Oh, Father – thank God, thank God!' I breathed. 'But for Phoebe, I might have been like all the rest. I might never have known!'

Slowly, painfully, he reached out his own hands and laid them gently on my shoulder. And from that single eye there came a tear that made its slow course down the destroyed face.

TWELVE

'Oh, Daisy, my darling – I'm so happy for you!'

The first person to whom I confided the wonderful news was – who else? – dear Florrie; we wept tears of joy together in my sitting room, with Felicity Denvers looking down on us – surely with approval.

'But for the miracle of Phoebe finding contact with father, he might have eked out the rest of his life in limbo,' I said. 'Imagine, Florrie, to have been locked inside the prison of a destroyed body; half-blind, robbed of the power of speech, deprived of the key to communicate by the written word, scarcely able to move without agony, let alone walk; confused in the mind and growing ever more confused as the shadows closed in about him. He could have become insane before merciful death. But instead – instead . . .' The vista of a new life for my father opened out before me. I saw him rising from his wretchedness to take his place by my side, to become a person once again.

'But – how was it done?' asked Florrie. 'How did that little child learn how to speak with him?'

'It must have been her own affliction – the shocking experience of the shipwreck that robbed her of speech for years – which made a bond between them from the first,' I speculated. 'And then, I suppose, she caught hold of a speech-pattern in the seemingly meaningless mumbling that is his attempt to express himself in words. In any event, she's able to capture even the most complex ideas that he throws out. They were gabbling away together like a couple of old biddies this morning, with me looking on spellbound. He has a sense of humour, too – though, not surprisingly, it's humour of the cynical kind. He said – and Phoebe interpreted for me: "An advantage of having only half a face is that one doesn't need to shave." '

'He was a brave man,' said Florrie.

'And still is,' I responded. 'I'm going to propose to him that he quits the west tower and comes to live like the rest of us. I shall get him a Bath chair, and Phoebe and I will wheel him out. Now that he's broken out of the bondage of his body and his mind is free to roam, he'll want to follow it. He has that kind of courage, Florrie.'

'Will he be able to bear the looks that folk will give him, though?' asked my friend. '*Ma foi* – that will take courage of the very highest sort.'

I nodded. 'That will be very difficult.'

'He could wear some sort of covering over his head. A mask, perhaps.'

The notion was appallingly depressing. 'I couldn't possibly propose it to him,' I said. 'It would be like saying: "Very happy to have you with us, Father, but people are going to point and stare when we wheel you out and about. Don't you think, for all our sakes, that you should cover up the horror that you are?" No – I couldn't do that to him, Florrie. Not when I've just welcomed him back to life. It would be like – like thrusting part of him back into limbo again.'

'I take your point, dear,' she said. 'It's a very difficult question and one which I'm afraid I can't advise you on. You'll have to make your own decision as to what's best for him.'

Yes, I would do that, but how to go about it was something I was quite unable to get straight in my mind. So I put it aside and turned to something else.

'I accepted an invitation to go up to London for the Diamond Jubilee, Florrie,' I said. 'Jack Todd is arranging for me to gain admission to St Paul's, and he can do the same for you, dear, I shouldn't wonder. Why not come with me? We shall see the Queen at close quarters. Poor old thing – she's very infirm, and I at least am not likely to have such an opportunity again.'

Florrie's eyes lit up, and she clapped her small, delicately-fashioned hands, waking Wink-Wink on her lap and causing him to bare his teeth in a snarl of annoyance.

'But that will be marvellous, Daisy!' she exclaimed. 'You know that Her Majesty is now acknowledging me after so long and painful an interval when I was ostracised following upon Sir Basil, my husband's, great misfortune. If her eyes light upon me, she will almost certainly incline her head towards me when I curtsy, and will smile. Though sometimes a very *severe* lady, she is really kindness itself at heart.'

'Then I'll have a word with Jack when he calls this afternoon,' I said. 'But one thing I would ask, Florrie – not a word to anyone about the trip to London. My – enemy – mustn't hear about it, or the danger that I live with will follow me there.

'For once, I would like to be free of fear – if it's only for a few short days.'

To this, of course, she readily agreed.

*

I had been guilty of a small subterfuge. On the pretext of seeing Jack to discuss with him the details of the London trip, I had sent him a note at the 'Blue Boar', inviting him to tea that afternoon. The Diamond Jubilee was the pretext; the reality was my scheme to use him as a stalking horse – if that is the phrase – for a meeting with Charles.

He arrived on his bicycle, and I was greatly heartened to see him and feel conscious of his strength and reliance, to hear his deep, booming voice echoing through the high-ceilinged rooms of the castle, and to savour his friendship and bathe in his obvious admiration.

'You're looking fine, Daisy,' he told me. 'Quite recovered from our small brush with the Grim Reaper the other day, eh? I had a word with that Sergeant Penbury – a very solid character, and I approve of him greatly – who seems to have the matter well in hand. He told me a certain amount of the background to your problem – in the strictest confidence, of course. He says that he's confident of making an arrest quite shortly, and I shouldn't wonder if he isn't right about that.'

257

'I devoutly hope so, Jack,' I said. 'I really do.'

'Well as regards London . . .'

'I wondered if . . .'

We both spoke together, and laughed – as one always does.

'After you, Daisy,' he said.

'No, you first, Jack. Tell me about the arrangements for London.' I could afford to wait to float the suggestion of a dinner-party at the 'Blue Boar'; the essence of a successful subterfuge is that one should never appear too anxious.

'The ceremony at St Paul's and the procession that precedes it being on Tuesday,' said Jack, 'my suggestion is that we travel up to London by the night sleeper on Sunday, arriving at Paddington Station in time for breakfast. I guess you'll be staying at your town house in Mayfair . . .'

With his deep baritone voice playing the background accompaniment, I let my thoughts stray to arranging the forthcoming dinner-party to my best advantage whilst exercising the uttermost discretion concerning my intent. It seemed to me that the pretext of the Diamond Jubilee and our departure for London might serve well as a reason for the event. Yes – that was it – Jack would give the dinner in honour of the 60th year of our Most Gracious Sovereign's reign – an elegant gesture from a former colonial, and sure to be well-received. I would float the idea when he had finished talking, and suggest a guest list . . .

'Don't you think, Daisy?' asked Jack from the background.

'Yes,' I responded stoutly. 'Undoubtedly.'

'Well, I'm glad we're both in agreement,' he said. 'As to getting from Mayfair to the City, I shall be on the cathedral steps awaiting my ambassador's coach. Your pass will enable your carriage to go through the police cordon at Temple Bar . . .'

As to seating arrangements, I, acting as hostess for the evening, would sit at the far end of the table from Jack, and Charles would be put on my right, and the lady on his other side would have on *her* right some very attractive man (Tristan Melmoth? – no, he had gone to Scotland), who could be relied upon to keep her engaged in conversation, leaving Charles exclusively to me. And I would say to him . . .

'. . . saw Arbuthnot on his way to the station,' said Jack, breaking in upon my reverie. 'He's off, bag and baggage.'

'Off?' I echoed. 'Off where?'

'To Italy,' replied Jack. 'Told me he's probably pulling out for good.'

'For *good?*' I experienced something like panic. 'You mean – he's not coming back to England?'

'I understand he's selling out his holdings in the family business and moving to a villa he owns near Rome. Not the sort of fellow I'd have imagined lotus-eating in the South, but there's no telling with folks. Well, we seem to have got the London trip fixed up to our mutual satisfaction. Hem – did you say something about tea, Daisy?' He gave me a greedy little-boy grin.

'I'm so sorry, Jack, I quite forgot. Pull the bell cord, will you please?'

Charles gone to live in Rome! For good. Never to see him again. The proposed dinner-party, the careful placements, my opening remarks, what might have followed – all washed away like children's sand castles with the outgoing tide.

*

That evening, I went with Phoebe to see my father. Here, at least, was a piece of my life that was a constant. Here, a person who needed me.

I was delighted to see that someone – it was Mrs Steeple, in fact, aided by Phoebe – had made some shift to tidy father up a little: his hair had been cut and brushed flat, they had put on him a broadcloth cloak that hid the worst contours of his poor, dislocated shoulders and hips, and a pair of soft pigskin gloves mercifully concealed his almost fingerless hands. That lively, questing blue eye met mine with a touch of jocularity.

I had in mind to introduce the idea of moving him out and taking him about; accordingly I tackled the subject right away, and Phoebe 'translated' for me.

'Good evening, Father. Had a nice supper?'

'Yes, thanks. Mrs Steeple feeds me very well.'

'Father, I've been thinking – wouldn't you be more comfort-

259

able with a suite in the keep? Somewhere close to mine, where I can look in on you regularly. And Phoebe too, of course.'

'That sounds very nice. No need to dance attendance on me all the time. I enjoy a bit of solitude occasionally, just like everyone else.'

'Of course. I'll see to it, then. Another thing – I thought to get you a Bath chair, so Phoebe and I can take you for walks in the home park. Also, we could go for carriage drives further afield. The village. Or even Falmouth.'

'I'm not so sure about that.'

'Why?'

'Why? Because I look such a fright. Scare everyone to death.'

'Well, Father, it's something we've got to face up to, isn't it? There's nothing either of us can do about it.'

'Course there is. I'll wear a mask.'

'A – a mask?'

'Yes. Fix it, will you, Daisy? Something in beaten metal. Hand-beaten in copper, or gold. Dull gold. Modelled like one of those Greek gods. Zeus, or someone. Might as well make a bit of a splash.'

'Zeus. Yes – er – yes, Father.'

'Get one of the best fellows around to do the sculpting. A Royal Academician – one of those Johnnies. Don't see why the hell I should stint myself.'

I think he laughed then. I know that I was between laughing and crying, and happier than I could have believed possible.

*

On the evening of Sunday, 20 June 1897, Florrie, Jack and I joined the night sleeper express at Falmouth. I spent a restless night, for I could not entirely rid my mind of the last time – indeed, the only other time – that I had tried to sleep on a train, and of my narrow escape from the hands of my faceless enemy (strange how I could not bring myself to think of him by any other name: Paul Studeley rang falsely in my ears, like a counterfeit coin), nor could I convince myself that our concerted attempts to keep our departure a secret could possibly have succeeded in a rural area where one could scarcely turn over in bed without the news being common knowledge by breakfast time.

London, when we arrived next morning, was *en fête*; there were banners in every window and streamers strung across all the main thoroughfares and every mean street and alley; jostling crowds spilled out on to the roadway, all in high good humour and sporting their red, white and blue. It took us nearly an hour to make the short journey by growler from the station to my town house in Upper Brook Street, near Grosvenor Square, for the traffic was almost at a standstill; wheel-to-wheel, patient horses moving from one leg to another, munching at their feed bags, everyone cheerful as you please. In Park Lane, we were further delayed by the passage of a troop of Life Guards in their scarlet and polished steel, who, led by a boy officer, were trying to forge ahead against the grain of the traffic and being roundly cheered by all and sundry in the process.

A Salvation Army band was playing outside my house; a little further down the street, an Italian organ grinder was churning out a tinny tune for a slow brown bear, who docilely sketched out the figures of an arcane dance, nodding his muzzled head in time to the music. And the crowds drifted slowly past.

My house was charming. The housekeeper was Mrs Welsh, a lady of middle years, whose husband had been a coxwain in the Royal Navy, and he had run away with a barmaid from Portsmouth, so the poor soul informed me. The furnishings and fittings, though not up to the high standard of Lansdown Crescent, were solid and impeccably tended, the fine woodwork waxed and polished to mirror brightness, likewise the silverware.

We breakfasted on eggs, bacon, toast and coffee in the morning room at the rear of the house, which had tall windows that looked down into a long, walled garden set with formal shrubs in stone urns, discreet statuary, a narrow strip of well-tended lawn, and a dovecote.

Jack had much to attend to at his embassy in preparation for the morrow, and begged to be excused for the remainder of the day. He was staying at his apartment in the embassy building, and it was arranged that we should rendezvous after the religious ceremony that was to be held at the foot of the steps leading up into the cathedral, since Her Majesty's advanced infirmities precluded her from almost any effort. (There had been some talk of carrying her bodily into the great edifice, but this had been dismissed on the grounds of the indignity attendant upon man-handling the tiny old lady who ruled over half the world.)

Faced with the alternatives of either going out into the streets on foot (a carriage being out of the question with the state of the traffic), or remaining quietly at home to rest against the exertions of the morrow, we plumped for the latter course. Accordingly, when Jack had taken his leave, Florrie and I settled down in the drawing room on the second floor back, she with the latest romantic novel, I with my petit point. There we sat quietly for half an hour or so, with only the distant murmur of the crowds in the street up front, Wink-Wink's quiet snore, and the discreet tick-tock of the French ormolu clock on the chimney-piece.

Presently, from out of the blue, Florrie said: 'You're not happy in yourself, my dear. Are you grieving over Charles Arbuthnot so very much?'

My fingers froze in the act of making a stitch. 'Oh, Florrie,' I murmured, 'is it as obvious as all that?'

'How long?' she asked.

'From the first moment I saw him, I suppose,' I answered, and it was an admission that I had not even made to myself before. 'And I knew for sure at Mr Melmoth's garden-party.'

'And he – how does he regard you?'

'As a potential conquest,' I replied dully. 'Along with all the others.'

'I see. You know about – all the others?'

'Not at first hand,' I replied. 'But I've been well-informed.'

'By someone who holds your well-being and happiness in very high regard, no doubt?'

I shrugged. 'By someone with cause to know him better than I.'

'I see. And now he has gone abroad – for good, we are led to understand – and you are at a loss to know what to do?'

'Yes. I rejected what I considered to have been his advances.'

'And now you regret having done so?'

I did not answer for a while, but fought with my conscience, my candour, my pride. In the end, I tossed them aside. 'Yes,' I admitted. 'I regret bitterly that I threw away my chance of having him for my lover – if only for a short while, and imperfectly.'

'And what would you wish to do now, Daisy?' she asked gently.

'I would wish – I would wish to have the strength, the lack of shame, the brazen effrontery – call it what you like – to go to him in Italy and say: "I will be yours on any terms you wish."'

'But you won't do that, will you, Daisy,' she said, and it was not a question. 'That's merely what you wish it was in your nature to do.'

'You know me too well, Florrie,' I replied, and bowing my head, re-addressed myself to my needlework.

Neither of us alluded to the topic again that day, or for some time after; but the conversation had had the effect of clearing my mind of much confusion and self-deception. But at some cost.

*

Tuesday dawned with a slate grey sky promising rain – a dismal prospect for the millions of people who had flocked to the capital, some of them having slept rough in the Royal parks or upon the pavements that lined the processional route.

Florrie and I were up at dawn and clad in costumes to suit all weathers, that's to say, summer frocks with cardigans carried over our arms in case of a chill wind, and rolled mackintoshes and sou'westers for fear of rain. We took with us a boy footman named Alec to carry any unwanted gear, together with a basket containing sandwiches, flasks of both tea and coffee, and a bottle of 'medicinal whisky' for my companion. The carriage was at the door promptly as ordered and we set off: eastwards to the City, along Park Lane and Oxford Street to Holborn and Temple Bar, where we were halted by the police and made to produce our passes issued from the United States Embassy, requesting and requiring that we should be permitted to proceed to St Paul's Cathedral, and duly signed by the U.S. Head of Chancery.

Beyond Temple Bar, down Fleet Street and up Ludgate Hill to where the steep façade and towering dome of Sir Christopher Wren's masterpiece was etched against the dull overcast sky, we passed unimpeded, with a sea of faces to left and right and in every window lining the route; under a continuous awning of flags and bunting that spanned the road, and the probing gazes and audible comments of the crowds:

'Who are they, then? Some big nobs, I reckon.'

'The old 'un looks like Princess Alice.'

'Too bloomin' old for Princess Alice.'

'Give 'em a cheer anyhow.'

On arrival at the cathedral, we were handed down by an anxious young officer in scarlet Guards' regimentals, our passes re-examined, and ushered to a vacant space on the steps before the great doors, where the notables of Britain and her Empire, foreign dignitaries both civil and military, white-skinned, black-skinned, yellow and brown, were assembled in all their personal panoply to do homage to the old Queen and Mother of her nation. And in the open space fronting the steps, a Royal Marine band played selections from *The Mikado*.

*

A while later, Florrie nudged my elbow. 'There's Jack Todd. Doesn't he cut a fine figure in naval uniform?'

Jack was with a group of officers gathered to await the arrival of the Royal procession. He was some distance away, his back turned towards us, though from time to time he looked round and scanned the ranks of the people massed on the steps as if searching for us; he certainly looked splendid in his navy blue and gold; so straight and tall – so like – someone else . . .

Presently, there came a group of men bearing a box-like structure on stilts, which they set up at the far side of the street, pointing towards the steps. A knowing gentleman standing beside me opined that this was a cinematograph camera for taking moving photographs, a new-fangled contrivance of which I had heard, but which had not then been seen in the West Country. Almost immediately after that, Jack's questing glance was directed so closely to where we stood that I tried to attract his attention by waving wildly, nearly knocking off the very complicated head-dress of a black gentleman standing immediately in front of and below me. He turned with an expression of some annoyance, which immediately softened into a broad smile and an assurance – in impeccable English – that it was of no consequence. And I still had not made contact with Jack Todd.

Soon after that, the murmuring and muttering of the vast multitude that spilled over the pavements, lined the windows, hung from lamp posts, even massed on the high rooftops, was stilled by the distant thunder of a gun, and then another, and another – the signal that the Queen had left Buckingham Palace and was on her way through six miles of triumphal procession through her capital.

And as if by special arrangement, the sun immediately broke through the tumbled clouds and shone down upon the crowded city in all the glory of an English summer's day.

*

Half an hour passed. The Royal Marine band played selections from *The Gondoliers*. Murmurings of hunger drove us to have a ham sandwich apiece. I had a swallow of lukewarm coffee and Florrie essayed a nip of medicinal whisky. The massed crowds grew if not discontented, certainly a little restless, like children bored with the tedium of a long journey. Even the grand folk about us, the high-ranking officers, diplomats and politicians, shuffled from one foot to the other, glanced for the hundredth time at their programmes, blew their noses unnecessarily, looked at their fingernails. My next door neighbour, he who had been so informative about the cinematograph camera, wore a cocked hat embellished with white ostrich plumes – and they were visibly wilting in the hot sunshine.

And then, like the rustle of waves spreading along a shingled shoreline, came the growing murmur:

'*Here she comes . . . here she comes . . . here she comes!*' As, far away at the other end of Fleet Street, by Temple Bar, we discerned the leading horses of the Royal procession. And all that great crowd took up the cheering that was already spreading from afar and tumbling towards us down the empty, long, hot street.

'I do so hope,' said Florrie, 'that she acknowledges me. I declare I shall be quite downcast if she doesn't.'

Minutes later, from our eminence, we could see almost the whole of the procession coming towards us: the scarlet and blue of the Household Cavalry regiments to the fore, led by the tallest man I ever did see in a saddle. 'That is Captain Ames of the Second Life Guards,' said my informant, he of the drooping plumes. 'Six foot eight, and the tallest fellah in the Army.'

The head of the cavalcade mounted the hill, the heat haze from the steaming street creating a mirage of horses seeming to walk upon air. Bands blared. The cheering rose to a crescendo that drowned fife and drum, trumpet and trombone, the clatter of hooves and the rattle of carriage wheels on cobblestones.

And then, in the midst of it all, the open carriage drawn by eight cream horses, and sitting within it, nodding and smiling under a black lace parasol, the dumpy little Queen-Empress in a tiny bonnet.

There was a surging forward of dignitaries. I lost sight of Jack Todd. Florrie clutched at my arm and urged me down the steps as the royal carriage came to a halt immediately below us. A group of vestmented churchmen were first to approach the Queen. They bowed and were acknowledged. I saw the Queen's brilliant blue eyes flicker over the crowded steps – and pause for a moment upon Florrie at my side. Instantly, my companion bobbed a curtsy, and won for herself a tired old lady's smile and a graceful nod.

'That made it all worth while,' breathed my friend, and unashamedly burst into tears of profound emotion.

*

266

The procession's pause at St Paul's was marked by a brief service – and then, so far as we were concerned, it was all over. The strains of the National Anthem having died away, the Royal coachmen urged forward their eight matched creams, and the Queen-Empress passed on her way to set the seal upon the conquest of London town that she had made sixty radiant years before.

'There's Jack!' cried Florrie, pointing.

I saw his tall figure in a group of uniforms moving up the steps towards the great doors of the cathedral, and set off after him, calling to Florrie to follow me; but there was a heavy press of people also moving up to go into the building, and no entreaties or protestations of mine won me so much as a foot of extra progress. The last I saw of Jack was the back of his head as he doffed his naval cap on entering. I looked back for Florrie, but she was lost to me in the crush.

Somehow, my part of the concourse managed to squeeze through the wide doorway five abreast, and the massive nave opened out before me, columned and arcaded, its long, domed ceiling hazed in shadow and sunlight from the deeply recessed windows on high.

The better to make a pursuit of my quarry, I broke away from the main body of people and darted to one of the side aisles whose shadowy walk was empty and oddly quiet. Somewhere along the way, I must have lost my bearings, for I very soon found myself in a silent transept, and the whispering footsteps of my late companions sounded very far distant. I paused and looked about me, finding nothing to indicate to which part of the great building my wandering had brought me; only the cold marble faces of the long-dead great in effigy were there to regard Daisy Friday – and with monumental disdain.

And then, turning to look behind me the way I had come, I saw – *him*!

I knew him by the strange hat that he had affected from the first time I had set eyes upon him from the window of my room at the counting house; as before, the wide brim shielded his countenance which, in any event, was thrown into deep shadow by the pillar beside which he crouched looking at me; yes, he looked straight at me, and though I could not see his eyes, I sensed the hatred and the malice there.

Escape! I was offered two options: to race across the length of the transept in the direction which I took to lead to the great open space under the dome, or to run in the opposite direction towards a low, open doorway that promised egress to the street outside. Because the former course would have taken me obliquely past the threatening figure, and possibly within the scope of his intercepting me in my flight, I chose the latter.

Accordingly, I ran. And sensed on the same instant that he came after me.

Through the doorway, I immediately discerned my error: the promising sunlight that had suggested the open air came only through a large, barred window set at the end of a small chamber with no other exit save an archway opening on to a spiral staircase that led upwards into unknown gloom. Pausing irresolutely for a brief moment, I heard the light patter of running feet approaching from down the transept, and I knew there was only one way of escape left open to me. In a trice, I was through the archway and mounting the stone stairs two at a time.

It was a long way up: round and round more times than I could count, till I was gulping for breath and my heart was pounding. I paused for a moment, and to my horror, heard my pursuer close behind: heard his menacingly light footfalls and his panting breath.

I sped on.

Presently, the half-gloom opened out ahead to a loom of sunlight coming through glass. One more turn of the stair and an open door was presented to me, which, when I rushed through it and out on to a stone gallery, I perceived to be one of many such doors that provided access to this gallery which entirely circled the base of the interior dome that soared above me, embellished with a gallimaufry of swirling and gesticulating figures painted on its underside. Far below, in a yawning abyss, a vast circular pavement was sprinkled with tiny, attenuated figures that moved slowly and with reverent awe, all unaware of the murderous drama taking place far above their heads.

Instants later, from the corner of my eye, I saw the dark-clad figure bound through the doorway behind me, and I took to my heels again. The next door I passed in my pell-mell flight was closed. So was the next. I had half-circled the gallery before I dared to check my headlong flight and throw myself upon the handle of another door – also closed. And, to my sudden, sick horror, locked.

Panic took flight in my mind with the realisation that I had offered a few precious seconds of life as hostage to freedom. When I set off to run again, I sensed that he was now very close on my heels. And so it was: I had not completed the circuit of the gallery before an iron hand was clamped upon my shoulder, powerful fingers bore into my flesh, holding me fast. And then another hand closed about my throat, choking me.

I fell back against the balustrade, fighting for breath that would not come, seeking through my fading sight to focus upon the face that stared down at me, but seeing only its outline and that of the sinister hat.

I think that, if I could have found tongue, I might have pleaded with him for my life, or, at least, for a few seconds to gaze once more and for the last time upon the sunlight and living things. No such opportunity was offered me: as my senses drifted away, I felt myself being lifted up, my scrabbling fingers trailed along the edge of the balustrade and then clutched at empty air.

I was being lifted over – to be dropped into the abyss, to the marble pavement far below!

Suddenly, it all ceased. The insupportable burden of choking fingers was relaxed from my throat and I slumped on to a hard floor, rolled over, and opened my eyes to see, not ten paces from where I lay at the base of the balustrade, two figures struggling frantically for supremacy: one of them black-clad and still wearing the strange hat, the other hatless, in navy-blue and gold.

'Jack!' I shrieked, and my cry echoed deafeningly along the gallery, was repeated, repeated and repeated all round me.

He turned his head for an instant at the sound of my cry – and it was his undoing: his opponent, taking advantage of that split second of inattention, wrapped one arm around the American's throat and bore him backwards towards the edge of the balustrade and bent him over. Next, quickly releasing his grasp, the man in black stooped and, taking his adversary by the ankles, *lifted* him bodily on to the capping of the balustrade so that the other's head hung downwards over the dizzy drop.

I cannot recall with any clarity the precise sequence of events that followed: suffice to say that Jack Todd the rock climber *par excellence* was not to be thrown off balance so easily. With hands, feet and the most excellent agility, he made himself a safe anchorage on the narrow ledge upon which he had been deposited, and having done so, he struck back.

It was like watching a trained climber making the initial hoist up a rock chimney: first, he secured himself with both hands upon the upper arms of his opponent; next, he made footholds against the upper part of the other's legs, one foot after another. And then, he *lifted!*

The creature who had been sometime known as Paul Studeley was borne on high and deposited across the body of his antagonist – except that he was further advanced by a head and shoulders over the abyss.

He screamed when he felt himself slipping, and had nothing to hold on to, for his hands were hanging free over the edge. Todd had only to wrench himself from under his living burden, and the doomed wretch was left to see-saw across the narrow ledge for a brief moment – and then to fall headlong, cartwheeling over and over to his swift end.

I looked down, wide-eyed, to see a circle of Royal Marine bandsmen gathered below. They appeared to be casing their instruments and putting away their music. Their astonished faces were upturned to the wheeling, screaming form coming down in the centre of them.

I closed my eyes then, and clamped my fingers over my ears to shut out the sound that must follow. Next, I felt Jack's arms about me and his soothing voice close by my ear.

'Be calm, little one,' he murmured. '*Le diable est mort.*'

*

Next morning, in response to my frantic telegraph, and on the advice of the police officer in charge of the enquiry, Giles Treacher, acting as my lawyer, arrived in London on the overnight express and accompanied Jack and me to the City mortuary, formally to identify – if we were able – the man who had fallen to his death from the Whispering Gallery of St Paul's Cathedral on the day of Queen Victoria's Diamond Jubilee procession.

The building that housed the place of the dead was hard by Wapping Old Stairs and overhanging the river. A white-coated attendant took us down gloomy corridors to a bare, brick-lined room where a still form lay under a sheet on a wheeled table that stood in the middle of the floor. Together, hand in hand, Jack and I approached the object of our attendance at that awful place, and Giles came with us.

The attendant lifted one edge of the sheet, revealing a strangely peaceful countenance that was unmarked by any injury and touched only by death's waxen pallor.

'I knew him!' breathed Jack Todd. 'He drank most evenings at the "Blue Boar" in Mortmain village!'

Giles edged forward, also in a state of astonishment. 'And I knew him as Hubert Trevis!' he exclaimed. 'For a while – immediately preceding the time when I was negotiating for your inheritance, Daisy – he worked in my office as a filing clerk. And that explains a lot!'

I, also, knew the face, though I had looked upon it only two or three times, and then without registering either interest or any lasting impression. It was a very ordinary face, an eminently forgettable face that one could pass by in the street and never notice at all.

'I knew him simply as Hawn,' I said. 'He was acting as Tristan Melmoth's valet – and I would have thought that he had accompanied his master to Scotland, only . . .

'Only, as we now know, he had business – elsewhere.'

*

All that week following the Diamond Jubilee celebrations, it had rained, blown and stormed in the West Country, so that the

271

panorama from the wide windows of the solar at Mortmain provided a vista of Nature outraged and an unforgettable spectacle. On the day that Sergeant Penbury came, a storm that had brought devastation to the small harbours and inlets of south Cornwall and driven several sizable ships on to the merciless rocks, was at its wild, triumphant height, and bellowed through the solar chimney as if through a pipe-organ.

The sergeant was giving his summation of the man I had briefly known as the valet Hawn:

'Like I said, he took after his actress mother in his ability – which must have been considerable – to be all things to all men, and yet remain inconspicuous. There's no doubt but that it was while working as a filing clerk with Treacher, Murdoch and Partners that he stumbled upon Mr Treacher's intent regarding your inheritance, ma'am; whilst, by insinuating himself into the employ of Mr Melmoth, he was able to bring himself very close to the inner knowledge of your comings and goings.'

'But, Sergeant, if he had been with Tristan Melmoth only a short while, why did he not come under suspicion after Lady Moira's murder?' I asked.

'He had been with that gentleman since the beginning of the year,' replied Penbury, 'and brought with him a set of most impressive references, including one from a member of the Royal family. With that sort of background – all false and forged in his case -- an upper servant's bona fides is never questioned, even by us. He was a cunning, clever devil, there's no doubt about it. But flawed in his judgement, like all the insane. It was the work of a madman to have recklessly killed Lady Moira the way he did, in that careless, slovenly manner.'

'Careless and slovenly' – I thought ruefully of the woman's appalling end, and shuddered.

'Well, ma'am, I'll be going,' he said, rising. 'But there is one thing, one request I would ask of you before I leave.'

'And what's that, Sergeant?' I asked, adding indulgently: 'And consider it already granted.'

He smiled. 'I've heard tell often of a portrait of the Honourable Felicity Denvers, that tragic young lady who died within these walls all those years ago. I have never set eyes on that picture, ma'am, and it would be a great . . .'

'Say no more, Sergeant,' I interposed. 'You shall see it here and now.'

I led him up to my sitting room, where Felicity looked down, as she had for nigh on two hundred years. Penbury met her gaze, staring up at her for a long time in silence.

And then, he said: 'Ma'am, there's a legend in my family, the Penburys, that Felicity Denvers' baby didn't die with her, but was spirited out of the castle by a kindly serving wench and brought to poor dead Richard Penbury's parents, where he – for 'twas a lad – was brought up as their own son. That same serving wench, who was ordered by his lordship to lay out the bodies for burial, did – so the legend tells – put Felicity's favourite childhood doll in her dead arms in place of her supposed dead baby.

'That's the story, ma'am,' he smiled. 'But it can't be true, or I would be a descendant of the gentry, and it's as plain as the nose on my face that I'm no such thing, but only a common fellow.'

I looked into his eyes – those undoubted Denvers' eyes – and made no attempt to contradict him.

*

At the end of that month, his span of duty at the embassy drawing to its close, Jack Todd received peremptory orders to rejoin the Fleet. Florrie and I had by then returned to Bath, and he came down for the day to see me. We had tea together in the Pump Room close by the Royal Baths, and he enlarged upon the news:

'There's a promotion in the move,' he said, 'and my first ship command. I should be throwing my cap over the moon, but I've a couple of causes for regret.'

'And what are those?' I asked.

'First, I'll not be seeing you again till heaven knows when,' he replied, 'since my ship is part of the Pacific Fleet and likely to remain so. And as if that weren't bad enough, I won't have the opportunity to climb the "Old Man of Hoy" – not for years to come.'

'You'll be back one day,' I said, reaching out across the table and fondly touching his hand. 'And we'll climb him together.'

'Mind you hold yourself to that promise,' he replied with mock severity. 'Don't you go sneaking up there to climb him before me. I know your kind, ma'am. You're your father's daughter – if I ever saw a father's daughter!'

We both laughed. He had met Father and 'spoken' to him, through Phoebe, in the fine suite that he now occupied in Mortmain. They had got on together splendidly, and – predictably – the topic of conversation had been largely about climbing. One exchange, in particular, had stayed in my mind:

'Tell me, sir. Did your tragic accident occur during the last part of the ascent, or on the way down?'

'What you're trying to ask is – did we reach the summit of the Jügspitz.'

'Sir, I cannot tell a lie – that's just what I'm trying to ask you.'

'All five of us reached the summit. The fall occurred on the descent.'

'It's one helluva misfortune that your conquest has gone unrecorded, sir.'

'It will be recorded in due course, Commander. The next party to reach the summit will find my signet ring up there – under a cairn of stones.'

'He looked great when I met him,' said Jack. 'It was like being received on Mount Olympus among the gods. That tremendous mask!'

'He's inordinately proud of it,' I said. 'He insisted on first putting it on himself, and his poor hands trembled when he did so. He's so proud of that mask. I think he wears it in bed. What a blessing that men – some men – are so vain. In Father's case, it has been the salvation of his self-respect – to be vain, and proud of his appearance in that beautiful mask of dull gold.'

(It had been modelled just as Father had ordered. One of our premier sculptors, Sir Dirk Marchmain, R.A., had fashioned it – and a pretty penny it had cost. Wearing it with a dramatic cloak and white kid gloves to cover up his poor hands, my father cut quite the dash, earning himself the envy of men and the admiration of women – for both sexes were full of speculation about the nature of the fascinating creature who must lie behind that god-like mask.)

All too soon, it was time for Jack to catch his train back to London on the first part of a journey that was to take him to the Pacific. We parted company at the table with a touch of hands and a chaste kiss, for I knew I could never bring myself to see his train steam out of the station.

'Goodbye, Jack,' I whispered. 'Thank you for giving me my life.'

'Not goodbye,' he said, laying a finger on my lips. 'Make it "till we meet again".'

He walked away, tall and straight, and did not look back.

I never saw him again. In the autumn of the following year, his ship foundered in a hurricane while attempting to take off survivors from a stricken cargo ship, and sank with all hands. The Pump Room at Bath will, for me, be forever haunted by his presence, by his deep booming laugh, his loving but undemanding friendship.

*

Later that summer – we were still together in Bath, and Father still at Mortmain and writing weekly through his enterprising young amanuensis – Florrie shyly suggested that, since I was now so very capable of ordering my own life both socially and in every other sphere, the time had probably come when she should go her own way. 'Not that we shall not always be the dearest of friends,' she hastened to assure me.

I had my own ideas about the reason for her scouting the notion; furthermore, I was pretty certain that the poor dear was quite penniless, and relied for her all on my hospitality and the small stipend that was paid to her by the estate to be my companion. So I tackled the situation in the only way that I know how – which is head-on.

'Rubbish, dear!' I told her. 'I should be lost – completely lost – without you, and a moment's thought would make it plain to you. The superficial airs and graces I have managed with difficulty to adopt would fly out of the window in weeks if I were

275

left to my own devices. What's more, my dear, I actually *like* having you with me. So let's have no more of this nonsense. This is your home, as are all my residences. And here you stay – so let's hear no more on't!'

My direct approach reduced her to tears of gratitude and – I suspect – relief, but I had got my way.

It was the same afternoon that Giles Treacher made his habitual monthly call regarding the administration of the estate: there were property and other purchases for me to approve, deeds to be signed, bank drafts to be endorsed, et cetera.

Giles always seemed to be overladened with work, and I told him so: 'Another twenty years of watching over my fortunes, added to whatever else you do at your office in Dorchester, and you'll be a candidate for an early grave, my dear,' I said.

His expression flitted from tragedy to a hesitant comedy. He shrugged. 'I could wish to be rid of some of the minor tasks that are thrust upon me,' he admitted, 'for it's truly said that it's the last straw that breaks the camel's back. And the matter of Charles Arbuthnot's latest request is a case in point – not, I hasten to add, that I jib at doing an occasional favour for Charles.'

My attention was all ears at the mention of that name. 'What favour is this?' I asked with elaborate casualness.

'Oh, it concerns Lady Moira Fame's grave at Weymouth Manor,' he said. 'The Fame family mausoleum being full to overflowing, she was buried in an adjacent plot. Charles is now asking me to arrange for a suitably inspiring monument, with statuary and all, to be erected over it. And commissioning high-flown monumental masonry is simply not in my line of country.'

'Mr Arbuthnot is quite unswerving in his devotion to the poor lady,' I commented tartly. 'I wonder he doesn't come over from Italy and arrange his late fiancée's high-flown monument himself.'

I did not at that time notice the swift glance of puzzlement that my companion threw at me then – or, if I did, I attributed it to his surprise at my vehemence.

'Perhaps Mr Arbuthnot is too engrossed in his other interests to busy himself so far,' I added for good measure.

'I'm sure that if the dowager Marchioness willed it, Charles would be over here commissioning the monument himself,' said Giles.

'And who, pray, is the dowager Marchioness?' I demanded. 'One of Mr Arbuthnot's new lady friends?'

Giles looked confused. 'Why, no, Daisy,' he said. 'Helena, Marchioness of Watermere is his godmother, and mother to the late Lady Moira. Charles is devoted to the old lady, who's had such a dreadful life with that family of hers, whereas Charles, who never knew his mother, has always been the one consolation of her appalling existence.'

'Tell me more, Giles,' I said, my jealous anger suddenly evaporating.

'Why, Helena was married off to a maniac,' said Giles. 'And perforce produced a maniac son, the present marquess, who was once allowed to leave the asylum where he'd been kept since early manhood – an act of enlightened charity which he repaid by strangling his mother's lady's maid. It was always the Marchioness's terror that her daughter was tainted with the same affliction – which was likely. And that's why Charles was always and forever touting her around wherever he went. It was because he had made a solemn promise to his godmother that he'd never let them take her away and lock her up like her brother.'

A great light was bursting in upon my mind . . .

'So he wasn't engaged to marry her after all!' I cried.

'Good heavens, no!' exclaimed Giles. 'Anyone who knew the family history would as lief have married a she-wolf. No, Charles took her on as a burden that he carried right to the end – and, being Charles, he carried it with a good will.'

'And now, being free of her, he's gone to live in Italy,' I mused.

'Mmmm. Can't imagine why he did that,' said Giles.

Regarding the manner in which I was going to order the rest of my life, my mind was made up on that instant – one way or the other.

277

'I must find out why he went to Italy,' I declared.

He blinked at me. 'I – I'm afraid I don't follow you, Daisy,' he said.

'You will, my dear Giles,' I promised him. 'You will!'

*

I tried to count, but lost track. There must have been at least a hundred stone lions' heads in one long line, and all spouting crystal water from their gaping mouths into a long trough that flanked the tree-shaded path through the garden. The trough fed other streams and waterways, runlets and rills, freshets, streamlets, channels and sluices – all descending the steep slope from which the water garden drew its impetus.

The sounds of moving water were all about me, and the only sounds to be heard: merry rushing, tinkle-tinkle, drip-drip, a torrential libation and – rising above all – the majestic hiss of the great fountains in the well of the garden, spouting tree-high, and reflecting the sun in a million droplets.

Without either explanation or prevarication, I had demanded Charles's address from Giles, and he had wonderingly given it to me without question. The villa – called the Villa Tortoni – was at Tivoli, which is twenty-seven kilometres from Rome, or so I was informed by the driver of the carriage that had conveyed me from my hotel.

Tivoli is a small town, or a large village, with a pleasant, sleepy-square, a church, two cafés, and a cluster of small villas clinging to a hillside that commands a splendid view of the Eternal City. I had quickly determined, from a useful-looking housewife out shopping, which was the Villa Tortoni: it lay at the end of a dirt road leading down the hillside. Long and low, with an ochre-coloured tile roof and surrounded by a lush garden, it had an instant appeal. My original intent had simply been to knock on the door and announce myself; brought to the test, I prevaricated. Better, I thought, to go for a little walk and put my mind in that state of calm and relaxation best fitted for the ordeal which lay before me.

After all, I told myself, I was making a very large assumption if I thought that Charles Arbuthnot had quit his home, his

278

native land, his business and all his friends simply for the unrequited love of Daisy Friday. He might extend to me no more than common civility: perhaps even take me out to dinner in Rome that evening. On the other hand, the discernible coolness with which I had sent him from my door might well still rankle with him; were he not a perfect gentleman, his inclination might well be to slam the door in my face!

No. Better, much better, to go for a short walk, put my thoughts to rights, and try my luck later. By such subterfuges do we deceive ourselves.

One of the largest villas in the place was, I discovered, open to the public. It was called the Villa d'Este and possessed a notable water garden. Accordingly, I paid a few lire to the attendant on the gate and went in. The villa itself was rather severe in appearance and not at all to my taste, but the water garden was a sheer delight.

I descended a flight of steps that brought me to a lower level, and came to a path that was overhung with dark greenery. A little further on, I went out into the sunshine and found myself standing on a balustraded terrace high above a complex of fountains, waterfalls, and sun-whitened stonework. And to my utter delight, there burst upon my ears every sound of water on earth, every note that it can make in movement. I was listening to a veritable water-organ.

A line of young seminarists straggled along the tree-shaded path below: black, like a party of wandering crows, their master leading them. They were the first living creatures I had seen since I had come into the garden; they pranced and chattered, as boys will, jostling and pushing each other, safe from their master's eye – ah, but yet not safe: there was one who followed after, beyond the tail-end of the unruly crocodile, and his eye would be upon them, and Nemesis must soon descend. Half-amused, I waited to see the outcome when the master bringing up the rear noticed how his charges were behaving.

He came out from under the shadows of the trees and moved into the sunlight – and I saw, with a leap of the heart, that he was no master of seminarists.

He was – Charles!

Moving quite quickly and looking about him. Anxiety written all over him. Looking for someone . . .

Looking for *me!*

He must have seen me up in the village. Perhaps even peering over the hedge and into his garden. And had come after me.

'CHARLES!' I shouted. 'CHA-A-A-RLES!'

He looked up. Even at that considerable distance, I saw the joy in his beloved eyes.

'DAISY!' He shouted in return. 'OH – *DAISY!*'

And then, he was running. And I was running, too, with joy and love in my heart; down the staircase that led to the lower level, out into the open space where the water-organ played, in and out of the flying droplets.

The seminarists and their master stopped and stared at my passing – as well they might, to see a woman in a formal crêpe de Chine afternoon frock and a powder blue picture hat to match, actually running like a love-sick schoolgirl to keep her tryst.

Charles's arms were open wide to embrace me as he ran, and mine were also. We met halfway along the line of ogling, open-mouthed boys, and a love that had had its mutual – if unpromising – beginning in the far-off chain factory was sealed with a kiss in what is surely one of the most beautiful man-made places on earth.

EPILOGUE

We were married when the leaves began to fall in the home park at Mortmain. I chanced my arm, as the saying goes, and ordered an attempt to be made again to raise a roof on the ancient chapel for the event. In defiance of legend and tradition, it stayed up long enough for Charles and I to be married underneath it – and it remains there still. I like to tell myself that love conquers all – even ghostly happenings from the dark ages of history.

Our first-born was young Charles, the bane of my life; takes after his grandfather. Charles, incidentally, became the only other one to master father's strange manner of speech; he learned it from Phoebe, who is now assistant matron of the General Hospital in Truro. Father died four years ago after a mercifully short illness, and remained mentally active till the very end, still quite absurdly proud of his gold mask and finding a source of constant delight in the stir he caused every time he appeared in public.

That year was a great sadness for us, for we lost baby Thomas Jack also, he who bore the names of two of the finest gentlemen I have ever known: Major Tom Bravingdon and Commander Jack Todd. May all three rest in peace.

The day I broke my train journey to Cornwall and went to have a look at the old chain factory in Mordwenn was the day I conceived the notion of hounding my Member of Parliament to death to set up a select committee to look into the whole rotten business of child labour. Those who have followed the story of my career thus far will not be surprised that I got my way – particularly since the Member of Parliament in question happened to be my old friend and legal advisor Giles Treacher. The committee was not a rousing success, it has to be said, but we did manage to cobble together some ideas which are already beginning to bear fruit, and I have high hopes of stirring our lords and masters into doing something really significant for those poor children in the next session of Parliament.

The charitable soup goes well. Charles ribs me unmercifully about it, but that doesn't stop him from putting his shoulder to the wheel, as anyone who has seen my darling husband at the unearthly hour of two in the morning, doling out hot soup and a hunk of bread to down-and-outs on the Embankment will know very well.

I remember dear Harold Nesbitt, the first man who ever loved me. It is my eternal regret that I never wrote in reply to his letter. Harold went to the South African war and was killed at Bloemfontein whilst dragging in his wounded officer after an attack. The fate that dictates the lives of mortals both mighty and humble had Harold marked out for a particular glory. The former draper's assistant turned senior clerk was posthumously awarded his country's highest honour for valour, the Victoria Cross.

Now they say there is going to be another war. The Kaiser, whom his grandmother Queen Victoria refused to invite to her Diamond Jubilee on account of what she called his 'fearfully and senselessly violent ways' will drive us into it, so they say. Well, I am glad that neither of my boys will be involved in it. If it starts this autumn, as they say it will, the war cannot last beyond Christmas, and my first-born, my rumbustious Charlie, whose only interest is in flying machines, is barely sixteen, so he'll never be called to the colours.

My dear, my sweet Florrie, who was to my later years what Meg Wolfingham had been to my earlier, passed away only last year at the very creditable age of eighty-two, praising old Sir Basil's name to the very last. It's very odd, but there appeared a report in *The Times* a couple of months ago about an Englishman of advanced years who was found dying on a remote island in the South Pacific. His native wife – or lady companion – paddled a canoe across a very considerable stretch of water, alone, to fetch medical help from the nearest centre of near-civilisation. The poor man was beyond help when the doctor arrived back, but – a very remarkable thing – the walls of the hut that the couple had shared were entirely papered with English twenty-pound notes.

Was *he* Sir Basil Wimsey-Fildes, I wonder? Stranger things have happened.

CM